Accolades

"*The Pleistocene Redemption* takes a giant leap beyond *Jurassic Park*! Its foundation in real technology and biology enables the reader to hurtle into this very enjoyable and intriguing fiction."
— William W. Hauswirth, Ph.D. and Erin L. Hauswirth,
Editorial Board of *Ancient Biomolecules*

"*The Pleistocene Redemption* is a thrilling, wild adventure. It uses just-beyond-current science to plausibly, forcefully and vividly place the reader amongst astounding extinct animals. As your muscles tense and your heart pounds, wipe the sweat off your brow and *try* to tell yourself that it's only a story!"
— Larry G. Marshall, Ph.D., paleontologist,
The Institute for Human Origins

"*The Pleistocene Redemption* is a fabulous, wild, fast-paced story that combines an extraordinary amount of research with a real narrative gift. The ending will leave you overwhelmed with its profound philo-sophical and spiritual implications. I highly recommend it."
— Douglas Preston, best-selling co-author of
The Relic (now a hit movie) and *Mount Dragon*

"With skill, wit and humor, Gallagher deftly propels readers. This fun and pleasurable tale is hauntingly profound. Accelerating powerfully within natural and supernatural realms, it enthralls, consoles and terrifies. This important thriller melds biotechnology, espionage, spiritual challenge, prehistoric adventure and more. A compelling and meaningful experience, *The Pleistocene Redemption* joins the ranks of Shelley's *Frankenstein*, Huxley's *Brave New World* and Miller's *A Canticle for Leibowitz*."
— Russell E. Smith, S.T.D., KHS, 1992-96 President of
The Pope John Center, a bioethics institute

"...a fascinating concept...the Preserve...the Neanderthals...all the perils. More authentic than *Jurassic Park*."
— James E. Gunn, author of *The Joy Machine* (Star Trek #80)
and editor of *The Road to Science Fiction*

More Praise

"A fast-paced and imaginative story, based on wide-ranging background research, that prompts one to wonder what it really means to be human."
— Ian Tattersall, Ph.D., paleontologist and author of *The Last Neanderthal*

"...hard to put down...hauntingly close to real possibilities...terrifying. I truly enjoyed the action, excitement, politics, human drama, all mixed with enough science to make me think that perhaps this could really happen."
— Scott R. Woodward, Ph.D., geneticist and microbiologist, Brigham Young University

"...thrilling new insight...Not only is the style of writing riveting, but the scientific and ethical infrastructure of this remarkable work is faultless. A brave new voice is heard..."
— Bernard N. Nathanson, M.D., author of *The Hand of God*

"This is not a story to put down, but you may wish it to last forever. A thrilling tale with a fine blend of adventure, politics, religion, and science. More scientifically plausible and better written than any other book I have read on regenerating extinct species."
Neil Clark, Ph.D., Curator of the Hunterian Museum (Scotland), and author of books on dinosaurs

"An engrossing confluence of cutting-edge science, thought-provoking ethics, and storytelling that moves at the pace of a Gatling gun."
Lincoln Child, best-selling co-author of *The Relic* (now a hit movie) and *Mount Dragon*

"...a gripping and highly entertaining yarn, matching *Jurassic Park* in accuracy and plausibility."
— John M. Harris, Ph.D, Chief Curator of the George C. Page Museum of La Brea Discoveries

"...extraordinary vision...well researched...intriguing..."
— William Sarabande, author of "The First Americans" sagas

More Praise

"...an important addition to science fiction... Others have tried... Now Gallagher...keeps the reader off balance with action: a plethora of very hungry Pleistocene megafauna, political tension and realistic military conflicts...a novel that is hard to put down."
— Thomas J. Bassler, M.D. (T.J. Bass), author of *Half Past Human*

"...intellectual...timely...wonderful humor, and a most entertaining story...a gripping science fiction...research, plot & character development, and intrigue are extraordinary...in refreshing opposition to the chaos-deterministic theme of *Jurassic Park* and the neopaganism of *The Celestine Prophesy*; ...I had a difficult time setting this fine work down and heartily commend it to the thoughtful reader."
— J. F. Bierlein, author of *Parallel Myths*

"Science fiction, anthropology, religion and thriller for fans of *Jurassic Park* and the human spirit."
— Lynne Bundesen, author of *So the Woman Went Her Way*

"...a high spirited, adventurous book worthy of the time and considerable thought readers will happily invest. ...readers will definitely have something to think about as they turn the last pages."
— Kelly Milner-Halls, author of *Dino-Trekking*

"I truly enjoyed it. *The Pleistocene Redemption* is a mind-opener, challenging religion and mysticism with 'new science'. It may make you angry but it will definitely make you think. A compelling read."
— Richard La Plante, author of *Tegné* and *Steroid Blues*

"Thoughtfully addressing critical issues confronting humanity, this science fiction/geopolitical thriller leaves *Jurassic Park* way behind. It's an intellectual adventure in...molecular biology, species regeneration, paleozoology, biomedical ethics, and spirituality. An assured classic and a 'must' read."
— J. Richard Greenwell, Secretary of
The International Society of Cryptozoology

THE
PLEISTOCENE
REDEMPTION

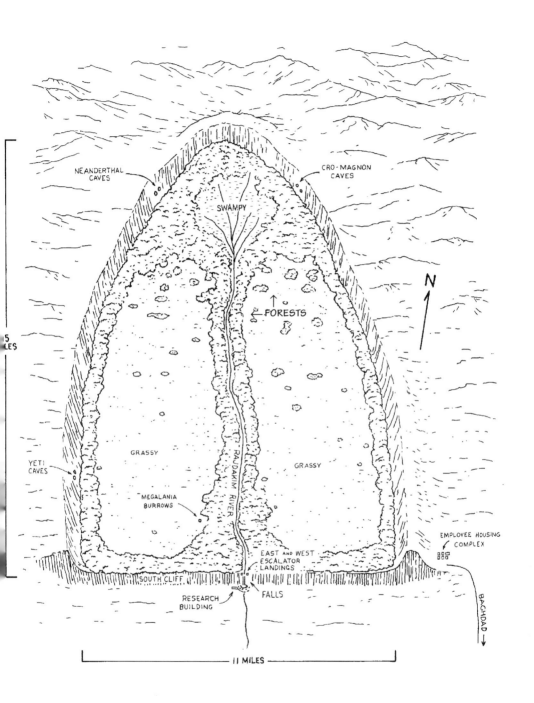

Al-Rajda, Iraq

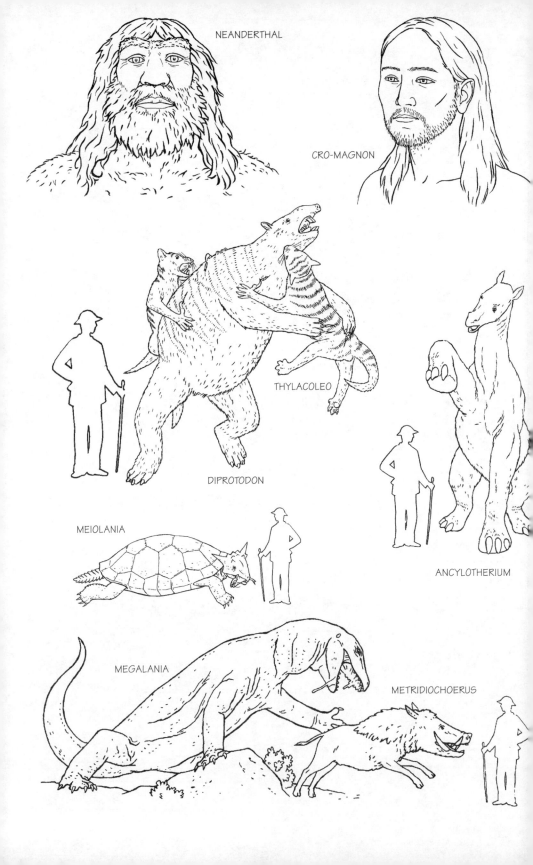

NEANDERTHAL

CRO-MAGNON

THYLACOLEO

DIPROTODON

ANCYLOTHERIUM

MEIOLANIA

MEGALANIA

METRIDIOCHOERUS

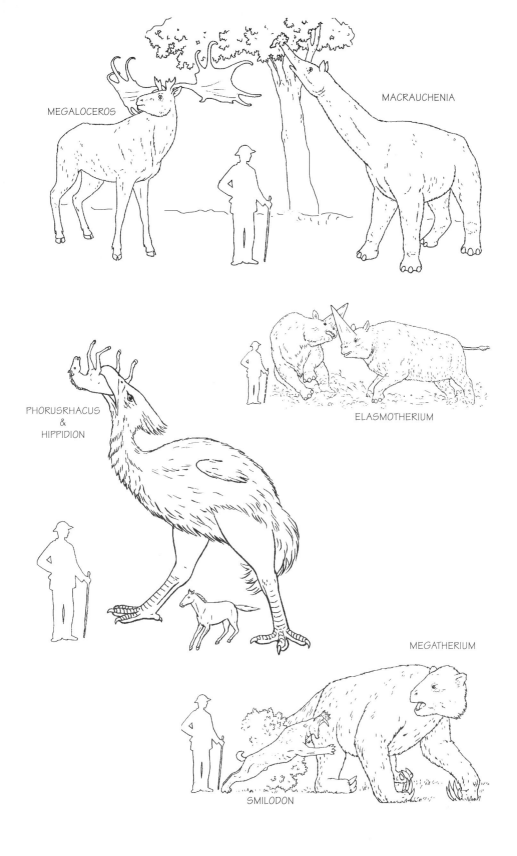

MEGALOCEROS

MACRAUCHENIA

PHORUSRHACUS
&
HIPPIDION

ELASMOTHERIUM

MEGATHERIUM

SMILODON

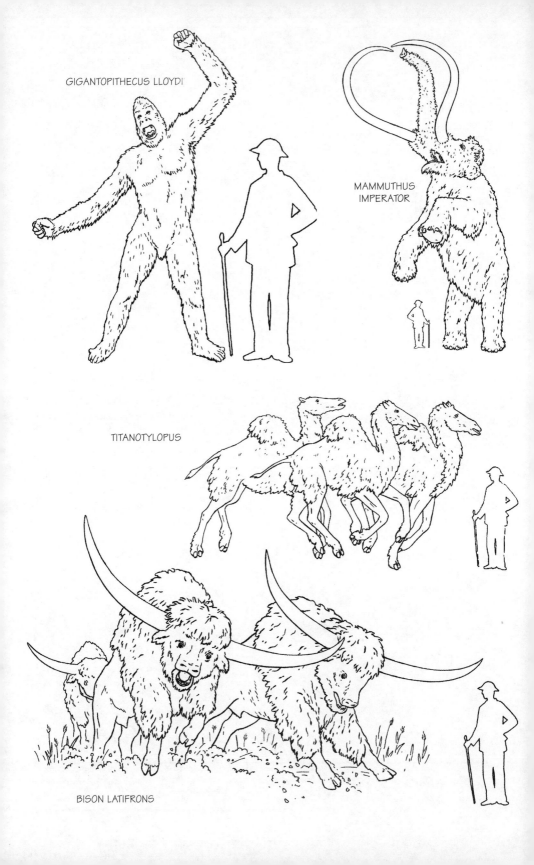

GIGANTOPITHECUS LLOYDI

MAMMUTHUS IMPERATOR

TITANOTYLOPUS

BISON LATIFRONS

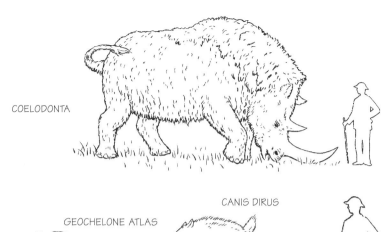

COELODONTA

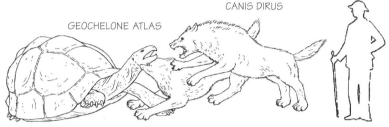

CANIS DIRUS

GEOCHELONE ATLAS

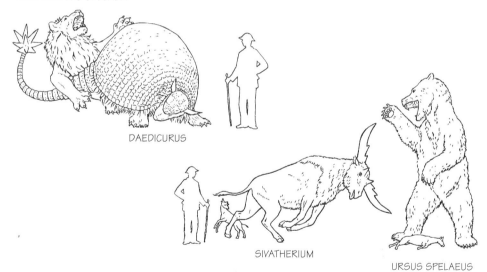

PANTHERA LEO SPELAEA

DAEDICURUS

SIVATHERIUM

URSUS SPELAEUS

MAMMUT (MASTODON)

THE PLEISTOCENE REDEMPTION

Dan Gallagher

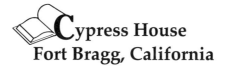

Cypress House
Fort Bragg, California

The Pleistocene Redemption © 1997 by Dan Gallagher

Cypress House
155 Cypress Street
Fort Bragg, CA 95437
1-800-773-7782
Fax (707) 964-7531

Bookstores wishing to stock this book, please call
Independent Publishers Group at (800) 888-4741.

Publisher's Cataloging-in-Publication

Gallagher, Dan, 1959–
    The Pleistocene Redemption / Dan Gallagher. — 1st ed.
    p. cm.
    Preassigned LCCN: 97-66273
    ISBN 1-879384-32-9

    1. Genetic engineering — Fiction. 2. Fantastic fiction. I. Title.

PS3557.A55P54 1997   813.54
                                           QBI97-40486

Cover design by Chuck Hathaway, Mendocino Graphics.
Inside art by David Narvaez of Williamsburg, Virginia.
Smilodon skull by Gene King, at Virginia Living Museum, Newport News, VA.

Note from the Author

Dear Readers,
    Thank you for reading my book. Perhaps someone you know would appreciate a copy of *The Pleistocene Redemption* as a gift. All owners of this novel are welcome to e-mail concise correspondence to me at webmaster@paleobook.com.

    You may also enjoy my website, www.paleobook.com, where you'll find intriguing excerpts, fascinating graphics, and critical reviews of other books in this exciting sub-genre of fiction, called "lost worlds" or "prehistoric adventures." Paleobook reviews and offers often hard-to-find paleontological and archaeological fiction and non-fiction, grouped by appropriateness for children, teens and adults. There are also links to other fun and informative web sites.

    Charitable organizations ordering for fund-raisers, please e-mail me. The electronic edition of *The Pleistocene Redemption* is $8.00 and can only be purchased through paleobook.com. Each download entitles you to one $5.00 rebate on the hard cover edition (restrictions apply, see details online). Thank you!

DG

Manufactured in the USA

1 3 5 7 9 10 8 6 4 2

Acknowledgments
&
Dedication

The author is indebted to scientists, theologians and others who contributed to this project through writings or personal assistance. The following is a list of those who provided assistance through conversation or correspondence; then general acknowledgments.

Sonney Cockrell for advice on fauna and specimen preservation media.

John J. Collins, Ph.D., for assistance with biblical questions.

Margery C. Coombs, Ph.D., for important help with *Ancylotherium*.

David J. Essex for very helpful editorial advice.

Eugene Gafney, Ph.D., for help with the *Meiolania*.

Nick Graham, Ph.D., for fascinating discussions on theoretical meteorology.

Jerry L. Hall, Ph.D., for crucial guidance on genetics: the possible and the impossible.

John M. Harris, Ph.D., for excellent advice on Pleistocene fauna.

William W. Hauswirth, Ph.D., for enlightening help on genetics.

Larry G. Marshall, Ph.D., for valuable advice on Pleistocene fauna and editorial help.

Paul S. Martin, Ph.D., for help with geology and fauna.

Greg McDonald, Ph.D., for extensive help with fauna.

Jim I. Meade, Ph.D., for intriguing examples of soft tissue preserved for millennia.

Geoffrey Pope, Ph.D., for help with our ancestor-races, the
    Neanderthal and Cro-Magnon.

Merritt Ruhlen, Ph.D., for linguistics facts and provision of a
    Nostratic Dictionary.

Tom Torgersen, Ph.D., for extremely useful help with geologi-
    cal issues.

Thanks are due to several NASA engineers for help with environmental and aeronautical issues. Through published communications, many scholars were of great help: Francesco Cavalli-Sforza,
Ph.D., L. Luca Cavalli-Sforza, Ph.D., Dougal Dixon, Stephen Jay
Gould, Ph.D., Svante Pääbo, Ph.D., Steven Pinker, Ph.D.; R. J. G.
Savage, Ph.D., Father Donald Senior, Robert Tjian, Ph.D. and the in-
trepid researchers of the International Society of Cryptozoology,
Tucson, AZ. Appreciation must also be expressed to these natural
history museums: The American Museum in New York, The Smith-
sonian Institution in Washington, D.C. and The Natural History Museum of L.A. County.

This allegory is dedicated to the reader.

THE
PLEISTOCENE
REDEMPTION

Prologue

Ancient Whispers

> IN THE BEGINNING, THE CREATOR LONGED FOR THE JOY OF
> CREATION. HE MEDITATED, AND THEN CAME RAYI, MATTER,
> AND PRANA, LIFE. THESE TWO, thought he, WILL
> PRODUCE BEINGS FOR ME.
>
> — PRASHNA UPANISHAD, FIRST QUESTION

Arrogant Answers

> . . . to prepare for greater enterprises, . . . to make use of the
> pretext of religion, [Ferdinand] adopted the piously cruel
> policy of driving the Moors from his kingdom and despoiling
> them; herein his conduct could not have been more
> admirable or extraordinary.   — Machiavelli, *The Prince*

One Final Call

> THEY PLOTTED, AND GOD PLOTTED. GOD IS THE SUPREME
> PLOTTER.   — KORAN, 3:54

Mankind struggled for millennia to survive in his world and to understand it. He battled and hunted fantastic animals; even his cousin-races. He sought insight into the *meaning and purpose* of life, suffering and death through superstition, religion and investigation. Have individuals, or humanity as a whole, progressed in this quest for true improvement? Do we view our progress, our science, as evidence that only we control our destiny?

Some say that there is a voice which calls our names before birth, as we mature, and which pines to call us home at death. Is this an archaic superstition, destructive of individual freedoms? Some assert that we have only a limited number of chances in which to turn our—and others'—lives enough to merit reward. Others see clear evidence that they have many years. Pontius Pilot, a man denigrated by history but well respected by his peers, asked the haunting question: "What is truth?" The query survives him.

i

New questions are presented by scientific discoveries: Are socially-erosive behaviors based in genetics and, hence, neither moral nor immoral acts? Were the Hebrews a people chosen by God or did they simply misinterpret several natural phenomena? How should we interpret what we learn from science?

Whence come our insights?

Who can discern meaning from the coincidences, personal changes and dreams which develop so subtly in the passing years of our human lives?

Kevin Gamaliel Harrigan, driven by struggles and longings deep within himself, pursued these and other questions of life. He sought the truth—or perhaps it sought him—about questions of the human animal, destiny and himself. A brilliant man, fit and resolute, he was well equipped to capture the answers. He was, he felt, a true leader and a man of superior vision. Many had good reason to accompany him on his quest. Manfred Freund shared many of Harrigan's qualities and curiosity. Freund, too, sought insight. He befriended Harrigan in their teen years and substantially contributed to Harrigan's projects. In a quest spanning twenty years, the two men ultimately *did* find the subtle answers.

Who could possibly have foreseen that such work would lead to the most ominous implications ever to confront humanity?

Chapter One

Medical Clinic, Al-Rajda
Zoological Research Preserve, Iraq
0742 hours, May 16, 2018

Harrigan awoke to now-familiar dull pain and penetrating cold. It was as if every joint and muscle in what was left of his wrinkled and decrepit body were rotting. His left arm throbbed from the I.V. that dripped the serum—the serum which was his and Freund's only hope to survive the rapid aging effects of this virus—into his frequently collapsing veins. He fumbled to manipulate the bed control button to raise his prostrate torso a few inches above the horizontal.

Harrigan's hazel eyes, sunk back inside his thick-browed skull, could barely open. He mustered just enough strength and coordination to wipe them free of crust. Once well groomed auburn hair now lay disheveled, graying and thinning on his scalp. Harrigan turned his head right toward the window and Freund's bed. He glimpsed a blood-encrusted *Megalania* lizard carcass, its shark-like jaw slicing a three foot wide rut as it was being dragged away by two straining Iraqi troop carriers. He sighed ruefully. The glare and irritation of morning sunlight through the milky haze on his eyes forced them to twitch closed. He jerked his head back to the left and down to his chest, squinting to see the rest of the sick room. From the crummy treatment he was receiving, it seemed to him that they had just stuck him in here to die. The room reeked of isopropyl alcohol, concrete dust and body odor. He mustered his command voice and tried to enunciate as perfectly as he could.

"System . . . Page orderly." Harrigan's intonation wavered despite the effort.

The reply took a few seconds but he supposed the computer was having trouble recognizing his deteriorating voice. The slightly metallic and distinctly non-gendered human mimic responded, "Assistance priority requires selection from the following choices prior to interruption of the clinic's human workflow: Say 'one' if your request is for supplies. Say 'two' if you need assistance visiting the lavatory. Say 'three' if—"

Harrigan quickly blasted: "System . . . Interrupt. Override . . . Page orderly!"

Harrigan suppressed another cough. He was disoriented and becoming almost as forgetful as Freund had become. Harrigan had had enough of this the last two days and was doubly irritated that the clinic staff ignored his request for a hand-held buzzer to the nurse and orderly station. Yet he distinctly remembered that someone here had even mouthed acknowledgment that his cough was exacerbated by using the computer voice system. *And the orderly station*, he steamed silently, *is only a few doors away!*

Down the hall, the soldier acting as orderly was still sleeping in his chair. Growth of his whisker stubble was prying dried gravy, a remnant of midnight snacking, off his chin. A computer screen before him blinked rhythmically and emitted a synchronous beep, both of which began to erode his slumber. He opened his eyes, grimaced and got up to attend to Harrigan's call.

Persistent cloudy patches in his vision irritated Harrigan and he could scarcely make out the door just off the lower left corner of his too-cold bed. He could see the faint reflection of the green and red lights of his status panel at the foot of the bed. It shone dimly off the white wall directly across the sparse twelve foot by twelve foot room. He realized now that the clinic rooms should have been designed so that a patient could read his vital signs.

The read-outs were all normal except for the iron readings from the bed's built-in Magnetic Resonance Monitor, which indicated that Harrigan's blood was becoming anemic. Not being able to see them made him more apprehensive.

He expected the orderly, Ron from Pittsburgh whom he knew to be quite considerate, to respond. Instead he heard hard boot steps approaching in the hall. The door jutted open and smacked against the rubber stop on the wall. He could just make out the man's features: he was one of those drab green clad, stern-faced Iraqi guards. It began to come back to Harrigan now: what had put him and Freund in this clinic. He hoped the soldier's English was intelligible but it turned out to be barely so. "What can I do for you, Doctor Harrigan?"

"Where is Ron?"

"Do you not recall? I am here to assist you. What do you *nid?*"

Harrigan did begin to recall as feelings of suspicion and animosity mounted. He cascaded into a sarcastic, venomous attack. "I *nid* my eyes cleaned out. I *nid* a blanket. I *nid* to see some lab results on Doctor Freund and myself. I *nid* the hand-buzzer I was promised would be installed. I *nid* the outside communication lines to operate. I *nid* something for this damn cough—h -hf, I *nid* some acetaminophen-III. I *nid* fresh water and there'd better be a little respect for the sick around here!"

The guard's face drew tight in anger . . . then relaxed, smiling. "You Americans and Europeans do deserve a *leettle* respect. Rest assured that you and Doctor Freund are our highest priority. I will see what I can do."

He left and returned almost immediately with a squeeze bottle in his left hand and a red pill in his right. Slapping the door open against the stop as before, he shoved the items into Harrigan's corresponding hands. Harrigan grasped the items and momentarily rested his arms limp at his sides on the white topsheet. He glared at the soldier, forcing him to answer for the absence of the cough suppressant, buzzer, blanket and drinking water.

"I am not authorized to administer eyewash nor provide narcotics for the coughing. You still have water there on the table."

"What about the outside lines and the bu- hu- zer?" Harrigan's cough took him again. "Minister Mon will learn of this treatment of the Project Director. I want to talk to Mon *now*. And what's your *name?*"

The guard smirked, realizing Harrigan's mind was beginning to fail. *"Premier Colonel* Mon is aware of your situation and he regrets the *incon-ven-ien-ces*. My name is printed on my uniform."

"You know I can't make it out, you poor excuse for a sol-"

The door closed on their confrontation and Harrigan had insufficient strength to engage the soldier through it. The guard returned to his console and called for his relief, due in minutes, so that he could sleep in a real bed without delay.

Harrigan fumed but yielded to the irritating film in his eyes and general ache of his joints, swallowing the pain pill with a sip of stale water. Next, Harrigan tried to clear his vision without poking the squeeze bottle into his eyes. He fumbled it and stuck them both. After pained squirting, wiping and rubbing, at least he could see clearly for awhile. Though renowned for its fast relief, the pill failed him. Yet it was the aching in his mind, tormented in dreams and in full consciousness, that hurt most.

He turned again toward the window side of the room. He did not notice the giant burn-scarred gouge in the grass beyond but would have recalled its significance had he focused directly at it. He concentrated on the hazy thoughts troubling him and stared at Freund.

"Mannie . . . Mannie are you awake over there?"

Manfred Freund looked as old and frail as Harrigan. His hair was not falling out but the blonde had turned a dull white. Slowly Freund awoke, blinked his gray-blue eyes and turned his head stiffly toward Harrigan. Freund started to stretch his limbs but grabbed the crook of his left arm violently as a sharp pain from the I.V. bit into his bruised flesh.

"Aaah; *OWW!"* Freund mustered his self control and struggled to clear the dull confusion from his mind. He glanced questioningly toward Harrigan: "Did you ask me some . . . Oh, uh, yes. Yes. Are you okay?" The rapidly aging German's accent was imperceptible in his weakened and quavering voice.

Harrigan's response was almost a whisper. "That depends, as you so often told me, on how one views life."

"So," Freund's shaky voice lifted to surprise, "you're getting philosophical in your 'old age,' eh, Kevin? That's a good sign. We haven't much time left for this serum to work, have we?"

Harrigan's lips and tongue shivered as much from guilt and worry as from chill: "I've been thinking about the things we talked about. I could never have said this to you before, Mannie. But now I have t-h-hoo."

Harrigan coughed from deep in his chest and spit into an already-used tissue. His tongue and throat felt almost too thick to function as he abruptly changed his own subject to blurt out more disgust and frustration. "Why can't the orderly at least bring new tissues in once in a wh-wh-while? No view-phones working. No nurses. Gotta beg for a glass of water around here."

Harrigan tried again to expunge the phlegm. It repeatedly seemed to leave some of itself inside him, no matter how many tissues he filled. Only the water gave temporary relief and the few mouthfuls left were beginning to taste like swill.

There was silence for a moment and then Harrigan began again in a subdued tone of worry that unsettled his hapless roommate. "Mannie, I've really screwed things up. My life, I mean; yours and everybody else's in the project. Me: 'the great overachiever.' I wish I'd never let Mon convince me to come out here. I wish I had gotten out of this project and listened to Tykvah when I had the chance. I always put myself and my work first. I have always been the center of my world, even *this world* we created. I placed so many important things secondary to this project . . . and through it I've . . ." Harrigan's feeble voice became a gruff whisper: "Mannie, I'm responsible for . . . so-o-o many deaths. If it hadn't been for me you'd be back in Megiddo with your family. My God, Mannie, I'm so sorry. I just can't purge myself of . . ." He trailed off, winded, worried.

Freund sat up awkwardly while Harrigan ineffectively fought the resumption of another cough. It took a minute or two for Harrigan to regain his tired and fearful voice. "An—And now it looks as if it may be over for both of us. Mannie, what if you were right after all about that anomaly in the girl? It was no statistical fluke, was it? I keep having ominous, horrible nightmares about what it could mean. And what if you were right all along about everything else?"

Freund began in a quavering, though warm and comforting, tone. "As for the anomaly, Kevin, how can we presume to know? And as for the rest, well, if I'm right, then there's hope for us yet, isn't there?! I've come to believe you realize that by now. All we can do is wait and think positively. It sounds like these events have all focused your thoughts, Kevin. That's good. Very good."

Harrigan fell silent, except for a few suppressed coughs. Then he turned his closed eyes toward the ceiling so Freund could not see him weep, one tear every few seconds. But Freund did see and had the feeling he understood—though he did not quite grasp all that Harrigan was getting at. Freund genuinely pitied Harrigan but knew his life-long friend would accept neither pity nor pep talks. Freund anticipated also that discussing his own sadness and frustration at being unable to communicate with his family would only serve to deepen Harrigan's sense of guilt and worry. *Harrigan always needed a challenge—even now,* Freund thought.

"Stop feeling sorry for yourself, Harrigan. And if you think I blame you for this, you're wrong. We all worked on this. We all acquiesced to Mon's agenda. You haven't even considered the possibility that all these things were *meant* to be; that someone else would eventually have done everything you've done in the course of scientific research. Is not the work that you're responsible for a legacy of achievement; of advancement toward the inevitable?"

Harrigan's quivering hands grasped the cup of water on his night table. He sipped for a moment, wiped his eyes and worked to draw in precious air deeply. Between sputterings, Harrigan marveled at Freund's lack of animosity; at the undeserved, kind consideration. Harrigan wondered, too, whether the absence of anger might be just Freund's mental faculties slipping further. *No,* he concluded, *but Mannie has indeed been deteriorating.*

Harrigan resumed. "You're just trying to make me feel better. And I appreciate that. But what I'm trying to say . . . this is not self-pity: All my life I've needed to prove myself; feel superior. It became a habit to always rank, ridicule and measu—hu -whu—measure everyone." He paused to wet his throat. "It was a security blanket for me. To me, the maintenance guys, the guards, clerks, housekeepers—they were all ignorant by choice, unwashed or crude. In my mind, everyone without achievement served to magnify mine. I rationalized that everyone with higher station than me got there through the poor judgment of fools. I even saw *you* as not up to *my* standards.

"I was never as good a friend to you as you—hoo—hm have always been to me. I'd always felt that your priorities in life were a waste: family and all your philosophizing. But you had the better priorities, Mannie, I know that now. I needed to feel above everyone else: the scientific community back home, even you, Tykvah; everyone. I could never be on a team—I always had to head it. Same even back in the Army. If I'd seen others as you did, Mannie, I'd have had more friendships. I'd have accomplished more—and for more honorable reasons. I'd have been happy; I'd never have . . ."

Harrigan's voice trailed to a low-pitched quiver. His tormented face and tone exuded a terrorized dread that chilled Freund to the point of alarm. ". . . killed so very, very many . . . and," he fought with no effect another eruption from his lungs and drank the last of the water as if it could cleanse him. "Now I've placed you in grave danger, too." Tears were pooling in his dark, wrinkled eye sockets.

Freund sensed that he could almost reach into the depth of Harrigan's remorse; almost fall into the abyss of his horror. He wondered what he could do for Harrigan. But now his own nerves were becoming unsettled. Freund felt the need to calm his friend—and himself.

"You know, Kevin, I guess I needed to hear you call me your friend. But how can I hold these things against you? You gave me opportunity and the means to support my family when I hadn't even a mark or a dollar to my name. You allowed me to peer into the very seeds of life."

Freund dwelt silently on the problem again: *Maybe just distracting conversation would soothe Harrigan, not to mention fill in the gaps I've caught in my own memory.*

"Kevin, you can help us both," he said attempting an upbeat tone, "I know my mind has been deteriorating. You can help me exercise it. Help me remember something stimulating; anything."

"My memory is going, too. Like what, the Megiddo Preserve?"

"More than that. How 'bout uh . . ."

Freund tried to recall Tykvah's face; he tried to remember this evil behavior Harrigan had just accused himself of—but was recalling only dim and perforated memories. Freund could not visualize many details of the past. Neither could he make chronological connections between the memories he did have from the past twenty years. Still, Freund remembered as if it happened yesterday what

7

Dan Gallagher

Harrigan had done for him and his family after the army or a research hospital—he could not recall which—had interrupted his career. His thoughts returned to the present and his growing suspicion of the Iraqis.

Freund believed that he had been shockingly proved wrong in his allegations and suspicions about Mon. He just could not figure it out. He distinctly recalled that he always trusted in the future. The very realization that he was no longer reacting with his usual calm served to exacerbate his mounting sense of foreboding. He was beginning to fight a rising but still controlled panic. Strangely, it now alternated sharply with vivid, calming flashes of confidence. The flashes felt vaguely as if he was a left-behind kid, just picked up and brought along by his dad.

He needed Gertrude. How he missed her. He knew his memory was going but whenever he thought of her, his impressions were vivid. He thought about when they had argued over his coming here and having to be away so much; how she wanted him to retire early. The trips back were always like honeymoons. And there were weeks at a time when he could stay in Megiddo and telecommute back here using his computer. He smiled, almost blushing, and was engrossed in these memories of now-rare clarity. The thoughts brought momentary relief from his unease and tension.

Now, Freund thought, *there might be no more leisurely Sunday rides along the mountain roads—here or at Megiddo. There might be no more visits with the kids. Perhaps never again will I hold her . . .*

Freund stopped himself. *I'm not one for self pity either. Still, what is going on? Why was there no reply to my fax home? Will Gertrude even receive my body if the worst actually happened? I should hear from her soon or the communications net will come back up and I can use a vid-phone.*

Freund's mind meandered still more: *The serum has to show some effectiveness soon! Harrigan and I might not even live a few days more and . . .*

Freund began to fight the mental fog. He needed to know *exactly* what was making the two of them look as if they were ninety years old. He needed to gain clear insight on where Ron and, he sensed, everyone else had gone. He *felt certain* that both he and Harrigan were only in their early forties. Freund silently searched his memory for the chain of major events that outlined his life. But his con-

8

centration so far only succeeded in conjuring unrelated memories, out of order, of people he knew had been part of his life. He had gotten several important events congealed correctly in time, only to sense that his concept of sequences would fall apart like ancient, crumbling flesh.

What, Freund puzzled, *had made me think of old and crumbling flesh?* Eerie, profoundly unsettling, thoughts flooded his consciousness. *There's something—I can feel it—some important event looming, beyond even this recent catastrophe, that my life and Harrigan's life have been building toward. Or have we been tools in some mysterious destiny? My God, I must be losing my mind! I've got to get a grip on this.*

"Kevin," Freund said in an insistent tone, "lets talk about something besides this hell-hole, for cryin' out loud! I think about how the heck we got here and even farther back—and everything's becoming confused. I *know* I should remember more details of what you're so agonized about, Kevin, but it's not falling into place. Are we prisoners of war? No, wait: We've never been in a war! But, I feel like . . . did all this start with the Army Medical Corps, somehow? No. No. Can't have. And what about these species preserve projects? That's where we are but . . . Kevin, I just can't get it straight!"

Harrigan was no better off, mentally or physically.

The guard set down his coffee and rose from the orderly station, visibly fearful, as his lieutenant and a Colonel approached. He had been nervous around the senior officer for years. The tired soldier offered a quivering salute and was dismissed. The two stern-faced officers halted, conversing at the desk. Then both stepped rapidly down the hall toward Harrigan and Freund's room.

Chapter Two

Ranger Training Camp J. D. Rudder, Eglin Air Force Base, Florida
1039 hours, December 15, 1997

The patrol crept wearily through the marsh grass and sparse pines. The soldiers began to slow their advance, dreading to cross the stream which they knew was now frigid from a week of unseasonable cold. The chill wind in this place, these sweat- and swamp-soaked trainees often complained, did not blow: *it sucked!* These men were almost all brand new second lieutenants; just out of college and the three-month Infantry Officer Basic Course. Yet even that rank had been removed from their uniforms as a reminder that the Ranger Instructors, seasoned Non-Commissioned Officers, or NCOs, were in charge. The Ranger candidates wore mud-splotched camouflage fatigues with patrolling caps of the same cotton material, bulging green ruck sacks, like back packs, along with numerous accouterments and weapons tied by 'dummy cords' to their bodies. The instructors carried small rucks or none at all.

Most of the twenty-five men in this class were West Point graduates, encouraged by tradition to accept the challenge of this the U.S. Army's most exhausting training course. They were within one day of completing it. Yet, they felt no comfort in this. The weather report asserted that an arctic cold front had moved south because of a low pressure system over the Gulf and a high one in Canada. But they strongly suspected that it had come intentionally; maliciously, because they had felt, for two weeks *already*, wet, hungry, long-overexerted and *highly* peeved in general. They were nevertheless determined to endure the extreme fatigue and irritation. Worse, the dog-tired Rangers-to-be were bunching up.

Senior Instructor Master Sergeant Gaines was in front of the formation. He understood the students' motivation acutely. He was known, his men would say, for possessing astounding powers of deduction approaching those of a brick. They felt, too, that he possessed all the grace and swiftness of a pregnant buffalo. But he was good-natured until provoked. Gaines sometimes joked, when this bunching up phenomenon occurred, that one grenade would kill them all.

Gaines smirked and let out a snort. It occurred to him that *women* would be perplexed to observe this sight: The extreme hesitation of these otherwise 'go-anywhere do-anything' soldiers approaching the edge of the frigid stream . . . which was just deep enough to soak their masculinity to the point of retreat, like a turtle cowering in its shell. The old Master Sergeant stood in the stream, precariously tip-toed and holding his pants up tight to keep his turtle and other equipment dry.

To the notoriously mean-tempered Junior Instructor, Sergeant Jenkins, however, this bunching up represented an intolerable lack of tactical discipline. Jenkins brought up the rear of the formation and, as an instructor, carried no weapon or ruck. With massive hands and a stern brow, he reminded some of a cave man. He wore three black chevrons on his sweaty camouflaged lapel and the coveted Ranger tab on his left shoulder. The bunching up irritated Jenkins. He found his anger building to rage.

Harrigan walked in the middle of the group, about twenty feet from the creek. He was intensely muscular throughout his five foot seven inch frame; a vigorous twenty-two year old. He had sought this school to prove himself, yet he felt close to the limit of his en-

11

ergy. Harrigan had lost his New York City accent due to living his teen years in Connecticut. But he had lost none of his feistiness.

Harrigan's ruck held blasting caps, used to detonate the otherwise inert plastic C-4 explosives carried by another ranger student. Just one of the finger-shaped aluminum caps could shred a man's arm and they were easily detonated by impact shock or by electrical charge above a low level. Harrigan's only friend was Manfred Freund, who marched just ahead in the formation.

Freund was a German exchange officer and Harrigan's classmate throughout their four years at West Point. Mannie had been just about the only guy who cared enough to address Harrigan as Kevin during the last four and a half years. Harrigan appreciated that, for nobody really warmed to him. Freund had applied to Ranger School as much because he could not shrink from Harrigan's dare as because he knew Harrigan would need a friend at Ranger School.

"Maintain your damn *interval,*" came Buck Sergeant Jenkins' angered shout. Venom began to build in his voice: "You scum-sucking *officers* . . ." He flung the last man in the formation, a second lieutenant being tested in the role of platoon sergeant, violently backwards several feet. ". . . think you can just have a damn preppy *frat party* . . ." The next soldier became a blur hurtling down to the ground. ". . . in *my* friggin' swamp and expect me to give you the tab." The volume and pitch of his abusive tirade continued to grow. "I'm sick of you privileged, pansy *dirt bags!*"

The furious NCO progressed swiftly, savagely, in gigantic steps forward into the center of the formation. He was ripping soldier after soldier off his feet—each landing askew under the weight of his sixty to seventy pound ruck—and viciously growling at them to "Put out security!" and "Get your interval!"

Now angered at the derision he heard behind him, Harrigan's thoughts turned indignant. *Somebody has to adjust this petty-minded buck sergeant's attitude, instructor or not.* He was about to turn around with a retort he had suppressed for days when he felt a slap on his ruck.

Suddenly, Harrigan landed hard on his butt and was abruptly energized by fear of the blasting caps. None having exploded, his fear turned to vengeful outrage at the degradation being imposed upon his fellows and himself, all officers. He did not care that everyone had, until now, been accepting Jenkins' daily abuse. Jenkins was already tossing Manfred Freund several feet to the right.

Harrigan shed his ruck by yanking the quick-release and sprang to his feet. He lunged at Jenkins. He grabbed the instructor around the waist from behind with his right hand and jammed his left forearm up into Jenkins' crotch. On pure adrenaline, Harrigan lifted the buck sergeant off his feet, toward their right, and slammed him head-first into a jagged tree stump.

Harrigan screamed his indictment. "Who the hell do you think you are? You think you can shove us around 'cause the rank is off our shirts?" With those words, a flash of fear gripped Harrigan: *This guy is going to cream me!*

Without a sound, the huge cave-man of an NCO ran his hand over his throbbing head and slurped up a mitt-full of blood. He rose in an instant and spit it into Harrigan's eyes. Momentarily advantaged, Jenkins snatched the rifle dangling from the 'dummy cord' which linked it to Harrigan. He thrust it, muzzle first, at Harrigan's teeth.

By trained reflex, Harrigan deflected the weapon just as it met his lips. He grabbed Jenkins' shirt pockets with both fists, excruciatingly mangling the right nipple. With his vise-like grip on the tormented chest clamped tight, he crashed his forehead viciously into the bridge of Jenkins' nose. Harrigan dropped himself backward to the ground, the NCO's chest irresistibly in tow, stabbed his right boot into Jenkins' solar plexus and crunched his other boot into his already-abused crotch; launching the windless instructor up into the air behind Harrigan.

Freund leaped onto Harrigan. "What the hell *arre* you doing?"

Master Sergeant Gaines saw the combatants and swiftly concluded that the fight had to be broken up. Even more rapidly, and applying his years of sure-footed outdoors experience, he leaped up the slick stream bank toward the tussle.

That first step did not propel him forward, however: Gaines plopped, nose first, into the pungent mud of the stream bank. His prominent facial bones absorbed most of the impact before the rest of him struck the ground. He perceived an odd but painless crunch and a momentary 'tickle' on his hammer-like chin. A nose-shaped rut was carved deeply into the mud as he slid face-down into the invigorating stream up to his neck.

Gaines pulled himself up and sprang forward with all the dignity he could muster, given his new face-camouflage. The fall left Gaines unavoidably in the dark about much of the fight, but he did manage to reach the scene in time to observe Jenkins curled up tightly on the ground. He grabbed both combatants by their shirts and hauled them upright.

"Stand at attention, you two!" It *doubly* irritated the insightful senior NCO that Jenkins was not bothering to stand up straight and was inexplicably caressing something in his right chest pocket. "Why the hell don't you stand up straight, Jenkins?!"

Just then, Gaines sneezed violently. One of the other ranger students, amused to see the plug of greenish swamp mud shoot out of Gaines' left nostril, answered for Jenkins: "He's unable to comply with your command, Master Sergeant Gaines, because he's become testicularly-impaired."

"Oh." Gaines winced, causing a squashed-flat bug to fall off his muddy chin. He pressed his mud-caked face almost into Jenkins' and bellowed menacingly. "Maybe you'd like to lose *another* stripe, Jenkins." Gaines paused to let his words sink in. "You two will separate and shut up—*Now!*"

With that, the two men each sailed off several feet as Gaines thrust them apart. They managed to remain standing, although their knees were knocking and their torsos were visibly quaking. "You two get where you belong, stay away from each other and report to the captain and me when we get back to Rudder. Now, get on with the exercise."

The patrol continued on, each man taking extra care to keep his interval. As they progressed, the ground became more swampy until they were waist deep in a mass of cypress tree roots grotesquely tangled and half-submerged in rancid-smelling reddish-brown water. The excitement of the fight passed quickly and seemed only to have drained them further. Soon, paused during a map check, a few of them succumbed to a common occurrence under conditions of sleep deprivation: involuntary sleep, even while standing in the water.

Freund rested only a moment against the base of the cypress tree but that brief rest became slumber. His hand, numb and wet could not feel the red, black and yellow ten-inch snake draped lazily atop the root upon which Freund rested his arm. Nature had given the snake tiny saw-teeth instead of fangs and only gravity to inject venom. Yet that venom would kill a man in less than a minute if it entered the blood stream. The reptile, feeling its strength sapped by cold, felt a dawning unease and the need to counterattack what it perceived as a threat. It sensed its inability to move quickly but could not think beyond its impulse to bite and chew, however slowly. Freund did not wake as the coral snake, almost leisurely, looped back and bit into his wrist with sawing motions of its half inch long jaws.

Farther back, Sergeant Jenkins could just recognize the snake on Freund's hand. Fighting to thrust himself over the tangle of roots and through the water, Jenkins approached Freund. Harrigan also caught an early glimpse of the snake, its jaws limply twisting left and right to saw an open wound in which to drop its venom. He had just one more thing to prove to Jenkins.

Harrigan arrived first, grasping the snake immediately behind its tiny head and by the tail simultaneously. He ripped it from Freund's wrist and turned to show Jenkins the prize. Freund dazedly jerked his head upright and opened his eyes, still groggy and unaware of what was happening. Glaring up murderously into Jenkins' eyes, Harrigan snapped his own jaws closed around the snake where he was holding it. He spit the bloody segment into Jenkins' face, threw down the remainder and turned to focus on Freund's wrist.

He squeezed the tiny incision tight with his front teeth, alternately sucking and spitting out any venom that might have seeped into the wound. He then thrust Freund's hand into the water and squeezed the wound violently. Another few seconds and the venom would have entered Freund's blood stream, killing him.

Master Sergeant Gaines got Freund out by medevac helicopter to 96th Med Group at Eglin a half hour later when they emerged onto fairly dry land. The temperature was dropping and Gaines did not want any hypothermia casualties. This last patrol of the course was essentially completed anyway. So the rest were also flown back to Camp Rudder, given hot showers and a chance to get into dry clothes before the final equipment turn-in. Freund did not return from observation at Eglin Regional until the next morning. Gaines reported the fight incident personally, but the captain did not take statements until early the next morning.

Freund rejoined the platoon just in time for breakfast and smiled at Harrigan as they sat at the mess hall table. The hungry Rangers did not eat just yet.

"Viel Dank."

"Stop with the Deutsch, already. You okay?"

"Yeah. You're lucky freakin' Jenkins didn't ram your teeth down your throat!"

"Jenkins is damn lucky I didn't *kill* him, the ignorant low-life."

"I hope he loses every stripe, Kevin. But you better come off contrite to the captain so he doesn't slam *you* for the whole thing."

"Gee. Thanks for the reassurance."

"I already told the captain what an unprofessional ass Jenkins has been. But everybody says you've got an attitude problem. Like you're the only one with the correct answer."

"I can't change everybody else's faulty judgment."

"Improving *their* judgment isn't what I meant."

"Can you keep your voice down! Anyway, Mannie, I generally make sure I *have* got the right answer! If you and I work our butts off and excel at stuff, why should we act like we're plebes or something?"

"Yeah, well, what I mean is lots of *other* folks are squared away, too. Having the right answer isn't *enough*. Look: I've heard guys say they'd want you with them in freakin' battle. But you still put people off. Intelligence and ability are not things to take pride in: you were born with them. They just represent responsibilities *you* have to those around you."

Freund halted his lecture to let Harrigan think, then resumed in a more soothing, jovial tone. "After four years at the Academy with me, you know I don't have any problem with you myself. I already cleaned your clock in boxing class enough to get out my frustrations! Lose the ego 'n the arrogance. It pisses a lot of guys off, Kevin; *Big Time.*"

Harrigan would never admit it, but he often agonized over whether his friend's advice was, at least in part, applicable to him. Harrigan returned only the good humor. "That's just 'cause you've got orangutan arms to match your face!"

"Maybe so! Don't get me wrong, Kevin, you're a good guy; smart as a brick and butt-ugly, though! You know I'm only telling you this because I give a rat's. It always seems that you're wrestling with yourself. I just hope the selfless Harrigan wins."

Harrigan's eyes widened without improving his vision. He was miffed at how well he had been read. Freund sensed that he had struck a nerve and changed the subject. "So we're both going to med school after this. We still have a long way to go and more dues to pay."

The conversation paused. Although he knew Freund was a true friend, it galled Harrigan to think: *Mannie, clearly second to me in just about all the evaluations we've been through—and helped each other through—in the past nearly-five years, is always giving me advice! As if he was elected to minister to me!* It annoyed Harrigan, too, that Freund always appeared serene before exams, deadlines or when there was some kind of trouble.

Still, the reminder about medical school itself saddened Harrigan, his fear of what the captain might do to him shifting to melancholy. He would not have his friend much longer. Freund would soon go back home for the same program Harrigan had qualified for, but with the German Army. Both would be captains upon completion of the medical training and owe five more years of service to their respective countries. Their next ten years were already mapped out for them, though Harrigan worried over his lack of official orders.

Freund had orders to return to his old Bundeswehr troop unit in January, followed by med school at the University of Munich in the fall. Harrigan had genuine esteem for Freund. Yet the American felt comfort in his belief that Harvard, to which he'd gained stand-by acceptance, had the better program. He had always competed hard with Freund and had generally come out on top—even though Freund, who was a couple of years older, had matriculated at West Point with two years of German army service already under his belt.

Harrigan believed that Mannie needed to focus on what was important. Freund spent an immense amount of time in the Newman Club even though he was Lutheran, not Catholic. Meanwhile, Harrigan had studied constantly to juggle engineering *plus* a minor (it *felt* like a major to him) in biology.

Both men were hungry, but Harrigan felt the need to defend himself before he ate. Freund did not feel it appropriate to eat while

Harrigan was upset, though he believed strongly that Harrigan *had* to learn some humility.

"I need a break on this 'ego' thing. Okay, Mannie? You're always beating me over the head with this 'arrogance' and 'humility' stuff. Like *I'm* gonna send the whole friggin' platoon flowers or something! Come on, just because I'm confident and do what I'm here to do doesn't make me arrogant. And you know I don't think I'm better than others, unless they're incompetent slouches, at least."

Harrigan paused and opened his watch cover, concerned. "Holy shhh-. . . . I've got to see the captain in three minutes. Man, I hope this doesn't screw up my application to the Medical Corps and Harvard. Wish me luck."

"Thought you made your own luck, Rambo! Don't worry though, you're already accepted to Harvard Med and they don't make federal cases out of fights during school assignments."

"Thanks. Just wish I knew that for sure!"

"Stop worrying. I'll bag your chow for you. Get going!"

Harrigan received Freund's hand shake and left. Freund bowed his head almost imperceptibly. Then he moved over a few seats, joined another conversation and finally snarfed up the creamed chipped beef, fondly referred to as S.O.S., which had been beckoning to him.

As Harrigan entered the camp's camouflage-painted administration hut, Master Sergeant Gaines grabbed his arm. "What you need to learn, Ranger Harrigan," Gaines said with almost evangelical fervor and concern, "is that we are here—all of us—to prepare for inevitable war. So you've got to be able to see clearly who your friends are . . . and who the enemy is."

The insight energized Harrigan like a dive into a cold river. But, for now, he dismissed the thought and continued into the building.

The captain had taken witnesses' statements before light. Harrigan and Jenkins sat silently outside the captain's office, thinking how they would plead their cases. But they were not afforded the privilege.

The captain came out into the anteroom. His tone was even and without emotion, at first. "Ranger Instructor Jenkins, Ranger Harrigan. This will be two *one-way* conversations. While I'm speaking, you'll be in the front-leaning rest and you'll low-crawl in and out of my office."

The two accused, terrified for their careers and not consoled by the fact that they were now clean, warm and fed, instantly dropped and assumed rigid push-up positions.

"Jenkins, you're first." The once-vicious sergeant now looked more like a guilty, cowering dog as he crawled through the doorway. "Jenkins, this is strike number two. You're out!" Contempt began to grow in his voice. "I hate to push you on someone else, but that's the system. So you're just plain gone. The adjutant will find you a home back at Fort Benning or somewhere. You have an appointment with him . . . *now*. Disappear!"

"Harrigan," the gruff summons was fired off like a rocket, it seemed, into his gut. Harrigan crawled along the floor into the sparse office to face the desk in the front-leaning rest. "Face forward." He could see only the lower half of the camouflage-painted steel desk. "An officer and a gentleman? Bullshit! You're no better than a brawler. You self-important, Napoleon-complexed, squat-bodied little leprechaun turd! I'm ashamed we came out of the same United States Military Academy."

Oddly, the captain's voice cooled to merely threatening. "You're hard to evaluate, as far as this course is concerned, though. Your peer evaluations were so lousy, you had to repeat the Benning phase and you've barely passed 'em in the mountain phase and here. But you risked your life to yank that snake off Freund and you passed every patrol with flying colors. So I'm letting you get your tab—not that it will matter where you're going next." The voice above the 'self-important, Napoleon-complexed, squat-bodied little leprechaun turd' calmed to a matter-of-fact tone. "Both incidents will follow you on your Efficiency Report but the fight won't kill your career. Which brings me to the next subject."

The captain's tone began to degenerate into disgust. "You got new orders faxed here day before yesterday. Seems you're having a few status changes. One: You will be a civilian on 'delay status' just after Ranger school graduation 22 December. Two: You are under binding contract to accept activation as a Medical Corps captain upon successful completion of your medical degree; as an Infantry second lieutenant should you cease to be in academic good-standing. Three: You will enroll at Harvard School of Medicine by Friday January nine."

The captain paused to take out his 'Red Man' chewing tobacco and bite off a chaw. It was an act quite common at the school as demonstrative of toughness. His words now became slightly muffled but still intelligible as cynicism: "You must be *special* just like you think you are. What a crock! Hey, don't medical programs start in the fall? You're in for a major ass-kicking, starting in the middle like that. You may speak."

Harrigan smiled broadly, thinking to himself that nothing and nobody ever *really* kicks his butt. He strained to turn his head and look up to hurtle his triumphantly sarcastic answer. It was pure glee to comply with the school requirement to shout loudly when addressing a member of the Cadre: "Yes, Camp Commander," Harrigan yelled as if the captain's authority hadn't even slightly shaken him, "Just like West Point, two academic majors, Officer Basic, Ranger School and Jenkins *all* kicked my ass."

It irritated the captain no end that he had let this apparently unfazed, sawed-off little whelp speak. Yet what really disturbed the captain was that the answer he had permitted left him, despite higher rank, with a distinct jolt of intimidation. "Dismissed, Ranger Harrigan. One of these days somebody's gonna *kill* you."

Chapter Three

Harvard University, Boston, Massachusetts
1238 hours, April 25, 2002

Bambi pranced into the doctoral genetics lab, her wavy brown hair wisping off her slender five foot, eight inch frame like a banner in a slight breeze. She alighted on a stool across from Harrigan and shed her white lab jacket, revealing a low-cut red blouse. Her face bright with an energetic smile, she leaned vivaciously toward him. She rested her chest definingly, and with an attention-capturing bounce, upon the shiny black laboratory table. It seemed to Harrigan that generous portions of her breasts were peeking at him even more engagingly than her flashing brown eyes.

"Hi, Kevin! There's not much going on now 'cause classes are over. And I, like, dropped a hint or two to Dr. Wentz that I finished all his precipitations and chromatographies and I even got myself to draw his mean-old blood samples from those cute little fuzz-bunnies and could I get the afternoon off?! And do you know what he said?" She paused to tempt a response. ". . . Kevin?"

Unsuccessful, she feigned a pout and resumed her twitter. "Well, at first he wouldn't pay any attention to me and pretended to be irritated so I wouldn't, like, keep begging him for the afternoon off. But I told him how hard I worked and how I even helped you in the lab sometimes; which I really enjoy, Kevin, really. And, so, like, can you guess what he told me?" She paused again, receiving no response, and tried to prompt Harrigan. ". . . Kevin?"

Mildly frustrated, she began anew. "Well . . . Dr. Wentz decided to be, like, *sooo* nice and he told me to take the whole afternoon off! Wasn't that nice of him? . . . Kevin?"

Harrigan managed an annoyed grunt and then a smile. The buxom lab technician's intentionally arousing posture and gaze were distracting Harrigan, despite his consuming need to concentrate on his study notes. Her perky voice was further coaxing him from attention to his reading.

"So Kevin, wasn't that like *really neat* of him? . . . Don't you think, Kevin?"

Bambi realized that she needed to relate better to Harrigan to gain his attention. "Hey, are you studying that DNA molecule print-out, Kevin? It just amazes me how a bunch of chemicals can form such a long bunch of strings and fit inside a cell! And, then, tell the cell to be whatever it's supposed to be; like a brain cell or curly hair or something! I just wish you people could make a gene that stops split ends cause they're really driving me crazy, you know? . . . Kevin?"

Harrigan was unable to resist correcting her, but employed as kind a tone as he could. "It's not DNA. It's RNA." His attention returned to the color print-out of an RNA molecule, that mysterious translator of genetic instructions. Harrigan thought, with great pride, that everyone except he and Wentz *believed* RNA functioned *only* to maintain DNA after an organism is formed and to translate DNA's instructions to the organism's cells.

Harrigan felt that he had no time for ditzy chatter after losing the whole morning to intermittently loud and quiet construction work outside his apartment. The library was full of whispering undergrads. *The only peaceful spot,* he had thought, *will be the doctoral research lab.* Now he complained silently to himself, true remorse and concupiscence beginning to grip him, *She really should have acted toward me like this months ago when I could have afforded to borrow a little time from sleep. Instead, she ignored my advances. It's just as well*, he concluded, *Celibacy, enforced by lack of time, will help me finish the doctoral program.* Harrigan did not deeply consider another benefit he prized above dating: his intriguing but conscience-wracking work on Wentz's clandestine genetics project.

The project consumed them both and demanded immense effort from them, in spite of Wentz's advancing age. It generated in them the serious fear of what would happen if the unauthorized work was discovered. *Bambi isn't aware of much—as a general truism*, he mused,—*but she's quite aware of my oral interrogatories tomorrow.* This thought irritated Harrigan and tempted him to just tell her to leave. He wracked his brain. *I need some way to put her off without burning the bridge to candyland!*

Now, exasperation mounting, he gave her a genuine response. "I really need to focus, Bambi. I've got . . . orals in the morning." Just *his own* mention of that simple plural noun further ripped at what remained of his otherwise studious train of thought.

"I understand, Kevin. I wish I had your brains and discipline. And your energy and your . . . Kevin, did you know I think you're really neat?! Lots of lab techs like me only have a 4-year degree but, even with partying *to the max*, I graduated very high in my class at UCLA. Did you know that? . . . Kevin?"

"UCLA? I'll bet you were, indeed, very high." Harrigan tried to hide the smirk by lowering his face to the page before him.

"Dr. Wentz says I'm the *very best* lab tech! Do you really think he's right? . . . Kevin?"

"You're the only lab tech in his lab, Bambi. But, yes, I wholeheartedly agree with him."

"I think he meant 'in the department,' *silly!*"

"Can I just finish this . . . Ah, do you mind if we continue this conversation later? I mean, I've really got to concentrate."

"Well, isn't there anything I can do to help? Like getting you some nice, fresh coffee or something? You know you need coffee to keep alert when you've had so little sleep. You must have been losing a lot of sleep, I guess. Hey! The stand outside even has cappuccino. I love how they make that creamy swirl on top, don't you? . . . Kevin?"

"Um . . . yes, what?"

"Would you like me to bring you some fresh cappuccino to help you study?"

"Ah, um. Okay. Thanks." He wasn't sure which distracted him most, her intense sensuality or her constant mindless yapping. He just wished that she would go but he could not bring himself to send her away.

"Really, Bambi, I would like nothing better than to spend the day with you . . ."

"I'm free tonight, too." Her eyes batted at Harrigan, teasing him further.

"I've got to brush up on my notes to defend my dissertation, Bambi, really. So, on second thought, why don't you just get yourself some? I'm coffee'd out."

The nymph scampered off, promising to be "right back." With that, however, Harrigan closed his notebook, sighed wistfully and left for his apartment. Bambi returned, only to have her warm but vacant grin droop to a saddened frown. She paused in thought: *Is Kevin being rude or is he just playing?* After looking everywhere, Bambi resolved to repay the former object of her interest. She wiped the single tear away with her wrist, her lower lip bulging outward. Then she pursed her lips tight and ground her pearly teeth together with the sort of anger men ignore at their own peril. "I'm never going to show any interest in short guys *anymore.*" Her foot stamped the floor and her fists clenched. "You'll get yours, Kevin *Harrigan!*" She ejected his last name from her mouth and sat down hard at the computer console. Punching in Dr. Wentz's private access code, she began to mutter quietly. "You *will* get yours."

* * *

No sooner was Harrigan inside his dentil-molded, tastefully appointed flat, than his phone rang. He banged the answer button on the keyboard, which was the only evidence that the massive cherry desk contained a computer. The monitor hung flat upon the adjacent wall, showing a screen-saver image of his initials, "KGH," in maroon block letters. He sank into the burgundy leather work chair, touching one of several control dots to prop up his feet. Just before speaking, however, he reminded himself to be courteous.

24

"Hello?" Harrigan closed his eyes and his light gray walls with their animal and microbe photos disappeared.

"Kevin!" The voice was upbeat and rapid. "It's Dave at Merrill Lynch. I waited all school year to call you on this so that I wouldn't disturb you during the intensity of your final-semester work." He continued his obviously prepared recruiting spiel; precluding interruption, save for the silent recollections sparked in Harrigan's mind.

Harrigan thought kindly of Dave. He had employed Harrigan part-time, and well more than full-time in the summers. Harrigan appreciated the fact that Dave believed in his determination to attain his long-shot goals. With Dave's help and contacts, Harrigan had earned enough to pay back the roughly eighty thousand dollars in student loans, which he had used to reimburse the army for his first year of medical school. That 'recoupment,' as the army termed it, provided him a release from his service obligation. He had needed that release to collaborate with Wentz. With Dave's coaching, Harrigan had learned the communication skills necessary to sell. At least as valuable, he had quickly acquired the knowledge required to analyze personal financial and estate problems, a prerequisite to acquiring wealthy clients and large cases. This, plus the student loans, had enabled him to pursue his new passion: genetic research.

Dave's persuasive but now slightly louder tone converted Harrigan's inattentive hearing into listening. "Kevin, I've always been in awe of how you could find major cases—while paying your way through a *doctoral* program. You're a driven guy, Kev. It's people like you that have brought sound, intellectual analysis to financial planning and that's what *we're* about. We need minds like yours. Now I know your heart is set on research. But, based on your past production, we can offer a first year draw of a hundred seventy thousand . . . plus your own assistant, your old clients back, your pick of prime clients to be assigned to you and a first-class, private office. Can't do better than that anywhere, Kev, especially when you're just out of school. What do you say?"

Harrigan felt bad turning down his some-times mentor, for Dave had made much possible for Harrigan. "I appreciate it, Dave, but I have no time to discuss it. It's been nothing but interruptions all day and I've really got to study for orals because, actually, I won't be awarded the degree until I pass those. Besides, I'm too focused on something I'm doing now. The money is tempting, but I'm working on something that's more important."

"Kev, I'm not making light of a Ph.D. in genetics from Harvard; by any stretch. But you *know* that research grants in that field are unreliable. And genetics is, for you, an untried career path. What you *do know* with certainty, Kevin, is that *this* is a proven career for you."

"Dave, I appreciate it. Really. But I can't. There's something I'm working on. It's really got me riveted. Gotta go. Tell Tom I know he's doing a great job for my old clients. Bye, Dave." Harrigan hung up without giving the frustrated securities principal a chance to speak further. He hated doing that. He realized with satisfaction, however, that the firm had helped him to relate politely to people. *Even*, Harrigan smoldered at the thought, *if most of them didn't deserve the patience and concern.*

Two hours later, just after four o'clock, the phone split Harrigan's renewed concentration. His mother greeted him with her warm and familiar whine and 'New Yawk City' accent, which complemented his father's Bronx growl so well.

"Hi, Kevin, it's Mom and Dad! We just wanted to call to congratulate you."

"I'm not quite done yet, Mom."

"You don't mean you have to go to summer school? Oh my *Gawd*, Kevin, you're going to put me in my grave! Are you *never* getting out of school?!"

"Nothing like that, Mom. I've got a big, final, oral exam tomorrow. It should take most of the day. So, I'm still studying."

"Well, we're so *very* proud of you, Dear. Would you like your father and me to come up tonight and take you to dinner and visit for a few hours?"

"Mom: It's a three hour drive, *minimum*, from Hartford. You'd get back home around midnight or one in the morning!"

"Oh, don't worry about us, Dear. We're just concerned about you. Are you eating right?"

"I'm fine. Really. Please don't come up tonight, Mom. I'm trying to study."

"Jean, Kevin's got to go. He's got to study. But quickly, Kevin; before we let you go: How are you set for a job afterward?"

26

Harrigan began to impatiently hover his fist over the phone button. "Well, ah, there's really nothing concrete. But I'm working on something, using my own resources, with Dr. Wentz."

His mother's tone began again, haughty but concerned. *"Well,* I don't want to see you selling stocks for a living anymore, Dear. You know there's no money in *that!* Listen to your mother on this. Your Uncle nearly starved doing that and, my *Gawd,* with the expenses, he almost lost his house!"

His father's low, grating voice confirmed the maternal judgment. "Pay attention to your mother on this, Kevin, she's right. I always said you should have completed the medical program. Army doctors make excellent money. Gotta be, what forty, fifty thousand, and it's a *secure* job! You could have been making a decent living . . . right now! Like your brother. You should . . ."

Harrigan's eyes rolled as he mentally predicted the words, *talk with your brother!*

". . . talk with your brother, Kevin. He wasn't too proud to accept a little tuition help from *yours truly!"* The voice hung a moment and resumed like an old truck engine revving three times rhythmically. *"You* should go *talk* to your *brother!"*

"Listen to your father, Dear."

"Mom, Dad: I've gotta study now. I've gotta go and finish reviewing my notes."

"You haven't even acknowledged what your father is *telling* you, Kevin. And that will upset him and raise his *blood pressure*, not that *you* should worry about *your father's* blood pressure!" Her indignation began to build. "Do you think your father's talking for his health? *Your father and brother* didn't spend their lives with their noses in a book; cooped up in some ivory-league tower!"

"That's 'ivy' league, Mom. And . . . Oh, gees. Never mind!"

"And I *worry* about you being around all those boiling beaker-bottles. They can blow up in your face, Kevin! Would you like to have a *fake eye*, never pointing in the right direction, like the *Harris boy?!* Gawd between us and harm!"

Harrigan opened his mouth to answer but his father, softening his tone, beat him to it.

"Can't be a student forever, Kevin. You've got to make a living. We'll let you go. Call if you need anything."

"Or if you just want to talk." The motherly voice began to quiver;

just enough to generate remorse. "Why don't you *call* once in awhile, Mister 'I don't need to call my own mother?' And it wouldn't hurt you to go to church, once in awhile, either. You'd meet a *nice* Catholic girl."

The rhythmic truck engine revved again. "Oh, *he's* too *proud* to take *our* advice, Jean! Now let's let him study. He told you *before* he didn't have time to talk now!"

The slight quiver in her voice rose, predictably, into pitiful stuffy-nosed sobbing: "I'm just afraid, Kevin, that you took a wrong turn when you got the army to release you." Her abrupt and powerful honk seemed to Harrigan to blast particulate-laden air right out of the computer speakers at him. "Well, Kevin, I'm *going* to send you some *healthy* foods! You know what happens to your hemorrhoids when you don't get enough roughage."

This phone line, Harrigan silently mused, *is a hemorrhoid in my ear!* "Thanks, Mom, but I'm eating just fine. Listen, I've really got to go. So you and Dad take care. Love you. See you soon. *Bye.*"

He gently pressed the phone control bar on the computer. Huffing at the wall, he hesitated a moment before shouting his frustration. "No more distractions!" Raising his eyebrows, he grabbed the phone cord and walked along the wall toward the jack to unplug it.

The next set of rings came just as he reached the wall jack. It stopped him in his tracks and, of course, worsened his already grinding headache. Harrigan stared at the phone plug in the wall, mentally debating whether to yank it out. Force of habit led him back to the desk. He closed his eyes, scrunched up his face and pressed the phone bar again. "Hello?" Harrigan's tone was less than friendly. The familiar voice bore the slightest trace of a German accent.

"Greetings from Munich, old buddy! It's a girl!"

Harrigan wanted to be mad but could not keep the grin from loosening his stern face. "Mannie, that's great. That's wonderful! Congratulations! How are Gertrude and . . . what were you going to call it if it was a girl?"

"We've named her Marian. And thanks! Gertrude is pretty tired but she's doing just fine. She didn't even threaten to 'alter my anatomy' during delivery this time! I had to tell the grandparents first but couldn't wait to let you know. We're truly blessed, Kevin."

Harrigan ignored the uncomfortable "blessed" reference, in favor of his own clear understanding the biological causes of babies and birth. "Do you think little Hans will like her or be jealous?"

"He's as excited as we are! Hey: I'll be a medical doctor May ninth and promoted the same day! Beat you, for once, molasses brain!"

"Only by a week, *'captain'* dog-face! And don't forget: the sleepless nights have just begun, lowly intern! But really, Mannie, this is wonderful news! Where will you be stationed, 'Hauptman' Freund?"

"Right here near Munich! I'll be assigned to the post hospital."

"So, are you and Gertrude house hunting?"

"Nope. I keep worrying whether we're overextended . . . but we *just closed* on that big brick house I told you about. It's like all our prayers were answered! Everything's going our way! I could just burst! But how about you: Are you through with the grind yet?"

"Almost. Orals tomorrow."

"If I know you, you're still studying. Are you?"

"Yeah. And, frankly today's been constant interruptions. But *your* call was a great pick-me-up! I should get a quick bite and get back to reviewing, though. It's great to hear from you, Mannie! Let's talk in a few days when the dust has settled for both of us."

"Exactly! And I know you'll wow 'em! Take care, Kevin. Later!"

Harrigan went to the freezer to retrieve the only meal available in his bachelor apartment: A Swanson frozen beef tips dinner. He was thawing it in the microwave oven, the wrong way as usual, when his mind made a random but morbid association. The thought caused him to trash the entire plateful. The half-thawed and leathery beef tips reminded him of his first look at the specimen Wentz had shown him three years ago.

Every time he thought of the specimen, he remembered how, as a medical student in Wentz's genetics lab, he had been riveted with fascination at the revelation. In the fall of 1998, Wentz took an immense risk in showing Harrigan the research he had kept secret since 1991. On September nineteenth of that year, a five millennia-old "Ice Man" had been found in the Italian Alps. Four days later the body was ripped from a prostrate, face-down position in its ice and mud sarcophagus. It was flown by helicopter to Innsbruck, Austria, and identified as Neolithic.

Wentz, then an associate genetics professor at Harvard, was on a one-year sabbatical at the University of Innsbruck to do research.

He had overheard discussion of the find when archaeological experts from his institution were called to examine the body at the forensics lab in town. What he found quite peculiar were comments that the genitals were missing from it.

The body had been inadvertently torn away from the penis and scrotum, which the recovery team had not noticed were still solidly frozen in the ground. Bypassing an opportunity to view the corpse, he chartered a helicopter ride to a nearby tourist spot and hiked, unseen, a mile to the mountain crevasse where the body had been found. He was alone at the temporarily abandoned and seemingly empty site. It took him only an hour to recover the leathery fossil genitals, hike back to the tourist landing and radio his pilot to pick him up.

Wentz was then sixty years of age and frustrated by a career devoid of truly novel discovery. He was soon back at Harvard, happy to have distanced himself from what he then feared would be inquiring officials.

He had confessed to Harrigan six years later that he was not proud of his theft but that it was irreversible. Studying this critically important specimen, he had told Harrigan, had given him a renewed sense of purpose and deferred his retirement from—what Wentz at least considered—an unremarkable career. Both researchers knew that their experiments could not be revealed to the scientific community—at least not any time in the foreseeable future. Yet they felt confident that the world would eventually owe them a debt of gratitude.

Harrigan was never comfortable with how Wentz had obtained the specimen. But he understood why Wentz needed him and why he had taken the chance to relate his secret: Though in good health, Wentz knew he could one day die, leaving no access to his work. It might become forever lost or discarded, since the frozen vials had to be intentionally mismarked and the computer files were accessible only by Wentz and would appear useless to anyone examining his computer accounts. Wentz needed to take on a trusted assistant. He had risked everything in telling Harrigan, the brightest and most intensely inquisitive mind in his class. Wentz revealed the secret to him when Harrigan confided that his fascination for the study of life was far more captivating than his father's near-directive that he become a physician.

Wentz's bet had paid off. Harrigan not only kept the secret but took the research a dramatic step further. Harrigan used PCR to replicate some of the undestroyed segments of genetic material from the "Ice Man" sperm. PCR, the polymerase chain reaction, produced viable copies of fragile DNA segments.

Harrigan had inserted these copies into modern human eggs whose corresponding genetic strands were removed. This was so that he could isolate the effects of the archaic genes. The eggs were purposely made incomplete in other aspects of their genetic coding so that they could not mature past nine or ten weeks. The resulting zygotic masses, essentially embryos, yielded clues to the evolution of the human organism; clues which no one else had ever found. Despite the danger to his career, Harrigan had become as addicted as Wentz. He was consumed by the desire to unlock the secrets of what made humans human.

Returning to thoughts of supper, Harrigan wished he could operate the "stupid" microwave without burning or drying out food. He decided he did not like beef tips, anyway. The frustrated bachelor made and rapidly devoured two peanut butter and jelly sandwiches. Then he sat down to quiet study. After a few hours, sleep began to seem more valuable than reading over material he knew anyway. It took almost an hour, for he still was nervous over the interrogatories and irritated by the interruptions that had plagued his day. Finally, he slept.

The ring seemed like some fire alarm as it roused him upright in his bed. He glared at the clock, mentally interrogating it, as if it owed him an excuse for the jolt made by the phone. *Three minutes to midnight! What—the—hell?!*

Harrigan pounded the white bar on top of his clock-phone on the night stand and barked viciously. "What *now?!*"

The Austrian's voice came fast, shaky and thick with accent. "Harrigan. *Ist* me: Wentz. Someone *hast* accessed the computer files. *The* files. *Und alle* the specimen flasks—They *arre* gone. I'm almost out of *meine* mind, for *Gott's* sake. Come down, can you?"

"I'll be right there."

Chapter Four

... FOR IF THEY HAD THE POWER TO KNOW SO MUCH THAT THEY
COULD INVESTIGATE THE WORLD, HOW DID THEY FAIL TO FIND
SOONER THE LORD OF THESE THINGS?

—WISDOM OF SOLOMON 13.9

... it is ... correct to record work, privation, misery, and
suffering, crowned by death, as the [purpose of] life as
Hinduism, Buddhism, and ... Christianity do; for it is these
which lead to the denial of the will to live.

—A. Schopenhauer, *The World as Will and Idea*

OTHER SEED FELL ON ROCKY GROUND ... BUT WHEN THE SUN
ROSE, THEY WERE SCORCHED; AND SINCE THEY HAD NO ROOT,
THEY WITHERED AWAY.

—MATT 13.5-6

Engkar Ridge, thirty miles west of Mount Everest, Nepal

0547 Hours, 12 June, 2002

Unsponsored British explorer, Dr. Bart Lloyd, awoke to his
Sherpa guide telling him they had to go back. Frustrated, Lloyd had
intended to get results and be taken seriously this time. A paleontologist and explorer, Lloyd specialized in the fauna of the late Ce-
nozoic era, especially the Pleistocene epoch which extended from
nearly two million years ago to about ten thousand years ago. The
children's books he had written did not sell. It seemed to him that,
when people thought of fascinating prehistoric animals, they
thought of the dinosaurs, long-gone by the Pleistocene. The creatures of the Pleistocene, or so most people thought, just were not
weird enough to sell. In fact, his theories were not taken seriously
by peers either.

Lloyd's parents were from Africa and very dark skinned. Despite some prejudice, they had built a modest fortune in England through a small electronics manufacturing business. They died in 1998, leaving their only son almost a million pounds and the electronics firm, itself no longer profitable. The money was now nearly exhausted. Lloyd viewed both the wealth and the electronics merely as the means to further his unsuccessful but undaunted digs and expeditions.

His company's most recent venture, at his directive, was to produce a gravity and magnetic wave distortion sensor. The sensor operated on a controversial and incomplete theory of how divining rods functioned to find water or underground formations of varying density: by detecting minute distortions in an area's magnetic and gravitational resonances. Lloyd called the device a tomographic sensor. He had brought the first doubtful prototype along. He was intent on finding something very special with it.

Lloyd believed that 'yetis' of Himalayan legend—and the 'abominable snowmen' of other central Asian and North American legends—existed and were related species on the verge of extinction. Lloyd studied drawings, photos and eyewitness accounts collected over the years. He felt certain that the yeti was actually *Gigantopithecus*. That animal was an ancient primate once assumed to have died out three hundred thousand years ago. Then, from skeletal finds only a year before, it was thought to have become extinct eight thousand years ago. Lloyd's research led him to strongly suspect that both animals were distant relatives of the modern orangutan. Few gave credence to his theories.

Skeptics! No respect for my work! Well, nobody believed in the snow leopard, blue bear, warm-blooded fish, sea-going lizards or the gorilla until some laughed-at researcher proved them wrong, he had often thought, smoldering. So he was determined to prove it. He had seen a yeti himself in the foothills of Tajikistan and wanted to search for them in caves there but fighting kept flaring up unpredictably. So the lanky six foot adventurer came to the Himalayas.

Lloyd was first out of the tent he shared with the guidemaster, Lonzing. Bitter northwest winds at first light shot stinging, dry snow at Lloyd's partly exposed cheeks. The sky had rapidly turned overcast from the crisp whitish blue of dawn. The northeastern horizon filled with dark, streaming clouds just above the valleys below him. Lloyd looked back thirty yards at the ledge they had crossed yesterday to get to this craggy, partially protected crevasse to make camp. Wondering if Lonzing was right, that the weather was getting too rough to continue, he walked back to the edge of the ridge. He peered out over the sides of the icy ridge; west toward still-dark Tibet. He began to feel nauseated but forced himself to check the eastern side as well. Both menacing gray slopes dove down steeply. Lloyd had the feeling that the wind might easily toss him over the edge, sending him scraping down along its abrasive surface like a carrot being skinned against a grater.

Lloyd imagined that a falling climber would grind against the sides until, two miles below, only remnants of the chopped and rock-planed body would skid to a stop, mangled and unrecognizable. He knew he was crazy to have been up here during the monsoon season. The Sherpas, never ones for fright, had warned him that the break in the weather would not last long enough to safely make the climb and detect any caverns or passages. Lloyd felt alarm constrict his breathing, and now realized that they had been right. He carefully backed away and returned to the camp, which was already almost packed up. Lonzing had told Lloyd when he woke that it was imperative they head back down. Danger, but prudence also, was routine for the Sherpas. Considering the fact that three of them, including his guidemaster, had long ago lost one or more ends of fingers to frostbite, Lloyd now heeded their advice. He approached his dismantled tent and spoke in a dejected tone to Lonzing.

"Ah, yes. Yes, you were right." Lloyd yelled, testing his voice to be sure he would be heard over the rising moan of the wind. "Let's leave. Now."

On the way out over the ridge yesterday, Lloyd had felt fine. He had walked behind the others and focused on the readout from his computer, rather than their precarious route. It analyzed disappointing data from his prototype tomographic detection unit. But now his attention was commanded by the stark danger of their position.

With one hand signal from Lonzing, the line of five men linked by a nylon life-line moved out. Lloyd had been up mountains before but never terrain this rough. There was no record of this particular spur near Everest having been scaled; undoubtedly because of its particularly sheer cliffs and dangerous ice formations. Slowly the expedition descended the ridge to a broader point they felt they could trust. Observing, too, that the map they used was inaccurate at this point and that a safer route down now presented itself to the southeast, a sense of confidence returned to the men. They anticipated being back in Chautara by dark despite the impediments of wind and snow. They were making good progress toward safety now through a small and gently sloping snow-filled chasm.

Lloyd was jolted by the loud beep from the computer strapped in the case on his left hip. The ray-gun looking sensor arms to which it was attached hung exposed and drooping from his other hip. The sensor arms were not very sensitive unless they were held horizontally, so he thought that it must be a malfunction. He had forgotten to turn off the sensor. Signaling for a stop, Lloyd grabbed the sensor arms and held them level to the ground, just to check.

"BEEEEEEP!" The computer blasted at him.

He unclipped the rope that kept him from ranging from the Sherpas and trudged away from the snowy valley toward the bare side of the chasm. The noise stopped. Curiosity began to pester him but his straying was plainly irritating the Sherpas. He trudged back toward the snow's edge and up onto a small boulder.

"BEEEEEEP!"

A quick disapproving look from Lonzing made it clear, though, that even if there was a crevasse or cave there, it was not to be dug out on this climb.

"Okay. *Okay!*" Latching the sensors back on his hip, Lloyd gave in to the disapproving glare and his own prudence and jumped down off the rock.

The collapse of the snow-dusted ice under his boots was instantaneous. There was no time even to reach out to stop himself from careening down through the shattering sheet. Lonzing's red face mask disappeared upward out of Lloyd's sight in a cloud of shimmering snow as Lloyd's knees buckled at the impact. The spiked crampon broke from his boot and he fell backward onto his huge back pack. The fall bruised his shoulders as the gasp of frigid air he had taken in a split second ago rushed painfully out of him—but at least he was on something solid. The rain of glittering snow cleared a bit and he could see that the Sherpas were on their stomachs above him, tossing down a line.

Lloyd rose carefully and reached for the rope only to feel himself slipping, slowly at first, backward and downward. He reached desperately outward to grab anything but lost his footing and fell again, onto his stomach. In a brief few seconds he slid down the icy tunnel seven yards and came to rest almost level but in near-pitch blackness. He could barely tell that there were rock and ice surfaces around him forming a widening tunnel.

A faint sound reverberated through the dark, so high-pitched and eerie that it paralyzed him with fear. It was almost birdlike in resonance but also had a distinctive growling undertone. He could not draw in full breaths and he felt unable to exhale. Lloyd swallowed hard and reached for his flashlight, rolling over to sit up and face the sound. It stopped. He perceived a very pale glow of light in the craggy tunnel ahead of him. He turned on the flashlight attached to his right shoulder as much to satisfy his frayed nerves as to see his way out. Back up the funnel which had landed him there, snow and ice particles were suddenly sliding toward him and he heard Lonzing calling that he was coming to get him. He turned to face the reassuring human voice with immense relief as boots and legs appeared in the chute. Lonzing crouched beside him.

"You are all-okay, Sahib?" Lonzing clamped a five yard safety line onto the back of his novice client's belt, so that it could not easily be removed.

"Yes. Just bruised. I heard a sound farther in."

"It is the wind, Sahib. We are under a very thin ridge and this cave must open eastward to the big valley."

"What if it's the yeti, Lonzing? That's what we're here for. We must get some video before we leave; at least record the sound for analysis."

Lloyd detached the small camera from his computer and mounted it on the bracket which he extended slightly out from a harness on his hood. He attached a seven-inch dish microphone to another harness on his left shoulder. Switching the apparatus on, he hoped the transmitter in his pack would reach the British Broadcasting satellite through the rock and would come to the attention of some editor back home. At least, he thought, the computer would record anything he might see. He knew it would be embarrassing if the sound were merely wind.

At that the shriek came again, shaking them both.

"No, Sahib. We must go *now!* That is yeti."

It seemed to Lloyd that he could barely catch his frightened breath. His elbows and knees were quivering as he forced himself to crawl slowly several yards toward the sound; around a jagged corner and . . .

The icy floor gave way, dropping Lloyd face-first into a gray abyss. With a gut-crushing yank, the safety line snapped tight. Lloyd dangled twenty feet above the floor of a house-sized cavern. Faint light penetrated a huge wall of ice shards, apparently intentionally packed snow, to dimly illuminate the cave. Most of the rock was covered with dense moss. But what literally kept his breath from returning was the utter shock of the scene in a corner below.

A massive red and black-haired figure gaped up at him and let out a growling scream, causing the repentant explorer to cringe with fear. It occurred to Lloyd that the ice he had dislodged must have struck the yeti. There was a bloody gash amid the long fur on top of its wide, cone-shaped head. He estimated that it stood over seven feet tall and had arms longer than half that. Lloyd immediately uncurled his body to attempt to climb back up the rope, too winded to even call for Lonzing or perceive meaning in any of the Sherpa's calls. Unable to right himself or to pull himself up the rope, Lloyd slipped back to face the screeching, flailing, man-like creature brandishing its prominent fangs and brownish molars almost directly below.

The yeti's body was arched back so it could look up at Lloyd. Its eyes flashed white in the swaying lamp-light and it held something shiny, jet-black and squirming in one of its claw-like hands; something limp and bloody in the other. Another yeti, just over five feet long, he guessed, lay crouching as if in fear against the near rock wall. Like the one threatening, screaming and jumping at Lloyd from below, it had almost no neck and a large, cone-shaped head. It was full-breasted and had blood matted throughout its leg hair. It must have just given birth.

"Oh my God: Lonzing! Lonzing: It's bitten the head off a *baby!*" Lloyd's mind flashed to interpret what he was witnessing. He had, on rare occasion, observed male apes attack and kill newborns in the wild. Sometimes it was to bring the female of a rival into estrus; sometimes it occurred during environmental stress and, he had once concluded, probably was an instinctive means of population control. Regardless, Lloyd knew he had to get out of there.

"Lonzing, pull!" Lloyd was already rising in short jerks.

The yeti was fiercely angered by the head wound which Lloyd had unwittingly inflicted. It hurled the bloodied and headless body at Lloyd and missed. Lloyd heard a splat on the cavern wall behind him followed by another as the tiny body struck the cavern floor. The female got up and threw a fist-sized rock which struck Lloyd's boot, dislodging his other crampon. Then, just as Lloyd was within a yard of the opening and escape, the massive primate threw the other baby at him. The baby had made no noise to this point. But as it slapped back-first into Lloyd's chest, it blurted out a single high-pitched sigh. As if catching a soccer ball to leave the game, Lloyd's arms closed around the shocked but squirming newborn yeti.

Lloyd realized in an instant what this could mean if he could possibly get it to civilization alive. The smallness and weakness of it tore at his emotion and he knew it needed close contact. Lloyd held it under its shoulder with his right hand and opened his parka, then jacket with the other. He stuffed the baby head-first down underneath his thermal-regulator undershirt and sealed the wet primate up within. As he did so, he chanced to notice that the orientation of the baby's feet was reversed, as if the left and right were transposed. The presumed mother and the adult male appeared in the dim light to have similarly reversed feet; Lloyd was unsure. There was no time for anatomical examination.

Lloyd felt confident that the huge primate could not scale the cavern walls or even want to pursue him. Just to be sure, he turned to look down as he scrambled back up into the tunnel. To his terrified shock, the furious yeti was only two yards behind him. It let out an alarming howl, sending Lloyd's feet scurrying frantically.

"It's . . . Lonzing: Go, Go, Go! . . . It's attacking! Pull! Get out!" The walls of the narrow passage now seemed to constrict maliciously around them.

Lonzing did not speak but scurried and tugged with everything he had to get himself and Lloyd away. Approaching the opening where he first found Lloyd, Lonzing screamed in Nepali at the three men above. "Help us! Yeti attacking! Pull, quick!"

Lloyd's own fear now heightened to panic as he realized that even Lonzing was becoming frantic. The pair was being pulled through the fissure. They were ahead of their pursuer by almost four yards. The force of the tug was so great that they almost lost their grip on the rope. The surface appeared just ahead. But the screeching was catching up. With uncontrollable panic rising in their throats, the two could hear clawing and slapping as the yeti followed them up through the ice-floored crevasse toward the broken opening at the surface.

Once atop, on the side of the rising ridge beside them, the pair thrust their fellows forward along the only ground on which they could run without being mired by snow. Limping in their running strides along the angled rock which offered better footing than the snow below and to their left, they paralleled the snow line. They were running, it seemed, right into the blinding sun but at least they could move almost as fast as they could on clear level ground.

One of the Sherpas, whose many observations of yetis led him to characterize them as timid animals, turned to see if his leader's reckless fear was justified; whether there really was anything chasing them. He glimpsed the monster, running almost silently but in great leaps. It was immediately behind them. It was almost upon Lloyd and reached out its huge hand at his pack.

The Sherpa sensed that he had missed a step and was tripping. But as he turned forward again to see the ground and guide a recovering step, his mind boggled. He shuddered with the sight which met his and his companions' eyes. There, below his feet, was over two miles of air. Terror momentarily kept him from gasping.

Several yards down along the fluttering safety line, Lloyd's plummeting form turned pack-down, face up, in the freezing wind. The yeti came into Lloyd's view, standing atop the cliff and shaking its fists wildly. Lloyd's tearing, quivering eyes beheld the cave, sealed up with glinting ice and snow, fast receding above him.

The horror piercing them cramped every muscle as if they were electrocuted.

* * *

On the other side of the globe in Boston, and while Lloyd had been waking, it was just after seven o'clock in the evening. The setting sun was making Harvard's new colonial style brick administration building deeper red than it already was. The old administration building in Cambridge was being converted to a dormitory. Harrigan sat nervous and angry in the white marble anteroom to the university chancellor's conference hall.

Too late and too rude of the chancellor, Harrigan thought, flexing his jaw in suppressed fury, *but I'll hold my tongue for now.*

Wentz had just left the conference room and sat next to him, tearful and silent. Harrigan felt like hitting someone for this humbling of Dr. Wentz but told himself to remain in control. He was angry and nervous; *very* nervous. The massive oak door opened and the chancellor's assistant jutted out what struck Harrigan as a pinhead and a pencil-neck.

"You may come in, now, Dr. Harrigan."

The assistant ducked from Harrigan's glare and yielded the passage.

Harrigan stood, rigid, defiant, before the Board. *Ethical-immaculates*, he silently branded them.

The chancellor, visibly tired, addressed the accused. "It's been a long thirty-some days with this, Dr. Harrigan, and it's late so I'll come right to the point. The Board has determined that your unauthorized and unethical research was independent of the research conducted to fulfill your doctoral requirements. As such, it has countermanded the Disciplinary Committee's proposal that the conferment of your degree be rescinded. I concur. So you will retain your degree.

"But it is a fact that you have participated in the creation and destruction of fetuses, using University resources including donor eggs not authorized by the donors for such a purpose. The university will, tomorrow, release a press statement of that fact and the fact that all findings, data and specimens involved are destroyed. Those items will be destroyed this evening after our meeting.

"You and Dr. Wentz might be relieved to know that we will not disclose the origin of the specimen, since it could not be verified. I believe it serves no purpose to lecture you. You are permanently barred from this institution and a summary of the case will be sent to several scientific societies and institutions. I doubt you'll ever be able to make anything of yourself in the field of genetics."

"Your opinion, Chancellor, of my career prospects is as wrong as are your ethics. You people are just trying to avoid lawsuits from me, the donors and even the Italian government. You may not be successful at that. As for your ethics, you have a lot of nerve. This institution teaches abortion techniques and pays, through the medical plan, for employee and student use of RU-586. All of this is quite appropriate. But you are hypocrites if you think that my research on fetal material is any different, ethically. You're absolute hypocrites."

Harrigan fought the impulse to violence and left the room. He grasped Dr. Wentz's hand firmly.

"You should *haf* taken my advice *und* gotten a lawyer. *Vill* you keep your Ph.D., Kevin?"

"Yes. They decided to avoid a suit but they'd better be careful how they publicize this. They've already bordered on libel with comments to the press. What will you do with your retirement, Dr. Wentz?"

"*Weis nicht*—I just don't know, Kevin. But I want to *shtay* away from the public for a very long time. Did you read the *Science Journal* article? They *arre* saying we made hybrid fetuses *und* killed them. Lies. How can they view it that *vay*, Kevin? *Vee* discovered gene repair occurring during the formation *uff* eggs. You discovered a *vay* to redeem archaic genetic material. This could be *uff* monumental importance. *Und* they *arre* destroying all the research. What imbeciles! What hypocrites! Man was meant to *shtudy* man." Wentz's voice was breaking down and clogging high in his throat. "Now it's all lost, Kevin. Your brilliant research career *ist vorbei* before it's begun—*und* mine is ended in disgrace. I can never face friends *und* colleagues again. We're beaten. We're both finished." His voice turned more melancholy and quiet. Wentz looked at the floor. "What fools. Absolute, *destructif* fools."

"*You* have long needed a rest. Take a cruise. Maybe put your notes back together just to defy these sanctimonious jerks. And don't be so sure they've beaten *me*. As for the gene redemption process and the meiotic RNA discovery, they can't take those things out of my brain."

"Vat vill you do now, Kevin?"

"I haven't decided yet. My folks have been great through the controversy. I think I'll visit with them for a few days. Then, maybe, go on vacation to plan my next moves careerwise; wait for the adverse press to die down. But if those bastards think they can wave a pen and stop *me* in my tracks, they're wrong."

"*Goot* luck, Kevin. I hope you can *buildt* a life after this."

"Thank you, Dr. Wentz . . . for everything. And don't let yourself get so despondent. Positive mental attitude. It's like a college buddy of mine used to say: 'It all depends on how you view life.' So chin up, okay?"

"Ja. 'Chin up.' That *ist* the *vay."*

The two men shook hands and left.

* * *

Lloyd fought the panic and screamed at his plummeting comrades: "Unbuckle the safety line *first.* Undo the line *first."*

Only Lonzing comprehended the English shout. He fought his panic just well enough to relay the critical message in Nepali to his frenzied companions as they accelerated and twirled down through the frigid air. The north side of the cliff face broke the northwest wind's fury. It also deflected gusts along and outward from the eastern-facing rock. This, combined with their forward momentum, carried the shocked explorers out and away from the sheer precipice.

Lloyd pulled his belt around, hard, and managed to unclip the safety line. Lonzing followed. The other three also forced themselves to do the same.

"Now—*lose*—the—*pack!"* Lloyd pulled a metal clip on his side and wriggled a bit. The back pack sailed off him slowly and began to spin as Lonzing translated the commands. *"Wait!* Fall away from each other. Away!" Lonzing repeated the shouts in Nepali as four more packs began to flee their owners.

"Now!" Lloyd held his breath, clamped his eyes shut and pulled his rip cord. The tiny nylon box behind his shoulders seemed to explode with color. He felt the painful tug and looked up to check the multicolored, squarish, puffed-up canopy which slowed his headlong descent from a hundred twenty miles per hour to about fifty.

That pain was desperately welcome, for it proved he had a chance to live through this. An imperfect chance, he knew, especially in these conditions.

He tried to control the risers with his hand still protected in the mitten. Gloves were never used in these conditions as they dissipated heat, leading to frostbite. The mitten's two appendages, in which wearers could place a finger and thumb temporarily, permitted only limited dexterity. Discarding the mitten, however, would rapidly produce frostbite *and* immediate tangling of its unremovable sleeve tether in the control risers. Lack of precise manipulation of the risers resulted in an uncontrolled landing; often in death. So each understood the deadly challenge that the mittens represented and focused attention on timing exactly when—or whether—to shed them.

They were scattered enough to avoid drifting into each other, which would have collapsed their canopies. The gray and white terrain they were approaching—now from two hundred yards above—rose up at them, it seemed, at an accelerating pace. The wind was threatening each of them and Lonzing had almost been buffeted up and swung onto his own parachute. This would have caused him to dart downward, wrapped struggling within it. Now the ground was not only rising fast but it was in clearer view.

Looking directly below, Lloyd gasped and squirmed. The ground was carpeted with closely spaced, one to six foot tall, thin razorsharp ice formations. They rose ominously each night from the ground as it froze and compressed its water upward and out of cracks. They usually melted by noon. It was not even close to noon.

The razors loomed up at them faster and faster. It would take expert skill and dexterity—something impossible now—to land on the tiny patches of safe, flat rock and avoid the scissor-edged ice. Their mittens started to be shed, tangling as feared in each man's risers, and all but stopping control of the direction and posture of the parachutes. And at the very instant of landing, a strong tug down would be required to counter downward momentum and land at a safe speed. Lloyd gauged the ice razors to be but twenty-five feet away. He tried to scream some expletive but, like his counterparts, was unable to stop panting with fear long enough to utter a word.

Lonzing would be down first, maneuvering by swinging himself with his feet and by pulling as best he could on his right riser. The circular pattern he made on descent would be responsible for a broken arm but it also enabled him to crash sideways through the blade-shaped icicles. Two of the others intentionally hit a vertical outcropping of rock, rather than be sliced up by the waiting crystal blades. Their bodies withstood the impact but their faces, bounced off crumbling rock, looked as if they had been mauled by an enormous cat's paw.

Lloyd looked down. He was skimming—backward and much too fast—about five feet over alternating flat areas and areas studded with ice daggers. He was completely unable to manipulate the chute in any way. He felt sure that he would be decapitated or sliced open and die watching his exposed entrails freeze. Lloyd closed his eyes—and his legs—tightly.

"Uuuh!" Two sets of lungs compressed out their air simultaneously as the Englishman and the Sherpa collided four feet off the ground; abruptly ceasing lateral motion. They fell dazed and sprawling upon the three yard square boulder. Landing with a crack and falling sideways, they toppled and crashed through the surrounding ice formations. The icicles were still intimidating, for they could easily have split a tall man from crotch to throat.

The Sherpa managed to get up and help Lloyd to stand. Nursing their bruises and minor cuts, each man gathered with the others to take account of themselves. They limped, moaned, bled and cried aloud. But they were alive, their radios and video transmitter worked, and they were only a few miles from a road.

Lloyd was about to keel over when he reached Lonzing, who held him upright with one hand and had the other Sherpas strip off his heavy wire-laced equipment harness. They set Lloyd's harness on a boulder, not realizing that the camera was still transmitting and that it was facing the group. Lloyd suddenly regained his senses with a very pained and surprised look on his face. Ripping his clothes open he grabbed the ravenous primate, now head-up inside his shirt. It was to no avail. The baby yeti was enjoying a fruitless but vacuum-tight suck on Lloyd's left nipple and a tight contingent grip on the other. Lloyd, hopping and hooting, quickly fumbled through a sealed, interior pocket and extracted a fortified milk pouch to protect both the newborn yeti's life and his own smarting chest.

The video, which included footage of the baby yeti latched onto Lloyd's chest, had been broadcast worldwide the very next morning. A week later, while meeting dignitaries and recovering his strength in London, he would realize that even the King of England could not avoid smirking. Lloyd was shy and handled it all quite awkwardly.

But to now-noted explorer and dreamer Dr. Bart Lloyd, royalty would not provide the most intriguing appointment of his life. That distinction would fall to his impending meeting in London. He would encounter an ostracized American geneticist who, the journals claimed, had found a way to redeem destroyed genetic material. Equally fascinating at the meeting would be a diplomat from Iraq's new government. As anyone who read the newspapers would recognize, this Iraqi was the man in charge of several joint peace projects with the Israelis. Dr. Bart Lloyd would come, through this new association, to experience in reality what he and millions of others had only dreamt.

* * *

Dr. Wentz did not go home the evening of his and Harrigan's confrontation with the chancellor and Board of Visitors. He walked toward the genetics lab, once reserved for him, across campus. On the way, he dejectedly watched the summer school students devouring an alcohol-soaked watermelon at a late night party. He tried to open his office and found that his key no longer fit. Wentz collapsed in tears still holding the key in the lock. He rose and walked to the men's room where the white painted water lines above the lavatories made a convenient tie holder. Wentz kept the tie knot in the front. So his step off the commode resulted in his head being jerked back. His neck did not break and he expired with more pain than he had anticipated. But his chin was indeed up.

That evening, Harrigan walked to the parking lot, considering what kind of future he would make for himself. He was doubly angered by the chancellor's prediction that his career would be stifled. He was stone-faced driving past the Cathedral of the Holy Cross toward his apartment on Union Park Street. He stopped and stared at its gray sandstone steeple, which dominated the gothic structure. Its huge circular window above the arched entrance caught his eye. He knew it bore the figure of an English King in the red stained glass. But it looked distinctly like a rose to Harrigan. He thought the impression was due to the scent of roses on the cathedral lawn.

That's odd, he mused, *my windows are rolled up.* He dismissed the thought.

Harrigan gazed questioningly for a moment at the cross atop the roof. His eyes filled with tears and he let out an awkward, pitiful moan that surprised him. He felt embarrassed at himself for momentarily yielding to what he thought of as superstition. Harrigan put the car back in gear and proceeded to his apartment where his phone had been disconnected for almost a month, since the press got the story. He wrote a few notes on a to-do list and slept. The next morning he left to visit his parents in Hartford for four days.

On his last morning at his parent's home, just before light, Harrigan sat nursing coffee in the small but cozy kitchen. His father was not up yet. This morning he felt guilty that he had anticipated an 'I told you so' attitude but encountered only moving support from both parents despite all the media criticism and debate of the last four weeks. He noticed his mother staring at him from across the kitchen.

"Kevin," She began in a simple, questioning tone. "The newspapers: They say Dr. Wentz killed himself and that the university has destroyed all the records. All the work you and he had been doing. Why would he do that? Why would *they* do that?"

"I think our work was the only thing that was important to him, Mom. He told me once that working on the specimen was what gave his life meaning. They disgraced him and he wasn't strong enough to take it and go on."

"Kevin, you don't feel depressed do you? You're made of tougher stuff than to do anything stupid like that!"

"No Mom. I'm fine. Just angry. I'll get my name back one day. You'll see. And those hypocritical S.O.B.s will see, too. As for the university, they said they destroyed everything because findings may only be added to the genetics body of knowledge if obtained ethically; by their self-serving definition of ethics. They didn't want anyone to have any possible incentive for doing unauthorized research; any possibility that their work would be kept. The real reason is that they didn't want an investigation which could enable the anonymous egg donors to discover if their eggs were used . . . and sue."

"The *Time* article said you were able to rejuvenate destroyed sperm. A Fossil Gene Redemption process, they called it. How could that be done, Kevin?"

"It can't, exactly. Wentz and I wanted to study how sperm and egg are produced; how the genes are assembled when they're first created. That production process is called meiosis. For boys, meiosis occurs when they're several years old and practically impossible to study. The sperm would have to be observed forming in *living* testicular filaments. But for girls, meiosis occurs while they're still in the womb. We can study fetuses in a genetically modified pig uterus. So fetuses are vastly easier to obtain and work with.

"Wentz had for years been unable to get permission for an unrestricted study of meiosis. So, he did it anyway and discovered an RNA molecule that occurs only *during* meiosis. I believe it inhibits certain types of mutation in humans. We could only find traces of it in animals.

"When Wentz found the specimen of the Ice Man, it was the chance he'd been waiting for all his life. He wanted to find out whether this molecule occurred only in humans and how far back in the development of sapiens this odd trait arose. He was unable to implant any of the genes from the specimen into a modern egg. What I did was to find a way to stretch out the long and convoluted genetic material without destroying it and enhance the way computer-controlled scanners could follow and read its coded segments. I enabled the computer and that PCR machine I showed you last year to reconstruct most of the genetic coding in the archaic sperm. It's like this, Mom . . ."

Harrigan grabbed a thin booklet, which his father had left lying on the table. It was the instruction manual for assembling a cabinet.

"Imagine you have instructions, say four pages typed, for making a cabinet. These printed pages represent the genetic blueprint of a possible baby the 'Ice Man' might have fathered, less the egg's half of course. Now imagine I tore each page into five or six pieces."

He ripped the booklet as his mother gasped but held her tongue.

"That tearing represents the damage done to the sperm's genetic instructions over five thousand years. Got it so far?"

"I think so. You could put them back together if you could read the language so you could tell which words and sentences would make sense as you put the puzzle together. Right?"

"Exactly. And we have a mental model of what these pages ought to look like. The words and sentences are like gene segments. The computer can read and make sense of them. That's because it has a database, like the language that the cabinet instructions are written in, from the recently completed human genome project. Remember I told you about that project to decipher and map human genes."

"Yes, but Kevin, there are many different children any given man could father. How can the genes be put back together with all of that complication?"

"First, siblings aren't as different as you might think. I've begun to suspect that there exist 'personality sequences' in genes and that these produce the most significant differences. Second, I discovered that all the potential instructions for slightly different potential children can be estimated by the computer. The genetic coding in each sperm is only slightly different. For any given man—and the 'Ice Man' was no exception—*most* segments in the genes of each sperm are identical.

"All of the segments were damaged, *but* that damage was never in exactly the same place for every fossil sperm. The computer read the instructions—the genetic sequences—in hundreds of sperm. It could discern what the destroyed segments were by reading the *corresponding intact segment* from a different sperm in the same sample.

"I had the computer build a model of what the most common configuration of genetic sequences were and compared its readings of each sperm scanned to the model. Like our mental model of what a page looks like. That way it kept updating and perfecting the model of the most common configuration. It eventually built a model of the coding that the typical sperm in the sample had. Like reassembling these printed pages by being able to read and know which words and sentence fragments would make sense if you put them together.

"Then, all that had to be done was to wait a few days while the enhanced PCR machine manufactured an actual set of gene sequences from that perfected model—the reassembled instructions. The last steps were to put the manufactured genes into a donor egg — a kind of artificial mating. The reconstruction was very good but imperfect. So, to avoid creating a freak, I inserted genes which coded them all to be female and to terminate just after meiosis would occur.

"Wentz was the first to observe the mutation-repairing RNA molecule. That molecule *only* appeared during meiosis and falls apart once the egg is formed. I think it's the same for sperm production. The evidence from doing this with donor eggs of several races suggests that it's present in every modern population. But we found that its prevalence was somewhat less in the human gene pool of five thousand years ago. The significance of this, Mom, is that a biological process *might* be occurring which is keeping humans from evolving further! None of this is published and I'm not *about* to give the press any interviews. These fools at Harvard won't even study it. Did I explain all this clearly?"

His mother was surprised at herself because she *did* follow at least the gist of it. Her motherhood enabled a deeper understanding even than she wanted to have. She looked at her son in horror.

"Then, Kevin, you created *human beings* using living women's eggs and a dead man's sperm . . . and prearranged for the little-girl fetuses to be unable to grow to experience a mother's love . . . while you studied what went on in the doomed fetuses' ovaries. Don't you tell *your father* these things. It would *kill* him, Kevin. And *Gawd* help you, son of mine. It's not for me to judge. I can only pray that God will forgive you."

Harrigan's face turned ashen and fearful. He realized his parents must not have completely read or understood the many articles that taunted him when they offered their warmth. Then his face reddened and hardened in an indignant frown, further evident in his voice.

"So you *are* judging me, then, if you say I have to be forgiven. Stop it, Mom. It's not against the law. And for good reason. Look: It's man's destiny and purpose to study every aspect of himself and his world. And anyone who studies history knows this 'god' stuff has always inhibited the progression of science and society—and even peace. It always has. Look at the crusades a thousand years ago and the Arabs and Israelis fighting until recently.

"Every day, it seems, you read of some archaeological discovery that proves the Bible 'right.' But 'right' about some recorded event which its authors *interpreted* in ignorance to be a miracle. These events *we now know* were natural occurrences. Like the discovery in the last couple years of Sodom and of the parting of the Red Sea. Both were *proved* to be natural geologic occurrences. Ancient people who saw these things just assumed some 'god' did them because they had no knowledge of science. So, don't lecture *me.*"

"All right, Kevin." Her voice was sad and quiet; almost defeated. "I won't lecture you. I'll just pray for you."

Harrigan noticed his father eyeing him from the kitchen doorway. The man looked to be on the verge of tears but his eyes were dry.

"I understand now, Kevin." And he walked, head low and silent, from the room.

Harrigan left within the hour and did not speak again with his parents, though there were many times later in life when he almost called and almost let them know his phone number. The fact always bothered him, but he had to move on with his life. He decided there that he would vacation for awhile by driving randomly around the South for a month or so. *I'll just spend some time considering my options*, he thought, *and find a way to bounce back. I will not let those S.O.B.s kill my chance at greatness. There must be a way to actualize my work's potential.*

Harrigan returned to Boston to pack, ignoring the pile of mail, despite an ornate invitation protruding from the stack. The following morning a man arrived with a sealed envelope. Inside was an intriguing note, which only hinted at a genetics project that a representative of the new Iraqi government wanted him to join. There were also tickets for a London flight which left that very afternoon. *Why not?* He thought on his way to the airport, grinning for the first time in weeks, *It can't hurt to check it out.*

Chapter Five

Heathshire Meeting Suite,
The Grosvenor Hotel, London, England
0859 hours, 20 June, 2002

His overdressed, over-polite Iraqi escort walked just behind and to the left of Harrigan as they strode briskly through the open doors of the meeting suite. Harrigan's gray pinstripe suit, traditional black Florsheims, starched white shirt and simple red silk tie were all spotless and sharp-looking. The escort smiled and took his place at the sumptuous breakfast cart nearby. The suite was impressively spacious and made a truly lavish conference room. A gleaming brass and crystal chandelier hung from the ceiling above the gold-leafed coffee table in the center of the opulent room.

Dr. Bart Lloyd stood munching on a grape jam covered bun. Highlighting his white cotton suit were half-inch wide light gray stripes. His simple flat-black shoes and gray no-button collar shirt were quite sporty. With one of the new mid-chest black ties which knotted several inches below the neck, Lloyd was clearly a modern dresser. Harrigan smiled warmly at the tall African-Englishman who looked to be about thirty-five, yet sported a graying mustache. It was noticeably thicker on the left side than on the right. Harrigan reached out his right hand.

"You English wake up at an ungodly hour! But it's an honor to meet you, Dr. Lloyd. I've read the accounts of your discovery with absolute fascination."

Lloyd's large hand tipped the croissant, dropping a clump of jam on the seat, as he swallowed quickly and set the morsel down. His hold was medium-firm against Harrigan's tight grip.

Lloyd's accent was refined and his tone was friendly. "Thank you. I'm over my jet lag, now, but you must be exhausted. What with being five hours behind England and arriving only yesterday. I've read of the controversy, such a ghastly affair, which seems to have befallen you. I must say, Dr. Harrigan: I think the university has been most unfair to one who has made the brilliant breakthroughs you have. And Dr. Wentz's death has been treated quite callously, if you ask me. My condolences; I understand he was a close friend."

"Thank you."

"By the bye, call me Bart, would you?"

"Sure. Call me Kevin. Bart, where is our host?"

"Oh you know these diplomat-types, busy busy! Hassan, the gentleman who met me in the lobby and brought you from your room, said that Minister Mon would be unavoidably late; not too. Well, let's have a sit, shall we?" Before Harrigan could warn him, Lloyd's white pinstripe suit gained a new purple design on the exact center of its seat.

Hassan offered Harrigan some breakfast but was politely turned down. Harrigan sat straight but not rigid on one of the three finely embroidered and plush armchairs which surrounded the coffee table. *Clearly,* he thought, *the setting has been carefully selected.*

"Hassan," Harrigan inquired, "would you mind if Dr. Lloyd and I speak alone while waiting?"

"*Noht* at all, sir." Hassan departed to the hall, shutting both doors behind him.

For about ten minutes further, Harrigan and Lloyd exchanged descriptions of their work and theories, though Harrigan was careful not to be too specific just for the sake of good policy. Their discussion became friendlier and livelier as they progressed.

"That's amazing, Bart. I've never considered that the atmospheric reactions which must have taken place when the meteor struck sixty-five million years ago could have destroyed the ozone. And you theorize that the only animals which survived the sun's unimpeded rays were those which burrowed and which lived in the very lowest depths of the ocean?"

"Indeed. I suspect that low-level exposure to ultraviolet and other radiation promotes speciation via mutation. High levels kill off whole species and can induce cataracts, a death sentence in the wild, more readily in reptiles than in mammals. Your work touched upon speciation—and inhibition of it, as the rumor goes—did it not?"

"To some degree. Have you published your theory?"

"Yes. And there are a few who have come up with the same suspicions independently. Still, almost no one seems to take me seriously on this. I think, Kevin, that I have found partial proof: An ankylosaur—a herbivorous dinosaur—which seems to be sixty-four million years old. That means its species, which dug burrows, survived nearly a million years after the other dinosaurs died in that horrendous Cretaceous-Tertiary event. Hence, its ancestors survived longer than other dinosaurs because they burrowed - like crocs - and rarely came out. The one I found, however, had evolved very small claws not suitable for digging. So, by the next round of ozone destruction, after a million years of recovery of the ozone layer, they didn't burrow anymore and the whole species was vulnerable."

Harrigan thought it was barely possible for the huge *Ankylosaurus* to construct a tunnel and he doubted the theory. "What about birds? They don't burrow. How did they survive?"

"I suspect the early birds and remnants of the smaller therapods did burrow, or occupied burrows of prey. I just haven't found the evidence yet. But look at alligators, frogs, small mammals and other species which survived from the time of the dinosaurs: they burrowed and hibernated. Modern penguins under the ozone hole produce a lot of non-viable eggs. Oceans provided better protection than the atmosphere alone. So more salt water species survived than land species. That much can be proved.

"There is also evidence that some volcanic activity alternately destroyed and helped restore the ozone, depending on the content of what was spewed into the atmosphere. Very deep-source eruptions and meteors that caused eruptions by striking deep enough into the earth's surface, I believe, caused sulfur dioxide to reach and deteriorate the ozone layer. Other reactions I'm still studying may have restored it by catalyzing oxygen-based gases into ozone. Even natural ignition of fossil fuel deposits could have restored the ozone layer within a brief number of years of this cyclical ozone destruction."

"Fascinating. You know, when I was a kid I used to go to all the dinosaur exhibits and collect models. Even the few models of animals that came later."

"Oh, well, my dear Dr. Harrigan! Then you must see my fossils from the Pleistocene epoch. That's my specialty. These creatures existed during mankind's own evolution. Most are in the Natural History Museum not two miles from where we sit! Yes, the Pleistocene was an amazing time! Why, there's even evidence of a predecessor race of humans living in a warmer Antarctica up to as recently as ten thousand years ago. It's theorized that they built cities in South America, Africa and Australia! They might have built the Sphinx twelve millennia ago and lost their grip, as it were, as their homeland iced over and their colonies experienced drought. I've wanted to investigate this theory but the field is now crowded, I'm afraid. But enough about my work. What I'd like to know is how that mysterious Fossil Gene Redemption process of yours works."

"Bart?"

"Yes?"

"Why do you suppose the two of us have been invited here?"

"I had supposed it was so Mon could buy the yeti and put him on display somewhere. He's developing all those joint projects for tourism and industry in Israel and so on. But it belongs to Oxford now, my alma mater from frosh year through doctoral work. The ungratefuls wouldn't even return my book rights when, not two days after I signed the papers, I told them I hadn't intended to include book rights in my donation! They'd been quick to draw up the papers when I informed them of my desire to establish a modest endowment. I suppose I should have read the documents or consulted a barrister before I gave away the yeti, the video and the story. They can bloody well write it themselves, now!"

"Sounds like a very tough break, Bart. I'm sorry."

"Indeed. And thank you. I must admit: I'm quite disturbed, too, by the fire that destroyed my electronics firm's only facility while I was in Nepal. It wasn't insured. The bright side, though, is that I still have the prototype of the tomographic detector, so things will be just grand financially someday soon, I should think."

It always irritated Harrigan when he failed to get a straight answer to a question. In addition, he had no patience with people who gave away so much of what they worked for to charities. Further impeding his concentration now was the odd feeling that they were being overheard.

"Hmm. Bart, let's just sit quietly until he gets here, okay?"

Lloyd was uncertain whether Harrigan was being rude or had a good reason for the abrupt request. "Well . . . fine. That's fine with me if you like."

Minister Ismail Mon strode in moments later alone, smiling, apologetic and complimenting the pair. The researchers stood as he entered and greeted them both.

Mon's accent was vaguely American yet still detectable as Iraqi Arabic. "Doctors Lloyd and Harrigan! Your *kind* consideration in agreeing to speak with me is *most* appreciated. Please accept my apologies for this unavoidable tardiness. Please sit and be *comforrtable*. I promise to take but a few minutes of your time. Let me say that I am hugely impressed by the work you two have done and that I take great issue with your obviously jealous and self-righteous *detrractors.*"

Both felt justified and somewhat more at ease. Mon was almost as tall as Lloyd and towered over Harrigan. The skin of his squarish face seemed a bit lighter than Hassan's and his close-cropped hair was graying-black. The famous diplomat had no mustache, unlike most of his countrymen. He appeared to be in his mid thirties; handsome and sophisticated. He wore an impeccable navy blue pinstripe worsted wool suit, blue shirt and a quiet-toned red, white and blue, traditionally western, thin tie. There were no pant cuffs calling attention to his maroon wing-tips. He wore no jewelry, not even a tie clasp. His manner was unpresumptuous, engaging. Mon seemed to be the type of well-groomed gentleman from whom another man could gain valuable advice without the slightest loss of respect for having asked a stupid question.

"Gentlemen, I will honor you with brevity in relating what I beg of you and what I can do for you: We in the *Meeddle* East are approaching a new era of peace. But it is incomplete and still demanding of many Herculean tasks in order to change hostility into cooperation and economic interdependence. You may be aware that the commission I serve is engaged in building up non-defense industry in several nations in my region. If we can enable the hungry to feed themselves, we can eliminate a major cause of strife. If we can better develop economies of the region to become both strong and dependent upon one *anotherr*, we can establish more safeguards against the senseless fighting of the past. And, finally, if every family can own and work land without crowding out neighbors, we can quell the hatred spawned by the coveting of land."

Harrigan and Lloyd were taken much aback by this articulate and apparently caring man whose fluency in the English language was undiminished by his slight accent.

"You may recall the risks which many in my Justice Party in Iraq took to forge a *day-mo-cracy;* to establish safeguards against the aggression of past regimes. Our nations *can* cooperate to assure permanent peace. We in Iraq are proving our *honorrable* intentions with action. You two can contribute greatly to that historic effort and be handsomely compensated for your work."

Harrigan responded first. "I commend you for what I understand is an emerging democracy in Iraq now. But I'm not very political other than believing in individual freedoms."

Lloyd added a small measure of joviality: "Neither am I very politically active, I'm afraid. But God save the King, nonetheless, *eh?!*"

Mon's eyes flashed with his smile as he turned to look Lloyd directly in the eyes. "Of *courrse*. God save him. Forgive me, gentlemen, for my exuberance has kept me from speaking plainly as I promised. One of our projects may be of interest to you. It is a planned endangered species preserve at Megiddo, Israel to be primarily funded by Iraq as a gesture of peace toward the Jews, ah, toward Israel. There, we planned many *de-ve-lop-ments* to include a monument to peace, a new college and a natural history theme park. Megiddo was the site of so many battles of old. It was therefore decided that no more *apprropriate* location existed for such powerful symbols of progress and peace; of man's defeat of aggression and his ascension to mastery of his world."

56

The two scientists gazed expectantly at Mon as he paused, leaned forward and resumed in an excited tone. "I offer you an opportunity to greatly expand the concept of the preserve recently approved; to do something never before attempted successfully. Gentlemen, if you would agree, we will expand the species preserve to include regeneration of extinct fauna. Yes, extinct animals for the enjoyment and *fa-scin-ation* of the world. The area has been a tourist attraction for years. Soon it will be much more: It will be a multi-faceted project for peaceful development and *zo-ological* research."

The two began to be taken up by the grandeur of Mon's vision. Mon looked squarely at Lloyd and continued.

"I have been reliably inforrmed that you, Dr. Lloyd, have developed a device that can identify subterranean formations if they are sufficiently different in density from the surrounding earth. This, of course, means you can quickly and reliably locate non-mineralized fossil soft tissue . . . like sperm and egg of recently extinct animals. Your own published research shows that it is the lack of mineralization, even if remains are crushed, which is key to redeeming any genetic instructions from a fossil *spe-ci-men.*"

Mon turned to Harrigan. "It has been likewise reported, Dr. Harrigan, that you have successfully redeemed non-mineralized fossil genetic *materrial* despite damage to the DNA strands. You have been successful in activating such replicated strands to produce life."

Mon opened his arms to the pair. "Gentlemen: I realize that you have other demands on your time. But we will fund this change to the species preserve project if you are willing to combine your talents and make the preserve one which *re-generates* extinct species."

Lloyd wanted to believe but found this idea of Mon's impracticable for several technical reasons. "My dear Minister Mon! Even if we could do something so fantastic, which I doubt since you cannot believe everything you read in the tabloids, you could never be able to provide an adequately cool and watered environment for that anywhere in all the Mideast. Why, I've heard of the Israeli's plans for a high-tech desalinization plant on the Dead Sea and the attendant dreams of reforestation and the like. But all of this seems impossible; sensational journalism, pie in the sky, that sort of thing."

"It will be my pleasure to *show* you how all these projects actually will bring *pro-sperrity* and peace to Israel and the entire region, Dr. Lloyd. Indeed, I have a fascinating surprise for you both regarding the water and environment for such a research preserve. Regarding the other issues, you are far too modest, Dr. Lloyd. I, for one, believe in your work and have been fascinated by it for years. You see, zoology and related sciences were for me hobbies when I was so long exiled from my country. I studied Civil Engineering at New York University and *Po-litical* Science in graduate school at the University of Tel Aviv but kept current in those hobbies.

"So, Dr. Lloyd, while some may not appreciate you or your work, I do. You are able to find such specimens in media which permit some soft tissue to survive thousands, perhaps hundreds of thousands of years. I understand that anaerobic sinkholes, petroleum seams, frozen tundra or desiccated sources all contain such partially-preserved *spe-ci-mens*. If you allow it, your talent can enrich the lives of children and adults alike by changing our faulty understanding of the past; your theories can be proved." Mon paused a brief moment and turned to Harrigan.

"Dr. Harrigan. I am one who has endured rejection in his own *prrofession*. Like you, I resolved to go on to accomplish my dreams. Let me help you actualize your dreams of discovery and accomplishment. I would be honored if you would personally recruit and lead a team, complete with staff I am *prrepared* to place at your disposal. Dr. Lloyd could be in charge of specimen location and recovery. As for lab facilities, I will see that you have the finest available. I understand such work can only be done with meiotic material, sperm or egg, rather than other tissue—at least once the animal is dead. This makes things difficult but far from impossible. Your expertise, Dr. Harrigan, and ability to lead are *in-dis-pensable*. You can make history and be unimpeded in your work. You have the opportunity to show a hypocritical scientific and academic community not only what *they* are made of . . . you will be able to dramatically show them what *you* are made of."

There was silence. Harrigan stared at Mon for half a minute, wondering how this man's words could be so well targeted; so persuasive, almost hypnotic. Lloyd was already fidgeting and focusing an expectant grin at Harrigan. The cautious yet excited American spoke as if he believed the regenerations which Mon envisioned were impossible. He realized that it might, in fact, be possible. Harrigan was uncomfortable with how much detailed knowledge Mon had about their work; about their inner feelings.

"Minister, all my work was destroyed by Harvard and non-mineralized fossil egg or sperm of such animals are almost impossible to locate. Non-mineralized fossil genetic material has been found but only from the mid-to late Pleistocene; within the last half million years; only *very* rarely and in near-useless condition. Then, too, is the problem of genetic compatibility. The extinct species would have to have close *extant* relatives, if not *direct* descendants. Finally, you still haven't explained how you can accommodate—if we ever could regenerate them—Ice Age animals in a relatively hot region."

Mon's uncontradictory tone avoided debate. "Manageable challenges, wouldn't you *agrree?* If I had a solution to the environment *pro-blem* would you join me in this historic endeavor?"

Lloyd blurted his answer even before the question was complete: "Yes! Yes, absolutely."

Harrigan hesitated and thought a moment. He sensed that something was wrong, somehow. Still, he knew that he could maintain control of his secrets if he was careful. Harrigan thought of the articles that had slandered him, his parents' reaction when he had explained his work, Wentz driven to suicide; that smug, hypocritical Harvard chancellor.

Harrigan spoke slowly, deliberately. "If I can run the show and maintain control, yes. Yes. We can give a shot at this. Oh, and one more requirement: For personal reasons, I'll need a salary of one hundred seventy thousand U.S. dollars yearly."

"I want to build a solid working *rrelationship* among us. Provided there is equal salary for each, I hope you, Dr. Lloyd, will not mind reporting, informally and with substantial autonomy, to Dr. Harrigan. The salary is two hundred fifty thousand. Reviewed annually, of *courrse.*"

Lloyd dropped his jaw a bit further. "Of . . . of . . . ah. Of course!"

Harrigan spoke up again. "So, what is this 'means' you alluded to for accommodating such animals in Megiddo? Climate-controlled warehouse set-ups?"

"Let me have Hassan describe it to you now. Hassan!" Mon called out into the hall and the escort appeared with a large suit case. "Thank you, Hassan. Set up the display unit, please."

Mon turned back to his guests. "We have some computer *simulations* complete with vivid scenes. I'll have him project these on a screen for you. Then, perhaps after preparations in Megiddo which should take at least the rest of this year, you'd like to witness how we intend to affect the climate. We're having a little demonstration *Janu'ry* second in Morocco."

Harrigan and Lloyd looked at each other, silently questioning Mon's sanity.

The two spoke in unison, incredulous as if Mon was playing some joke. "Morocco?!"

The presentation was quick and hard-hitting. At its conclusion, the amazed pair stared at each other and at Mon. The announcement of the Atlas mountain range project was scheduled for the next day. It was clear that the execution date, a mere six-months away, was set to minimize protest or protracted controversy.

Harrigan sounded almost winded. "My God, I didn't even know Israel was developing a weapon like that, let alone intending to use it for this kind of a purpose! When do we begin our work? Are there facilities for us in Megiddo now?"

Mon reassured them both. "This is a massive effort, gentlemen, to *co-operate* toward lasting peace; to forge spears into plow shares, so to speak. Israel is as serious about this as we are. There are *mo-dest* offices waiting for you both now in Megiddo. In six months, you will likely have your teams together and you will all be my guests to view the Atlas project from a safe vantage point. Its effect in the eastern Mediterranean will be less than we'd like. So we're installing a unique supplemental misting and cooling system at the Preserve. The Atlas program will nevertheless be *drramatic*. We can depart for Israel whenever you like. Temporary accommodations are available."

Harrigan had not felt such giddy anticipation since he was a boy visiting Dinamation's life-like prehistoric animal robots at Dinosaur World. He and Lloyd left for Megiddo the next day and began to recruit the personnel they would need. He was amazed to see the once-undeveloped valley studded with new, mostly unfinished, buildings. Pipes were being buried everywhere. Several miles east of the archaeological dig of Har-Megiddo was a massive north-south tear in the earth and a huge sign. It read, in three languages, "The Highway of Peace: A triumph of Arab-Israeli Cooperation."

The intervening six months saw the building of many of the facilities at Megiddo but Harrigan's lab was the priority. The facilities, at
least, were scheduled for completion in ten months. The time
would pass quickly.

Lloyd arranged access to several sites he suspected would yield
fossil soft tissue, specifically genetic material, and had several
back-ups of his detector manufactured in Israel.

Several interesting specimens were found and recovered: A
Smilodon, the saber-toothed cat, and an Imperial Mammoth were
located pinned beneath four yards of stone in a shaft of Lepkin Cavern, California. A cave-in, geologic evidence showed, crushed the
Smilodon's body over twenty thousand years before. Oddly, it had
been found in two pieces and wrapped in a mammoth pelt. Oxygen
was almost non-existent for decomposition in the inch-high, collapsed cavern. The animals were mummified, as the rock above
them never compressed the carcasses more than enough to remove most of the oxygen from the seam. The mammoth specimen
was a juvenile with little more than legs and the front half of a
torso; no egg or sperm.

Lloyd was confident of finding a usable specimen mammoth
somewhere, perhaps frozen in Canadian or Siberian tundra. Also
during this time, the mummified carcass of a massive and grotesque moose-like animal was recovered in India. Discovery of this
twelve thousand year old *Sivatherium* meant that its species survived several thousand years longer than previously thought. It
was found fairly well preserved at the bottom of a sinkhole that
had high concentrations of tannic acid, a byproduct of rotting
leaves, and almost no rot-permitting oxygen. There were plans for
an expedition back to Nepal to recover another live yeti, a mating
pair if possible. Specimens purchased from existing collections
were mounting up; stored adequately at the lab.

No genetic manipulation could take place yet, however, for the
lab would not be fully operational until mid spring, 2003. Things
were progressing well, despite the debris, mud and dust that permeated the soon to be bustling valley. New Years would come
quickly.

* * *

June twentieth was a painful day for Manfred Freund. He could scarcely believe his new orders. They struck him hard as he reread the single, terse page. His commanding officer was handing out white sheets to every military member of the hospital staff. The hospital, indeed the entire post was closing. The hospital was to be among the first facilities closed since it was one of the most expensive. He stared at the others in shock. One of his fellow interns started to cry.

"Why?" Captain Freund's voice was soft, clear.

Colonel Weiner seemed stolid, cynical. This in itself was a great disappointment for Freund, because he had come to admire the man for his compassion throughout their six-year active and reserve duty relationship. "Everything is going to the dogs, people. Our services are no longer required. This entire division and, with it, the post is no longer needed. It seems Germany hasn't the funds to maintain much of a military anymore, now that it's committed to buying into the American fusion reactor boondoggle and that stupid space station. I'll bet they won't even work when they get them on line. Space?! Cheap energy: It may prove to be very expensive energy one day. God help us if they're wrong and the Russians become tempted by our weakness. You and I do not make these decisions. The patients will transfer to Munich. The hospital closes August second."

Freund could not remain silent. "Sir, what of the interns? How will we finish our internship and residency?"

"Perhaps you and the other interns will be hurt the worst. There will be no transfer. The severance will be only six month's base pay in lump. We have all been totally abandoned by a government that overspends and overcommits—then reneges on its promises. You will have to find a job at a civilian institution to finish. And *good luck*, since there are already too many fully qualified doctors flooding civilian hospitals and other institutions. What a fiasco. That's it. You all have your orders. We will all, including me, be discharged with no reserve assignment August second. Good luck." The Colonel turned away from his personnel and left.

Arguments began to brew and some officers even started to break down. Freund silently went to a desk he shared with another intern and took out a book on how to write a *Curriculum Vitae.*

Freund, third in his class of over three hundred, recaptured his confidence and determined not to let this stop him.

August second came and went for Freund, his wife and two children. The August fifteenth mortgage payment was the last he could make. A number of other bills went unpaid. He had paid nearly all of his widowed mother's nursing home and funeral bills, which were substantial with the demise of Germany's socialized medical system. Relatives were unable to assist. In addition, he had borrowed heavily for family needs against the promise of his future captain's pay. Except for the mortgage, these were high-interest, short-term debts. The loan for the nursing home alone well-exceeded the severance pay. That note had a single balloon payment due September first unless it could be converted to a monthly-paid note. Freund could not qualify for that conversion now. Soon, past due notices, even foreclosure and car repossession threats would torment Freund and his young family.

Freund applied for internships at hundreds of institutions at home and abroad, but he received only a constant stream of rejection letters. It became clear that there must have been more interns in Germany—even in other nations—than institutions wanted. No one was hiring. He thought about third world nations. They needed doctors badly, even ones who had not completed all their training. But that would mean that he might never complete a proper internship and residency. In the last couple years, he had read about cutbacks occurring elsewhere in the military and government but his optimism kept him from translating such news into actual planning.

Gertrude had no marketable skills and had to care for the babies anyway. One final shock hit him when he attempted to sell their wonderful house: He had overpaid for it and improvements to it. It seemed to Freund that every fifth house in his area was for sale. He could not even get an apartment with his credit rating gone. A mountain of debt was crushing, grinding down upon him.

*   *   *

In November, Harrigan and Freund spoke by phone. Harrigan felt genuine compassion for his friend. However, Freund's request of him struck Harrigan as asinine: Freund had asked only that Harrigan "pray that God's will would be done." Harrigan thought, *If prayers could do any good, at least Freund should pray for a job.* Secondly, it seemed to Harrigan that it was always *people* who answered prayers; people starved awaiting divine intervention. Harrigan had some selling to do.

On Christmas day Harrigan got up from his highly organized work station in one of the few buildings actually completed at the Megiddo Species Preserve. He was the only one in the building. He donned his heavy sweater, put a pen-shaped computer chip in his pocket, grabbed the two wide printouts from the oversized printer and strode confidently to the jeep outside. Work crews, mud, plumbing fixtures, fencing and mass quantities of hardware were everywhere around him. The parking lot was mush. The grassy plain around the Megiddo archaeological mound was transforming daily into a mix of red-domed, pinkish-tan-sided buildings and western-style brick homes.

Harrigan wondered if it would get even muddier after the Atlas project. Minister Mon's office was a mile east toward the new highway, itself still unfinished. He parked right up on the new sidewalk, changed into clean boots and entered the glass and granite building. The secretary gave Harrigan access with a silent smile. Mon's oak doors were wide open and the visionary Iraqi looked up from his computer monitor.

"Come in, Kevin. I thought you'd be in the states celebrating *Chriss-mas!?*"

Harrigan placed the charts on the desk. "Just had to finish up these schedules and ask you a few things."

"Thank you. Is this a PERT chart or something?"

"It's similar. It's a new multidimensional scheduler. Most-likely-case is printed out for twelve month and five year projections and the program will run itself for you. Best and worst cases are on the chip. You can even put on the view-visor and visually walk through the Preserve as it gets completed phase by phase. I've checked all the inputs for this with the contractors and it's accurate."

"Wonderrful. I'll have a look."

"First, though, about the medical staffing. The Megiddo hospital has only one doctor and . . ."

"She's the finest. You hired her!"

"Yes, but she might leave one day and we need a back up."

"Kevin, the patient load isn't large yet and the Commission isn't made of money."

"I'm speaking of an intern, but the best. He was RIFted from a German army hospital five months ago and he's willing to work cheap. Ismail, he was third in his class of more than three hundred at the University of Munich last May. He even took extra courses. He can work half time here and you can arrange to find him some experience at Tel Aviv. Then, by the time he's finished paying his dues, the patient load here will be three times what it is now. See? There on the projections."

Mon studied the paper covering his desk. "I see. You really do think ahead don't you, Kevin? How cheap is cheap?"

"Sixty thousand, U.S., and he'll need a bump in the usual relocation package. Fifty thousand to settle a loss on his house."

"Well, at least the salary is *rea-son-able*. And you vouch for him? You've checked him out?"

"I went to college with him. His name is Manfred Freund. I know his family. He's dedicated. The best. He should even turn out to be a major asset on the research end, after his residency. His forte is neurology. He'd be a big asset."

"*Neur-o-logy*. Top one percent. Inexpensive backup. Interesting. Okay, Dr. Harrigan. You have asked and, this time, you shall receive. You know, Kevin, you and *your* research have enormous potential. *You* are going to have the scientific community, maybe all mankind, in the palm of your hand one day. I'm just glad to be a patron; no, a bit of a mentor for you. If men like you and I could have true freedom to create, the world would be a *su-premely* better place! But one step at a time, eh? As I said, the Commission is not made of money. Half from your budget and I'll get the rest from the theme park or something. All right?"

Harrigan felt, oddly, both exhilarated and uncomfortable. Only Mon gave him such high praise or exhibited faith in Harrigan's ability to attain glorious achievement. "Thank you, Minister. Now about these projections: I think you'll be pleased with . . ."

*　*　*

It was a massive and historic effort, combining mostly Arab oil revenues with previously secret Israeli sound-beam weapons technology to change a major planetary feature. The nations involved intended to finally produce permanent peace through reclamation and distribution of land made newly fertile. The thirteen hundred mile long northwest African mountain range called the Atlas chain was going to be reduced in height by at least a third. This had been carefully computer-modeled until the result was certain: The reduction would permit rain to pass eastward from Atlantic weather systems to quench the barren Sahara and even improve precipitation somewhat as far east as Iran. Many nations that were not involved impotently issued formal protests at not being included in the decision process. Although funds were set aside for claims resulting from erosion and other side effects, the decisions had been made and committed to, at the highest levels, irrevocably.

Local forces did a relatively humane and efficient job at clearing the small populations of villagers from the target areas by mid-December. By the New Year the thousands of protesters, scruffy Berber villagers along with radical environmental and human rights groups from around the world, had also been cleared. Moroccan troops manned posts in segments of the range within their borders. Iraqi contingents accompanied those of each nation whose soil was affected: Morocco, Algeria and Tunisia. Cooperation was mandated: Even the Israelis usually spoke Arabic around Iraqi and the host troops.

Everyone in the stands was issued ear plugs even though they were out of reflective sound blast areas. The blasts would come primarily from the desert southeast of the mountains. A few would emanate from airborne platforms to ensure adequate coverage. From the VIP observation stands set up several miles from the foothills, it was not hard to tell that this range was indeed a barrier to rain clouds which swept east from the Atlantic. It was calm; almost no breeze. The insulated red souvenir jackets provided to chattering dignitaries in the stands were hardly sufficient to keep out all of the morning cold. The low temperatures lingered well past seven o'clock in the morning in this part of Saharan Morocco. Coffee and even blankets were being distributed, though they would soon be unneeded when the rising sun would scorch the area.

Spaced at twenty mile intervals along the southeast sloping foothills were huge tan trucks. They each held one cube-shaped sonic blast weapon. They could be easily seen from the stands by using binoculars. Behind the bleachers, farther to the east, the desert was covered as far as the eye could see with a dark gray foam. Two of the mammoth spreader-activators were still spewing more foam along the near edges. It was artificial topsoil made from petroleum and corn stalk fibers. Though a product produced by a joint venture between two American firms, Archer Daniels Midland and Texaco, it was licensed for manufacture by Islamic League nations. Already it covered the worst of the sandy and rocky central portions of the huge desert, where there had not been topsoil for ten thousand years. The Megiddo Species Preserve staff, already up to seven specialists, had their own seating cordoned off. Forty yards away, beyond the large concrete helicopter pad, a dusty tent and trailer command and control complex had been set up.

Lieutenant Colonel Mon stood at the elaborate command post listening to the field reports from security forces posted all around the range and in helicopters above it. His Israeli counterpart, Colonel Shomran, stood a few yards away, focused intently on weapons data. Liaison officers from Algeria and Tunisia sat at video consoles at the complex's center, monitoring activity in their respective domains.

The tan and brown camouflage-clad Moroccan liaison turned suddenly back from his screen toward Mon. "Minister, Unit Seven reports five Berbers remain in the El Althal village mosque in sector Delta eight-seven."

Mon's voice rose rapidly from disapproving to furious—and very uncharacteristically so. "I thought you posted an all-clear status yesterday, Lieutenant?! We can afford no delays! The monsoons have begun and they *must* be allowed to pass or an *entire* crop year will be *sacrificed.*"

"I'm sorry, sir. I will have them picked up immediately."

"No. Get *your* men out. *My people* will take care of it."

The Moroccan lieutenant knew that splitting off tandem field forces was against procedure. But, having already been disciplined by his own superiors for questioning instructions from a junior Iraqi officer, he was more than a little intimidated. "Yes, sir. Right away."

Shomran, concerned, ceased speaking with his people at their weapons control screens. He eyed Mon suspiciously but respectfully despite the fact that he held higher rank. Shomran's voice was firm and clear. "The guns remain under Israeli command, sir. I must now halt countdown per the joint command procedures. I cannot re-initiate without complete evacuation confirmation."

Mon glared at Shomran silently. "Of course, sir." It seemed ridiculous to the Moroccans that Mon, who was really the man in charge, addressed Shomran as "Sir" while Shomran, who outranked Mon addressed the Iraqi as "Sir." Mon looked at his watch and left the tent to enter the separate command and control trailer for Iraqi units. The door shut and locked behind him.

The mosque was the only refuge the frightened Berber family felt they had. The father looked elderly at thirty-five and his wife, twenty-seven, was also aging fast. She hugged the three ragged children, now eight, ten and eleven, who had not died in infancy. They did not trust the announcements and promises of land for everyone. Neither did they want new neighbors with whom they were not familiar: Palestinians, who were said to be willing to move from Israel. The Moroccan troops had been kind enough but the Iraqis seemed to look for an opportunity to shove people around.

Suddenly, the doors of the sacred refuge slammed open and a group of Iraqi soldiers ran in, rifles already firing over the family's heads. The father yelled at his wife to run. He shut her and the children into a hallway and turned to block the troops. She and the children ran frantically out the rear of the mosque and through a door in the village wall. They heard several guns fire, and a single scream from the father. She thrust her children down the steep dusty hill until they all rolled to a stop forty yards below. The old cave was not large but it offered the only way to hide. Quickly gathering scrub, she obscured the small opening and pushed her children far enough in to be sure their breathing would not be heard.

The Iraqi soldiers saw the retreat into the cave. The leader had two of his men drag the father's body down the hill and shove it just inside the opening. He placed a small explosive charge atop the brim-shaped boulder above the mouth of the cave and detonated it. The tomb sealed, they returned to the town square, mounted the lone helicopter and headed west.

The Moroccan lieutenant thought it odd that the message he now received was on his own force's radio frequency rather than that reserved for the Iraqis. He relayed the message just the same to the Israeli colonel and to Mon, who was reentering the tent. "We have them all and will drop them off at the temporary housing facilities on the west side."

Shomran suspiciously eyed Mon but gave the order to resume countdown on the original schedule.

Mon took the microphone which connected him to the observation bleachers and to radio news programs worldwide. The speech was brief but inspiring. Even many who opposed the project were moved to admit the whole thing might work and relieve not only hunger but pressure for Arabs to fight Israelis—and each other. Another voice resumed the countdown. It was five seconds before the 9:00 a.m. blast. Four. Three.

Shomran began to sweat as he released the safety hood on his hand-held activator. Two. One.

There was only the slightest high-pitched sound. The air seemed to become refractive. The long mountain range blurred a bit, as if heat was rising through the air and distorting the view.

Suddenly the whole range exploded in a long cloud, which was actually composed more of gravel-sized particles than sand or dust. The rumble followed moments later. It grew loud in a few seconds. Already it appeared that the steeper faces of the range were pouring like liquid down their slopes. Portions of the peaks collapsed slowly, flatter and wider. Then the high pitched sound ceased and the rumble continued only briefly, quieting. The air calmed and was clear in an instant. The dust settled quickly, revealing that the once awesome peaks and ridges were flattened at the top and heaped at the sides as if ground with a router.

Dark clouds invaded slowly from the west. The humbled mountains grew dark within minutes and became striped along their slopes with what could be seen through binoculars as mud slides. Aerial viewing by the speechless crowd was canceled as the advancing rains soaked everyone and grounded the observation helicopters.

The Berber family, though trapped, was not crushed by the crumbling rock above them. Instead, the molecular-level vibrations penetrated the earth around them and disintegrated their bodies into microscopic shards a half-second before the gravel fell down upon their remains.

In the developed world, the jubilance seemed boundless. Even the tragic accidental electrocution of Israeli Colonel Shomran, the day after the razing of the Atlas range, barely made the news. The whole project was celebrated and envied throughout the world. Even *Time* magazine's special issue almost ignored the loss of Shomran, celebrating Ismail Mon as its man of the year, 2003—with eleven months left to go *in* that year. Mon continued to supervise the Atlas project through the remainder of the year. It resulted in the cheap recovery of billions of dollars worth of copper, zinc and other previously hard-to-reach minerals from the remnants of the mountains. He was praised in the media everywhere for his fair and well-organized management of land distribution as well as Berber and some Palestinian relocations. The affected areas of now-fertile desert initially totaled as much land as the whole of France but eventually amounted to more than twice that.

Later, in December, there was more 'good' news: Ismail Mon was elected Chairman of Iraq's moderate Justice Party.

Chapter Six

LOOK UNTO THE ROCK FROM WHENCE YOU ARE HEWN, AND TO THE HOLE OF THE PIT FROM WHENCE YOU ARE DUG. FOR THE LORD SHALL COMFORT ZION, HE WILL COMFORT ALL HER WASTE PLACES; AND HE WILL MAKE HER WILDERNESS LIKE EDEN, AND HER DESERT LIKE THE GARDEN OF THE LORD.

— 2 NEPHI, 8:1; 3

Man does not live by bread alone, but also of the meat of good lambs . . .
— F. Nietzsche, *Thus Spake Zarathustra*: Fourth Part

ROAM THE EARTH AND SEE HOW GOD HAS BROUGHT THE CREATION INTO BEING. THEN GOD WILL INITIATE THE LATTER CREATION. —KORAN, 29:20

VIP Pavilion, Megiddo Species Preserve, Israel
0735 hours, April 3, 2008

Bright sunlight and small grills warmed the crisp morning air. Past the servers, hungry guests could see that the sun was glinting off the tall cone-shaped aluminum spire which was the Monument to Peace and Man. It stood defiantly beside the ancient symbol of warfare, the Har-Megiddo archaeological mound, also visible from the serving lines. The smell of eggs, steak, lamb, blueberry sauce on cheese crepes and a host of other aromas almost made some of the lucky visitors forget they were at a zoo. The rectangular yellow pavilion was filled with nearly three hundred gabbing, laughing and eating VIPs.

Each set of three white cotton-draped tables had eight to ten settings and signs on poles displaying the group numbers of those who were to spend the day together. A concrete stage was centered on the pavilion's long side, nearest the brick administration building, just inside the preserve's main gate.

The largest table, nearest the stage, was reserved for political dignitaries and a few military personnel. However, the crowd was composed primarily of well-screened private individuals who could afford the trip, accommodations and five thousand dollar special two-day pre-admission price. People clustered between tables but were beginning to take their seats and eat.

Harrigan stood alone at the microphone and began to speak just slowly enough to accommodate timely translation. "Good morning, everyone. Please: go right ahead with your breakfasts! I'm Kevin Harrigan. I appear to run this preserve. I say 'appear' because, in fact, it's my wonderful staff, whose members will guide you through today's touring, who make my job almost unnecessary. As you may have surmised, you are grouped by language preference. Please note that each staff member speaks English and most of them speak other languages, too."

Harrigan first thanked the Arab-Israeli Mutual Development Commission, having Minister Ismail Mon and the Israeli Foreign Minister Benjamin Heitzman, the Commission's Vice Chairman, take bows. "Thank you, Minister Mon, for taking time from your duties in Baghdad. Thank you, Minister Heitzman for likewise putting us on your busy schedule."

The crowd was quieting down to listen to Harrigan but the clinking of glasses and silverware continued. "I'd like to introduce the staff now for those of you who haven't met them yet. So, group leaders, please stand as I introduce you.

"Escorting Group One will be Dr. Bart Lloyd, who hails from London. Bart is in charge of our amazing globe-trotters who find most of our fossil specimens.

"With Group Two is Dr. Tykvah Strauss. Dr. Strauss joined us not even a month ago from the University of Haifa and she is performing almost magical feats with our computers. She already knows our work and this place like the back of her hand.

"Group Three is with Dr. Paulo Cabral and his lovely wife. Dr. Cabral is an outstanding geologist from the wilds of Brazil and has been of invaluable help on Dr. Lloyd's expeditions.

"Group Four has Dr. Simone Kairaba from Senegal. Dr. Kairaba handles the genetic scanners you'll learn about in the orientation room.

"Group Five should be well entertained by our Australian biologist and veterinarian, Dr. Carl Smythe. Carl can be quite a card!

"Dr. Yoshiko Oda, our resident chemist and Lab Director, is from Japan. Dr. Oda will lead Group Six.

"Group Seven: You will be with Dr. Claude Olivier, formerly with the Tyrrell Museum in Canada. Claude is of immeasurable help with the specimens which Dr. Lloyd's team recovers.

"Group Eight will be exploring today with Dr. Stefan Woj. Some of you may have seen Dr. Woj's nature documentaries on recovery of the wildlife populations in his native Poland. He conducts most of our zoological research.

"Dr. Gregor Ruliev, from Moscow, is a senior geneticist who, I can tell you, has taught me quite a few things. Dr. Ruliev will escort Group Nine.

"Now, last but far from least is one of the brightest geneticists I've ever had the privilege of working with, Dr. James Fong of the People's Republic of China. Dr. Fong has Group Ten."

Gertrude Freund waved her hand anxiously.

Harrigan started again. "Oh. Excuse me, I forgot: Those of you with small children are welcome to join Dr. Manfred Freund's group, which will—I believe—be spending most of the morning at the petting zoo beyond those signs. Then, I understand they'll be joining the rest of us in the Preserve." Harrigan pointed westward with his flattened hand. "The animals there, including a three-foot tall dwarf mammoth, have been engineered to remain cute and juvenile. Don't worry, they enjoy their lives greatly! You can cuddle a baby saber-tooth and he will *not* eat you!"

Light laughter reverberated throughout the pavilion.

Harrigan continued his jovial mood. "Even you *big* boys and girls we call adults will have a chance to visit it at as you exit the tunnels. Dr. Freund and his wife, by the way, are from Munich. He is doing some fascinating work for us in the area of genetic transmission of instinctive behaviors and his bride of nine years is pregnant with their third child!" There were claps, several "aws" and the clink of silverware continued.

"We do ask that you stay in your groups throughout the day. Of course, tomorrow will be non-scheduled. The tours will begin in one hour in numerical order at the Welcome Center—the one with the porcelain animal scenes—where you will also access the conveyor tubes. Concessions with *excellent* food, all free during your visit, are located at rest stops in the tube hubs within the Preserve. Supper will be here at five thirty this evening, followed by the Monument tour at seven. When you return tomorrow, you may pick up your interactive guide devices at the Welcome Center and enjoy more of what you'll see today or take the trams to Pleistocene Safari Theme Park. *You* are our very appreciated guests, so please feel free to ask our staff about anything which interests you. Thank you and enjoy your visit."

Harrigan returned to the table marked "Reserved," rather than with a group number, and sat among bodyguards and personal secretaries; across from Mon and Heitzman. The conversation turned to the protesters outside the outer gates.

Heitzman's voice sounded almost jovial to Harrigan. "The police better have some order restored at the monument and outside the preserve gates by this evening at least. I think we ran over somebody's foot driving in here! I don't know who these fundamentalists hate worse, Mon or myself! But it is time, is it not, for this monument?"

"First, Mr. Heitzman, let me say that I do appreciate you and Minister Mon allowing my staff to have the spotlight at both tour sites today. I hope you can stay and enjoy the theme park tomorrow! As to the monument, sir, I'm not sure I'm comfortable with all of its messages. It reminds people of the Tower of Babel. With essentially the same meaning to fundamentalists of several faiths, it's quite a magnet for controversy."

Harrigan hated implying that his staff wanted to be "allowed" to serve as tour guides but he knew some of his people were excited by the festivities. He had no qualms voicing reservations about the monument's proximity to his preserve.

Heitzman appreciated Harrigan's candor but diplomatically avoided controversy. "Thank you for your frankness. Indeed you are right, Dr. Harrigan. And it's not even quite finished. The theme park is ready now only by the skin of its teeth, as you Americans say. Yet, I understand *your* facilities were scheduled to be ready this June but they are obviously ready now. My compliments!"

"Thank you, sir." Harrigan finished a few bites, excused himself to visit the other tables and checked on how his people were doing. He stopped first at Olivier's table just in time to hear an unwelcome grumble from a hippo-looking guest with her nose in the air. She was Mrs. Banks of Seattle, here with Jeffrey, her fourteen-year old, and her flat-expressioned husband. They were very proud that they had taught their son French as a second language.

"I understand the animals are cooped up in narrow lanes for viewing, rather than roaming a decently large area. The temperature is still too high for these types of animals. They've got a lot of nerve calling this a 'preserve.' It's a zoo!"

Harrigan read her name tag and responded to the criticism good-naturedly. "Yes, you're quite right, Mrs. Banks. But we've engineered the animals to better withstand the heat and we have been able to bring the average summer temperature, at least in the lanes, to about eighty. That's midway between what most of their modern counterparts like and what we think the Ice Age fauna enjoyed." Harrigan kissed her hand, gently pulled a bit of wrist flab and whispered not too-privately to her, "You know, we can fix this now, too!" He winked and left. The woman tried to look unflustered as the guests laughed at her under their breaths.

Harrigan went to other tables, cheering his tolerant staff-turned-tour-guides. He stopped to speak with Mannie Freund, who was now a part of the research team and its exclusive physician. Freund knew Harrigan had been attracted to Tykvah since she joined the team three weeks before. He laughed at his friend.

"Kevin, she won't go out with you! She's on staff. She's with a tall, handsome date, too. She's as likely to sue for sexual harassment if you wink at her as to stomp on your foot! Good looking, too, and taller than you. But, then, everyone's taller than you! Nope, Kevin, not for you!" Gertrude giggled and gently slapped her husband's hand.

Harrigan looked Freund squarely in the eyes and stated his prediction without humor. "She's for me, Mannie. You watch. I'm going to marry her."

Freund's orange juice came spurting out of his nostrils as he and Gertrude both burst into laughter. "Oh, gees, Kevin," Mannie said snorting and wiping up, "and I'm the Easter Bunny. You vacillate so much, Kevin. You don't even know your *self!*"

"Mannie, if a dog-faced clod like you can interest a stunning woman like Gertrude, I can go out with Tykvah Strauss!"

"Kevin, if I had a dog that looked like you, I'd shave its—"

"Yeah. Yeah. You watch!"

Harrigan proceeded directly to Tykvah's table, stood between her and her date and began to engage her in flirtatious conversation. Tykvah enjoyed the competition but, when Harrigan whispered in her ear and gently massaged her neck, she decided to step on her boss' foot anyway. Harrigan laughed it off and limped back to Freund's table, vowing to try again.

At five minutes to nine, Harrigan escorted his unnumbered group into the Welcome Center. It was flanked outside by adjoining thirty foot tall, thick glass walls which surrounded the animal pens. The impressive acreage beyond was studded with even taller yard-thick concrete columns. Each of these spouted plumes of fine, cooling water mist. These reflected some heat and carried more away by evaporating before reaching the ground. The plumes covered essentially the entire thinly-forested, grassy preserve.

Inside the Welcome Center, most of which was the huge Orientation Room, the VIPs saw holograms depicting evolution. They felt the models that actually moved when touched. Cladistics charts mapped out which modern species were related to others and to more archaic ones. The charts traced each taxon, or species, by genetic similarities all the way back to the simplest life forms. Quite a few cladistics branches had no surviving, modern limbs.

Nine foot square, high-definition wall monitors showed films of genetic scanning and injections of synthesized chromosomes into either egg or sperm. The clips also showed subsequent artificial inseminations and then phases of embryo growth. Other monitors showed photographic-quality, computer-generated depictions of tribal hunts. The genetic engineering which enabled fast maturation of both the animals and plants at the preserve was shown with diagrams. Yet most of the genetic methods revealed were not detailed and no actual viewing of the labs or nurseries was provided.

Harrigan had insisted on technical secrecy. This was partly because the huge size of some of the babies and eggs necessitated horrific, bionic modifications to the mother animals used for gestation. Such facts would not produce a good public reaction—and there were enough 'tough realities' of animal life the public would see. Actually, some of the work was done only by him—and in seclusion. The groups nevertheless found interest in the film clips of modern mother animals weaning and training their hybrid archaic/modern young.

Many of the specimens from which the fossil sperm and egg had been harvested were specially treated with preservatives and displayed in total vacuum containers. A few still had pelts or scales. Still, most visitors were itching to see the actual animals. Maps were handed out, revealing the immensity and layout of the maze; the locations of restrooms, concessions and animals. Then they headed for the entrance to the viewing tubes.

There were three entrances to the preserve along the opposite wall from the Center's entrance. Each was a thirty-five foot wide, ten foot tall glass domed tunnel. They were complete with footbars, hand rails, air vents and occasional benches placed at the vertical supports. They were drenched in sunlight. A sign above each reassured visitors that the special glass could withstand an impact even from a four-ton truck crashing into its side—or top—at fifty miles per hour. A small box containing a glass cleaning apparatus perched outside the tunnel on top of each support. The floor had slow-moving, off-white, non-slip panels that interlocked and could even turn corners like airport luggage conveyors. Many would have fun bouncing on them. One conveyor led into; one out of, each tube. Three seven foot wide strips of black, shock-absorbing, polymer flooring lay fixed, bracketing the two conveyors of each tunnel. The grinning VIP group members stepped onto the moving walkway, just a bit nervous about the integrity of the glass, despite the signs.

It was nine thirty before Group Seven, led by Paleolab Director Dr. Claude Olivier, entered a tunnel. The thirty-two person group spoke mostly French. Group Seven stepped, almost giddy, onto the conveyor.

The first pen held two Indian elephants. They lumbered out from behind a clump of trees and bushes. Their respective nine and eight foot tall frames were actually quite imposing to most of the group. They strolled toward the hay dispenser, which popped up as Jeffrey glided past. His mother pulled him from the conveyor to stand against the glass and watch the pachyderms eat. The oblong pen was a fourth the size of a football field; larger than many zoos provided but certainly not a wild preserve.

Olivier began in French. "Ancient proboscideans, including

mammoths, migrated from Asia into Alaska, Canada and down into South America in *several* waves. Most species of mammoths lived in fairly open areas like tundra and savanna. They had flat, rippled teeth to grind grass. Mastodons, which the Preserve does not yet have, were forest-dwellers with cone-shaped teeth. We don't know why mastodons are extinct but we believe that man hunted mammoths to extinction. Debate continues to this day."

Jeffrey complained in English, "Oh Mom! I've seen elephants before. That's nothing."

Mr. Banks was aggravated. "Fifteen thousand dollars to listen to you complain! And we're speaking French now, Jeffrey. Pay attention and *learn* something!"

Mrs. Banks attempted to soothe. "Now Jeffie, you can learn a lot from this. Let's move with the group to see the mammoth. *My*, perhaps I was too hard on this place. There's quite a bit of land for roaming, isn't there?"

At Olivier's summons, the group glided toward two Imperial Mammoths, still out of view, in the adjoining enclosure. He related his discovery, made in a Sierra Madre sinkhole, of the fossil soft tissue from which the mammoths had been created. Jeffie's eyes rolled in exasperation—then bugged open wide.

"This is just another eleph- Oh! Ah! Maaaa!"

A deafening, dull *bong* shook everyone's ears as the shaggy, matted female burst from behind trees to charge the tunnel. She was more than twice the height of the female elephant seen moments ago and appeared to attack the tunnel repeatedly with her massive feet, wider than Mrs. Banks. The female jumped desperately upon the tunnel, directly above the group, faltered and crashed left side down, upon the glass. They could glimpse her head, huge and with a radically heightened forehead. Her ears were smaller than the elephants' and her tusks were about the same as those of the bull elephant. Her left eye, as big as a fist, darted in every direction. She rolled kicking and trumpeting to the opposite side of the tube.

Olivier crouched to the floor like the rest, scanning the glass for cracks. He found none. Then a deep roar, more like a tank engine than a trumpet, turned every head.

The bull, his eyes widened and crazed, crashed his front feet into the shaking but unyielding glass. His tusks were nearly twenty feet long. They curled downward, then twisted up and inward, to a dull but frightening point. The bull mammoth struck the tunnel with such speed and force that it leaped right up onto and over the top of the tube. It lost no rhythm in stride as it caught the female from behind and mounted her with hammering force. The cow withstood the collision, buttressing herself from falling forward by spreading her front legs well ahead of herself. Her bleating was only slightly higher in pitch than the bull's.

Gasping, Mrs. Banks covered her son's eyes. She stared, like the rest, in shock at the sight of the two. Unlike the rest, she began to gag and bulge out her eyes from the volume of egg and sausage pumped up through her esophagus. As her humphing and choking subsided, yielding to big, full-throated gulps, she began to calm. Only Mr. Banks had noticed his wife and it converted his tongue-hanging, open mouthed smile to a firmly disapproving grimace.

"Well!" Olivier, red-faced, managed to address the group. "As you can see the glass is very sturdy. Let's take a peek at the next enclosure, shall we?"

Everyone rose dusting themselves, though there was no dust. Most lowered their eyes as if this action could keep everyone else from noticing that blushing and embarrassment were replacing the fear of being crushed to death.

Next came *Titanotylopus*, the original camel. It looked almost exactly like the dromedary whose pen adjoined it—but was almost twice as big.

Olivier explained the sample's origin. "The source fossil for this animal came from Arizona. It had been wedged between 'horst and graben' formations, in a crushed-down and sealed-up crevasse, apparently washed down river into the cave at death. It must have been quickly desiccated. The formation apparently collapsed and was thrust upward above the water close to a hundred and sixty thousand years ago. Coming up after *Titanotylopus* is the modern bison and then *Bison latifrons.*"

The next area contained a bull American bison, two cows and two calves. They were majestic animals, five feet tall at the shoulder and over six feet long. They only appeared aggressive. The bull had a large brown head and a long black mane. Its ten-inch horns curled up close to its skull from behind its large, dark eyes. Its shoulders hunched up like a furry boulder atop front legs, which were twice the size of its rear legs. The herd was placid, swatting flies with their tails and each cow suckling one calf.

Latifrons was nearly twice the size of the American Bison. Upon seeing the visitors, it thrashed its frightening horns—thirteen feet long, tip-to-tip—against a bush near the glass. The horns were not curled but stuck almost straight out from the sides of its snorting, fear-inspiring head. The visitors could feel the threatening vibration as it reared and stomped the ground.

Mr. Banks grabbed Olivier's arm. "Are most of the regenerated animals more violent than their modern relatives?"

"Oh yes, indeed. Most of them are. We're trying to determine whether our own genetic techniques have caused this or whether they were just more aggressive tens of thousands of years ago. But the evidence so far is that even the herbivores were *quite* vicious."

The brat, now intrigued, broke in. "Woah! What about *carnivores*, then?!"

"Let's just see! We pass the dire wolves shortly."

The wolves, unable to range and hunt, seemed docile to Master Banks. He gawked, curious, at their bulging, nearly hyena-like shoulders and wide, long-fanged snouts. Olivier delighted in describing imagined confrontations between dire wolf packs and prides of *Smilodon* in the savanna of the American southwest thirty to ten thousand years ago.

They rounded a corner to see big cats. A lion pride enjoyed shade in a too-small pen of a hundred feet square.

As they proceeded to the adjoining section, Olivier provided details on *Panthera leo spelaea*. "This prehistoric lion, what many have called the 'cave lion', ruled Eurasia *and* North America for tens of thousands of years. We found both egg and sperm in a frozen Siberian bog to produce this lion, so we know there is no possibility of genetic dilution from the current species. The specimens were only four thousand years old. As you may have read in the papers, there is quite a bit of criticism of our work here because half the genes come from distant modern relatives. Actually, it's not that bad, since we analyze the archaic sequences thoroughly and modify the modern host egg or sperm before uniting it with the redeemed archaic chromosomes. So, such criticism is misplaced—but especially false in the case of this animal. It is exactly as it was four thousand years ago. That's technically the Holocene epoch but this species thrived well back into the Pleistocene in this very form."

The cave lions were almost identical to the moderns except for their thick black manes, smaller but distinctive on the females, and their half-again size superiority. They were imposing creatures. But they were lying farther away than the modern lions, so their immensity was lost upon the visitors.

Just before the next corner was a South American jaguar. It looked nervous and paced back and forth along its fifty foot range. Olivier admitted that *Smilodon*, it's counterpart, was one of the most uncertain of their regenerations because its line had completely died out and had only a very distant cousin, the jaguar. Indeed, it could not fully distend its jaw and had to be fed sliced meats. The male saber-toothed cat became, nevertheless, quite a spectacle for the group.

Two long, flat, banana-shaped canines extended down from its snarling muscular snout well below its lower jaw. It had a short, fluffy tail. It was the size of a modern female lion but as bulgingly muscular as a male lion. The head was vaguely like a modern cougar, though half again as large, and the paws and legs were thick, massive. It eyed them from on top of its rock and snarled repeatedly.

"We will soon have a female to mate with this one," Olivier informed them. "We recovered the twenty-two thousand year-old hind quarters of this one's 'figurative' father in Lepkin Cavern, California. It was better preserved than those in other such formations because it was mummified in mammoth skin and never subjected to running water. It appeared, upon excavation, to have been chopped in half and meticulously wrapped in the bones and skin. I think it was ceremoniously cut in half and buried by *people*. Just some of a *growing* amount of evidence that humans lived in America *well* before eleven thousand years ago."

* * *

Half a block from the Preserve's main gate, a large, white utility van pulled into two empty parking spaces. It had normal Israeli plates. Large panels on each side read, in Hebrew, Arabic and English: "Institutional Refrigerated Vending, Ltd." Inside, a lone black-haired Syrian turned off the engine, got out of his seat and shut himself into the dimly lit cargo area. He booted a small computer.

He spoke into a microphone. "Number Two, are you on line and moving in the group?"

A moment later, the screen of the portable computer facing him flashed two words, TWO: AFFIRMATIVE.

"Number Three are you on line and in position?"

Immediately the computer screen changed to read THREE: AF-FIRMATIVE.

He smiled then clamped his teeth tight, emitting a muffled growl. "Your highway is an avenue of the last invasion and your unfathomable hate . . . I will reflect back to you!"

He closed the screen, made his way past the freezers and exited the rear of the van. He placed four cases of pizzas, which were sliding down from its automated load/unload bay, onto a hand truck. He wheeled the cases a few car lengths toward the main entrance and stopped to show the guard his ID and the purchase order, and silently walked to the administration building.

*   *   *

In the Preserve's glass tunnels, Dr. Stefan Woj was enlightening his English- and Polish-speaking group near the rhino area. This section contained a huge black rhino. It was five feet tall at the shoulders, ten feet long and had a head nearly a yard long. Dark gray, with two horns, it stared at them vacantly and returned to tearing at the bush which it preferred to its mechanical feeder. Its eyes seemed small and insufficient for such a large animal.

Woj broke the group's silent awe with an odd anatomical fact, in imperfect English. "And this brute is none other than a *moh-dern* black rhino! It may surprise you to know that its horns, like those of its archaic and *moh-dern* relatives, are made of *ke-ra-tin*—like your own hair and finger nails!"

The conversational buzzing, which the revelation caused, was brief. Gliding into viewing range of the rhino's once-extinct and very distant relative, *Elasmotherium*, they stared, silenced. Mouths dropped open and eyes gazed fixed. Astounded, they were unsure whether the sight was real or faked. The monstrous beast stood over eight feet tall at the shoulder and was over sixteen long. It was covered everywhere except its face with thick, wavy, two-toned hair. The sides and belly were shining auburn. The top third of its back, neck and head were a rich golden tan. Its broad, flatish neck seemed to be one unit with its shoulders due to its great muscular bulk. Its head was twice as large as the rhino's. But its single conical horn was unbelievably massive: Its circular base spanned almost four feet in width. The giant spike jutted imposingly upward six feet and was rutted like the slopes of a volcano.

Woj commented in a quiet, reverent tone. *"Majay-stic*, isn't it? We only have one adult but there is a baby in the petting zoo. This female is generally docile but males . . . never cease if they decide to charge! We had a male a year ago that killed itself trying to beat through the glass wall to head-butt the rhino. Since then, we've replaced many of the wall segments with opaque glass so that such mistakes would not be again made. We hope to mate her when we've got a male which is enough mature. We found the specimen for it in a Carpathian salt seam, quite well preserved, actually. We believe early man hunted this beast across the vast steppes and forests stretching from central Europe to Siberia. A few paleontologists have suspected that *Elasmotherium* evolved into the Indian rhino. But our research shows that it has no descendants. Its closest relative is the black rhino of Africa."

The next glass pen held a close but slightly smaller relative of *Elasmotherium*: *Coelodonta*. Woj continued, "This animal—I will for you pronounce: 'seel-o-donta'—was the famous woolly rhino. It was hunted to extinction in Europe. It is aggressive *much* more than *Elasmotherium* and I would not want to have needed to hunt it for a living!"

The animal resembled a rhino but held its head higher and farther out from its shoulders. It had a thick, dark brown coat like a horse in winter and a scruffy black mane. The mane trailed rearward and down from its forehead to the middle of its undrooping back. Its head was four feet long, and boasted two horns. The horn at the nose was as tall and big around as a weight-lifter's leg and the second rose half as high from between the eyes. After eyeing the visitors, it charged the tube—causing screams—but stopped short of striking the glass. The group rushed onward.

The next pen held a handsome pair of fallow deer. In an adjacent pen just beyond, stood the once-extinct *Megaloceros*. It had been generated from a three thousand year-old specimen found in a Welsh bog. "The common name, Irish Elk, misleads," Woj explained, "since this immense animal ranged *over all of* Europe and parts of Asia for ten thousand years."

All were impressed by its bulk and grace. The proud animal brandished massive wide-dished, sharp-pronged antlers. These spread up and out six feet on each side of its huge, stately head— which itself towered twelve feet off the ground. *Megaloceros* was ten feet tall at its powerful shoulders.

"We believe," Woj explained, "that this species became extinct because forests grew thicker as the glaciers receded. Trees may have caught its antlers, impeded mating, migration; even from predators: escape. And what predators there were! One of the most frightful—and one which our own ancestors knew well—is coming next: *Ursus spelaeus*, the dreaded cave bear."

The European and Asian cave bear was, as were most of these animals, more vicious than his modern cousin, the grizzly bear. Since none of these visitors had ever seen a grizzly, or any bear which could tower to stand twelve feet tall, both omnivores were intimidating.

The gargantuan cave bear rose ominously, clawing the air, and roared. Its jaws gaped wide enough to sever half of a man's torso in one chomp. In an instant it launched itself upon the glass, trying to claw and bite through the tunnel. Everyone but Woj jumped or fell back in fright.

Woj continued unfazed. "Intimidating in the extreme, no? Paleontologists have long debated whether *spelaeus* was carnivorous. The venerated Björn Kurtén thought it *vahs* herbivore. Well, we gave this one a deer once. I'll tell to you: a *horrendously* vicious predator is this bear!"

Everyone stared, breathless. No one dared inquire about the deer to which Woj had referred.

Dr. Carl Smythe waived at Dr. Woj as the Australian passed at a hub. Several people, slightly shaken, asked Woj to make a rest and snack stop there. Woj returned a wide-arc wave as his Group Eight began to sit, calming and munching.

Smythe brought his Group Five past the concessions, vociferously sharing his enthusiasm for the fauna of his part of the globe.

A very bright and bubbly thirteen year old girl named Linette Wu was in Smythe's group. She was visiting from Hong Kong with her parents but changed from Dr. Fong's group to Dr. Smythe's in order to practice her already-excellent English. She soaked up every bit of knowledge Smythe imparted.

"Look here, mates! This fuzzy Australian marsupial, *Diprotodon,*" Smythe explained, "is related to *air mod'n* giant wombat. Anyone like to cuddle it?! No takers, eh? Right you are!"

Diprotodon's pig-like appearance, great clawed hands and long, curious snout was a visual treat. It had thick, brown fur with two gray stripes along its sides. The pouch-riding baby hung securely, even when this eleven foot long creature stopped eating from the box on its pole to lower itself and walk on all-fours.

Geochelone atlas was next. It was an eight foot long, six foot high version of the Galopagos tortoise. Smythe continued. "We call this *laynd* reptile '*G. atlas*'. It ranged from India to Pacific *eye-laynds.*"

Linette was impressed. "Dr. Smythe! Tortoises don't swim. How did they get on islands?"

"Some *eye-laynds* were connected to *laynd* before the glaciers melted. The melting raised the sea level. So animals got stranded. But that doesn't explain animals on *eye-laynds* that were never part of a continental mass. So *he-ah's* my theory, young lady: Evidence keeps mounting up that primitive humans as *fah beck* as fifty thousand *ye-ahs* used boats to populate the Pacific, spreading species to cultivate a food source. Polynesians repeated the *patt'n* in more *mod'n* times."

"Fascinating!"

The group passed a colorful, three foot long side-necked turtle from Australia without much notice. The next stop gripped them with mounting fear. They peered nervously at a partially ob-scured bright green and drab orange lump. It was over eight feet long, excluding the head and tail. The lump was *Meiolania*, a squat-shelled Australian turtle. Smythe spoke into his wrist watch and a box released a six foot snake near it. Immediately, the lump rose three feet higher and advanced. Its horrendous claws and grotesque, sharp-spiked black head suddenly shocked the visitors. The head was three times the size of a man's and, mov-ing from side to side, jutted far out of the shell. Its tail was also spiked. A triangular and toothless beak suddenly opened and snapped up the doomed snake with a thunderous clamp. The turtle shook its hideous head and flung half of the snake onto the glass as the crowd cringed. In a second, the other half was gone. Then, the *Meiolania* lay motionless.

Everyone's facial and neck muscles remained tensed, their gazes fixed upon the frightening spectacle. Linette gulped and she looked as if in disbelief from the turtle to her father and back again.

Smythe broke the alarmed silence. "Dr. Lloyd and Dr. Cabral found the fossil tissue of this one's '*fah-tha*' so to speak in an outback Australian bog. It was at a depth that dated its genes to ten-thousand *ye-ahs* ago. Bogs preserve tissue amazingly well. This creature's *very* fast and attacks *anything* that moves!"

Linette shrieked in utter exuberance. "Wow. I'll bet nothing could eat him!"

Smythe inflected his voice like a game show host. "Don't be so *shore*, mate! You haven't seen all the predators, or even some of the more fascinating *herbie-vores*, yet!"

* * *

Hassan sat waiting, stolid and stern at his desk in Baghdad. His small, Spartan office adjoined Minister Ismail Mon's office suite. He wore a black pinstripe suit that belied his rank as a major in the Iraqi army. At precisely the appointed moment, two trusted officers reported sharply and closed the door behind them.

Hassan neither greeted them nor returned their salutes. He spoke quickly and, as he had learned from his mentor, without discernible emotion. "The minister will be back in two days and will require your report. Review it with me now."

"Sir, the only site with sufficient seclusion, water supply and moderated temperature is too close to a Kurdish village, Al-Rajda, in the foothills. If we relocate the villagers, we will need to comply with the new protocols. And that may create suspicion in the West."

"That can be dealt with. I'll take it up with the Minister myself."

The second officer began. "Sir, four specimens have been located to date. Three are thirty-five thousand years old and were found together in a collapsed shaft of Shanidar Cave. These were just recently found by Lloyd's team. Our own people found one in the Pyrenees mountains. I am informed that it is nearly forty thousand years old. We have confirmed that each is *Homo sapiens neanderthalensis*. Our lab assures me that these are usable . . . if we can get Dr. Harrigan to cooperate or clarify his methods. However, we do not think Harrigan will cooperate, as his dossier indicates he would be suspicious of any genetic research within our borders. I regret that I do not have a solution. Our people are not ready to do this kind of work alone."

Hassan's words were flat-toned but menacing. "Harrigan is a self-centered fool. The Minister has informed me that he is willing to personally work on him, now that Harrigan has proved his potential in Megiddo. However, *you* will continue search efforts for additional specimens and you *will* find and recover at least one Cro-Magnon. You have both disappointed me. That is unwise. I want this program isolating the traits you have on 'the alpha list' within a year. Do you understand?"

"Yes, sir. Un- Understood." The first officer's voice quavered.

The second hoped that he could gain distinction above that of his comrade with a more committed assurance to his superior. "I understand and will not fail, sir."

"I will report to the Minister myself when he returns. You two will be busy creating solutions, rather than reporting problems. Dismissed."

* * *

All groups took noon meals at concession hubs in the tunnels. Dr. Paulo Cabral's Spanish and Portuguese speaking Group Three ate fast, impatient to resume "the trip back in time." The common language for the group was Spanish. They resumed their journey quickly even though they'd been enthralled by Cabral's engaging lunchtime stories of hair-raising cave explorations all over the world.

The next area displayed a two foot tall, gray-brown South American bird known as a seriema. It stared stone-still and pointed its thick, sharp beak at them as they passed.

"The seriema," Cabral said, "is a surviving relative of our next resident. You will find it *most* interesting!"

Cabral spoke with typical flair. "The source of this one's genes is a *forty-five thousand year-old* female *embryo*. We found it in a cave on a submerged island off Argentina—quite usable, the rot arrested—*still* in the egg shell. It was a dwarf, so we suppressed the nanism genes to get the one you'll see in a moment. You may call this ancient bird . . ." Cabral's tone lowered to a deep, ominous whisper, *"Phorusrhacus*, the 'terror-bird' of legend! We are unsure if man ever dealt with this one. But evidence from *fifty thousand year-old* camp fires and boat parts from Chile show that there may have been early settlers in South America *that* long ago. If so, they would undoubtedly have visited coastal islands and encountered the last remnants, close dwarf cousins, of the terror-bird!"

A male *Phorusrhacus* glared at them through electrified fencing near the tube as the gasping visitors approached. The immense bird stood ten feet tall at its small-winged shoulders and looked nothing like the seriema. It's bulky neck and massive head arched, poised to strike, four feet above its back. Its sharp, overbite beak was almost two feet long and ten inches wide. It eyed them a moment before attacking viciously with its dangerous red and yellow striped head. The electric shock drove it back and served to infuriate it all the more.

Cabral activated the box and a small brown pony bolted out. The bird reminded more than a few in the shocked crowd of a vicious theropod dinosaur but with red, yellow, tan and black feathers. It reared back, leaped at the pony and crushed the equine's back within its huge beak. The bird raised the squealing mammal thirteen feet in the air and slammed it to the ground three times. Next, it carried the limp and bloody form to its mate at a nest farther out from the tunnel edge. It and a light gray and tan female dismembered the mammal with apparently effortless pulls of their beaks and lightning slashes of wide, hook-shaped claws. Then the pair fed the shreds to three squawking, turkey-sized gray babies.

Mrs. Rodreguez, a previously quiet lady from Mexico City, stared aghast at Cabral. "You horrible brute, to do such a thing to a pony!"

"I'm sorry, Mrs. Rodreguez, but this is one of our animals that will only eat live prey. The feeding demonstrations for today are set to enable two groups to observe simultaneously. We cannot deny this educational opportunity to Group Four. Most animals die by violent predation, Mrs. Rodreguez. A fact of prehistoric life— and of modern life!"

Next came a donkey followed by its neighbor, *Hippidion*, a four foot tall primitive horse. It seemed to smile at the visitors. Cabral explained that, along with smaller predecessors, it was food for some of the later-surviving dwarf terror-birds and for the saber-tooths of North and South America millennia ago.

Farther on they were awed and calmed to view two herbivores, the giant ground sloth *Megatherium* and its close—but far from obvious—relative *Daedicurus*, a glyptodont.

The formerly-extinct sloth bore little resemblance to its modern descendant, the South American tree sloth, which Cabral delighted in referring to by its scientific name *Bradypus tridactylus*. His curling 'r' sounds were accompanied by a warm, entertaining and toothy smile. *Megatherium* was brown with faint yellow stripes, vaguely in the pattern of a zebra. The animal was over twenty-two feet long with a thick, conical tail. Its head was over three feet long and bulged with powerful jaw muscles. Its ears were five-inch long ovals and its eyes were the size of baseballs. It moved on its bent-back hand-like paws and yard-long hind feet. There were four claws on each hand and three on each leg. The hind feet looked out of place as such, for they were so big around as to appear to be bent-forward shins. The rear claws pointed up and inward. The animal had surprisingly quick reactions, evident when catching vegetation dropped from the feeding box. As it ate, its characteristic peg teeth could be glimpsed.

"The nine thousand year-old specimen for him came from a sink-hole in Argentina. Its smaller cousins populated Florida and the American South and Midwest. They migrated across the Panama land bridge and, we have recently discovered, via the once-dry isthmus to Florida. *Megatherium* and our next exhibit, *Daedicurus*, are 'xenarthans'. Xenarthans are among the most ancient of mammal groups, with an inferior ability to regulate body temperature."

Cabral now focused on nearby *Daedicurus*. The tortoise-like mammal had brown hair protruding from under its shell and from its two-foot long, conical face. Its tail was long, thick and scaly. The egg-shaped shell extended six feet above its stubby claws. It was covered in rows of three-inch hexagonal brown scales.

"Die-dick-a-rus," he carefully pronounced, "is among our most *fantastic* animals. This Patagonian oddity is most closely related to the armadillo but it obviously dwarfs our little friend next door! It had many relatives as far north as the southern third of the U.S. As you can see, the mace-like club at the end of its powerful tail is two feet wide and would be most unpleasant to be struck by. It burrows and sometimes digs for roots with its bony snout and claws."

Mrs. Rodreguez shuddered to envision the Pleistocene world, gaining new respect for her host's work - and for the people who once lived in that world.

* * *

The black-haired man had been waiting by his computer in his parked van, with delicious-smelling, collapsed pizza cases, most of the morning. Now, well into the afternoon, he glanced at his watch, looked out his window at the shiny monument and grimaced. He opened his computer again and spoke coolly to his operatives through a microphone on the device. "Number Three, check door codes again and report."

It took over a minute. Then, the screen flashed CODES OPER-ABLE.

The man smiled again as he left the vehicle. He delivered cases of food, this time to the buffet tables being set up in the VIP pavil-ion, and returned to his van. As he drove off, he eyed the brass and steel revolving door at the base of the Monument to Peace and Man, only a few blocks away.

He muttered self-righteously, hatefully, "Sacrilege! You who would be gods in God's land deserve no mercy! You will be sacri-ficed. For I know your secret abomination and am he who stops you. Wolves, masquerading as lambs! It is my sacred will that your time is never to come. All of you go to the slaughter."

* * *

Dr. Yoshiko Oda, the Chemistry Lab Director, had been among those who complained at being assigned to act as tour guides. Nev-ertheless, she found that the afternoon was now ending quickly and that she had enjoyed the people she met. She also relished the chance to again speak in her native tongue.

Oda quizzed her already well informed Japanese VIP guests.

90

"What do you suppose we made from the likes of these lizards coming up?"

Ikuko Matsu, the jovial lady of the group, whose husband kept trying to silence her, spoke up. "A giant man-eating dinosaur!"

"No, Ikuko, *silly!* But you're reasonably close! It's a reptile you will think went extinct, yet has *always* been with us—only smaller during the last couple of thousand years."

Oda resumed her revelation. "Notice these two thick gray-green Komodo dragon lizards, at twelve and ten feet in length. They're members of the monitor lizard family. You all probably know that these are the second-largest modern lizards. They were discovered about a century ago on islands near Java. They mainly eat deer and scavenge but there are several documented cases of them killing and eating humans.

"What we found interesting in our genetic analysis is that they are thinner-framed *dwarfs* of a very ancient species. So, like the yeti you will see later, their larger ancestors never went extinct. Nanism, or dwarfing, occurs when a species becomes isolated, such as on islands, without the ability to roam for large food supplies. Only the small ones survive when food is scarce, though the natural tendency otherwise is toward giantism. All species have numerous genetic sequences for nanism. Nanism genes are generally suppressed by certain types of RNA molecules until the trait is allowed to become expressed through environmental pressures.

"The next animal we will see was produced by suppressing the nanism genes of the very pair you see before you. We were able to verify the genetic authenticity when Dr. Lloyd and Dr. Cabral, accompanied for this special expedition by Dr. Olivier, made one of our most interesting and *controversial* discoveries: On an expedition to Iraq, they found a small buried palace under fifty feet of desert sand. It had a man-made pool in the center, covered up with granite blocks. The structure was only about three thousand years old. It contained the half-decomposed body of a *thirty-foot* monitor lizard—with a huge copper chain around its neck! Dr. Olivier and Dr. Woj later verified that the archaic species was *Megalania*. We think the Babylonian kings imported the beasts from the Pacific for entertainment or worship."

Oda continued. "As a check on the accuracy of the genetic redemption process, Dr. Fong created this one by suppressing the nanism gene segments in the modern monitors' egg and sperm. It grew up very similar to a *Megalania* which Dr. Harrigan created using FGR. Using two different methods, we know that the Fossil Gene Redemption process is valid—at least for these reptiles."

Ikuko could not resist the question. "Did you imply that there is only one *Megalania* ahead?"

"That's right."

"Then, Yoshiko, what happened to the other you just spoke of?"

"The one you are about to see . . . ate it."

The group gasped but remained enthralled as the four foot long head came into view, and then the rest of its awesome, horrific profile. As they passed near it, the titan thrust its body from the ground and tried to bite the electrified fence surrounding this segment of the tube. The gaping mouth revealed fist-length, serrated, triangular teeth and a thick purple-red forked tongue. Its growling hiss was deafening, even inside the glass. It held its tail above the ground, swiping it side-to-side while it alternately eyed the huge feeding box—and the group members.

Oda began to elucidate as she activated a feeding box, launching a thick leg of lamb into the air. The meat was immediately inhaled by the monstrous lizard. "No telling what man's encounters with this thing might have been like. Grisly! This one kept breaking its teeth on the glass, not learning. Very stupid. Please don't taunt or excite it as we pass! Ah . . . We really shouldn't impede the next group."

The VIPs shivered visibly. They moved on, trying to continue glimpsing the fearsome giant reptile through the increasingly distortive angle of the glass tube.

A large boar and then *Metridiochoerus*, an ancient boar, came into view. It stood five feet at the shoulders and snapped ravenously at them with two-inch fangs. *Metridiochoerus*, which Oda pronounced "meh-tridio-keer-us," sported two ten-inch spiked tusks protruding from each side of its snout. The two in the upper jaw curved forward and up, like horns, while those in the lower jaw jutted menacingly straight out to the side. It ignored the group and fought its three pen-mates for dead meat and vegetables.

"This animal ranged from East Africa to Polynesia, in cousin-species-form, some forty thousand years ago. You may not be aware of this about boars, but they are *most* vicious animals."

Dr. Lloyd led his group around and ahead of Oda's. His voice was naturally louder and deeper than hers as it drowned hers out. "The next animal is one you'd never see in jolly old England, I can tell you that! I came upon suitable remains of it after weeks in the bloody bush! If you think this upcoming giraffe is impressive, look farther ahead: *Sivatherium!* What a devilish brute, eh; what?"

The English-speaking group almost ignored the huge giraffe and even the odd-looking, stripped okapi in its pen. The VIPs trained their eyes instead on *Sivatherium* with intense interest. Lloyd told its story as simply as he could, given its more complicated genetic makeup.

"Our *Sivatherium* was created from redeemed fossil genes, of course, joined to the genes of a giraffe. However, sivas were also related to okapis. So, certain genetic sequences were taken from an okapi, too."

The beast was impressive with its two yard-long, foot-wide and six-inch thick ossicones, which had the appearance of downy antlers. It appeared to be a cross between a bull and a moose but was gargantuan: seven feet tall at the shoulders. It had a conical snout and viciously-displayed cutting teeth. It began stomping hard enough to threaten even these 'experienced' veterans of the preserve tour.

Around the corner, they saw a large seven foot long tapir with its abbreviated-elephantine trunk. Its short black fur was divided by a white band extending from its pig-like shoulders to its rump.

"This next one is a Malayan tapir. It's a modern relative of the next animal coming up, *Ancylotherium*." Lloyd stated the name slowly. "Ans-eye-lo-thee-rium."

"We call it an 'ancy' for short, and it *is* a bit antsy and occasionally erratic. It was a savanna animal, able to browse high or pluck grass. Its genes came from a deep, three hundred thousand year-old, oxygen-free sinkhole on a small island off East Africa. Its discovery made all the papers, as its extinction was previously placed at about nine hundred thousand years ago. Recovering this one was quite a fright, what with the dark water, sharks, and the scuba gear getting caught in among branches and bones! There is a disputed fossil of it at a higher strata, which could mean its kind survived on the island to about a hundred thousand years ago.

"It's a member of an extinct family of species called chalicotheres, which are distantly related to tapirs. They were odd toed, giant plant eaters, attaining massive size in Africa and North America. Chalicotheres like our ancy ranged from Europe to North America. It is our most ancient resident here at the Preserve."

The gargantuan, tan, vaguely horse-like creature stood ten feet tall at its intensely muscular shoulders; eight feet at its tiny-tailed rump. Its front legs were a third longer than the rear ones, giving it a gorilla-like stance. Its hind legs bent backwards and down towards claws, rather than hooves. Each set of three claws looked like two-foot long, hairy primate hands resting long-fingered and palm-down on the ground. They had three-inch thick sickle nails, four inches long. The front claws were like the back but were twice the size. It dragged its worn-down claws on the ground and the staff suspected that this was one of many minor flaws caused by archaic/modern hybridization in the Preserve's species. Its head and neck were twice the size of a horse's and there was a strong resemblance, even as to posture. It rose on its haunches to eat from the bail. When nervous it stomped and sprang up bipedal, threateningly clawing the air.

Lloyd shared his fervor for Pleistocene life and early man's place in it. "We believe that most of these animals, even the next which we're about to visit, were contemporaneous with *Homo sapiens sapiens*, modern humans. All of them were probably well known to our close cousin species. In his several subspecies, man roamed the globe stalking, worshipping and being stomped or eaten by these and other fantastic animals. The fossil record clearly indicates that humans battled related species, like *Gigantopithecus* and closer extinct subspecies, like *Homo sapiens neanderthalensis*. We are coming up on our last exhibit, a close relative of *Gigantopithecus*, also called the yeti, just past the orangutan. Except for having almost no neck, this silly-faced orangutan looks nothing like its tall, menacing neighbor, I assure you! But repeated genetic analyses prove that yetis and orangutans were very close cousins to each other and to *Gigantopithecus*. Dr. Woj, Dr. Cabral and I captured this family. They were not genetically hybridized."

The yeti's area included a manufactured cave designed to enable viewing. The seven and a half foot tall male was deeper red in color than the thinner, six-foot tall female. As Lloyd came into its view, the newly-enraged male viciously hammered a tree limb at the glass and ripped at the tube's overhead cleaning box. Then it suddenly rotated an inside bolt on a door plate, nearly panicking the group. In a shaky voice, Lloyd immediately called for both maintenance and security. The yeti abandoned the bolts, thereby calming the crowd. But it continued screeching threateningly and scrambled up along the tube until Lloyd glided out of its sight.

"Uh. Yes. Now then. As I was saying: a very close relative of *Gigantopithecus*, if not the very same species." The group began to calm. Lloyd swallowed hard and regained his composure. "We've checked x-rays and bone sample analyses against the fossil record and we're quite satisfied that they are direct descendants, probably dwarfs of the ancient primate."

A fellow Londoner, Reggie Walsh, queried Lloyd. "Why isn't this glass coated with a one-way mirror substance so the animals won't be upset by our presence?"

"I . . . why I don't know, Reggie. That's a marvelous idea. I'll take it up with Dr. Harrigan this very afternoon!"

Lloyd looked at his watch. "That yeti and I have never seemed to get on. Gives me the creeps, I must admit. They do mate, apparently in the fall but she's not pregnant yet. We intend to isolate him if his behavior doesn't moderate soon. And we'll inseminate her artificially if she isn't pregnant by November. Despite suspicion some years ago that the yeti might be a 'missing link' they're obviously not very human-like are they?! Let's get on to the pavilion, shall we? And then there's that monument which I understand is so controversial. I'm eager to see it myself. Haven't so much as peeked inside yet!"

The groups assembled for a buffet style dinner. They enjoyed sumptuous rack of lamb, lobster Newberg, chicken dishes and a cosmopolitan selection of sauces, vegetables, fruits, wines and beers. Then all were led past the dwindling groups of protesters, through the huge revolving doors and into the massive, windowless, aluminum structure.

Chapter Seven

... he shall make sacrifices and offering cease; and in
their place shall be an abomination that desolates ...
— Daniel 9.27

Lo, Soul! Seest thou not God's purpose from the first?
The earth to be spann'd, connected by net-work,
The people to become brothers and sisters,
The races, neighbors, to marry and to be given in marriage,
The oceans to be cross'd, the distant brought near,
The Lands to be welded together.
— Walt Whitman, *Passage to India*

So when you see the desolating sacrilege standing in
the holy place ...   — Matt 24.15

The Monument to Peace and Man, Megiddo, Israel

1910 hours, 3 April, 2008

The handful of press and protesters were shooed away. Each tour group passed security to enter the two hundred twenty foot tall aluminum tower. The setting sun beamed pink and orange radiance off its gleaming exterior walls. The outside of the massive vessel had been meticulously cleaned and polished to a sparkle. It rose in smooth, helical form like a tightly rolled silver scroll whose center had been ceremoniously pushed up. Crowning the narrowed pinnacle was a United Nations flag. A huge gleaming brass revolvable door provided exit; another permitted entrance. The spiraled roof formed less-reflective, non-skid ramps, bordered at the open outside edge by a sturdy balustrade all the way down, over top of the entrance, to a small, adjoining domed shelter.

The shelter contained administrative facilities as well as a large bank of computer terminals provided free to visitors who wished to debate issues raised inside. Visitors would be able to type directly onto the linked monitors which were among the displays within the monument.

The monument had no windows, even on the doors, for it was well lit and the inside wall space was needed for displays. Its inside walkway up was of generous but narrowing width. Its center was a one hundred eighty foot cone; almost a cylinder twelve feet wide at the top and thirty feet wide at the base. This center shaft was empty except that the sides were laced with steel supports, long, exposed bolts and electrical wiring. In the long, curved display hall, most kiosks were animated with 3-D TV or robotic exhibits. The painted wall displays, lush blood-red carpeting and bright glare-free lighting were very pleasing to the gabbing visitors.

Harrigan had taken a quick look at the inside weeks before and had a fairly complete idea of the exhibits. His group led the way, discussing points broached by the displays. The VIPs leisurely ascended from the base toward the top. Freund's group followed. Gertrude, barely showing in her third month, had no problem negotiating the gentle incline of the long, curved hall. Restrooms and benches were available at the base level, before the floor began its angle upward.

Just past the restrooms, various displays portrayed issues confronting man's ancient ancestors. These were depicted, as were all displays from bottom to top, by a wide variety of media, including paintings, interactive screens and mounted artifacts such as spearpoints. Exhibits began with depictions of survival challenges facing early simians. The ape-like creatures were shown evolving societal and other traits. These characteristics were explained as compensating for hominid vulnerability to monstrous creatures, even bigger and more vicious than those which had astounded the visitors earlier in the day. The prehumans were shown to have formed bands, divided labor—at first between the sexes—and to have learned to use deadly force against other species and each other to gain food or shelter. The abilities to think symbolically, imagine, cooperate, vocalize and manipulate tools all were touted as key attributes contributing to sapien survival and continued development.

Still, as the displays made clear, evidence of brutal individual and group fighting and killing had been unearthed. Wall placards and displays broached the issue repeatedly: Whether the urge to kill—and any other propensity in humans—might be genetic and, hence, merit no moral judgment. Following closely behind Harrigan's group, Freund grimaced at the premise of the question. He knew that evolution theory was sound. However, he was quite vocal in his disapproval of the implications asserted as he glared at Mon.

"These displays *obviously* promote the assumption that acting on genetic proclivities is morally neutral. I'm sorry but the truth is *not* established by rationalist philosophy, opinion polls or political correctness. Stand in the truth, sir!"

Mon listened to Freund's comment and returned an apparently unemotional response. "Dr. Freund, *sir*, what is truth? You must admit that this concept of 'morality' differs from society to society and is an imperfect *human* construct. This monument, however, should please you: For you will see as you walk on that it celebrates man's conquering, by reason, technology and societal evolution, his most dangerous inherited traits—such as the propensity to kill his fellow man. We are at that threshold now, Doctor, and neither religion nor morality has brought us here. Civil, secular mastery of ourselves has."

Quite a few in the spiraled hallway clapped and cheered the impromptu speech. Freund did not choose to respond but did appreciate Harrigan breaking off and stepping back to speak with him.

Harrigan had been surprised at himself in the months preceding the monument's completion. He had wanted to see. He had wanted to understand its meaning and why it was so important to Mon and other bureaucrats. It had even haunted his dreams as it began to take form. A few weeks before, he was permitted an early look inside. Harrigan felt uncomfortably and profoundly affected by the issues broached within its walls but he kept his private debate to himself. He sensed Freund was unfairly put on the spot by this encounter.

"Mannie, I saw this thing three weeks ago and, frankly you're right. This thing was designed by Mon's Commission and reviewed by zillions of UN committees. It's kinda like the International Public Radio news, you know? Promoting *its agenda* while only appearing to impartially inform. But this next area looks at how religion developed and, here, I think they're on target. Just look at it impartially."

"Okay. Impartially. I can do that."

The group wound its way past the most primitive simians toward depictions of near-humans, such as *Homo erectus* and *Homo ergaster*. One theory, based on recent finds, asserted that *Erectus* continued to survive, side-by-side, with Neanderthal and Cro-Magnon man and that the Cro-Magnons deduced that they and the Neanderthals both were the children of the more primitive species. It postulated that stories, like that of Cain and Abel, were orally handed down as Genesis-like myths. Other such theories were in the displays but all had a common thrust: Man's history was not revealed to him, rather, he created it.

Freund looked irritated as he passed the only reference to creationist views. "I really wish the fundamentalists wouldn't be so literal. Their black or white interpretations are like declaring that they know the mind of God—when no one can presume that. They get so wrapped around the creationist axle, that they can't find the true meaning of the Genesis allegory! As if someone who believes in evolution *and* God must be going to hell or something! So, now they've provided ample material for the rest of us to be ridiculed!"

Freund pointed to direct his wife's attention toward the collage depicting numerous examples of shoddy science once used to refute the theory of evolution or, before the theory, to discourage scientific investigation. These included a fossil shell coil, which Irish monks, rather than studying them, had carved at the blunt end to appear as Satan's snakes turned to stone by divine punishment.

Gertrude frowned at her husband. "Manfred Freund! I'm surprised at you. That's mean! We may not share fundamentalists' views, but their hearts are righteous! You corrected Hans for talking that way to playmates yesterday. Remember what you told him? 'Try to live each moment as if you had only a few left.' Practice what you preach! Besides, maybe the Creation Story is true and evolution began afterward." He was embarrassed but did not retract his words.

* * *

99

"Number Three, test the door codes."

In an unfurnished apartment opposite the monument, a young Israeli woman with curly brown hair adjusted her headset to hear the command clearly. She tapped several keys on her computer and awaited the test result. She observed the phrase CODES OPERABLE on her monitor and smiled. She typed again to relate this status to her comrade in the white utility van.

The black haired man in the utility van received the status and nodded to himself. He had planned every detail. He had known that, if charges were detonated near the monument's pinnacle, only the top or the door might blow off.

His plan to maximize damage, therefore, relied upon the monument's design: The walls around the center, forming the cylindrical core were made of relatively soft plastipanels mounted on steel supports. He wanted the force to be as evenly distributed throughout the superstructure, from the very center upward. Killing power would be most effective when everyone was spread throughout the building. The doors were to be remotely locked by radioing the compromised security code from a nearby apartment. He checked another operative's status.

"Number Two, how close are you to the platform?"

The computer screen in his van flashed one word: IMMINENT.

* * *

The two lead groups moved on, and the others followed. They saw depictions of Neanderthal and Cro-Magnons. These common names were explained as being derived from European valleys in which the first specimens were unearthed. *Homo sapiens neanderthalensis*, extinct, and *Homo sapiens sapiens*, essentially the same as modern man, were depicted on a time chart. Neanderthals were shown as arising about two hundred ninety thousand years ago and Cro-Magnon about thirty-five thousand years ago. Within five thousand years of the arrival of the Cro-Magnon, the Neanderthals were gone.

Displays evidencing spiritualism among both human subspecies were prominent. Spiritual practices were interpreted to be tools by which the shamans and leaders manipulated their tribes, reinforced authority and secured the best possessions. Warfare, based on recent and twentieth century finds, was depicted between these two groups. More theories were espoused as to why there are no Neanderthals today and why some people had Neanderthal features.

One, illustrated with manikins, had a strong archaeological basis: The recent French Alps find of five Neanderthals, tied together at the ankles and buried under a rock slide. A juvenile male among them had both Neanderthal and Cro-Magnon skeletal features. The theory asserted that enslaved Neanderthals interbred with their captors. This adjoined and led to displays depicting slavery, governmental development, organized warfare and, eventually, modern civilization.

Conflicts and societal change from mammoth-hunting, nomadic lifestyles to agriculture-based villages were shown. The stories of the first settlements, then city-states of Sumaria, Egypt and the rest of the world were told. Repeated destruction and migrations of Hebrew tribes were traced as the history lesson continued to progress on through the Roman, Aztec and other empires.

Progressing farther up the incline, the groups viewed representations of the medieval crusades. These were vividly shown with Christian fighters massacring whole Moslem towns and Moslem knights also using religious fervor to justify disemboweling Balkan women and children. Mankind's religions were shown as worse than no help in this matter. Indeed numerous and undeniable facts were presented for consideration: The near-modern Catholic Church's virtual silence during the Holocaust was prominently portrayed. Representations laid bare centuries of Buddhist, Hindu and Islamic impotence at restraining warring behavior against followers of competing sects. Displays indicted organized religion as the source of deadly religious fighting and terrorism. The gist of it all was clear: That man progressed technologically and socially primarily when religion was rejected and that mankind needed universal, systemic and enforced safeguards against his own propensity to covet, hate and kill.

Mon pointed at depictions of the modern wars and terrorist incidents. "Note the abuse of religious and governmental powers. Mass killing to solve the problems of competing moral systems and uneven distribution of resources. The prevalence today of war and religious terrorism proves the destructive influence of nationalism and religious fervor. Only a world government, properly led, can free mankind from the bane of hypocritical god-centered systems."

Freund turned red and shouted. "No! Destruction comes from man's own judgment of God and his will to *be* God. History is rife with *leaders* who distort the divine in the name of rationalist progress. It has always been *leaders*, terrorist or governmental, who use force in God's name, discrediting genuine fervor – not organized religions!

Mon's voice rose inspiringly. "Humankind will only be free when it rejects the oppression of clerics and focuses on making a good living within the rules of one global society. The UN and we, in progressive governments, are attaining that goal now. Not in compliance to the dictates of some *ayatollah, pope or swami*—but through the scientific creativity of man. We will build peace, accomplishment and wealth, conquering the very *stars* to carry the torch of the supremacy of *man.*"

Applause and cheers from most of the crowd were loud and spontaneous.

The remainder of the displays portrayed the work of the Arab-Israeli Mutual Development Commission, other groups like it and the progress which they had achieved. Mon stepped just ahead of the crowd to a level-surface which formed the ten foot diameter, round room at the top. Between the exit and a maintenance access door, an impressionist painting hung bathed in bright spotlights. It showed a nude, racially-vague couple stepping out into bright stars from a dimming silver-gray volcano, spiraled like the monument, in whose bowels boiled symbols of religions, nations and wars.

Harrigan disliked politics and had never completely warmed to Mon, either. Yet he couldn't help feel a shiver of inspiration. He thought to himself, *This proven get-back-up-and-keep-going leader painted the future and nailed the past almost right on the head.* Freund felt fear, loathing. He and Gertrude had placed arms around their children and each other during Mon's proclamations.

As Mon turned, a red light lit on a control panel beside the huge revolvable door. Two loud metallic clangs rang out as steel bars jutted out a foot from inside the walls of the exit's curved turnstile, locking it.

Then machine gun fire suddenly burst from behind Freund. As he threw his family to the floor, Freund saw Mon fly backward;

blood splattering from the right side of his head. Everyone dropped, screaming. This shooting took only a few, horrible seconds. Mon's bodyguards and two Israeli soldiers scrambled to their feet. Freund could not see the gunmen behind him but their work was evident: Mon's bodyguard trained his pistol down the walkway past Freund. But before acquiring a target, the guard fell immediately to the ground; his neck ripped wide open at the left jugular by rapid-fire. The two Israelis threw Heitzman behind them and sought targets, also without results. Their heads were almost immediately snapped back, blown open.

The gunmen turned and fired down the hall toward the crowd, most of the bullets embedding in the ceiling due to nervous aim. The thugs ordered silence. Most screams quelled but moans continued. Then, Heitzman stood to surrender as a hostage, screaming that they could take him. As he rose, a single pummeling spray of bullets opened his skull at the center of his face. It tossed him back down, silent.

Two men in jeans and cotton sport shirts—one dull red, the other navy blue, jumped over Freund and pulled a fat-looking man in gray slacks and a black parka-style shirt up through the crowd. As they bounded past Heitzman's body toward the maintenance door, Harrigan screamed and hurled himself at the three, bowling each to the floor. Harrigan was only able to hold down the two in sport shirts. With the butt of their small machine guns, both men in jeans immediately clubbed Harrigan, knocking him unconscious.

The 'fat' man rose to his feet, his open shirt revealing recessed foam padding and flaps in which his and his co-conspirators' weapons had been smuggled. The smuggler saw that his comrades were about to kill Harrigan. So he turned back toward the maintenance door. He pulled a small white putty cube from his false belly, slammed it onto the bulky door handle, drew away and pushed a small green plunger linked to the cube by wire. The explosion blew the door open but it remained on its hinges. The other two assassins raised their weapons to Harrigan's head and . . .

"Aaaahhh!"

Freund's yell distracted the two long enough for him to close his distance and pounce upon them. He landed also on Harrigan, who began to regain consciousness. Shots ripped a quarter inch-deep valley across Freund's left side below his ribs. The noise jolted Harrigan who wrenched the weapon from the second assailant's hand, which had been immobilized below Freund's heavy shoulder. The fat man turned back and pointed his gun at Freund, who was on top of the two accomplices, and fired. The pinned attacker was rising to throw Freund off and recover his weapon from Harrigan.

But the rising attacker met his death, as a short burst from the fat man's weapon ripped directly through him. It split his backbone and exploded shreds of his stomach out onto Harrigan and Freund. The other prone gunman tried to push Freund off and take his weapon back but Harrigan fired, at a range of only seven inches, into the terrorist's forehead. The spray of bone shards, bloody skin and hair was shocking. It only appeared to frighten the explosives man. He disappeared into the maintenance room as the door automatically closed behind him. However, he did not enter it to escape.

Freund and Harrigan scrambled to their feet to pursue him through the mangled door. Others behind them rushed to the revolvable door but began panicking and screaming as they realized they were unable to control or budge it. The foam padding fell off the assailant, revealing rows of C-4 plastic explosive embedded with wire-connected blasting caps. Freund gasped, now realizing why the man had shut himself inside the utility room.

Freund screamed at Harrigan. "He's wired! Caps *und* C-4 all over him!"

"Jesus Christ! Get him."

They sprang through the door but the man was already climbing over the railing of the maintenance platform which overlooked the monument's deep center shaft. He was about to jump down onto the roof of the base level, a hundred eighty feet below.

"He's jumping!"

The suicide bomber was in the air and falling. Harrigan lunged for the man's arm and missed.

Freund dove for the floor, almost sliding out himself into the dizzying shaft. He managed to hug the falling man's right arm and waist. The hold was not sufficient. The terrorist continued to fall forward out and away from the railing—pulling Freund precariously out over the edge. Harrigan kneeled to grab Freund and pull the two of them back through the railing. Freund was losing his grip on the deadly, struggling terrorist.

Bart Lloyd suddenly rushed into the room and leaped onto the platform. He flung his body directly onto Freund's with a painful thud to them both. He reached over Freund and through the railing to grasp the killer's left arm. Pulling back against the terrorist's substantial strength, he got within reach of a headlock and began to strangle the "filthy blighter," as he called him.

Harrigan and Lloyd quickly pulled the man in now, throwing him back against the workbench. He slid back sitting upright, feet toward the railing. Harrigan accidentally tipped the bench over, spilling tools and thick extension cords everywhere. Harrigan, still on his knees, grabbed a long torque wrench and quickly pushed Freund and Lloyd out of the way. He swung the heavy steel club to his right, then slammed it with his remaining strength into the man's left ear. The bomber started to tip over, as if dead, but Freund gasped and held him before the C-4 and basting caps covering him could strike the floor. Then Freund laid the body down very carefully, announcing that the man was still alive but out cold. Harrigan dressed Freund's painful but superficial wound with one of the clean work rags and his belt.

"Shouldn't we, uh, tie him up or something?" Lloyd was almost out of breath.

Harrigan took charge. "Do it now! No. Wait. Get everyone to move to the lower levels—slowly. I don't want any stampedes!"

Bart opened the door to leave and begin the operation. There was already a stampede. He chased the sound of the screaming crowd and was gone.

Freund and Harrigan began to wrap the man randomly with knotted, confused hundred foot electrical cords.

"Vee need to tie him *bedder* than this! He could wake up any min—"

The man's eyes opened and he shot up, pulling a detonator from his right side. In a flash, he dove for the railing. Harrigan went for the man and Freund reached for the detonator. Freund grabbed it around the sides but the man was already pushing the plunger down on the top of the device. Harrigan caught him just at the edge of the platform. But the detonator plunger was already almost all the way down to its base.

"Ahhh. Aaah." Harrigan's finger felt as if it was crushed but it did effectively block the plunger from its base. His other fingers wrapped around Freund's on the plunger base. The terrorist held it too close to wrest free, and tied up Harrigan's other hand too effectively, for Harrigan to reach and break the wire. The men struggled as Freund, noticing Harrigan's safety-grip on the green box, released his hand and grabbed a carpenter's hammer from the floor.

Freund struck the man twice with the heavy blunt end but the bomber was kicking Harrigan away and was almost over the edge. Freund spun the hammer in his palm and crashed the claw end down, gouging the top of the skull. The man continued to struggle; he was out over the edge again. Freund struck again, harder; well into the brain, and pried the hammer back viciously. It cracked the skull and spattered a red and gray jam-like substance on his face.

The man began to convulse wildly. He floundered out under the railing and away from the two; through the air and down, five feet, then ten; twenty feet; more. Harrigan and Freund blanched. Both knew the man could, in seconds, blast up at them and kill hundreds.

Freund saw it first. Then Harrigan. One of the cords they had tied him with had fallen over a banister post, providing a chance to halt the deadly fall. It draped around the post about twenty feet down but was already taut; being pulled back up, around and off the railing. The two got in each other's way grabbing for it. Only four feet remained and they still had no hold.

Harrigan reached out around the pole to grasp the cord. He pulled it back in, forming a single twist around the base of the post. Harrigan pulled it tight and wrapped it one more twist around the pole. All he had left to grip was the prong and about ten inches. Freund clutched this remainder. Together, they held it fast.

"We've got it! Mannie!"

The binding was holding easily. Too easily. They stared in horror: The deadly, explosive-laden body was still falling, spinning furiously as it unwound.

Then the line tugged. The body bounced. They held their breath and Harrigan even prayed, "God *help* us!" out loud. The prayer was not answered: The body slipped the confused loops and began to fall again; to lurch and flip. There was very little cord left wrapped on the body, now tumbling eighty feet below.

A tug. A snapping sound, like bone cracking. The cord appeared tangled about the neck. The hanged, bloody bomb bounced and swung. A moment passed as the two men quivered and took their breaths in short, halting gasps. Tears as much as sweat dripped from their cheek bones as they knelt gripping the cord and staring down, terrified. The body dangled. Another moment passed. It swayed. A few moments more, and it hung almost motionless.

Harrigan could only whisper. "Mannie. We've gotta go down and get it. The cord's binding around his neck but it could let go any minute. We can't just wait for the outside guards to figure out that what's going on in here. You know what will happen if it falls."

"*Ja*, I know. We have to secure the cord but there's not enough to tie it. *'nd* if we pull him up, the disturbance could unbind him."

Harrigan drew a breath and saw the duct tape near his leg. He pulled it to himself with his foot and a free hand. Then, with that hand and his teeth, he unwrapped a foot of it. He wrapped it around the twist at the base of the pole, almost dropped it, and continued to expand his bind. Within moments, he released his other hand and accelerated the taping. They were satisfied. Freund released his grip.

They looked around for more extension cords and found one, a hundred foot roll. As they searched the lockers, they found three more of the same and tied four into two single lengths with knots they had been taught years before. They raced to secure the lengths to the railing, three feet on either side of the pole to which they had taped the dead man's line. There were three empty tool belts with a few hinged 'D' rings, four small room extension cords and several pairs of heavy duty gloves. They rapidly donned these and wrapped the cord once each around the 'D' rings clipped to their tool belts. With the cords pulled around their right sides and held centered on the small of their backs by their right hands and the taut upper end with their left hands, they dropped from the railing. They rappelled down more quickly than they knew was safe but they could not afford to assume the binding around the bomber's neck was secure.

At the one hundred foot point, they breathed sighs of relief because the tangle around the man's neck looked temporarily secure, yet far from permanent. Freund and Harrigan reached the corpse and began to re-secure the small extension cords on their own bodies and tether the other ends to the dead man's arms. They tried but realized that they would not be able to haul him back up. So

107

they unhooked their 'D' rings, hung on precariously with one hand each for a moment and resecured it below the start of the next cord. They could hear moaning and crying though the walls below them. They were all still locked in.

Freund smiled at Harrigan. "Okay, ready to untangle his neck 'nd lower him down?"

"Let's do it."

The eighty-foot journey was exhausting and painful, especially at Freund's wound and where the small tether cords constricted his side. They reached the bottom slowly and without dropping the body. They set it in the sitting position, its head resting on its chest and the bloody skull gouge no longer leaking due to coagulation, lumps of brain matter and clots matted in the hair.

"Okay. Now: We're safe from this guy! I think it would be easier to break through that heavy plastic wall than to climb back up, don't you Mannie?"

"Absolutely!" Freund's accent was dissipating as his confidence bolstered. He rose to look for something with which to attack the wall. There was nothing. They both wished they had thought to bring tools. Freund examined the wall bolts. They were not removable by hand. Harrigan did not assist but remained at the body. Harrigan looked the dead man over between the layers and rows of C-4, even down to the ankles, and listened.

"Kevin! Are you going to keep gawking at that horror show or are you going to help . . ."

"Holy sh- . . . Mannie! This thing's got a back-up detonator. I can hear it."

Freund didn't hear it. His nerves were frayed and he was getting irritated at Harrigan for pulling his leg. Harrigan grabbed the corpse and carefully rolled it on its side. He put his ear to the middle of its back. "Zhzhzhzhzhzhzh." He snapped back his head and tore the shirt open with his teeth, being careful not to disturb the hundreds of sensitive blasting caps. If just one went off, it would detonate everything. Freund heard it. Then they both saw it: a red box with two blinking green lights.

"It *could* be a battery pack," Freund said, now petrified and knowing he was wrong.

"Its a friggin' timer, Mannie, and we don't know how to turn it off. If we disconnect it, it could detonate right then."

The realization that they knew neither when it would blow nor how to disarm it shook them visibly and they both began to sweat profusely again.

Harrigan was fidgeting, frantic but not panicked. "It could blow any minute or *any second!* What can we do?"

Freund thought a few seconds, grinned and announced his idea to Harrigan. "Pull the C-4 from the blasting caps *'nd* separate them. He blows up but the C-4 isn't detonated. We *wouldt* need at least fifty feet distance, though, with this many caps on him."

Harrigan gave Freund an irritated look. "I was gonna suggest that next!"

Freund spoke quickly, flippant but friendly, already loosening blasting caps as he had been taught long ago. "I *know* you were, Big Guy. Let's go!"

The two knew they would have to rib each other later, if there would be a later. They feverishly ripped tape from the rows and layers of C-4, avoided pulling wires, and wiggled the deadly blocks off the corpse. They stuffed them into their shirts. Breaths were getting shorter. Sweat was dripping into their eyes, dangerously impeding the accuracy of their manipulations of wiring, bricks and volatile blasting caps. The cries and moans beyond the wall continued without relief.

Finally, Harrigan took the last brick, sweaty and smelly, off the man's lower buttocks. There was no room in their shirts or pockets. Freund already had a brick in his mouth and was mounting the cord. No bricks could be left on the bottom, as even one would blast through the plastipanels and kill several in the huddling crowds below. He had to follow immediately. Harrigan grimaced, disgusted; wiped the brick and stuffed it in his mouth. The two men climbed as fast as they could. But it was slow going and they were exhausted, sore and cramping.

The two groped their way about forty feet up and absolutely had to rest, catch their breath, momentarily. They knew that a delayed blasting cap could be launched upward by the others detonating and then explode on *them*, in contact with the C-4. They were not getting enough air with those bricks in their mouths. Freund looked almost as if he was having breathing convulsions. Harrigan was concerned and mumbled to him through the impediment of the smelly C-4 block in his mouth. Freund saw it and winced.

"Mannie: Breathing problems? Not far now 'till we get this stuff out of range. You can do it!"

"I'm okay, Kevin. Just winded. I was laughing."

"Laughing?! We could die any second and you're laughing?"

"You know, Kevin, all you had to do to keep that butt-sweat soaked C-4 out of your *moutt* was exchange it with one in your shirt!"

Harrigan's eyebrow popped up. He frowned at Freund again but said nothing and resumed the arduous climb.

Freund followed, calling to him. "I know, Big Guy: You were going to think of that any second but you *hadt* to get climbing immediately!"

They were about forty-five feet up when they saw Lloyd pop his head over the side of the platform above.

"Are you chaps all right? We're still stuck in here and I don't think anyone knows were locked in. The crowd has some serious injuries, I'm afraid. The outside guards will probably soon notice that we're late in exiting, though. Hey, can you hear me?"

Harrigan and Freund had no more energy to respond. They were straining too much and could easily fall back down—and that would result in worse than a nasty fall. They knew they were still within the range of what could easily be an ejected, live cap.

Lloyd realized they needed help and prepared to come down. He overestimated his rappelling prowess, however. Lloyd was forty feet down when the pair passed the self-declared but uncertain safe range of fifty feet up. All three met at the half way point, ninety feet. That was where Lloyd slipped. He swayed too much and tangled his feet in the wiring along the plastipanels, lost his grip and hung upside down by one leg. He struggled to pull himself upright. Harrigan and Freund tried but could do nothing for him.

The blast came at that moment, when they least expected. The blasting caps surrounding the body detonated within milliseconds of each other, creating the effect of one big explosion and ejecting four delayed blasting caps. It melted and shattered the surrounding plastipanels injuring several people on the adjoining hall. The shock knocked the weakened pair into the steel supports, spilling the blocks. Both lost their grip on the cords but almost instantly regained stability by instinctively reaching for it at the 'D' ring. The dead man's arm bones, shattered and stripped of meat, slammed against the wall. Similarly, the feet were blown off, ripping almost intact through the plastipanel wall and into the crowd on the other side. The chest shredded as it imploded from the force surrounding it. The shattered head and some of the neck rocketed upward.

The bloody comet lost speed just as it reached Lloyd. Shocked, he gasped and struggled. He witnessed it temporarily lodge on a nearby bolt extending outward from a beam; then fall to the ground. Harrigan and Freund recovered their senses in seconds, waited a full minute to be sure no late-fuse caps remained and then tossed away the C-4 they carried. They managed to help Lloyd right himself. All three were shaking uncontrollably from both fright and muscle fatigue when they finally reached the top and clambered onto the platform. After lying still and panting momentarily, they exited the room to walk, weak-kneed and bloodied, to join the others below.

"Who were those murdering bastards," Harrigan asked Freund as they stepped down the curved display hall, "and what were they trying to accomplish with this attack?"

"Who knows. And what does it matter, anyway? It's always been like this. Look at those depictions of holy wars through history. If 'religious' warriors, the IRA, Jihad and the rest, genuinely subscribed to their beliefs, they'd bury the hatchet and work for peace. God sends iterations of prophets, like John the Baptist and others. Humans persist with arrogant answers. God keeps trying— but there *is* a final call and I'd bet the human race is approaching that point."

Harrigan dismissed the thought. The pair could hear cries and moans more loudly now. As they reached the huddled group below, they saw Gertrude tending to an ugly bullet wound which had destroyed Mon's ear. A blow torch was flaring inward from its user outside. He was half-way through cutting a three foot by two foot opening in the outside wall.

Within twenty minutes, everyone was out. There were nineteen bodies for the morgue. Three were religious terrorists. Eight were murdered by the devout deceased. The remainder were trampled by the stampeding crowd or crushed against the unyielding entrance door.

Most did not realize, until the next day's news, how much danger they had faced or who had saved their lives. Henceforth, Tykvah would not stomp Harrigan's foot. In fact, she developed an entirely revised attitude toward her boss. Harrigan assumed that Mon felt indebted to the hero-scientist for his life; that he was now Mon's confidant. Mon would soon reinforce this belief by offering Harrigan a reward: Protected and apparently unrestricted research facilities, soon to be constructed, so Harrigan could continue the work he had put on hold years before.

Chapter Eight

. . . FOR NOTHING IS COVERED UP THAT WILL NOT BE UNCOVERED . . .   — MATT 10.26

The foulest of the carrion are those who come clothed in the cloak of humility.
— A. Hitler, Dinner Speech, 11 August, 1942

AND AMONG HIS SIGNS IS THE RESURRECTION OF THE EARTH. YOU SEE IT DRY AND BARREN; BUT WHEN WE SEND DOWN THE RAIN UPON IT, IT STIRS AND SWELLS. HE THAT GIVES IT LIFE WILL RAISE THE DEAD TO LIFE.   —KORAN, 41:39

Al-Rajda Village, Northern Iraq
0934 hours, 12 September, 2008

Major Hassan eyed his commander from his seat in the roomy ten-passenger jet. He admired the work done on Mon's ear and scalp. The segments had been regenerated in Harrigan's lab from Mon's own cartilage and flesh but attached by Mon's personal physician. Mon had chosen to wear his crisp, forest green, medal-laden lieutenant colonel's uniform for the trip north. It was uncharacteristic of Hassan's mentor and political party leader to sit idle peering through a window. Hassan was curious now but had always wanted to know Mon's mind.

Perhaps, Hassan reasoned, *Mon is surveying the somewhat enhanced greenery of his realm. No, that couldn't be. Iraq hasn't been much of a beneficiary of the Atlas project; the area is still sparse. Ah! Yes. He is angered by this very lack of improvement when the computer models had projected great benefits here at home.* Hassan was avoiding the obvious. Mon made him nervous by his ominous reticence. Yes, indeed, Hassan wanted to be able to read his mentor.

113

The research site still had not been cleared of Kurds. The project was three months behind schedule. He dared not engage his master in idle or probing conversation. Hassan watched as sparse desert turned to dry grassland, then became greener as the plane approached the plateau and the rugged green-gray mountains which surrounded it.

As they passed a bend in a tributary of the river Tigris, the tiny village came into view near the cliff base of a high plateau. Up on the plateau, mountain ridges formed a northward-pointing angle bracketing sparse grasslands and a small river. Since the ridges opened and ended at the plateau's southern cliff line, they framed a nearly triangular area with the southern cliffs forming a curved base. The modest river on the plateau cascaded into a beautiful waterfall that provided water to the village.

It seemed to Hassan that the ridges were jaws closing on the settlement. Most of the military vehicles were parked in a deep ditch along the dirt road approaching the village to make room for the construction equipment convoy. Huge tan bulldozers, power shovels, cement mixers and flat-bed trailers stacked with heavy construction material formed a line pointing toward the gray brick homes. Four large, dark blue school buses were parked at the head of the construction convoy and turned around, facing out of the village. Armored personnel carriers and trucks surrounded the area.

A few stragglers were being shoved into the crowd of two hundred or so Kurds. Most of them bore heavy sacks on their stooped backs and waited in uneven ranks for the order to load the buses. Guards stood bored in two lines, leaning on their weapons or lazily hanging them muzzle-down from their shoulders. Soldiers bracketed the Kurds left and right while armored vehicles formed the ends of the troop lines to guard the front and rear of the ragged ranks of villagers. The jet had already slowed to a crawl a hundred feet above the grassy plain as its wing tips rotated its quiet engines so that the exhaust would support the aircraft's vertical descent.

Upon landing, Mon descended the staircase to stand facing the battalion commander assigned to clear and secure the area. Mon returned Lieutenant Colonel Vaj's salute. Mon enjoyed being saluted by peers-in-rank. He even demanded it of superior officers by his station as party chief responsible for the election of the current president of Iraq. Vaj began to rattle off excuses as to why the relocation was late but about to get under way.

Mon passed and ignored the babbling site commander, proceeding beyond an old but refurbished BMP armored troop carrier crowned by a small gun turret and its unhelmeted operator. He stopped to face the executive officer, Major Najik, standing at the edge of the rut which hid the bottom half of the BMP. The officers were fifty feet from the vagabond-looking ranks of wailing babies and other unhappy, captive members of humanity. Najik and his officers snapped to attention as Mon approached. Vaj rushed ahead to stand beside his executive officer and again greeted and reported to Mon.

Mon finally addressed Vaj. His words betrayed sarcasm but his tone was flat and quiet. "Have you been standing here looking at each other for three months?!"

"No, sir. Only today have we had the support necessary to force these filthy, stubborn—"

"Shoot them."

Those near the front of the crowd heard Mon's soft-spoken command and gasped, eyeing the officers and buses in disbelief.

"Sir, we will have them out in mere moments. The buses are—"

"Give me your sidearm and you will observe the correct method of control."

The commander hesitated, mentally debating whether there might be a way to keep his leader from making an example of some unfortunate in the barely cooperative crowd of Kurds. He had no time to think. Vaj took out his pistol and handed it to Mon.

"Minister; Colonel: If you will allow us but a mo-"

Mon turned to Najik and placed the pistol in his hand. "You are now the commander of this battalion. Shoot Lieutenant Colonel Vaj and execute the order I gave him."

Vaj did not actually believe Najik would do this, kill him with his own weapon. His mind raced to find a solution to the deadly dilemma. *Yes*, he thought, *take my pistol back and immediately kill one of the Kurds. One of the old ones.*

The crowd began to back up nervously. An old man near the front shook his fist and swore at the officers, not considering that he was neither understood nor given notice. A young mother at the front focused her quivering blue eyes on Najik in horror. Her baby

Dan Gallagher

boy was quiet now, half asleep. He rarely cried loudly, for his mother had tended him dotingly and continuously since his birth a week before. She clutched the peaceful, suckling newborn tighter to her breast within the covering blanket. This did not stir the infant, since his mother's warmth and tight embrace imbued security and a sense of well-being to the child.

Najik was stunned. Then, he realized that opportunity had knocked. In a spit-second, he raised the pistol to the center of Vaj's forehead and fired. Vaj sensed the nine millimeter round, which bore but a small hole in his forehead yet blew out the entire rear of his skull, as bursting shock within almost immediate darkness. Vaj's body hung for a few second's along the edge of the field table, then collapsed face-down beside it on the grass.

Najik pointed the pistol at the left side of the Kurd ranks and traced an arc across them as he ordered the BMP's gun turret operator to fire. The Kurds abandoned ranks and cringed into a tight crowd. The operator of the turret gun did not understand that he was to fire in an arc, left to right. So he fired into the center and then sprayed in a zigzag pattern, careful to avoid shooting his stunned comrades. His rapid-fire, three-quarter inch wide rounds were designed to pierce light armor.

The blanket covering the mother and her nursing baby received the first round. The deadly projectile split the skin of the infant's head, then the tender skull between as yet unjoined bone. What seemed like an explosion to the soldiers actually sent such powerful shock ripples through the tiny brain as the bullet progressed, that the head seemed to burst from within. The sleepy infant perceived a quick flash of light and became more at peace than it had ever been. Ripping through the breast, rib, heart and spine, the mother's torso ruptured outward and splashed back toward the men behind her. The round moved much faster than her flesh, pierced seventeen in the packed crowd, seventy feet of air, a mud-brick exterior wall and finally embedded deeply into an opposing wall. It's path and effect were essentially paralleled by hundreds more rounds which followed in the spray. Despite the carnage, not every Kurd was dead and Najik ordered his lines of soldiers to use their rifles to quiet the moaning, screaming remainder.

Displaying efficiency and initiative, Najik greatly impressed Mon by immediately issuing orders. He ordered the power shovel to dig

116

a mass grave, the dozers to push the Kurds into the hole, and his men to burn the contents. Gasoline fumes, burning flesh and ash permeated air, lungs, equipment, buildings and uniforms. Searing reflections of the flames glinted off each officer's eyes. Mon noticed that only he, Hassan, Najik and half of the soldiers appeared tolerant of this change in their environment.

Mon spoke again to Najik. "You will watch your 'weaker' men carefully after this. You will assure complete security."

"Of course, sir."

"Your unit, *all* these men, will remain here throughout the building phase and will become the security garrison."

"Yes sir."

Mon's voice skewered both of his officers' attention. "This project is of paramount importance to me. Therefore, it is of paramount importance to you. I will remember you two as I rise to my rightful place as president and, ultimately, even greater leadership."

Najik and Hassan thanked their teacher. Mon turned and led Hassan back to the aircraft, tasting the ash on the stair rail with his finger. Hassan was astounded, amazed at his mentor's grace and confidence. He wanted Mon's vision. He had long sought insight into the mind of his mentor. He wanted for himself, whatever mysterious mettle enabled Mon to be so resolute, so successful, so impervious to adversity and opposition. Yet no man or woman could ever penetrate Mon's mind. None. Were any ever to gain even the first insight, they would be unable to conceive or endure the unspeakable immensity of its seething and insidious malice.

Mon addressed Hassan inside the plane. "Your people are still ignorant. So I must personally convince that fool, Harrigan, to head the project. Are your scientists ready to learn from him and accomplish my assignments?"

"Y-yes sir. They are."

* * *

Gertrude, nude except for a towel across her protruding belly, screamed so loudly that she startled even her husband. He was the physician assisting her labor at the gleaming new maternity center in the top floor of the Megiddo Hospital. The only assistance she had wanted was almost constant massaging of her pained lower back. This massaging effort became, eventually, painful for Mannie. Gertrude was propped, almost sitting, on a mechanical bed formed into a large chair. The baby still sensed the warmth and security of Gertrude's rhythmic heartbeat but he became very much ill at ease as her heart beat raced faster. He began to sense being squeezed. With the constriction of his head in the birth canal, temporary loss of consciousness was induced and he felt no panic or pain.

Freund encouraged Gertrude in German. "The head is out now, my Love! A few more breaths. Now, push!"

"Hhuh. Hhhuh. Fff. Fff. Ahhaaww! Ohhw! Hhnnn . . ."

The wax and clear fluid-covered baby boy was out in the world. The nurse wondered, for the several hundredth time, why suffering was so much a prerequisite to reward. She put vacuum tubes momentarily up the infant's nose as Freund beamed from ear to ear and placed his fussing new son gently upon the towel below his wife's breasts. Freund clamped and cut the cord. The very competent nurse was soon working to remove the placenta—thus resuming Gertrude's pain. Baby Otto had already regained consciousness to sense unfamiliar fright; what he perceived as loss. His ninety-eight point six degree, securely-pressurized environment had been so quickly exchanged for one which was seventy-nine and open. The comfort of lying upon his warm mother and instinctively sucking sweet colostrum finally calmed him.

"You take it from here. I'm exhausted!" Freund smirked at Gertrude and waited to be rebuffed.

"You can be such a jerk, Manfred, but I love you. Just look at him! Such a beautiful little *person!*"

I'll never fully understand, Freund mused despite his profession, *women's need to coo and say stupid things about how beautiful these sinewy, wrinkly little kinder are!* Neither did he really fathom how it was that a mother could bond so tenderly to a baby while the father needed weeks, even months of contact to do so. But that was life and life thrilled him, though he refused to jump up and kick his heels while anyone was watching. He began to gently clean slimy, young Otto, his fourth child, when he got his hand lightly slapped. The infant resumed crying as loud as he could, yet it was still a very minute voice.

"We'll do that soon enough! Let him be to nurse, will you?" She paused, quelling the tiny cry with a nipple. Then, her face turned slightly rueful as she thought of her mother. "It's sad *Mutti* could not have lived just one more month—and your parents to have lived longer. So sad."

"No reason why *we* should be melancholy. *They* aren't. It just depends on how you view life. Everybody sees death as horrible because we fear suffering and the unknown. But it's a necessary passage, even if painful."

"Oh, please, Manfred. Stop. It's still sad."

Freund held Gertrude again, got her to smile and cleaned himself up. He turned on the video camera on top of the phone screen, considerately pointing it away from Gertrude.

He called his brother in Stuttgart, a few other family members, and began to call friends.

"Megiddo Species Preserve. May I help you—oh. Hi, Dr. Freund!" The Preserve's switchboard operator smiled. She knew Dr. Freund by sight and voice.

"Hello Susan! May I speak with Dr. Harrigan, *pleass?*"

Susan did not immediately grant the request. "Boy or girl? And how's Frau Freund?"

"It's a boy. We named him Otto. And thanks. They're both doing just *grreat.*"

"We knew it was getting close! Best to Gertrude and Otto! I'll transfer you now, Dr. Freund."

Freund waited to be connected to the preserve's genetic engineering lab.

*   *   *

As Gertrude had been writhing in pain, Harrigan and Tykvah's blood pressures had also been rising. They were barely paying attention to the computer screen—and less to their coworkers. Tykvah sat before the screen nuzzling her head under Harrigan's chin. Harrigan's arms embraced her shoulders as he stood leaning forward from behind her, resting his hands lightly upon hers. Tykvah had already fallen in love with him but Harrigan denied his own developing feelings.

They stared at the computer analysis of differences between the DNA of two *Panthera leo spelaea*. One had been created using both

119

modern and archaic genes while the other was completely archaic. The analysis was another attempt to determine whether the building criticism of Harrigan's FGR was justified. A plethora of adverse articles blasted his and his team's work as creating only hybrids—new species—rather than regenerating the extinct ones. The *Smilodon* and *Elasmotherium* recreations were particularly lambasted. The criticism, Harrigan knew, might be at least somewhat valid. This was because Lloyd's team had only once found *both* egg and sperm of any one species, the cave lion. In its current state of refinement, FGR otherwise required use of modern egg or sperm for half of the required chromosomes. The issue continued to plague Harrigan. It humiliated him publicly and detracted greatly from the prestige of his preserve. The Preserve, to him, was to be his vindication to the academic community which had jealously spurned him years before and never really let up.

Tykvah's voice was always soft and feminine but she spoke particularly alluringly as she pointed to the numbers on the screen and rendered her conclusion. Her New York Jewish accent had diminished after nearly a decade living in Israel yet she still inflected the last words of most statements. "This new statistical program says, Kevin, that it's almost exactly a match. It's a match except for the base pairs shown in failures window B, and those are unique to the sampled fetus anyway—its individual characteristics. The next screen shows that the modern lion is quite distinct from these two. So, I'd say all that criticism of *my* hero, Dr. Kevin Gamaliel Harrigan is bunk!"

"I told you I can't stand my middle name, Tykvah! Gees! We're not paying attention and doing this right, Babe. It's Friday. Let's just take the day off and . . ." Harrigan put his lips to Tykvah's ear and whispered, causing her to giggle merrily.

"I'm game," she said. Music to Harrigan's ears.

The video phone beside the computer rang and its own small screen flashed from black to showing Freund's smiling face. Harrigan turned on the small camera on top of the screen.

Freund's accent was again imperceptible. "Hey, Big Guy! Hello, Tykvah! It's a boy! When are you and Tykvah gonna tie the knot and have one?"

Freund knew that would pester Harrigan but such digs were, to Freund, great fun. He had been proved wrong when, soon after the monument incident, Tykvah and Harrigan had hit it off just as Harrigan had predicted. He would not let Harrigan forget the rest of the prediction: "I'm going to marry her."

Harrigan stewed; even more so when he noticed Tykvah blushing and looking at him expectantly with a toothy grin.

Harrigan spoke his mind with joviality. "Yeah! Like I need to get married and tied down!" He paused and returned to the main subject as Tykvah tried to look as if she was not disappointed in that statement. "So! Great news! Congrats!"

Tykvah broke in, inflecting and elongating the names. "And how's *Gertruuude* and . . . I guess it would be *Ottooo?*"

"They're both doing fine. Can't put 'em on screen just yet. It was a rough labor. I've got cramps in my arms!"

Harrigan took his turn. "Better not let Gertrude hear that stuff!"

Gertrude called from across the room: "Your arms are not *de* only appendages *dat* will be hurting you, *eef* I get my hands on you!" Freund laughed sheepishly.

Tykvah reinforced the admonishment. "Guess *you've* been told."

"When can we visit?" Harrigan inquired.

Freund was conservative but considerate of Gertrude. "Supper time, I would think—" He glanced over toward Gertrude and received a nod. "Yes. Five or six, if you like."

Harrigan sealed the agreement. "Great. We'll see you then." Freund smiled and the image went black.

Tykvah reached up and grabbed Harrigan by the ears, pulling him to her for a serious, deep kiss. "Isn't that exciting, Kevin?! A little baby. They've got a *house* full!"

"I don't know how they all fit in that little house, now that you mention it! I think he must give all his pay away or something! Well, let's take off. Want to swim at my place?"

"No. Why don't we just go for a walk around *here*. Have you even seen your own petting zoo?"

Harrigan looked disappointed. "Petting zoo?! That's not the kind of petting I had in mind." Tykvah pouted at him and it worked. "All right. Okay. We'll go to the petting zoo."

Harrigan sighed and wondered to himself, *Why are women, especially gorgeous ones, such outrageous teases?!* Yet, he knew he was addicted to this one; to her long brown hair, her mesmerizing eyes, her challenging intellect and her caring passion for him. She could always make him laugh and forget himself. Her engaging conversation was so natural; so soothing and familiar now to him. *All right*, Harrigan admitted to himself, *I love her.*

"I love you, Tykvah. Do you know that?"

"I knew! But it took you long enough to say it!"

They shed their jackets and silently crossed the tourist-packed quadrangle, walking hand in hand toward the sun-drenched petting zoo. Scattered white clouds against inspiring sun beams and the vivid blue sky caught them both. Tykvah smiled and kissed him as they approached the pens filled with baby animals and laughing, scampering children. He knew exactly why she was leading him there but, for now, he would let her lead.

"Kevin, look at those *silly kids!*"

A group of young girl scouts was screaming and hopping as they chased a soft, furry pygmy mammoth. It had tiny, blunt tusks and was about two feet tall. The animal squealed and jumped with them like a frisky dog used to playing gently with children. The girls could not resist flopping its ears. The sign on the pen clearly read "Do Not Pull Animal's Hair, Tail, Trunk or Ears." The attendant pointed at it and yelled at the mischievous girls, who flopped its soft ears again when he was not looking. Tykvah laughed and motioned for Harrigan to watch their antics.

Nearby, a little boy in a red striped shirt and too-big, rolled-up jeans sat in another pen hugging and feeding a bottle to the baby *Smilodon*. Its downy fur was shedding on the boy's clothes. It already had the famous canines showing but, like the rest, had been engineered to grow only slightly larger and, hence, not mature to become aggressive.

They drifted to the marsupial section. Despite the fact that there was no regenerated predecessor in the main preserve, a baby koala clung to a motherly three year old girl. The girl was trying unsuccessfully to get it to drink from her doll's 'pretend' bottle of milk. The attendant eyed this carefully for possible inadvertent abuse as the enraptured parents took pictures from every angle. A five-year old boy was trying to ride the baby ground sloth, whose claws had been clipped. Suddenly caught by the stern attendant, the boy adopted a puzzled, sheepish expression which almost made him appear innocent.

Harrigan could not help but become caught up in the charm of it all and even directed Tykvah's attention to a young couple kissing on a bench near the exit. Tykvah's response was predictable. They embraced and gazed into each others' eyes. Slowly, they stepped apart, still holding hands, and strolled toward the preserve's main gate. They walked left out of the exit and continued several blocks past the greenery which had been planted along the preserve's property limits.

"I came here to get the Preserve going when I was twenty-seven. Tykvah, this place was just an archaeological dig and a few poor farmhouses then. Look at it now! In only six years, it's become a beautiful town of fifteen or sixteen thousand. Things are always changing."

"And you? Have you changed? Will you change more in the years to come?"

"Me? I don't change. Same old, same old! Still work out daily. Still like my hair short. Still wear the same thirty-two inch military belt I had in college. I've noticed a few gray hairs, though!"

The relative cool of the late summer morning tempted them to brave the theme park's exhausting safari adventures and thrill rides. Talking and laughing intermittently, they entered the park, showed their passes and proceeded directly to the "Time-Safari" area.

The giant structure reverberated with recorded bird calls and scary growls. The ceiling was painted and illuminated to look like the sky but actually was composed of computer-controlled tracks. These tracks could move riders in special harnesses across the make-believe earth of a hundred thousand years before. The floors sensed impact, absorbed it and sprang back at twice the force so that one could jump very high to avoid the fairly realistic robot animals and pre-humans of the Pleistocene. One could counter the bouncing by buckling the knees, thus reducing the thrust-off reaction of the sensitive, computer-manipulated flooring.

They donned the padded harnesses. These enabled them, along with the hand-held controls, to rise even higher, hover and glide over and through the make-believe world. This expertly recreated environment was composed of forests, swamps, jungles, glaciers and other creature-filled 'dangerous' terrains of the massive fun house. Of the many diversions at the theme park, Harrigan and

Tykvah enjoyed this ride best. He laughed and made airplane and condor noises like some kid. But he realized that it was Tykvah, not the ride per se, who could bring out the giddy kid in him. Their turn was eventually over and they and the other 'time-travelers' had to yield their harnesses to the next people in line.

Harrigan and Tykvah continued on. The lines were not too long since the school year had resumed and families were not vacationing. They rode roller coasters through fake but intimidating volcanoes. Tykvah marveled in the shops at the realistic toy animals, some collections of which even interacted. Eventually, they noticed that they had missed lunch and it was nearly four o'clock.

They entered the more modern Holocene History Restaurant, whose theme was the natural and man-made history of the last ten thousand years. Dinner was excellent: tender Australian emu steak stuffed with cheese and crab. Harrigan paid the bill and they left to visit the Freunds. Harrigan picked up flowers and a card on the way. Tykvah waited in vain all day for the marriage proposal but did not press the issue. They parked at the hospital and went up to Gertrude's room.

The Freund's other children, Eva, Hans and Marian, along with a neighbor, were there. The visit was brief since the small room was getting too confused from adults talking and children running around. Tykvah was enraptured by the baby. Both Freund and Gertrude winked at her, knowing how Harrigan had earlier discussed his feelings with them.

Freund, as he often did, philosophized to Harrigan despite the latter's rolling eyes. "It's a big parlor party thing to wonder about the meaning of life. But, ya know, Kevin," Freund directed his hand toward his wife and children. *"This* is the meaning of life."

Harrigan grimaced slightly and wondered momentarily if Freund might be on to something or just irritatingly parochial. Tykvah stared in wonder at Freund's insight.

Tykvah observed Shabbat each Friday with her father in preparation for the Sabbath. It disturbed her that the man she loved was, from all appearances, atheist. She knew she could work on that problem. Now she weighed today's momentum with Harrigan against her conscience, called her father on the way out of the hospital and canceled.

Harrigan and Tykvah returned to his house, a truly stately mansion in the midst of Megiddo. The security gate, erected after the monument bombing attempt, was controlled from his car. They parked below the gray brick structure and took the oak-paneled elevator up to the foyer. They silently crossed the green marble floor and walked into the adjoining cherry-paneled study. Harrigan motioned for Tykvah to sit on the plush burgundy leather couch opposite the black and white marble fireplace.

Harrigan's voice seemed deeper than usual. "Fireplace on three."

The fire glowed softly as Harrigan selected a spicy Australian Shiraz from the cabinet and returned to the couch with two sparkling glasses.

"Tykvah."

"Yes, Kevin?" Her voice was worried. She sensed that a let-down was coming.

"This is . . . well, I feel as if . . . I mean, you and I come from totally different backgrounds . . ."

Tykvah felt this was definitely it: *The big 'This can't work for us' line*, she thought.

Harrigan continued. ". . . but I have this sense that you need to be; you *ought* to be . . . cherished by *someone*. I love you and I feel I've . . . like I've needed you all my life. *But mine* has always been a life alone, despite appearances."

Tykvah lowered her head and began to weep silently. Harrigan got up and immediately sat down again.

"Tykvah!" Harrigan called to her loudly, surprising her. "Will you marry me?"

Tykvah was bleary eyed. She forced herself to breathe. The breath was more like a sigh of relief from fear that she would remain lonelier than Harrigan well past her advancing thirty-two years.

"Yes." She whispered, finding no other words. "Yes." She repeated herself slightly louder. Harrigan's smile and kiss released tears for both of them; then laughter. He breathed deeply, wiped her eyes gently with his thumbs, picked her up in his arms and carried her into the foyer. To Harrigan, the elevator to the second floor seemed inappropriate to use now. He carried her up the stairs. The night was like magic, gentle; then torrid, passionate. The weekend seemed like a lifetime of joy and communion. Harrigan and Tykvah had created meaning.

Dan Gallagher

* * *

Harrigan spent a good part of Monday morning grinning, some-times staring, at objects on his desk at the Preserve. He was alter-nately fearful and excited by his question and Tykvah's answer. Tykvah tried to focus on work but kept giggling and smiling at eve-ryone and misplacing lines of computer code. Every twenty min-utes or so, the two would wink and whisper, unsure when to tell the staff.

Just before lunch Mon appeared at Harrigan's office door unan-nounced.

Harrigan looked up. "This is a surprise, Minister! We don't see much of you these days. What can I do for you?"

"May I close the *doorr*, Kevin?" Mon's accent was now slightly more noticeable due to his time in recent years being predomi-nantly spent in Baghdad.

"Sounds big. I'll get it for you. Please, sit. Coffee?"

"Yes, thank you. Kevin, our intelligence feels *therre* will be an-other attempt on my life . . . and yours as well."

Harrigan shrugged his shoulders. "There's always going to be that kind of thing. Security's been totally revamped here. I think we're okay and you have even tighter security than we do."

"Kevin, *therre's* more."

"Sorry. Please go on."

"Your work is too important to risk vulnerability to terrorists, Kevin. You're still refining the FGR *prroh-cess*. You need a labora-tory where these jealous academics cannot intrude to ridicule. To the extent that your people have been largely unable to find both egg and sperm of a given species, the criticism is right. But both can be found with adequate supplemental support *forr* Lloyd. You need a bigger, more able staff. You need a true preserve where the animals can interact. And, above all, Kevin, you need prehuman DNA to continue the work you left behind six years ago! Only *then* will you be able to further refine FGR and show those self-righteous *bah-stards* what you really *can* achieve. Like the genetic improve-ment of mankind itself."

Mon waited for his words to be considered and resumed speak-ing. "My people have found more fossil egg and sperm to mate with some of the samples you have redeemed here. And, Kevin: We have

126

also found both egg and sperm of two *Neanderr-tal* females and a male. Thirty-five thousand years old; among the last of their breed. You have a chance to study man's genetic development in the natural environment of one of the warmer interglacial periods. We have *prrofessional* researchers waiting for the privilege to make history as surrogate parents—under your direction. The facility is completely secure north of Baghdad. It will be ready in eight months. Our people want to do it all themselves without you but I insisted on giving you a shot at the *prrogram*. All of this, Kevin, I will give *you*. What do you say?"

Harrigan did not know what to say. His heart started to race with excitement and worry simultaneously. *Fantastic*, he mused, *like a dream come true*. Yet something bothered him. He generally trusted Mon but was keenly aware that, not so long ago, America and its allies had had to destroy biological, chemical and nuclear facilities in Iraq. But that was under a completely different regime. Those in charge seemed to be proving that they were of genuinely peaceful intent. *Got to talk to the feds on this one*, he reasoned. *Could be in over my head, this time. Mon is probably right about the terrorist threat. Two technicians left after the attempted bombing, despite our best efforts to tell them that the only threat is to the monument. Still, the prospect of this type of research is enticing! Very enticing.*

"Minister, I'm really caught at a bad time for thinking right now. I just got engaged. May I consider it for a few days?"

"We only have one day, I believe, Kevin. I have been assigned to staff the *prroject* with Iraqis. National pride and all that. But I have asked permission to put *you* in charge. I was given until tomorrow morning at nine, your time, to obtain at least *your* commitment."

"I understand. I can decide by then."

Mon abruptly rose, shook Harrigan's hand and left. Harrigan's heart raced even more as he considered how to report this; whether it even required reporting. He decided that it did. Harrigan phoned the American Embassy on a public phone at the concessions. The officials knew who he was and verified his voice by computer. He was called back twenty minutes later and instructed to meet an American and an Israeli near the phone at three thirty.

Harrigan strolled around the preserve alone, stewing over his impression that the foreign service officer must have already had him under surveillance. He returned at the appointed time. There they were. They sat and discussed his work in more detail than Harrigan wanted but he felt it was necessary. The Israeli said practically nothing the entire time. Harrigan thought that these guys already knew more than they let on, but spooks were supposed to act like that.

"You did the right thing, Dr. Harrigan. We've been instructed to ask you to accept the offer and continue the project as you've described it. After all, we have no reason to suspect that your work could or would be misused for military purposes. We have no way to monitor Iraq since sanctions were lifted and the new government took power. So, in a few days, you'll need to interview and hire a man we'll send you. He'll be your only contact after that. His name is *New-nez*. I mean, *Nuhn-yez*. Dr. José Nuñez. He's a computer scientist and he's good with models. He'll be a genuine help to you in your research anyway. If we conclude there's no threat— and that may take quite a long time—we'll just withdraw our man and you'll hear nothing further from us. You should proceed with a *genuine* assumption that there is no threat. Nevertheless you and Nuñez must be the only ones on your team who are aware that the project is being monitored. Try to maximize your people staffing the Iraq facility. The fewer Iraqis the better. Any questions?"

"No. No, I don't think so."

The men got up and left via conveyor through the tube. Harrigan knew that he would have no trouble selling most of his staff on the idea. He walked around the Preserve wondering about Freund and worrying about Tykvah. *Both of them are religious types and they'll go through the roof if I ask them to participate in experiments involving prehumans. But I've got to try. Not sure what I'll do if Tykvah refuses.*

Tykvah! Harrigan suddenly realized he had just disappeared for much of the day and said nothing to her. He quickly returned to the lab, thinking about her and considering how he would recruit Freund, on whom he would more heavily depend to assist him in exploring prehuman development. He felt he needed Freund for more important reasons. He was again gripped by struggle within himself: *This work must be done. This frontier must be explored. And, yet, I will be leading my people and their families . . . into a potentially enemy nation.*

Chapter Nine

I WENT INTO A FOREST OF TREES OF THE PLAIN, AND THEY MADE A PLAN . . . SO THAT [THE SEA] MAY RECEDE BEFORE US AND SO THAT WE MAY MAKE FOR OURSELVES MORE FORESTS.

—2 ESDRAS 4.13-14

Once one said God when one looked upon distant seas; but now I have taught you to say: overman. God is a conjecture; but I desire that your conjectures should not reach beyond your creative will.

—F. Nietzsche, *Thus Spake Zarathustra*: Second Part

MICAH THEN SAID TO HIM, "DWELL WITH ME AND BE A FATHER AND A PRIEST TO ME, AND I WILL GIVE YOU TEN PIECES OF SILVER A YEAR, A SUIT OF CLOTHES, AND YOUR MAINTENANCE." SO THE LEVITE WENT IN.

—JUDG 17.10

Main Conference Room, Megiddo Species Preserve

1134 hours, 22 September, 2008

The conference room was only slightly dimmed for the visual presentation which Hassan was to make after Harrigan's well-received description of the Iraqi preserve project. English was always spoken in work settings at the Species Preserve. The room was filled with every technician and scientist affiliated with the facility. Even Lloyd's team had been recalled from its searches in the cold north of European Russia.

Harrigan continued his portion of the presentation. He anticipated objections and provided reassurances. "So, for those of you who worry that the hominids we will create and study might be maltreated, let me summarize the plans. Despite romantic presentations of Neanderthals you all saw in books and movies when you were growing up, these animals are not entirely human. We will, however, treat them with greater care than the other species to be released into the Preserve.

"We intend to accelerate their growth and maturation so that adulthood is reached within seven years. *But* this applies only to their pre-adult years since the gene coding will cause the maturation rate to be three times normal during gestation; slowing to a halt at adulthood. That way, they will not entirely miss growing up and will not lose years of life in adulthood. Remember, these sapiens once died young due to unpredictable food sources and worse winters than they will experience here. They'll live quite satisfactory lives, comparatively speaking. If you still have heartburn with this, just think back to when you were a child impatient to grow up."

All seemed to relate to this youthful desire. So Harrigan tried to head-off any more objections before they could arise. However, Freund was still unconvinced; bordering on horrified, in fact: "What about medical care for them, especially in event of injury from the animals?"

"There will be extra protection during initial formation of the tribes. After that, Mannie, there *is* likely to be physical danger—but they will have been taught to fear and respect the various taxa introduced there. You cannot tell me there is no danger in our own modern world: only danger of a different kind than was present during the Pleistocene. We have considered the need for safety and training.

"We will utilize surrogate parents, just as the animals will have. This is to help develop basic behaviors like hunting. Human surrogates are being selected based on stocky build, scientific credentials—such as psychology, medicine, anthropology—and other criteria. They'll receive hormones for more body hair and cosmetic treatments to look like Neanderthals. They will conduct all on-site observations and raise cohesive clans in semi-protected ridge areas of the new preserve.

"The young prehumans will be taught a basic vocabulary of Nostratic, which is our best reconstruction of the root language of all Indo-European tongues. The sapiens will also learn to make basic tools and hunt under controlled conditions. So, when they are finally left to themselves, they will have all the basic cooperation and other skills necessary for survival in their environment. It replicates conditions which existed between a hundred thousand and thirty thousand years ago.

"Wide strips of forest, which our next speaker will show you shortly, are now being planted with the help of supplemental underground irrigation. They will be quite dense, discouraging predators from reaching the sapien and yeti ridge areas. Anyway, the herds should stay near the river and sparsely forested plateau while predators will keep near them. A robotic heavy-lift suit, disguised as a large cave bear and rigged with tranquilizer darts, will be available for maintenance people to use in removing predators from the ridge areas when necessary.

"Caves will be provided for Neanderthals, yetis and possibly other sapiens. These clan homes will be equipped with hidden surveillance gear and anesthetizing gas outlets in the ceilings. They will even have warm water springs. Any serious medical problem will be observed and treated by disguised removal of the prehuman. They will never know what we are or anything about our culture. Once a community is established in five or six years, we'll turn off the sound walls, another barrier to predators, and permit more interaction between fauna and prehumans. Don't be alarmed: These sound devices are not like the famous Israeli weapons! Periodically, some of the sapiens will be drugged and removed for study and then replaced back into their tribe. So this preserve is humanely designed, I assure you."

Olivier was still concerned. "What of *'omo sapiens sapiens*, Dr. Harrigan, *s'il vous plait?*"

Harrigan knew that was not yet a problem but addressed it head-on nevertheless. "Of course, we have no Cro-Magnon specimens now. But Dr. Lloyd's team and an Iraqi team will—I believe—have success soon. So that's a good question, Claude. Let's keep in mind that, despite continued debate, Cro-Magnon is not exactly human—hence, regeneration and study of that species cannot be said to be some 'barbaric' act. The preserve is massive and, when the sapiens mature, they will be permitted to roam within its boundaries. We think they will not roam, however, if we keep adequate food sources near the ridges. We will do the same with the Cro-Magnon as with the Neanderthal, although we will separate the two subspecies to avoid any possible conflict. The yetis, by the way, are naturally reclusive so we see no problem including them in the preserve for study."

Cabral understood culture shock and had seen the destructive effect on isolated Amazon communities when moderns were in close contact with them. "How will we keep from—eh, avoid—ruin of their way of life or invalidating our study of their behavior due to contact with us and our technologies?"

Harrigan was getting uncomfortable but was unwavering in his response. "We don't want prehumans to have conscious contact with any aspect of our world, Paulo. Therefore, all field contact will be disguised or done while the subjects are sedated. Drugs will be used to inhibit memory in event our safeguards fail."

Tykvah was hostile toward the project, despite her intimate involvement with Harrigan. "What about our lives and duties here?"

Harrigan was irritated and sweating but still confident. "The Committee will hire replacements for us here. We will have to keep flying back to get them up to speed and obtain certain specimens but eventually we will work only in Al-Rajda. It's actually quite nice; almost as lush as Megiddo and cool enough—due to its location and elevation, to dispense with the cooling plumes.

"There will, of course, be liberal furloughs accommodated at employee expense. I'm certain none of you will have a problem with expenses, given the compensation packages described earlier! Travel back to this 'zoo' for research purposes or to work with your replacements will be at the expense of the Al-Rajda Research Preserve. You are all free to publish findings but only per the contract rules. By the way, the FGR process software and some of the equipment will move to Al-Rajda. This is because I own the rights until they revert, under the contract, to the Iraqi government ten years from now. So, Megiddo will lose most of its capability as a genetics research facility."

Fong looked nervous and raised his concern. "What if something of military value is discovered, Kevin? Are there safeguards?"

Harrigan hesitated a moment, careful not to appear excessively arrogant or to argue. "An important question, Jim. This project, though closed to the public, will not be used in any way for military purposes. Iraq has many times proved itself worthy to rejoin the world family of nations! And you all know that I would never permit that kind of thing, anyway."

Tykvah was glaring at Harrigan. He returned the look but she did not shrink from his stare. Harrigan turned on the projector again and began to waive his pointer. "I want to conclude my portion of this discussion by re-emphasizing our primary objectives and what this new venture means. The objectives are: a) to create authentic regenerations; self-sustaining and interacting populations of Pleistocene fauna for study; b) to map the genetic evolution of subject species, especially sapiens, and to determine the instinctive versus cultural basis of behavior; c) to discover the basis of positive and negative genetic traits and behaviors through direct observation and evolutionary comparison. We now know from Dr. Lloyd's and many others' recent discoveries, that early humans and near humans ranged all over the world during the mid- to late Pleistocene. So we will attempt to recreate taxa from the six temperate continents. Most trees and plants, though, will have to be deciduous to withstand the winters at Al-Rajda."

He lowered his pointer, turned off the projector and looked directly into the eyes of his staff, one researcher at a time. "My friends, respected colleagues: You have a once-in-a-lifetime chance at a truly historic venture; an ad-venture. You will be making some of the most profound discoveries ever made about life. You will witness life interacting freely as it did at the very dawn of man's emergence. You may even discover ways to advance the human genome and expunge genetic defects from it. And your work will be conducted without superstitious or doom-sayer interference. You are the finest, most competent team ever assembled to engage in such discovery. This is a journey of discovery for which mankind will one day owe you all a permanent debt of gratitude."

Harrigan surveyed the silenced room triumphantly. "So, now, I'll let Major Hassan, who is our liaison with our sponsors in the Iraqi government, describe the preparations and physical layout of the Preserve. Major!"

Hassan, smiling and relaxed in his white cotton blazer, gray cotton pants and solid blue tie, thanked Harrigan for yielding the floor. His accent was heavy and he had difficulty phrasing. An aerial view of the valley at the Al-Rajda site flashed up on the screen. He stepped to the podium.

"Forgive my English, please. I will be brief. The valley area you see here is fifteen miles long from north to south *by* eleven miles east to west. It is mostly flat and grassy in the center—though *brro-ken* up with small hills and stream . . . bottoms? No, *stream beds*—yes! We have already planted fast-growing trees in areas along the Rajdakim River, which is a *not-well forrdable* tributary of the Tigris. The preserve has also been forested in a five hundred foot wide band along the foothills, along edges of the cliff and along each bank of the river. Eventually, this band will be expanded to as much as a half mile along most of its length. Hence, thick forest ringing and . . . *bi-secting* . . . the area provides you concealed access to the entire preserve. This also deters animals from approaching even the minor cliff edge. It *in addition* provides the sapiens some barrier to the large animals even after the sound walls are *per-ma-nently* disabled.

"The river divides the valley roughly in half and is fed by numerous streams from the mountains. It also forms a barrier between the Neanderthal and, *we eventually hope*, Cro-Magnon domains. Valley ridges, as you can see, form a *down-upside* 'V' opening southward until they connect to the southern cliffs of the Valley plateau.

"Notice now what this area will look like in a few months: The ridges are cut to a *very sheerr* face, forming an *impreg-nable* barrier to escape by the animals. The cliffs of the valley plateau have been cut, forming also an impassable barrier. A minor five-foot high cliff will be cut twenty feet deep into the entire length of the plateau edge as an escape stop—deterrent—and so that the larger plateau cliff will not endanger the animals. Similarly, the waterfall will be re-formed to this contour and, how to say: with submerged catches equipped. It empties into a huge net which will not be visible from the plateau above.

"Formed to *rresemble* boulders, there *arre* additional sound generators along the bases of the mountain ridges. For about the first five years, these will keep away predators from the sapien clans. It is not *destrructive* but will make any animal approaching it to turn back. It will be turned off whenever the surrogates permit the tribe to enter the valley to teach them to hunt or trap food. Eventually, the surrogates and the sound walls will be removed altogether.

There are ample caves in both ridges and none of them extend near the exterior of the preserve.

"At intervals of about a mile all around the outside edge of the ridges and plateau edge, we have *cam-ou-flaged* and computer-controlled repelling units. These are permanent sound generators. They automatically repel animals which the system's surveillance finds are on the verge of breaching the *pe-rim-eter*. They also repel intruders to the preserve. We anticipate no such breaches in either direction. Troops patrol outside the plateau with . . . what is called *real bullets?* Yes: *ballistic* rounds. Tranquilizer rounds, by the way, are for use on the plateau and these degrade to dust in a few days so the sapiens will not find one.

"The buildings of the research complex are just west of the river, hidden along the base of the plateau cliffs. These will not look like man-made structures if viewed from above. This is in case any sapiens manage to reach the second cliff edge *forr to* look down. Labs, offices and most rooms in the clinic will with voice-actuated *mi-crro-phones* be equipped. This is so you can use the computer without needing to reach a keyboard. *Only* the work areas are made in this way, so personal privacy is assured!

"There are two one-hundred foot long, thirty foot wide escalators—conveyors, actually—for veterinary and research access by vehicle. They open well-concealed upward into the floor of small clearings near the edge of the forest. One on each side of the falls. Below the plateau, the road along the river will be replaced with a tunnel leading behind the east ridge; then out onto a paved road southward toward Baghdad. Your personal homes will be built to your own *spe-ci-fi-cations* along this highway on the eastern face of the east ridge. The research and support facilities are superior even to those in Megiddo, *which you have here*. This facility will be completely ready by spring but quite functional in only three more months.

"Eventually, my *go-vern-ment* will have to recoup its investment by turning part of the preserve into a park and exporting some of the creatures to zoos. We promise you exclusive scientific use for ten years. You will be able to publish articles concerning the animal research. However, given the commercial potential of this work, we retain the right to control material which would essentially give away the *e-co-no-mic* benefit of our investment. Also, nothing may be published about the sapien research until the contract ends. It will be *fan-tastic-ally* important work but we simply don't want the *contrroverrsy*. Specific terms of the ten-year contracts are in your packages. *There are any questions?"*

The researchers had read the contracts earlier. Restrictive publication clauses in commercial and other contracts were common. None of the scientists had any objections to what they had read, especially given their excitement at becoming genuine scientific pioneers. They had questions about entertainment diversions at Al-Rajda and about the small residential community which was planned for them. Hassan answered these to everyone's satisfaction.

Freund and Tykvah, however, had privately been objecting since Tuesday to the entire concept. Harrigan closed the meeting by telling everyone to take the rest of the day off and the weekend to decide. He knew he would have a tough job with Freund and Tykvah—and this troubled him greatly.

Harrigan was scheduled to interview Nuñez that afternoon and share Shabbat with Tykvah at her father's house. So he accepted Freund's invitation to visit the next morning, Saturday, to discuss the new project. He took lunch and returned to his lab where Dr. José Nuñez stood waiting for him at the entrance to his office.

Both men knew the interview was a formality. Nevertheless Harrigan thoroughly quizzed the amiable Mexican, who was most recently a resident of Toronto, Canada. Harrigan was impressed with this thirty-two year old's grasp of the computer modeling which would be required of him. Harrigan would have to see it for himself but Nuñez asserted that intuition and even logical conjecture could now be teased from some mainframes with proper programming.

"That might come in handy as we try to isolate which gene sequences are involved in particular traits," Harrigan told him when the meeting concluded.

He took Nuñez for the usual new employee orientation. He pointed out along the way how better facilities—and a genuine species preserve with actual regenerations of extinct species—would be provided soon at Al-Rajda. He was uncertain whether Nuñez's interest was primarily because he was on CIA contract or due to the fact that Nuñez was a first-rate scientist.

Regardless, Harrigan concluded to himself, *Nuñez will be ex-*

pected to deliver hard scientific support for his team's research. They finished the tour of the lab and computer archives by five-thirty and departed the Preserve for the evening.

Harrigan met Tykvah at his house. The Brandenburg Concerto, Number Three, was playing on his stereo. Tykvah was already seated on the couch in his study, flipping through a pile of unopened letters.

Harrigan was immediately angered. "Tykvah, what are you doing with those?!"

Her end-of-sentence almost-a-question inflection was becoming more pronounced. "Well, Kevin, you said before that I could *roam free here;* that you had no secrets or *old girlfriend photos!* Anyway I haven't opened them. But why haven't *you?* They're from your *parents.*"

Harrigan tried to force the anger from his voice, succeeding only in making it icy. "I just don't have the relationship with my parents that you have with your father. Look, Tykvah, those things are mine. Put them back, please."

"You don't communicate with your parents, but you *keep their letters.* You must still love them. Couldn't you patch things up and *let me meet them?*"

Harrigan's voice approached anger again. "Tykvah: Put those away; change the subject. You pick and pick. Like when you kept pushing me about my middle name. Some things inside me are not for you—or anyone else, okay?"

Tykvah knew she could get farther than this. "You were going to tell me why your dad gave you 'Gamaliel' for a middle name. At least you *have a middle name!* Mannie hasn't got one and neither do I. But I told you on our first date that Tykvah means 'hope.' My parents had tried for years to have a child and I was their hope, so to speak. Can't you share yourself with me *even that much?!*"

"All right! Look: My mother told me that Dad had gotten on this religious kick after my brother was born. He wanted a name that would remind me I was Catholic—which was stupid, 'cause it's a Hebrew name, anyway. It means 'The Lord is vengeance or recompense.' Mom said *that* would be *my* choice. They wanted me to be nagged about going to church and all that—even when they weren't around. Clearly, it worked since you are nagging me now!"

"There. That didn't hurt so bad, did it? Come here and kiss me!"

Harrigan smiled and gave her a deep kiss. "We've got to get going if you want to be at your father's on time."

"One more moment, hero." She subdued her inflection, lowered her gaze and then looked directly into his eyes. "Kevin: How do you feel about kids?"

Harrigan was tiring of her 'get to know you better' premarital probing. "Tykvah, we've been over this. Kids are okay, I guess."

"You're going to be a father. I checked today with a 'Knownow' pregnancy test kit."

Harrigan held his breath for a moment. A tinge of anger struck him, followed by joy. Then he thought of the Iraq project and whether she would refuse to move with him. He became worried and outraged.

"That's it, isn't it?! You don't want us, *me*, to move to the new project!"

Her tone was surprisingly relaxed, almost sexy. *"We* go where *you* go, Kevin . . . if you want us." She sat silent, staring.

Harrigan knew she was testing him; looking for verification of his commitment to her; now 'them.' *"We* go, then. I love you! I'm sure I'll love *the kid*. What are you going to tell your father?"

"The truth. He'll blow up but what else could we tell him?"

* * *

Later that evening at the Strauss residence near Tel Aviv, Harrigan observed that Tykvah was wrong. Her father did not get angry. He looked shamed and his eyes filled with tears until he had to leave the table.

The aging Orthodox Jew returned soft-spoken, less sad, from the kitchen to address his daughter. His gray beard and temple braids bracketed a kind face. It was obvious where Tykvah had gotten her habit of speech inflection. "Tykvah. *Tykvah*. A generation is lost; but, I pray, *not you with it!* You have shamed yourself, me *and your mother's memory*. And, yet, that slap at God and His Law has served to implement his will. You have made a child. *A child*, Tykvah! Are you ready for *this baby?* And you, Kevin, are you ready to care for it?"

Even as an adult, Tykvah sought her father's approval. She was in tears. "We *are* ready, Father."

"*Speak for yourself*, my daughter. Kevin, have you saved my daughter's life only to *stigmatize it?* Will you be a faithful husband to her and a dedicated father to this child—a *dedicated* father?"

"You can count on me, sir. I will."

"You have no regard for my daughter's faith; *nor for your own.* If you would not become a Jew, you would *still* find your way . . . *if . . .* you would practice the faith of your birth. Will you reconsider *this?"*

"Sir, you demand what you cannot. You are wrong if you feel we are—I am—lost. But rest assured I will love Tykvah and our child. If she wants a Jewish wedding and to raise the child in your faith, I have no objection. You have *my word."*

"Tykvah, you will abandon the faith of *Abraham?"*

"No, Father."

"It is *enough.* You have *my blessing."*

The old man knew Harrigan had not asked for his blessing but raised his glass and smiled. He hugged Tykvah and even Harrigan. His grin was contagious, then his laughter. "Mazeltov, children. *Mazeltov!"* They finished the meal with a new sense of happiness and Harrigan did not even steam at having placated Tykvah's father.

Harrigan and Tykvah stayed the night at her Father's house—in separate rooms. Harrigan could not remember upon waking all of the dream which plagued his slumber that night. He awoke at four in the morning feeling tense, worried.

Harrigan got up and went to the living room, adjusted the rheostat to dim so as not to wake Tykvah or her father. He sat in a plush easy chair, trying to remember; drifting asleep again. The dream embraced him once more, brushing him with cold exhilaration.

"I am . . . creator," he mumbled, "my will . . . supreme."

Suddenly, he jolted awake, oppressed by a panic akin to a child's first roller coaster ride yet different: It was as though he sensed that a parent could save him from the accelerating descent . . . yet as if he had just realized that no parent was with him on the ride. As he woke, Harrigan retained from the dream only accentuated fear and shocked loneliness.

He stood, nervously inventing a reason for these feelings. *My parents. Yes, that's what this is about. Maybe I need to reconsider the rift . . . or something. Yes, that's it.*

Dawn burned away some of the fog obscuring Harrigan's view of the horizon as he stared out the large picture window. The slightly improved view, far from clear, felt tentatively reassuring to him.

Tykvah and her father knew he was driving back to Megiddo for the day. He left them both considerate notes about missing breakfast. Harrigan drove north toward his house. He began putting the remnant emotions from the dream behind him.

On the highway, he even smiled, considering the irony of his Irish Catholic upbringing—and his love for a Jewish woman. He felt almost exhilarated to have established a good relationship with his future father-in-law, for he had anticipated animosity. The more he considered his new life and family, the more he thought of his parents. He began longing to just forgive them and be forgiven. He hoped they would accept Tykvah. Harrigan began to remember and sing the words of a tune which his family used to croon at weddings and reunions: "H—A—double R—I—G—A—N spells Harrigan. . . . Proud of all the Irish blood that's in me. . . . *Divil's* the man can say a word *agin* me." He surprised himself, for he found that he was shedding tears. He happily resolved to drop his rejection of his parents and visit them before he began the new project.

Harrigan pulled into his garage and went up to check a few things in his study before showering and leaving for Freund's home. He started to put away the pile of letters which Tykvah was supposed to have put back on his desk. The hand writing on the latest one, which arrived a month before, he noticed, was that of his brother—but the return address was that of his parents. He opened it. The smile generated by his new resolution in the car fell from his face. Tears began to stream and he knelt on the floor from weakness in his knees. Sobs and one long, trembling moan tore from deep in his chest. An auto accident had claimed them—and he had missed the funeral. Harrigan would never have the chance to act on his resolution. He had believed that he had more time. And, in his shame, he gained a critical insight into the nature and meaning of time.

Harrigan finally composed himself after an hour, showered, dressed and left for Freund's home. He felt humbled, thoroughly reprimanded but he had a job to do—and made himself focus on that.

He drove up the flower-edged driveway and parked behind Freund's five-year old Ford minivan. Harrigan wondered why Freund did not get himself a sedan—and a bigger house; he paid Freund *more* than enough! Freund came out to greet him and they strolled to the rear of the house where the entrance was not strewn with toys and screaming kids.

"Want some breakfast, Kevin? It's still hot."

"No thank- Well, yes. Thanks. Whatever you're having."

Gertrude greeted him warmly. She had the temporary maid place two meals on a folding table between a pair of simple reading chairs in their small study. Gertrude and the maid left the men alone.

The room was neat and utilitarian. It was formed with white painted walls adorned with pictures of ancient family members, friends and scenes of mountainous southern Germany. There was no fireplace but it had a beautiful black leather couch facing a small, flat, antique mahogany desk. The desk area was a ten foot wide bay, enclosed in window panes which rose to form a partial roof over the desk. Bright sunlight was filtered by the topmost panes, which were polarized to avoid sun damage to the computer and desk.

Freund knew exactly what Harrigan was here for and preempted his long-time buddy. "This is our home now, Kevin. We thought last year of moving back to Germany but decided to stay. The kids and Gertrude have friends. We're involved in the Lutheran Church outreach program. Beyond that, Kevin, I cannot participate in genetic manipulation or discarding imperfect embryos."

"Mannie, that activity will take place whether you join us or not. You can fly back here frequently and even telecommute much of the time. But if you don't come, you'll never get to discover the genetic basis of behavior and instinct as it has evolved through the millennia. You'll never be the one to discover what gives humans individual personalities. Whatever we discover in that area can't be released for ten years. And don't forget the pay bump." Harrigan could see no change in Freund's concerned but reluctant expression. "Mannie, look: I really need you with me on this. As a researcher *and* as a friend." Harrigan stewed silently: *I wish I could just knock some sense into this closed-minded, superstitious yokel!*

"I appreciate that Kevin. I suppose that zygotic and fetal research will inevitably happen. At least you're right about my desire to solve the neuro-genetic puzzles. But I *can't* participate. It's against everything I believe; everything I know."

Harrigan thought hard. He needed more to convince *this big knucklehead*. He began to look nervous and got up to close the shades. "Mon says his government is going through with this with or without us. He also said that I can bring whomever I want but he'll have to fill vacant slots with Iraqi researchers. That, and the remote possibility that the project and a few of my methods could be of some military value, made me nervous. I talked with the U.S. Embassy. You can't know any of this, by the way. Their people see no threat but they feel that we still need to accept the project and minimize Iraqi researchers on the team. I need you, Mannie."

"I see. Let me think a moment." Freund stood and paced. He did not want to reject Harrigan out of hand, even if Harrigan did generally ignore his counsel. After all, Freund thought, he has Tykvah to work on that amoral ego of his. Freund frowned and sat, again disappointing Harrigan. "Kevin. I cannot do this. You may think it's organized superstition, but I cannot work there."

Harrigan contained his tone but not his words. "Man, this religion thing has impeded more scientific, sometimes crucial, discovery than any other factor in history! Mannie: If there is a god, don't you think he wants humans to understand and improve themselves? Don't you think he would want us to use abilities he gave us to advance man's own genes? Don't you believe he would demand that we use those skills to alleviate suffering, prolong life—perhaps even uncover evidence of his divine hand in our own evolution?"

Freund smiled and his tone was warm, yet his words were a direct challenge to his friend and employer. "You sound like a New Age preacher, Kevin! Those are intriguing questions. Do you think about them often or are they prepared for my recruitment?"

Harrigan felt inexplicably guilty. "I think about these things . . . sometimes, Mannie. Between you, Tykvah and her father, it's impossible to go a day without being reminded of this god-thing. Look, I don't believe it but as a scientist, I'm open to new evidence. Maybe there is evidence of God. *You'll* have to show me. Maybe *this* is your chance."

"God would not provide evidence of himself, Kevin, or at least not enough for proof. He wants us to just accept the faith he offers. Once in awhile, though, he'll bonk someone like you in the head with a two-by-four if it serves his purpose. As a matter of fact, even if genetic engineering's a sin, it might actually serve his purpose. I don't know."

"Well, obviously you're not coming." Harrigan resigned himself to the fact and relaxed to enjoy breakfast and the pleasant but challenging debate Mannie usually offered.

"No, Kevin, I can't participate. Sorry."

"It's odd." Harrigan looked absorbed in thought.

"What's odd?"

"That's what Tykvah's father said last night."

"You asked him to go to Iraq with you?!"

"No, I mean . . . oh, gees, Mannie! I didn't tell you: Tykvah's pregnant. I'm happy about it, actually!"

"That's great! But you two are getting married in the spring. Should make for interesting wedding pictures!" Freund began to laugh until Harrigan's humiliated look stopped him. "Sorry. Are you moving the date up?"

"Yes."

"Well, what was it that he said, *anyway?!*"

"He said our sin was God's will."

"I'm sure he didn't say it like that!"

"No. He said *the child* was, even though we shouldn't have been doing the dirty deed!"

"He's right. I met him once. He's really a very devout man."

"I thought Christians think Jews are going to hell; like me, the Buddhists, American Indians and so on, for not accepting Christ?!"

"Do you think God never spoke to people before the days of Christ or even the days of Abraham—or that he spoke only in the Holy Land?"

"No, I thought *you people* thought that!"

"Some do. They're wrong. God speaks unrestricted by time or prejudice to everyone in every language; in every age. The problem is that people in each culture write down the accounts or create religions with cultural bias. People interpret things through their own paradigm. The abuses within religions are man's doing and, as such, able to be reconciled if we would change our imperfect paradigms. Even *my* church is reconciling with the Catholics and vice versa. So, it's man's imperfections and perspectives which divide, not God's."

"Well, what about the people who lived before Christ or who never heard of the New Testament? Isn't it true that you folks think they're going to hell?"

"You fail to see the nature of God's bridge to heaven. We may not know the mechanism. But we do know those people will have a chance . . . someday."

"I see. And you have this directly from God?!"

"In a way, yes. Kevin, last week Hans tried to convince Marian that the map of Europe is not the entire world; that the model globe in his room was. She wouldn't believe him because she was proud of the perspective she had gained. When Gertrude used the computer to show them a representation of the earth within the solar system, and then the Milky Way and so on, they still hadn't stopped fighting and wouldn't budge from their beliefs. It took days before the two would even speak to each other, let alone believe Gertrude.

"You and I have to accept that we, even the human race, are not yet mature or evolved enough to accept successive revelations of greater truths. We never stop to realize Who is revealing these truths, often through—as you assert—explainable, physical events. Our egos demand that we believe we've done or learned everything ourselves. As adults, we tend to believe the apparent expert of the day, the investment experts, even the bogus churches if they tell us what we want to hear. Yet truth simply is. Truth is immutable."

Harrigan thought about this for a moment. Freund had stumped him. This bothered him, for he knew he had always been a better debater than his less-empirical buddy. "If that's what you believe, Mannie, I'd have to conclude you think the older religions are wrong. And, by further implication, modern science is more right about things than any religion—since it has access to successively greater truths. So, you've defeated your own argument." Harrigan smiled triumphantly and took another bite of scrambled eggs.

Freund knew his point had been distorted for the sake of argument. "There may *well* be more revealed in the later religions which the older ones would do well to consider; even accept. That doesn't change the fact that they were genuinely inspired at a very personal level; that they continue to be conduits of revelation and even the very Spirit of God for their followers. As for science, I see nothing that usurps the core, the heart, of *any* religion. Discovering the physical world's mechanisms, which I believe are subtly *used* by God, does not validly lead to the conclusion that the spiritual world is bunk."

Harrigan would not let himself be defeated in debate. "Mannie: Science has found physical explanations for hundreds of things you would say have a divine nature. Remember that Red Sea discovery? The Hebrews who originated the Exodus story saw the natural draining of water and subsequent tidal wave—and mistook it for God's work. Another example: Every day there's more evidence from chimpanzees that behavior like theft, violence, even homosexuality is genetic and, hence, morally neutral. Not that I want to kiss you or rob a bank or something! But the world is now emerging into an age of peace and prosperity—no thanks to the major religions. No thanks either to people who are informally religious. Government and business, armed with scientific breakthroughs, are the ones making these improvements."

Freund poured coffee on Harrigan's eggs and smirked.

Harrigan blotted his eggs, taking it correctly in jest. "Thanks, jerk!"

"You're welcome! Kevin: Prosperity is only an improvement from the incorrect perspective of what *we* value, in our immature state. What if God expects individuals as well as society to evolve spiritually by rising above our physical nature, rather than using the example of chimp behavior and genes as a self-justification? You can't validly assert that if something occurs in nature, it's morally neutral for humans. What if you see it from this perspective: That our genetic make-up is merely a way for God to *challenge* us to *choose* to deny the physical in favor of the spiritual; to grow spiritually toward becoming more perfect?"

"Right. And if pigs could fly . . . Look, Mannie: This faith thing is contrived, even though I don't doubt the evidence that Jesus actually lived. You've got to admit the New Testament contradicts itself: Priests tell us that God has a loving nature. If so, how can it *possibly* be that he demanded the *cruel, protracted suffering and death* of his own son as atonement for our sins? That would amount to an *unjust* shifting of revenge against mankind to one man. I really never could reconcile that, Mannie."

"Kevin: one's paradigm is key here! You see a cruel death demanded by God as contradicting his nature. Has it never occurred to you that such a death was *necessary* to get mankind's attention; to demonstrate to the extent of his love?! He chose to suffer human trials. His suffering was all about gaining mercy, another chance, for humankind. Perhaps he needs us to humbly *attempt*, according to our gifts, to emulate his example. A sacrifice that isn't just a ritual.

"And suffering, well Kevin, it's like sacrifice. It's meaningless unless one chooses to *make* it be a sacrifice to gain genuine life. Mercy and going the extra mile when it's more expedient to hurt or ignore others, that counts even more. You will not see that if your eyes are fixed on the comforts of your current life more than on those of the next. Perspective, Kevin. Like Hans and Marian."

Harrigan dismissed what he felt was a trick of semantics and began to see a way to get Freund to participate in the project. "You're really into conjecture, now, Mannie! If you really believed that man is supposed to use his 'gifts' to improve both spiritually and physically, then you would come with me and explore both processes. This is your opportunity to see how religion developed, to observe behavior and traits which could literally be evidence of divinely-promoted evolution in mankind."

"We'll never find proof of God, Kevin."

Harrigan tried again. "Remember when I told you about those RNA molecules which form and operate only during meiosis to inhibit major changes in human genes? Well, you can study these now and find out whether your belief, that God's hand is evolving us into something better, is valid. You may alternately discover that you're wrong and that, to evolve further, mankind must take charge of its own genetic makeup. I hope you're not afraid to discover that you're wrong! This is your chance, Mannie, to bring *your* perspective to the work we will be doing *anyway*. It's your only chance to change *my* perspective or prove *me* wrong!"

Freund felt compassion for Harrigan, despite their disagreement. He paused, deep in thought. *This challenge to faith is hard to ignore. He's clearly harassed and helpless. Guess I'd better go out there with him; he'd be lost out there alone.* Freund always knew he was his brothers' keeper. He smiled tentatively.

"Possibly an interesting adventure, Kevin! I'll do it on one condition."

"What's that?"

"You have to remain open-minded to other perspectives on spiritual reality. Think about the issue every time you witness either death or birth: embryonic or mature, animal or sapien."

"When you plant a suggestion in my mind that way, Mannie, I guess I won't be able to help but be reminded in the course of this work! But *you* promise not to lecture me! I've got to shoot you straight on this, Mannie: My perspective is that of a scientist. Yours should be, too. We'll *both* keep open but empirical minds, all right?"

"Okay, Kevin." Freund smiled and shook Harrigan's hand. "That is enough."

Chapter Ten

AND THE DEVIL SAID TO HIM, "TO YOU I WILL GIVE [ALL THE KINGDOMS OF THE WORLD] . . . IF YOU WORSHIP BEFORE ME, ALL WILL BE YOURS."
— LUKE 4.5-7

. . . the Jews are the most catastrophic people of world history: by their aftereffect they have made mankind so thoroughly false that even today the Christian can feel anti-Jewish without realizing that he himself is the ultimate Jewish consequence.
— F. Nietzsche, *The Antichrist*

CHILDREN A YEAR OLD SHALL SPEAK WITH THEIR VOICES, AND PREGNANT WOMEN SHALL GIVE BIRTH TO PREMATURE CHILDREN AT THREE AND FOUR MONTHS, AND THESE SHALL LIVE AND LEAP ABOUT.
— 2 ESDRAS 6.21

The Ministry of the Interior, Baghdad
1417 hours, 19 August, 2009

Major Hassan's palms were damp with sweat as he closed the door to the brand-new, lavish but windowless, subterranean office. He nervously took his seat facing Interior Minister Ismail Mon, a man becoming feared even by the elected Iraqi president. He felt Mon's eyes burning through him and was unsettled about why the Minister seemed to be displeased.

Mon queried his Special Activities Chief in a calm, almost friendly tone. "Hassan, your people are integrated with Harrigan's team and learning his FGR process?"

"Yes, Minister. However, the techniques we have gained from his success with the animals in Megiddo and at Al-Rajda have so far failed at our lab here. It has been most frustrating. He is hiding something. He has been using FGR for the past eight weeks on the

148

Neanderthal genetic material specimens. We have been monitoring him and the computer system more thoroughly than ever before. We will have it soon. And *then*, Minister, we will be able to replace dwindling oil revenues with a myriad of commercial applications! We will not need to wait the ten years of the contract. We can *dispose* of Harrigan and make it appear that FGR was lost with him and *we* discovered the process independently!"

"Listen closely, Hassan. I will confide something to you so that you will be more effective in directing the efforts of your people at Al-Rajda . . . than you have been to date. You will *not* share this with anyone."

Hassan looked puzzled.

"Hassan, we are *not* after Harrigan's secrets to make money; even to compensate for diminished oil demand."

"But, sir! Funding for the project is based on—"

"Are you questioning me, Major?"

"No sir."

"The Arab nations have been kept at each others' throats for centuries by the West. They have made us dependent upon their increasingly meager oil purchases and forced us to accept those filthy Hebes dominating Palestine. They would soon have us catering like groveling servants to their fat, spoiled children in tourist parks. Eventually, they would not even need that. I will *not* allow this to happen, Hassan, to *my* people. Those who follow me will never die. I will perfect, evolve mankind. With greater mental capacity and longevity, our descendants will experience a truly higher plane of existence. Now, open your Alpha list and follow along with what I tell you."

Hassan flipped open his notebook computer and touched the Alpha icon. Immediately a summary of research objectives for his main area of responsibility was displayed.

"Would you like to live a thousand years, Hassan?"

"Yes, sir!"

"Do you suppose we could gain the loyalty of leaders of the Arab League if we could control their longevity, reward them with better health—or punish them with the opposite?"

"We have discussed longevity, sir. My scientists place a high priority on tracing genes related to longevity."

"Hassan, it is not wise to tell me what you are aware I know."

"Yes, sir. I didn't mean to—"

"Scroll to the last item, priority twelve: Meiotic Research. This one is your highest priority, Hassan."

"I do not understand, sir."

"That is because you are an idiot who will become more effective and insightful . . . if you wish to live. Those RNA molecules described there in the section marked 'confidential' are key. According to his notes, Harrigan believes that some of them inhibit mutation and evolution while most inhibit ancient traits. They must control whether traits, inherited from as far back as our reptilian ancestors, become expressed in a fetus or not. Why, Hassan, do you think Harrigan has unsuccessfully attempted to keep that information in his ciphered files?"

"I supposed he felt sensitive about it. Studying those molecules requires destroying fetuses—and that's illegal here and in most countries now that RU-586 is distributed free."

"Don't be a blind fool, Hassan. RU-586 is but a convenient rationalization. The world can proclaim innocence for having outlawed abortions. Harrigan knows he is safe from prosecution here even if he obtains aborted fetuses. No, he is not so sensitive! Harrigan knows these RNA molecules can trigger or inhibit traits which are dormant, carried forward from past generations. What would happen, Hassan, if *the West's* women suddenly began giving birth to imbeciles or tiny apes like our ancestors—while *our* women produced fearless, strong, fast-maturing children? What would happen if the non-Arab world's military personnel suddenly aged decades—in days? How difficult, then, would it be for Arabs—*led by us*—to inherit the entire earth?"

"Uh. How would we, I mean what vector could carry such genetic triggers?"

"*You* will have *your* people develop the answer; then provide *me* with that capability, Hassan. I want techniques which can be controlled and selectively activated. I want them in a form which is easily, effectively and exclusively dispensed, at *my* command—just like any weapon or reward we are now able to employ at will. I want enhanced intelligence, rapid aging, greater longevity, disease resistance and everything else on your list."

Mon took a page from a file, walked out from behind his desk and placed it on Hassan's keyboard.

"I will simplify things for you, Hassan. If you are successful—and I mean meeting the generously flexible schedule on this sheet—

you will rise with me. I will give you Iraq as your personal domin-
ion. But if this assignment is beyond your ability, you will die. Do
you comprehend your assignment more clearly now, Hassan?"

The awed and intimidated Major realized he could not turn
down this responsibility and live. The realization of what he could
gain, however, enticed and exhilarated him.

"You have honored me with your confidence, Minister. I will
even *surpass* your expectations! In fact, I will start by eliminating a
spy."

Mon's eyes flashed at Hassan. "What spy?! For whom?"

"This morning I received this report from Toronto. I wanted to
give it to you myself."

Mon read the hand-written note from his North American Bureau
operative and handed it back to Hassan.

"Don't kill him, you fool! Not now. This Nuñez could be valuable.
Keep him away from your researchers—and monitor him. Feed him
the confidential portions of the Al-Rajda commercial plan. If he
makes the Americans and Israelis think we're only out to make
money, they'll recall him and leave us alone. If he appears to be
communicating anything else, kill him."

* * *

The previous two months of preparations had been exhausting for
nearly every technician and scientist at the preserve. Yet almost no
one seemed exhausted. Each step in the process had been more exciting than the last and the atmosphere of exhilaration was such that
these professionals appeared almost giddy. Implanting four Iraqi surrogates with thriving Neanderthal zygotes the day before had been
the crowning achievement of this phase of their endeavors. The surrogates and their husbands were behavioral specialists, psycholo-
gists and other professionals. They seemed to Harrigan, when he
had helped interview some, to take seriously their new responsibilities to train and raise Neanderthal children in a realistic manner. Everyone treated the artificially impregnated mothers like
fragile queens; practically smothering them with attention.

Although a great amount of work loomed before them now, Harrigan wanted to give his team a break. He arranged for a late afternoon cookout and had even asked Major Najik to allow the guards

to participate. It would be outside a hundred yards south of the complex so as to provide a better view of the awesome plateau cliff and waterfall at which he loved to gaze. The plateau reminded him of a story he had repeatedly read and seen depicted in old movies: *The Lost World*. Of course, the ecosystem his team was creating was far from lost. He was glad, though, that its isolation from the rest of civilization was so well enforced because this enabled the work to progress without disturbance.

He would soon be joined in his office by Dr. Freund for a private conference. But now Harrigan wanted to just sit for several minutes and contemplate the project so far. The past two months' intense work, the nearly finished construction, forestation, and the fabulous lab facilities, was a great source of pride. He was particularly happy with the quality of his labs and the amazing feats which had just been achieved in them. Only thoughts of the impending appointment marred his satisfaction at the last two month's accomplishment.

The Fossil Gene Redemption process had been executed assembly line fashion, using three in-line laboratories. These were the Paleontology, or Paleo Lab, the Genetics Lab and the Biology/Cryogenics, or BC Lab. A sweet, minty odor permeated in each work area. The mint had been Dr. Oda's idea. It was based upon several Japanese studies of the positive effects of certain subtle odors on mood and alertness. This proved to be a big help, for the process had been demanding:

First, the Paleo Lab isolated and recovered nucleotides, pieces of gene strands, from damaged fossil egg and sperm. In the first five weeks, Olivier's team had separated and prepared specimens from the four fossil Neanderthals. Seven technicians, laboring six weeks, tediously extracted damaged but redeemable fossil cells. The cells were then re-hydrated and processed so that their chromosomal residue could be embedded along a thin bar of non-reactive clear gel. Faint electron beams were used to manipulate and straighten crossed strands in the gel without modifying the nucleotide. The still-aqueous gel bars were then semi-hardened and passed via a yellow, one foot square, port into the Genetics Lab.

Windowless and eighty feet square, the Genetics Lab was twice the size of the other two main labs. Its walls were covered with generous-sized monitors. These hung like pictures and displaying en-

larged computer-colored scans of DNA segments, whole chromosomal depictions, RNA molecules and statistical analyses. A set of
wide double doors was the only authorized entrance or exit from
the room, though there was an emergency exit leading to the administrative office hallway. Work stations along its walls were
plush and spacious, each with oversized monitors and virtual reality headsets and gloves. The center of the Genetics Lab held Harrigan's most highly guarded equipment, starting with the genetic
sample scanner module.

This module, whose operation took only a day, received the gel
bars from the Paleo Lab. One of its components, the Terahertz illuminator, the T-ray illuminator, looked like a three foot long silver
bar with hundreds of emitter diodes. It emitted very low-level energy which, while not affecting the reconstituted fossil nucleotides,
functioned like a camera flash. Parallel to it, one foot above and below, two black bars produced a null-magnetic field which held the
gel bars fixed in mid-air. The stationary gelled sample was then T-il-
luminated and the deflected rays 'read' by the surrounding two
halves of a clam-like blue ceramic globe, called the T-ray receptor.
This receptor was the computer's eyes into the fossil gene segments so that it could create a model, or map, of the genetic sequences. These scanned images were also transmitted to the wall
monitors.

The key to proper computer modeling of these genetic sequences was that few samples were damaged in exactly the same
place. During this mapping, the computer compared strands for sequence patterns, identifying thousands. These patterns were compared to determine which portions were common but missing.
Hence, missing segments were identified in the scanning and mapping steps by comparing those of each fossil egg and sperm reconstituted in the gel bar. Processing of these genetic maps had taken
a day. The computer then required two weeks to control synthesiz-
ing and assembling of raw genetic material into replicated sets of
chromosomes for implantation into an actual egg.

Water and nucleotide storage tanks, raw materials, along with
cable bundles and a temperature control unit were the next components in the line of machines which bisected the Genetics Lab.
These were mounted above a door frame-like gap so that the center of the lab could be traversed.

On the opposite side of this gap were the genetic manufacturing devices. The first of these was a nucleotide base-pair synthesizer. The synthesizer drew the four component nucleotides from the tanks to make DNA strands. Adjacent to the synthesizer was a gene strand assembler. It manipulated these strands of base pairs into complete genes and, then, into twisted sets of genes called chromosomes.

Two years earlier, a research team at Stanford had discovered human gene segments, called "growth microsatellites," which control maturation rate. Harrigan's team inserted copies of these to code the fetuses for fast gestation and development. Except for the fast maturation genes, the synthesizer had produced genuine Neanderthal chromosomes.

These chromosomes were migrated to the BC lab's microscope-crowned implantation station. Each completed set of twenty-three chromosomes was then placed in a gelatinous, artificial cell nucleus. The nuclei mimicked those of human eggs. Each such nucleus, of which there were ninety-one, was immediately inserted into an egg. The eggs, nuclei removed, came from four human surrogates. In just two days, nine artificial wombs received eighty-seven of these zygotes.

The forty-five female zygotes would all attain the developmental state of ten week old fetuses within three weeks and produce their own eggs: the process of meiosis. These girls in the artificial wombs would be terminated during meiosis and their eggs harvested to discover the secrets of that miracle. Forty-two males were frozen for later study. The remaining four zygotes, two of each sex, were implanted into the surrogates' uteruses to be born after a gestation period of only three months. Careful to use the four fossil sources from two locations, the zygotes would be cousins to each other. Recessive genes were identified and repaired, as these four Neanderthals were intended for natural breeding years hence.

Harrigan and his team had been confident throughout the long process because of previous successes with extinct animals. What had really charged the air with barely-controlled exhilaration was the fact that they were accomplishing a feat previously only dreamed of: The researchers had not just authentically regenerated another extinct animal from both fossil egg and sperm. They had not simply recreated an extinct, higher-order primate. These men and women had created viable embryos of genus *Homo:* the once-extinct *Homo sapiens neanderthalensis.* Only one thing dampened the joy: Freund had refused to perform the implantation and was now at Harrigan's office door to answer for that refusal.

"Come in, Mannie, and shut the door. Have a seat."

"Thanks." Freund suspected he was about to be fired but was more sad than nervous.

"Mannie, I was going to fire you for not doing the implants. But I need you to monitor neurological and other physical development."

Harrigan touched a console on his desk and a dull vibrating sound made it difficult to hear speech more than three feet away. He got up and pulled up a chair next to Freund.

"Mannie, I don't trust these Iraqis. I found they've been into my personal computer files. For all I know, the whole building is bugged. So, this irritating buzz is necessary. Mannie, I . . . I need your insight on something."

Harrigan took a wide, folded computer printout from his pocket and showed it to Freund. Freund studied it for a moment, sadness giving way to startled intrigue, and stared at Harrigan.

"Kevin, have you run this analysis a second time?"

"I've run it three times, each with the same results."

"Could be a statistical fluke, of course, but the odds are several million to one. What do you think it means, Kevin?"

"Well, obviously implant number two—what were they naming it?"

"Kora. It's a modern name close to the Nostratic word for lamb."

"We got half her genes from the Pyrenees male specimen and half from the fossil girl Lloyd found at Shanidar. He thinks the three found there were a family. But, Mannie, Kora is genetically identical to the fossil mother of that fossil girl."

"An identical twin to the presumed mother . . . from the daughter's genes? The fossil sperm used was five thousand years older and from an unrelated specimen! Any matches among the other fetal or fossil Neanderthals?"

"None."

"Hmm. Matthew Eleven reveals that John the Baptist was Elijah. Maybe . . ."

"Oh come off it, Mannie!"

"There *could* be spiritual forces which we cannot understand interacting with physical laws. Maybe the essence of the Neanderthal mother has been recalled *for a reason*. Perhaps it's a sign . . . or perhaps Kora has some mission to our world. Kevin, have you given what we talked about any thought? We agreed that—"

"Yes, yes, I have. Look, Mannie, I can't see how it could be a 'sign' or how she could be bearing some divine message. Why do you insist on making me uncomfortable? Who elected you to minister to me?"

"Seeking that which is comfortable has never been your style in anything but spirituality. But, okay, let's just look at this from a purely scientific standpoint for a moment, Kevin."

"Thanks. That's what I've been asking you to do!"

"If you shoot X-rays or T-rays through a box and get a round image, what would you suspect was in the box?"

"A ball. Is there a point, Mannie?"

"Why do you assume it is a ball and not a disk?"

"Uh. Well, I guess I think in three dimensions. Wait. Four, including time."

"So your interpretive frame of reference comes from your experiences of this world during your life. If you were really determined to find out what was in the box but couldn't touch it, what would you do?"

"I'd employ probe after probe, using the resulting data to build a list of known possibilities and eliminate the possibilities which were inconsistent."

"So, then, is reincarnation—or some process of God's grace that works like that concept—at least a possibility? Even if it never happened before, do you have evidence that can eliminate it from a list of possibilities?"

"Okay. *Something like that* is a possibility—and no more. But what could possibly be the mechanism for spiritual occurrences like you suggest? It's just not a supported hypothesis, Mannie. What I want is the list and the probing tools! Will you track her neurologically and psychologically? It really gave me shivers when I saw this."

"Certainly I will. Kevin, I don't believe that reincarnation has ever occurred before . . . except for the Elijah and John the Baptist connection. Well, look, you keep the resulting children well cared for and I'll have this phenomenon pegged one way or the other:

Random or otherwise. Now, what about this Iraqi prying? Are they trying to steal FGR?"

"I think they're after FGR because they don't want to wait the ten years under the contract before I have to give it to them. I see no evidence that anything we're doing has military value but I do know there is *no way* they can get FGR!"

"Why not? The interpretation and mapping program is at easy access for them to copy and they have physical access to the equipment now!"

Harrigan's increasingly amicable voice signaled clearly that the two men could be friends again. "I had some computer science grad students help me write parts of the program years ago at Harvard. They didn't see the whole picture so they don't have my program. But their help enabled me to integrate a security precaution into it. The error checking subroutine only uses the correct algorithm when I *personally* include a password in my voice commands. Otherwise, or if it's copied, it ends up introducing serious errors into the gene production. Another password permits correct operation for anyone but keeps the copy protection enabled. That's why the Iraqis can use FGR in this lab without me and still not suspect that I use a code word. It's in the design of the program so there's no virus to detect."

"You're a sneaky dog, you know that, Harrigan?!"

"Arf! Got to be around these people! One last thing, Mannie: I need to track down these meiotic RNA molecules to discover their function in humans. Your and Ruliev's work implicates some of them in preservation of characteristic behavioral and personality traits, at least in sapiens. If we are going to understand what made Kora the same as her 'fossil grandmother,' we're going to have to study human and Neanderthal meiosis. Are you still going to work with me to examine their function?" Harrigan often agonized silently over the 'side issues.'

Freund sighed heavily at the reminder. "Termination of fetuses is something you're going to do anyway, Kevin. I guess if I want to be a part of the discoveries here and get you to consider deeper meanings, I have to participate. At least I admit *my* rationalizing. What do you have in mind?"

"I've asked Major Najik to arrange to obtain female zygotes from donors all over the world at illegal abortion clinics. But before you

157

say 'no': I told him to use only women who are already intent on getting illegal abortions anyway. We will end up with enough specimens to answer quite a few questions. Like which traits are preserved by the meiotic RNA; in which groups of people. I want to know what change has been occurring in these molecules since the time of ancient humans. And I want to know what instructions they are blocking from being expressed in modern human egg and sperm."

"That's a tall order, Kevin. I have to admit, though, I'd like to know the answers to those questions. And any implication for modern behavior and personality traits. All right, Kevin. I said in Megiddo I'd do it and I won't renege."

Harrigan got up smiling and turned off the buzzer, which he hoped had been unnecessary. The two men walked together through the halls toward the exit and the cookout. Freund was not happy with himself. He was not happy at all.

Harrigan turned hesitantly toward Freund as they walked. "Mannie, I think I need a vacation or something. Too much stress. I keep having these dreams every few months or so."

"Dreams? Of what sort?"

"It's nothing, really. I can only barely remember anything that happens in them. They're always different but they leave me with the same odd exhilarating, yet fearful and lonely feeling. Like I've gotten myself into something too big, too . . . well, ominous."

"Dreams scaring *you?* What are they about."

"Well, last night, it was the escalator. Like I was on one of the escalators; half way up, alone. And I had to pick which way to go. There was a sense that if I picked the 'up' button, I would lose everything: myself, my family, the research—just a sad sense of loss. The 'down' button was no better: I sensed everything would prosper, like I could accomplish great things and be with my family—but the feeling of accelerating dread just chilled me. I couldn't really find or understand the right answer on my own. Just . . . I don't know. You're the doctor: Too much stress?"

"Stress, all right. Maybe something more. Maybe you should . . ."

Harrigan's voice turned to uncertain cynicism. "You think it's spiritual, don't you, Mannie? Everything is spiritual with you!"

"It's *you* who say *that*. Actually, I was going to suggest pentathol-II to dig into your brain."

"Woah! No thanks on experimental procedures! Look: Forget it. I'm just too stressed lately. I'll take a vacation. That should help. Right?"

"It might. But, somehow, I don't think a vacation will be enough."

Sounds of fast-tempo music and raucous laughter, interspersed with childrens' happy screams, greeted the pair as they left the building. Absent, were the flutes and striped Arabic robes which characterized recreational gatherings elsewhere in Iraq. Indeed, with no mosque, with western-style architecture, food and even deciduous plants being propagated, many in the Iraqi contingent here had become substantially westernized in their style of living.

Now the smell of barbecued chicken, beef ribs, corn and other delights made both Harrigan and Freund homesick for their respective native lands.

Harrigan dismissed his melancholy and worried thoughts from his mind just as he and Freund reached the picnic tables and were cheerfully greeted by Gertrude and Tykvah. He and Tykvah had moved up their marriage date to avoid having an embarrassing photo album. Tykvah had decided to take her husband's last name, pleasing her father as much as Harrigan. Now, perhaps more beautiful than ever to him, she was holding their sleepy two-month old son, Benjamin.

Gertrude used mock criticism and let her accent predominate in an attempt to get the two men to grin. "Look at you two *zow-er-pusses!* Get *mit* the program *und* have a beer!" The comment made both men grin from its ridiculousness. None of the four drank much alcohol.

Tykvah feigned annoyance. "It took you long enough to get out here!" She gave Harrigan a kiss that made him blush in front of the entire staff. Gertrude was not to be outdone and disentangled herself from the children to nab Freund.

"Hi, Tykvah! What's to eat around here?!" Harrigan had missed lunch.

"Oh, nothing. Looks like you don't throw much of a *party!*" Tykvah and Gertrude prepared tempting plates for their husbands and resumed talking. Harrigan and Freund spoke mostly with each other about American football and other pursuits in the West. After eating and several minutes of conversation, Harrigan smiled warmly and excused himself to visit the employees.

As he rose and turned, he glimpsed the cliff face. He turned to look at it straight-on. The sun was glinting off the waterfall to his right front and approaching the tall mountains to his left. The compound was built from concrete and gray cinder block. He could just make out new grass growing on its roof. Measures to keep the hominids from viewing the complex seemed to him quite premature but the whole place was shaping up nicely. Tractors and shovels stood idle, an extreme rarity, along side huge cylinders. The cylinders would soon cross under the river to form a subterranean driveway to and from the housing area east of the preserve's research facilities.

A feeling of awe at what he and his team had undertaken flooded his consciousness as he stared at the cliff itself. The ridges to the east and west were still being carved to enhance steepness but he was unable to see that from where he stood. Their southern ends, however, were within view and would clearly combine seamlessly with the natural cliff and its small man-made cliff border to preclude movement into and out of the preserve. He imagined the adventures he and the staff could have; the exploring, the danger and narrow escapes from vicious animals of the distant past. Then he stopped himself. He was not a romantic and knew this place was purely for research, at least for ten years.

Lloyd walked up to Harrigan. "There you are, Kevin! Don't like to talk shop at social affairs, but I've *got* to tell you about that Swiss glacier. The tools we scrapped out of it are definitely Cro-Magnon and I'm *most* confident we'll find a specimen soon!"

"Excellent! Keep at it! But you ought to relax here a day or so and get to know the facilities, especially the Paleo Lab. Besides, look: Kairaba is calling you to join her. I think she likes you!"

Harrigan grinned and excused himself to speak with the surrogates and their husbands. He had been impressed by their resumes. Now, as he spoke with them socially, he felt they were a bit too professional and not at all warm personalities.

Harrigan strolled over to address Nuñez, who was standing with Cabral; both slightly tipsy. "Hello, Paulo; José! How are you getting on, José, working with Dr. Freund?"

"He's a great *hombre* to work for, Dr. Harrigan. I like to bug him by telling him that the world is just one big probability model waiting to be solved! Complexity theory *esplains* . . . explains more than scripture. He takes it well *enough.* The work is more fascinating than any assignm- ah—I mean any work I've ever had! He's got me modeling gene *fun-tion . . . erp . . .* sorry! *func-tion-ali-ty.* We're going to be able to simulate genetic chemical reactions cascading in sequence or *simul-taneous-ly* to *espress* . . . express individual traits. We're linking the model to the traits database and getting most of the errors out at a pretty good pace.

"I think, between the two of us, we'll be able to tell you *wish* . . . which kids will grow up to be a party animal—like *Paulo* here—and which ones will be ogres like Major *Nashi* . . . Najik! Eventually, he wants me to model human population progression, starting with *Ne-ander-th-th* . . . those short hairy people. It's to predict what effects that RNA thing you discovered might have on future humans—or might have had in the past."

Harrigan laughed and moved on. He wondered nervously what such a simulation might reveal and predict, if it could be done accurately, about moderns, Neanderthals and, he hoped, Cro-Magnons.

On the way back to his own table, he overheard Corporal Abrih, one of the soldiers assigned to Preserve maintenance, complaining about the robot suits not being purchased. The large heavy-lift suits were, in Major Najik's view, overpriced and easily substituted by the far less expensive cargo tractors with heavy lift attachments. Harrigan was glad he no longer had any budget or administrative duties. Yet Harrigan strongly disliked the fact that for every money issue he had to go through *that thorn, Major Najik*, as he considered him. Harrigan had seen both items demonstrated by the vendors. The tractors were clearly obsolescent, far less flexible, less maneuverable and less durable than the suits. But the suits cost six times what the tractors cost. It was not an issue on which he chose to oppose his hosts.

Returning to his table, Harrigan offered a hearty smile and addressed Gertrude. "So, Gertrude, how do you like it here so far? Do you think you and the kids might *stay* here past next month—like permanently—so Mannie can save on air fare?"

Harrigan got a nasty look from Freund and realized that he had hit a nerve. "That's a point of contention right now, Kevin." Freund answered for his wife, winning himself a dirty look for so doing.

Gertrude responded for herself and lowered her voice to a whisper, "Kevin, it's not that we don't appreciate everything you *haf* done for us. But, frankly, I *belief* the family will be safer in Megiddo. I don't feel *comfort-able* in *Irraq.*"

Harrigan wisely avoided the debate. He felt he could relate to her feelings because of his own misgivings, which often plagued him. "As you wish, Gertrude. I see your point."

Chapter Eleven

Neurological Research Lab, Al-Rajda Zoological Research Preserve

0923 hours, 7 July, 2012

Dr. Ina Singh, the Preserve's anthropologist from Bombay, had been on the job only a few months. She was hired to assist Dr. Freund with his neuro-genetic studies of the hominids. This morning she was particularly excited, for she was participating in the first examination of a *living* Neanderthal. Thanks to well-planned teaching—in Nostratic—by the surrogates, this opportunity had finally arrived. Kora was the name they had given to this Neanderthal female, now the physical equivalent of an eight year old.

Kora had been removed under anesthesia very early this morning from her cave to spend a day in Freund's lab. The gas was already discontinued and would soon be replaced by sodium pentathol-II, a deep trance inducing drug which would facilitate study of her subconscious mind.

Singh eyed Freund somewhat nervously, unsure how deeply she should address a question which arose in her mind after reading the surrogates' reports on Kora. "Dr. Freund, what *d'you* make of her episodes of trance?" It was obvious that Singh had learned to speak English from a British teacher.

"I have an opinion. What is your interpretation?"

"If it were not for her healthy neurological condition, I'd infer epilepsy. But you are the medical authority. A recent report has an account of the sun changing color during one of her trances. Poppycock and hallucination on the part of the surrogate, I'd say. What do you think?"

"Yes. I must agree. I'm sure that's it."

"Well, then. Shall we begin?"

Freund smiled warmly. He had a strong sense that his response to Singh's inquiry was incorrect. He dismissed the thought from his mind and dropped his eyes. Stretching wrinkles from his surgical gloves and closing his white lab coat, Freund noticed that he was developing a very slight paunch. He momentarily recalled with mild chagrin how his children had enjoyed finding his few gray hairs and plucking them out before his trip back here five days ago. He refocused on his task and started the audio recording.

"System: Begin Recording, Kora One. Output to screen."

The large screen on the wall silently flashed three words. RECORDING: Kora One. The computer automatically recorded numerous monitored data, such as drug flow rates, Kora's blood pressure and her brain waves. It also recorded all sounds in the room.

"Present with me to conduct this experiment is Dr. Singh and Nurse Haddad. Nurse, please turn Kora on her side a moment as I begin the pre-experiment physical examination."

Kora lay nude and motionless on the cushioned tan examining table. Freund could not decide which emotion he now felt most strongly: awe at the very presence of this cousin of mankind, or sadness. He had been distinctly saddened when, often over the last three years, he contemplated her primitive, homely and fragile condition. He knew her surrogate parents were only barely loving and accepting. Freund often begged them to hold her and her siblings more, to be more patient with them. He even appealed through Harrigan to their employers to force a change of attitude but they both were bluntly told that parents did not read Doctor Spock's classic advice tens of thousands of years ago.

Kora had thick brows, a receded chin and her eyes were slightly smaller than those of modern children of her size. Such features had proved a century of artists' impressions of Neanderthals substantially right. Her eyes were gray-blue with surprisingly short black lashes. The girl's cheek bones were very prominent. Her neck was short and thick. Her lips were over-full and bright red. Her fingers were slightly thick and stubby by modern standards and her legs were noticeably short and muscular. The hips were much wider than modern girls' of any race and her skin was nearly void of pigment. Her wide feet were covered with thicker hair than her hands and arms but, overall, she still presented far more of a human appearance than that of an ape.

Besides the facial features, Kora's hair was most remarkable. It was quite thick on her head and was becoming so in the groin. Only the hair of her head grew longer than an inch. It extended nearly two feet and seemed to have splashed upon the table, forming a reddish-blonde corona about her head. It was uniformly soft. She was covered with the same reddish-gold hair over most of her body, except for her chest and somewhat bulbous buttocks which were nearly hairless. Kora's appearance had created contention among the staff. Some theorized that modern humans, especially Europeans, had gained her genetic lineage.

"Thank you, Nurse. Now please release five milligrams pentathol-II into the stream."

Singh and Freund waited for the pentathol-II dripping through the I.V. to take effect. Freund glanced alternately at Kora, nurse Haddad, the vital and secondary signs displays and the computer monitors. Kora twitched her eyes and began to frown slightly. The REM sleep indicator on the secondary signs display lit. Like her siblings, Kora's articulation of the vowels a, i and u was shallow, slurred yet recognizable. Neanderthal voices were low, rough and scratchy. She opened her mouth and emitted a startling moan.

Kora's tone became suddenly loud and fearful. "Sera! Sera! Mana! Gandi palu bisa. Gandi qohl! Telh-laki; karipunyi qohl! Khayni qohl!"

Her heart rate, blood pressure and breathing shot rapidly up to alarming levels as she began to scream and contort on the table. Freund instinctively held her arm and hand but knew she was not aware of his touch. His eyes darted back and forth from her tormented expression to the frightening blood pressure readings, now at 181 over 143. She continued to moan and scream, no longer articulating anything like words.

"Twenty milligrams of labetalol *NOW!*" Freund was alarmed, taken entirely by surprise. The nurse drew the required amount from a small bottle with a needle and began to insert it into the hanging I.V. dispenser. Freund snatched the syringe from her hand and plunged the needle directly into the port at Kora's wrist.

The screaming stopped almost immediately but was followed by continued moaning and a couple of words. Her blood pressure was back into a safe range. Freund breathed a loud sigh, quickly wiped his beaded forehead, and addressed the other two staff members in the room.

"What *de* hell was tha-"

Kora's low, scratchy voice seemed relaxed, quiet. "Gepeh . . . gilda!"

The researchers' eyes now stared at the computer monitor in amazement. The analysis of the translation appeared almost instantaneously as Kora spoke.

VOCALIZATION SET 1, PHONETIC: "Sera! Sera! Mana! Gandi palu bisa. Gandi qohl! Telh-laki; karipunyi qohl! Khayni qohl!"

(AS ONE) ANALYSIS:

PROBABILITY IT IS A STATEMENT. 98.23%

PROBABILITY IT IS A QUESTION. 01.41%

PROBABILITY IT IS RANDOM. 00.36%

SYNTAX CONFORMITY TO ENGLISH. 80.00%

MODERN LANGUAGE. . . . . none

BEST FIT. . . . Nostratic (90.91% match to etymology)

PRONUNCIATION CONFORMITY TO. . . . . Nostratic Model. 35.12%

ALL POSSIBLE MEANINGS OVER 10% PROBABILITY THRESHHOLD. . . . . One at 92.77%:

"Wake(!) Wake(!) Men(!) [Big men] many crush. [Big men] kill(!) Long-legs; black-hairs kill(!) [Khayni UNKNOWN PLURAL] kill(!)"

VOCALIZATION SET 2 (Y / N) ?

Freund stared incredulous at the monitor. Then it dawned on him that Harrigan might have programmed the computer to read out a bogus analysis as a joke. But neither man knew for sure Kora would say anything at all while unconscious. Indeed, this deep an access of her mind could have produced silence.

"Yes."

The screen blanked and then displayed the second vocalization analysis.

VOCALIZATION SET 2, PHONETIC: "Gepeh . . . gilda!"
(AS ONE) ANALYSIS:
PROBABILITY IT IS A STATEMENT. 99.81%
PROBABILITY IT IS A QUESTION. 00.00%
PROBABILITY IT IS RANDOM. 00.19%
SYNTAX CONFORMITY TO ENGLISH. 100.00%
MODERN LANGUAGE. . . . . none
BEST FIT. . . . . Nostratic (100.00% match to etymology)
PRONUNCIATION CONFORMITY TO. . . . . Nostratic Model. 38.57%
ALL POSSIBLE MEANINGS OVER 10% PROBABILITY THRESHHOLD. . . . . One at 94.29%:
"Light [PAUSE] shine(!)"

NO OTHER VOCALIZATIONS RECOGNIZABLE. SELECT MAIN FOR OPTIONS.

Freund shivered visibly and turned toward Singh. "Ina, would you get the hard copy Nostratic Lexicon, please."

Singh left the room and returned with a thin booklet. "Here, Dr. Freund. Is this some *form* of joke? An error or *somesuch* thing?"

"Perhaps. More likely someone taught her this. The surrogates have been teaching them our best model of Nostratic. But I don't think all of these words were in the lesson plans. If they've tampered with these children's minds and our ability to gain valid insight, I'll . . . I'll have their jobs!"

Freund silently thumbed through the lexicon, checking each translated word. "She pronounced these words differently from the lexicon, on which the computer language model is based—and a few of her words are not in the lexicon."

"What does that mean?" Singh was becoming confused as well as angry about the suspected tampering with the children's development.

"It means that we need to check the records on how she's been using these words to determine whether she's been coached. She would pronounce these words the same in waking speech as when she's in this subconscious state—if she's been coached in some unauthorized way by the surrogates." Freund paused and addressed the computer.

"System: Compare Vocalization Sets 1 and 2 to the model and to Kora's recorded usage. Time frame: last twelve months. Summary only."

SUMMARY COMPARISON. . . . . Neither Set 1 nor Set 2 Pronunciations match the model; no matches to any previous recordings (time = last 12 calendar months).

SUMMARY NOTES. . . . . The following words have not been recorded used by Kora previous to recording of Kora One:

Set 1: bisa, qohl, khayni

Set 2: gilda

. . . . . The following words are not in the model:

Set 1: khayni

DETAIL OF COMPARISON (Y / N)?

"No." Freund stared again at Singh and at the nurse. His jaw hung open a moment and he began to speak again. "Her pronunciation for each word is different in her waking state from her subconscious state. No one has taught her these things, Ina. She knows words never taught her at the Preserve. Yet all but one match Nostratic."

The nurse scowled in disbelief and disapproval as Singh whispered a Hindu interpretation. "Dr. Freund, Kora has spoken words from the last moments of her life—nearly forty millennia ago."

Freund was surprised by Singh's unscientific interpretation. "System: End recording of Kora One. Nurse, Dr. Singh: Neither of you will discuss this, even between yourselves, until Dr. Harrigan or I authorize you. Nurse, please go down the hall and *physically* get Dr. Harrigan in here. Stat!" The nurse scowled again and disappeared. "And Ina, you and I can discuss this later . . . but please don't elaborate on your interpretation with Dr. Harrigan or the Iraqi staff."

* * *

The two Iraqi privates assigned to be a permanent arboreal maintenance crew were led by highly-dissatisfied Corporal Abrih. Abrih's only significant moment of pleasure in this unit was when he was a BMP turret gunner four years earlier. His men, Privates Farhim and Jehmut, dutifully threw the last can of sap-like artificial bark into the tractor alongside seventy-five fast-growth cedar saplings.

Farhim and Jehmut, like most of this installation's soldiers, had been continually intimidated and watched since the massacre. Devout Muslims, the two remained frustrated and aghast at what they witnessed years before. Yet they could not use their knowledge as they wanted. Subtle threats to soldiers about how whole families could—and did—disappear were not idle. The secret of what they had witnessed remained intact.

It was close to ten already and they were only now being cleared through the dispatch inspection to ensure that their vehicle would not break down inside the Preserve four hundred feet above them. The Motor Pool Inspection Bay housed numerous jeeps and utility tractors. It and the escalators were the only portions of the complex which extended under the base of the plateau cliff. Iraqi military policy called for vehicle storage sites to be underground when possible. The huge concrete bay was the building's only access to two diagonal vehicle escalators leading upward to the Preserve.

The sides of the vehicle were poorly disguised to make it look like a *Megatherium*, somewhat oversized at thirty-feet in length. Its grass-camouflaged treads could be recognized within fifty feet, so crews were required to keep it from sapien view. However, the impressions it left on the ground did look more like paw prints and shuffling than track marks. Its top half, from the mock rump to just under the neck, was equipped with a protective cage, covered with realistic fur. The cage was the only door in this model and functioned like the top of a convertible automobile.

The crew disliked everything about the Preserve and their exile here. Furloughs beyond its gates were rare. Abrih was bored and impatient with the slow pace of the inspection. He longed for bygone days when he had ridden atop the turret of his old BMP, pretending to be a nineteenth-century U.S. cavalry soldier like those he loved to watch in the movies.

Corporal Abrih barked cynically at the Mechanic, who returned an angry glare. "I wish you would finish so we can replace the trees that these brainless mammoths and elks keep destroying . . . so we can keep replacing them . . . so that the stupid mammoths and elks can destroy them again! Maybe we could have some real fun if you people could finally get in the heavy-lift robotic suits we were promised four years ago! And this disguise thing is stupid since the ape-children can not see us on our route! And what harm could there be if they do anyway?!"

"Silence, Corporal! You know all the regulations. Just let Major Najik hear you talking like that. He would tear off your head!" The mechanic was almost through. He checked the cage latch under the phony animal head. "There. Cleared. You are logged out."

The sloth tractor suddenly jerked forward onto the west escalator ramp.

The mechanic shouted, worried. "Abrih! Never thrust it through gears like that! You could crack the final drive!" He always had a frustrating time compensating for their shabby design when he had to repair them. He could not make out the corporal's muffled response but he knew it had to be something cocky. *The lout is correct about the heavy-lifters, though*, he complained to himself, *I will be glad when they finally replace these tractors!*

Abrih was supposed to have Private Farhim drive but liked to speed up the ramps himself.

Farhim tapped Abrih on the shoulder. "Corporal Abrih, we did not fill our canteens. And, are we not we supposed to be in park while on the escalator?"

"Just shut your mouth, Farhim! I heard water sloshing. You will be fine with what remains from yesterday."

"Yes, Corporal."

The tractor moved at top speed, twenty-five miles per hour, while the escalator added another ten. "Hold on, Jehmut! You too, Farhim! Yee Ahh!" It reached the stationary exit platform beneath the hydraulic trap door with a loud thud and wild bounce. Abrih thought to himself, *I will have some fun today even if these two are gutless!*

The trap door opened automatically and the mechanical sloth headed out onto the grass on its own treads. The vehicle slowed a bit on the uneven terrain.

"Take over, Farhim. Follow the river line—do *not* get too close and flip us in! North for two point three miles. Then track due west and stop just within the tree line."

Even Abrih, a cynic, was impressed by the plateau animals—and feared them. He had compared Megiddo Preserve photos and videos with his own observations of these genetically genuine animals. Subtle features of Al-Rajda's animals were different: ancys here held their claws well off the ground, mammoths' tusks curved more inward at the ends, *Megatheriums* had swifter motor control, *Smilodons* could swing their jaws fully back to their necks and were a bit smaller—though an Iraqi researcher's briefing described one which experienced odd growth spurts—and all the mammals shed and grew fur more in synch with the seasons.

The three drove onward uneventfully until the point on the river where they were to turn west. Suddenly a four foot long, tan *Smilodon* lunged up from the lush bank and confronted the mock sloth. The men tensed, far more impressed with the great cat's threatening, ears-back, jaw-distended display, muscle-bulging crouch and vicious snarls than with their vehicle's armor. Confused by the lack of the usual pungent odor of sloths, it eyed them from forty feet ahead and directly in the crew's path. The ten-inch fangs always struck fear into the crew when they encountered these killers, but never once had one attacked them.

Abrih believed that this was either because the sloth form was that of a very large adult male or because of the lack of sloth odor. As the crew had personally seen before, adult male sloths were more than a match for lone *Smilodons* and even hunting pairs of the giant cats tended to avoid them. The men nervously turned west and continued, unmolested.

They arrived at the patch of damaged trees near the edge of the grassy plain, stopped and dismounted to begin work. The rolling green valley was dotted with bushes and patches of trees. It was bordered on the west by the scruffy pine-filled foothills of an imposing rocky ridge, which formed the yeti and Neanderthal domains. A herd of about a dozen shedding mammoths a mile away was heading north. Two of its cows were running ahead, forcing a harem of black-maned *Coelodonta* out of their line of march.

Abrih handed electric chain saws to his men. Then he sat guard atop the sloth with his tranquilizer rifle, reminded of the irritating prohibition against ballistic rounds. "You know the routine: If it is straight yet lost bark, patch it. If leans badly, cut it and put acid on the saw cuts. Load saplings into your planters and plant. Then we get out of this place!"

Farhim pointed to a pair of tall oak trees. One tree had sagging leaves and a single greening branch. It leaned precariously into the other, which had four vibrantly green limbs and seemed to catch the faltering tree.

"I would like to try to save that one, Corporal."

"We are not here to make extra work for ourselves, Farhim! It still has roots in the soil and it might survive. I doubt it, though. Allow the vines and bugs kill it!"

The men labored hard with their assigned task for an hour, exhausted their canteens and needed a break. Farhim made the request. "Corporal, what of a break and some more water?" Abrih's rump was getting numb from sitting in one place so long and he saw what he believed was a chance to endear himself to his command. He glanced over at the dirty, amber colored pond fifty feet away.

"Fine. You two climb up here with the rifle and *I* will refill *your* canteens at the pond. It looks stained by roots or iron but that is no problem. Get me the purification kit, Jehmut."

The reddish pond was little more than a widening in a small, slow-moving creek just off their work area. Abrih hung the purification kit and three canteens over his head and across his chest. He walked sixty feet south through the tall grass, regretting his offer as the ground became mushy and sucked at his boots. He hoped there were no ticks but knew otherwise, so he trudged out of the grass directly into the cool water. As he turned to look back, his foot slipped off what he supposed was a submerged ledge. Abrih fell into the water and sank. He immediately imagined numerous tentacles, snakes and monsters reaching for him. He thrashed and struggled to reach the ledge. Gasping desperately and on the verge of panic, he hauled himself back up onto the ledge and glared at the two privates, who were almost falling off the tractor-sloth's neck with laughter.

"Assholes!" Abrih shouted as he tried to look dignified and composed. He decided not to disinfect their water. *I hope they puke their guts dry!*

Abrih turned and impatiently contorted in an attempt to untangle the canteens from each other, from around his neck and from under his epaulets. Finally he gave up the frustrating endeavor, knelt nervously down in the water at the ledge and submerged all three canteens. He positioned himself so that he could watch the shore to his right and the water to his left simultaneously. The bubbles coming up from the fill-necks chirped like birds and glinted sparkling sunlight in his eyes. Their popping spit droplets up into the air just short of his pointy chin.

Abrih saw the fast-approaching, drab orange and green image slightly to his left in the rippling water. He shuddered with the thought of something looming over him from behind. Instantly, he dropped himself into the water to escape whatever might be sneaking up on him. But the image was not a reflection. Submerged and at zero distance, he now saw the *Meiolania's* face and horns more clearly. The monstrous turtle's triangular jaws opened a full twelve inches. It sliced off Abrih's entire jaw from ear to ear, just missing the carotid artery and jugular vein. Abrih's upper larynx, ripped completely out of his neck, formed a lump of bloody sinew and cartilage floating from the right side of the hungry reptile's hideous head.

Since the slice was lightning-fast and almost clean, Abrih initially sensed more of a crunching, ripping pull than pain. Water rushed immediately through his abbreviated trachea into his lungs. Coughing into the water, he pushed himself back up and away from the denizen and jumped to a standing position. Spouting bloody water up onto the exposed back of his palate, Abrih groped for his now excruciating lower skull. His hands shook as he frantically grabbed at the dripping void which had been the bottom third of his head. He back-peddled and fell on his right side in the grass hoping for safety and able to make only a splattering, gurgling sound to summon his men.

But the attack was relentless. The eight foot long horror hesitated a moment, still submerged, then thrust itself upon the ledge and tossed the regurgitated and gangly jaw past Abrih's own eyes and up onto the grass. The voracious monster lunged as Abrih rose to escape, and caught a hunk of the corporal's left calf. Again the slice was swift and nearly clean. Abrih was able to tear himself away from the vice-gripped remnants of his sacrificed calf muscle. Farhim fired at the vicious animal but the dart stuck Abrih in the chest. The dart injected its contents into the bronchial tube of his left lung, missing all veins and tissue so that almost no tranquilizer entered his bloodstream. Abrih's breathing immediately became painful, labored, barely adequate wisps. Still gushing blood and gurgling from the remains of his throat, Abrih desperately hopped and stumbled toward his comrades. They were rushing to his aid.

The soldiers, paralyzed with awe and horror, halted barely twenty feet from their corporal. Hooked claws on the nightmarish turtle's massive, scaly paw sliced down through Abrih's right heel, nailing him to the ground. Abrih fell, hinged at his skewered foot. He tried again to scream, but the gaping wound which had been his jaw and throat continued to emit only bubbling noises and whisper-like puffs of air. The privates gasped, petrified; riveted by the sight: In a second, the *Meiolania* lurched forward upon Abrih's impaled leg, tore off half his right buttocks and gulped the meat unchewed. Relentlessly and continuously, it thrust its beak into Abrih's thigh, raised its head up to swallow; then reiterated the greedy bites. While Abrih contorted almost silently and pounded the ground, the horrendous eating machine tore off the remaining muscle with its claw and finished most of the leg, leaving the bone and femoral artery untouched. The privates simply could watch no more and dashed, vomiting violently on themselves as they ran back to the tractor.

They started up the machine and did not even bother to close the top. Slamming the treads into opposite spins to pivot the vehicle around, Farhim popped the gears too hard. They spun once but the gears cracked with a minor explosion, yielding no more power but only a gut-wrenching, grinding whir. The men forced themselves to look back at the carnage, expecting to see Abrih dead and the monster coming at them. Instead, the thorny head was still gashing and snapping, now into Abrih's gut, while the tormented corporal's arms still thrashed the ground. In a moment, his arms only twitched, then lay still, then were devoured.

They jumped up inside the tractor to feverishly yank the stubborn protective cover closed. The *Meiolania* stared at them for a brief moment . . . then charged at them. The cover was ten inches from closing when the grotesque turtle abruptly halted only twelve feet away. Through the gap, Jehmut and Farhim eyed the gigantic spiked turtle as it hesitated and stared beyond the vehicle. The terror suddenly lifted itself well off the ground, turned and bounded back toward the pond. The quivering soldiers sighed loudly and collapsed their tense shoulders, concluding that the *Meiolania* had been intimidated by the nearly-closed sloth form.

174

* * *

Harrigan rushed down the hall and into the neurology lab. "Sorry I couldn't get here faster. What the heck is it, Mannie? Is there something wrong with the Neand-, uh, Kora?"

Freund was silently pleased with the increasingly numerous signs that Harrigan viewed the Neanderthals as humans. He momentarily ignored Harrigan, stepped behind him and closed the door. "Kevin, you need to hear this. System: Replay Kora One. Output to speaker and screen."

The computer played back its recordings of every sound and every command which had taken place in the lab an hour before. It synchronized these with a reenactment of the displays and computer screen read-outs. Harrigan stood silently taking in the replay of the events and frowning at Freund.

"I'm not amused, Mannie. We do science here, not practical jokes." Harrigan's cross tone was followed by a knowing smile and the look of triumph on his face. "Mannie: I've got you now! System: Run my validation check, code seventy-two." He glared at Freund, expecting to prove the ruse.

The metallic voice responded almost immediately. "All components of Kora One were created in real time and have not been modified."

Harrigan's grin fell and his face blanched. He stared at Freund, then at Haddad and Singh, embarrassed. "I owe you an apology, Mannie. I should not have suspected you of manufacturing phony results or of playing a joke. But this 'previous life' thing is garbage! I suppose you agree with Dr. Singh's comment at the end?"

"I'm not sure but I lean that way. Still, I wouldn't rule something akin to that out."

Harrigan's rage built but distinctly lacked any confident tone. "Well I would! This is a research facility, Mannie! Not a *damn* theology discussion group. We don't jump to the conclusion that hocus pocus is responsible for an observation—just because we can't immediately identify the mechanism causing a result!"

"Find the mechanism, then. Or continue to rationalize."

Harrigan bristled at the terse challenge and began to turn red.

"No, *Doctor* Freund, *you* will find the mechanism; you and Dr. Singh will prove *yourselves* wrong or . . ."

"You sound more like you're worried that *you* could be wrong about there being spiritual traits which define humankind. And these children *are* human, physically 'nd spiritually. Would you have us manufacture evidence that supports your position—*und* shield you from that which weakens it—or would you like us to learn about all aspects of human evolution? Perspective, Kevin! How one views life. View it *mit* open eyes."

Harrigan felt caught in the wrong again. What he particularly disliked was Freund trying to force him to admit it. Harrigan refused to do that. He did not respond to the questions but just glared at Freund in silence.

Dr. Singh was unaware of previous disagreements Freund and Harrigan had had over interpreting discoveries about Kora. She broke the tension between her superiors diplomatically and courageously. "Gentlemen! I apologize for sparking this argument by jumping ahead to conclusions. But, *really!* Come now: Let's just focus on studying her and—when they're ready—her siblings, shall we? We have a lot of work to do: We need to find a way to keep her stress in check during these subconscious accesses. We need to build up a sufficient number of observations. *Then* we can determine *whether* this is just a fluke; an anomaly—or something more substantial. Please: *Gentlemen!*"

The two men began, reluctantly, to calm to the point of debating civilly. Harrigan felt that he needed to convince Freund of the logic of his own strictly scientific point of view.

"Look, Mannie, no disrespect to the Pope or the millions of devout, but we already saw last January how it's *man* who saves himself."

"I suppose you mean when they discovered the asteroid that was due to hit earth sometime this coming December."

"Yes. And it was superpower cooperation and nuclear technology which diverted it; not the millions praying for Mary and Jesus to intervene."

Freund's tone became more ominous. "Don't be so sure of yourself, my friend. The episode served to polarize people. It definitely had meaning and purpose beyond technology averting disaster. But individuals *interpret* it differently, depending on how they *choose* to view life. More has been revealed to mankind now. So, more is expected of us and merely living decent lives is no longer *enough.*"

Harrigan felt the impact of Freund's concerned stare and agonized again over the correctness of his position. He momentarily averted Freund's eyes but offered a small concession to the physician's ongoing concerns about how the sapiens were treated. "You're right, Dr. Singh: We can't sacrifice Kora or the others to a stroke during research. I suppose you're right in *some* respects, too, Dr. Freund: She *is* essentially human. Let's get Oda—her entire Biochem Lab staff if necessary—in on re-analyzing what levels and combinations of drugs are safe. Safety is *primary* at my Preserve!"

* * *

Farhim and Jehmut felt that they could not have seen more welcome sights than the splash of the *Meiolania's* tail and the disappearance of the beast beneath the surface of the dark, amber pond. The two men slouched in their seats, emotionally spent. Drops of sweat on their trembling faces glistened in the sunbeam infiltrating between the chassis walls and the cover.

Jehmut composed himself enough to speak. "As the monster, Abrih, deserved!"

Farhim could summon no calm yet. "We cannot think about him now! We are stuck here! How do we get out of here *now?!*"

Jehmut reached for the radio microphone but froze, listening to sounds outside.

They both heard the panting. "What is that sound, Jehm—"

A dozen vicious growls erupted almost in unison as the vehicle top rocked violently. The artificial fur covering on the cage above their heads ripped open in several places, admitting snapping gray muzzles with menacing two-inch white fangs. The din of overlapping barks and growls was shocking.

Farhim grabbed for the handle to pull the top the rest of the way down. "Close the—Aahh, you—ghaaah!" Farhim felt a penetrating crunch in his right hand and yanked back half of it, bloody and searing with pain. The massive gray head of the wolf, *Canis dirus*, did not withdraw with the morsel. It hung its two fist-sized paws inside the open lip of the tractor and thrust itself in, forcing the top open two more feet. There, facing Farhim and crouching to leap, was the largest canine the man had ever seen – almost a third larger than the largest modern wolf. For a split second, Farhim noticed its head, flat and almost streamlined, and its broad, rapidly snapping jaws lined with huge sharp teeth. Landing squarely on the soldier's chest, the immense wolf knocked him backward to the seat. It attempted a gouging wound to Farhim's throat but clamped instead on his upraised arm. The powerful bite sliced through skin and muscle to crack Farhim's forearm along two lines of crushing contact. Farhim's scream was deafening.

Jehmut jabbed the rifle muzzle between the beast's ribs and fired. The needle-round pierced through its heart, killing it instantly. He smiled triumphantly as the beast dropped beside Farhim. Jehmut spun around to face the front of the vehicle. He felt the reassuring vibration as his weapon automatically reloaded from its large magazine.

"Who will taste *this* next?!" Jehmut shouted, reaching for the handle to close the top. Immediately three more dire wolves leaped into the chest of the sloth vehicle at him. He was shocked: three, and he had one chance to fire. In an instant, two more were inside. Jehmut gasped and fell backward, stunned and cringing toward the rear cargo area. Then three more were crowding in. As the growling, menacing pack advanced, Jehmut froze in panic and his bowels cramped with wrenching pain.

Farhim crawled rearward, screaming. "Shoot! Fire *now!*"

But even with auto-reload there would be time for only one shot before the pack prevented more. The men knew they would be fully aware while being ripped to shreds and eaten. An ominous choice forced itself upon Jehmut: only one of them could have a painless death. A brief prayer flashed through each man's mind. Suddenly, yet two more hungry dire wolves jumped into the tractor. In that instant, the eight already in surged. As the animals leaped, Jehmut turned the rifle to Farhim's temple and fired.

Chapter Twelve

Only now the great noon comes; only now the higher man
becomes—Lord. . . . God died: now we want the overman to
live.   —F. Nietzsche, *Thus Spake Zarathustra*: Fourth Part

"YOU ONLY SEE LOGS; YOU FAIL TO SEE THE BRIDGE OF
CHAO-CHOU." ISAID THE MASTERI
"WHAT IS THE CHAO-CHOU BRIDGE?" ASKED THE MONK.
THE MASTER SAID, "CROSS OVER! CROSS OVER!"
                          — CH'AN MASTER TS'UNG-SHEN,
              THE TRANSMISSION OF THE LAMP, CHUAN 10

U.S. Central Intelligence Agency, Langley, Virginia
1447 hours, 16 October, 2014

Dr. José Nuñez was escorted at a brisk pace down the brightly lit
hallway leading from the Human Intelligence Department. He carried a burgundy leather briefcase which held the laptop computer
and antenna he routinely used in Iraq to beam files and reports up
to the CIA's Information Acquisition Orbiter, or IAO. Recessed ceiling lights reflected off highly polished white floor tiles and silvery
framed wall hangings. Most of these photos and paintings honored
spies while others depicted scenes influenced by American intelligence, such as the departure of U.S. aircraft carriers from Pearl
Harbor just before the 1941 attack. Nuñez and his Contract Coordi-
nator, Michael Abscome, rounded the corner to the administrative
wing of the building. Adornments in the hall changed to pictures of
former CIA directors, deputies and presidents of the United States.
They headed for the last door on the left. A foot long black and

white placard on the massive red oak door read simply, "Deputy Director, HUMINT." They entered Deputy Director Fording's office anteroom and were ushered by his assistants through two more doors to be greeted by the Deputy Director.

Fording was a friendly, silver-haired giant who appeared as if he would be as much at home coaching a football team as managing spies at the CIA. He seemed well complemented by his massive cherry desk, bulky file cabinets and numerous tall book cases. Fording reached over the desk and gave each man a powerful handshake. "Good to see you again, Joe! Good morning to you, too, Michael!"

Nuñez bristled slightly and recovered his smile. "José, sir. My name *ees* José. Good to see you also! It's been *six years."*

"Yes, of course. Sorry, José. Well, let's get right to it. I have to leave in five minutes to brief the Director on the Cuban situation. Sometimes I think the press has more influence than we do in preserving democratic governments—but not this time, eh?!"

Abscome smiled knowingly. "You're right about that one, sir. Not this time!"

Fording immediately recognized Abscome's attempt to ingratiate himself. "Thanks, Abscome. Well, we've got to put our resources where they'll be most effective. You've both done a good job. But that's why we're terminating the Al-Rajda assignment. Unless you two have dug up something incriminating on the Iraqis, I've decided to declare them harmless—at least as far as the Al-Rajda research is concerned." He stared at Abscome and Nuñez and waited for the evidence he had just solicited.

Nuñez spoke first. "Nothing I can put my finger on yet, sir. But Harrigan's ciphered personal files *and* his FGR program have been copied. All of their work on humans and human ancestors *ees* secret and the Iraqi researchers are using Harrigan's process in an attempt to isolate longevity genes."

Fording was not impressed and his tone slowly worsened, revealing his irritation. "All of that is old news. José, if you were in charge of revitalizing a war-torn, backward country which was able to sell *less* of its *only* resource, oil, every day, wouldn't you be tempted to steal high-potential commercial processes? Half the scientific community would be in an uproar if it were publicly known that they were growing ape-men over there. The other half would be hounding them to be part of it all. And everyone is researching the fountain of youth! Who knows if they'll ever find it! In addition, Nuñez, if they *were* developing germ or genetic weapons, they would be using modern human subjects. *Not ape-men!"*

Abscome spoke up for his operative. "Sir, I think what José is saying is that they need to be continually watched."

"Abscome, Nuñez: You two have had funding to monitor these people for six years. You've produced *no evidence* of dangerous activity. If you cannot provide me with evidence after *that effort*, then you cannot make me believe."

Fording paused to let his subordinates consider his line of reasoning and then revealed his higher priorities.

"Gentlemen, we don't fund permanent moles to just *live* in a country and watch things anymore. I've only authorized it this long because Iraq was a priority country. Iraq is no longer a priority! Look, Nuñez, it's not as if I'm cutting off your second paycheck. I need you in Cuba."

Nuñez was thoroughly insulted by the perennial references to his receiving two paychecks over the years. He cared about his missions and never got much of a chance to spend money. Given his now genuine interest in Harrigan's project, he was just as happy to cut the strings that controlled him. "So *thees* assignment is at completion?"

"Exactly. As of right now."

"Then I do not have to accept any more orders. Find someone else to do your dirty work *een Coo-ba*. I quit for good. *Don'* call me anymore. And, for your information, I'm happy with my work *and* my pay with Harrigan."

Fording glared at Nuñez and gave Abscome a menacing frown. "That will be all, *Mister* Nuñez. You are released. You can leave the IAO communicator and complete the paperwork on the way out."

Nuñez silently placed his brief case on Fording's desk and left to enjoy what would now be a real vacation split between Mexico City and Toronto. Abscome remained standing before the Deputy Director's desk. He was mustering courage to speak his mind without ending up being assigned to some satellite tracking station at the South Pole.

"Deputy Director Fording, your policy is that we should speak our minds, sir."

181

"Okay. Get it off your chest, Michael."

"Sir, Al-Rajda may well be no threat. But we don't really *know* that . . . and now we're blind out there."

* * *

Harrigan awoke sweating, quivering and in tears. He glanced, still shaking, at the clock and noticed that it was midnight. He felt a tremendous impulse to wake Tykvah, to have her reassure him that he was all right. He decided not to disturb her. Instead, he resolved to defeat his tremulous dream-induced feelings by confronting them.

He opened the covers and strode to the bathroom, closed the door and rotated the rheostat to produce the most light his eyes could stand. He stood at the marble sink, looking into its gold fixtures to see if the small reflection would replicate the first half of his dream. Only looking in the mirror would meet this requirement but he hesitated, staring below it still.

He debated silently with himself. *You, Harrigan, are not a wimp. So why aren't you looking in the mirror? Why are you even going through this exercise?!*

Harrigan jerked his head up and peered suspiciously at his dim reflection, then deeply into his own eyes. He scolded himself audibly. "Nothing! What the hell are you doing?"

He turned out the light and walked to Ben's room. He stared at his beloved five year-old, remembering how he had vanquished the boy's nightmare with a hug only last night. Now Harrigan was reminded, by recalling that event, of the rest of his own dream. Harrigan concluded that his subconscious had simply let Freund's superstitions and his son's fears get to him. He returned to bed and accidentally woke Tykvah.

"What's the matter, Kevin?"

"Just a bad dream, Babe. Let's go to sleep."

"You never have bad dreams! At least you've never said you did. Wanna talk about it?"

"No, but it was *soo* realistic. As if . . ." Harrigan began to weep involuntarily, feeling again the emotions of his dream.

"Honey, are you . . . Kevin, you're crying! What's the matter?"

Harrigan related what had disturbed him. He repeatedly referred to the images, feelings and his waking reaction as "silly," and "stress-related."

"Kevin, you have been working too hard. Look, *tomorrow* is *Friday* . . . we'll just take off for a long weekend back at *Megiddo* . . . *youu* . . . *mee* and *Ben.*"

"Can't. The last of the meiotic specimens mature Sunday and can't be frozen at this stage. If we're going to get any observations from them, we have to use the thirty-hour egg formation window—which should begin late Sunday morning. Then Mannie, Gregor and I have some gene-tracing work scheduled for Monday afternoon."

Harrigan paused a moment and expressed a long standing desire he had been harboring. "But I might well take tomorrow off. Just enjoy the fall colors. I might even have some fun in the Preserve."

"*Inside* the Preserve?! With predators *roaming free?!* Isn't that against *your own rules?*"

"The predators stay near the herds most of the time. Besides, I'll take some of the staff, like Bart and Mannie—they'd love that—and some guards. The heavy-lift suits are impervious to attack anyway. We'll just explore. Only for the day. Like a safari and we might get some useful observations out there to boot."

"*I'm* not going there! And I thought you might enjoy some time *with Ben and me?* I mean I like being able to take off whenever I'm not scheduled to work with José or Mannie but . . ."

"I assumed you wouldn't go with me. You've always been scared to death of the place! But you're right about the stress. So tomorrow, I just want to do what strikes me. *We* can do something together in the evening, and Saturday morning."

"Okay. Maybe you do need to have some 'big boy' fun. Good luck getting past Ben *in the morning!* But, if you do go, you'd better not get eaten! You're okay *now?* With this nightmare thing, *I mean.*"

"Yes. Thanks. Aside from feeling childish, I'm fine. Let's get some rest."

* * *

The rising sun illuminated the bedroom as Tykvah ordered the computer to open the drapes and the sliding glass doors they covered. She rose to stretch on the patio adjoining their bedroom, enjoying the scent of the flowering hedges nearby. Ben was already up, digging up part of the lawn with his toy construction vehicles and making his model prehistoric animals fight. The new day was breaking with clear, crisp weather.

Harrigan did not wait to get out of bed to arrange clearance and two guards through Najik. Then he called Freund and Lloyd simultaneously on the phone. They both jumped at the idea of exploring the Preserve and agreed to meet in two hours. Harrigan dug holes and tossed Ben around for an hour between bites of breakfast. He showered and dressed in a tartan cotton shirt, blue jeans and a tan, multi-pocketed thermal vest.

Harrigan picked up his son in the hallway and held him upside down by the ankles. "You look funny upside down, little man!"

"You're the one who's upside down, Daddy! *You silly!*"

Harrigan righted the boy and held him up at his chest. "Ben, can you take care of Mom today until I get back?"

"I thought I was going to school today?"

"You are, but no day care before or after. Mom's staying home today! You and Mom can have an adventure! I'll be back for supper."

"Okay, Daddy but I want to go with you!"

Tykvah stood by the kitchen door in her tight-tied, pink silk robe and eyed Harrigan with her 'I told you so' look. She changed it to a pout and tapped her finger to her open lips. "It's still not too late to spend the day with *us,* Kevin!"

Harrigan stopped and considered his options but narrowly decided in favor of his original diversion plans. "Mannie and Bart are probably already at the vehicle bays. I'll see *you* tonight, Tykvah. Bye Big Boy! Be good for Mom!" Harrigan dispensed kisses all around and left, driving through the access tunnel to the research complex motor pool.

Harrigan greeted his two friends as he the exited his car in the motor pool. The smell of grease and electrical charging filled the stale, subterranean air. Freund and Lloyd, grinning from ear to ear, were already being secured into the cushioned interior of their heavy-lift suits.

The chest-doors of the suits were open and his friends' appearance reminded Harrigan that he was no longer the spry young man of his self-impression. At forty-one, Freund had a few age wrinkles and gray hairs but had kept his paunch almost unnoticeable. Lloyd had managed to stay in excellent shape for a forty-seven year old man but his mustache and short hair were now graying noticeably.

The battery-powered robotic suits were only slightly larger than the cave bears they resembled: twelve feet tall. Their high-tech armor and bear-like appearance were responsible for the complete lack of casualties, or even injuries, by research and maintenance personnel since the loss of three soldiers two years before.

The light gray interior of the mechanism was interspersed with latches and control panels. Many of its systems, from the radios to the equipment and cargo holds to the temperature controls, were automatic. The device was animated by its ability to sense, replicate and intensify the force of its operator's body movements with almost no delay in reaction. Hence, the instant the user made motions of stepping, the suit around him walked. The operator could adjust the default strength of each of the four limbs by blowing hard or softly into any of five air tubes, one for each limb and the torso. An "auto-pilot" could also be activated if the operator wished to remove his arms from the sleeves.

The mechanism was water-proof, if correctly latched shut. However, most models on hand could not be submerged because the wire-mesh view ports, which were part of a hinged visor-like door at the simulated neck, did not seal.

The foot-square visor component held a set of telephoto lenses and a small video camera in addition to the mesh view port. The entire visor unit could be retracted upward like a door. A swiveling telephoto lens permitted wide-range viewing and was in addition to that used for the video camera, which itself had a monitor for the operator. Most of the staff enjoyed training on the suits periodically. Freund, Harrigan and Lloyd could not wait to play again with the artificially-enhanced strength and speed.

The disguise for the suit was of reinforced, real bear skin. Unlike a bear, it had dexterous mechanical fingers. Suit operators usually walked erect for comfort. Some occasionally had to pick up animals for evacuation to the veterinary clinic or to perform other duties. This practice was deemed to have no impact upon the behavior of the sapiens, even in the unlikely event that a clan member might chance to observe the suit being operated. Still, no one in a mechanical suit or tractor was permitted to approach too close to the sapiens.

Two Iraqi guards from the maintenance section were also suiting up as Harrigan approached. Chatting with Freund and Lloyd about their work and families, Harrigan climbed into his heavy-lift suit and had the technicians conduct the check-out procedures. The techs clamped and tested his access door, verified food, water and emergency supply stocks and tested the electrical, video and radio systems. Peering out from the brown mesh neck of the bear, Harrigan saw the group was ready and gave the radioed command to depart.

Their tour was to include only the eastern half of the plateau. The route was tentatively planned to run north along the wood line bordering the river, then loop south around the eastern edge of the open areas and return. The Neanderthal and Cro-Magnon families were now well established in the northwestern and northeastern areas, respectively. Both communities were still supervised by surrogates, who were alerted to keep their adolescents inside the caves for today. This was important because sapien contact with vestiges of the outside world might trigger behaviors which could compromise the validity of Singh's and Freund's studies.

As they ascended the east escalator, Freund considered the crowning achievements of the Preserve, the sapiens, whom they did not expect to glimpse today. He thought with satisfaction how the sapiens had developed reasonably well and generally safely under his and Singh's direction. It was, however, not the best system possible. The surrogates were the primary researchers and caregivers for the sapiens. Freund remained concerned that the surrogates were less than loving parents, impatient to receive bonuses at the end of their stints.

The Neanderthal clan was now composed of thirty-eight total members. These were comparable, in physical maturity, to modern humans from newborns to sixteen year-olds. They were to have surrogates for two and a half more years. Then they would be led by Kora and her three siblings, now nearing physical maturity. The Cro-Magnon clan had thirty-five members, ranging, in human-comparable ages, from newborn to twelve year-olds. Neither clan had any mated members but this would begin soon for those reaching maturity, after genetic screening and before the surrogates were withdrawn.

The sound walls had been gone for almost a year now without

any predator intrusion into the sapien areas. The barren rock of the mid-level slopes, where the sapien and the yeti populations resided, enabled the clans' continually-posted guards to give early warning of animal approach. The open rocky area itself discouraged predators because it offered no concealed access.

After the all-clear check, the five bear-like figures emerged in a line from beneath the trap door at the escalator exit. Harrigan called for his companions to walk abreast with him and for the guards to trail them. The trees were like majestic torches and the breeze scattered bright red and orange leaves across their view.

Harrigan switched on his video camera. "Look at those colors! Smell the fallen leaves! This reminds me, Mannie, of the forest and grassy areas at Fort Benning—remember?—in Georgia."

"Yeah! Beautiful!" Freund agreed.

"Ablaze! Marvelous! Like the autumn English countryside, I should think."

Harrigan resumed. "You guys want video for posterity? Switch on! But you can't get any sapien clips out of here 'til the contract's up—unless you want to risk Najik confiscating it and docking pay!"

Najik was indeed personally monitoring their transmissions from the Preserve's control room and spoke up. "That *ees cor-rect*, gentlemen! Have your *prrivileged* fun today but keep to the rules. A contract is one's word and one's word is . . . as you people say . . . one's bond, yes, Dr. Harrigan?"

It was standard operating procedure for communications within the Preserve itself to be monitored. The control room was generally forbidden to clutter the channel by talking when personnel in the field were conversing or dealing with an emergency. So, personnel in the control room seemed to be silent eavesdroppers.

Nevertheless, Harrigan always wanted to know when an officer was monitoring him. He did not appreciate this request being ignored. He brought his mechanical hand up to the camera lens near his mesh viewing port. He retracted four of the fingers on the paw. This was for the benefit of his ever-irritating eavesdropper but Harrigan knew Najik would not understand. Lloyd and Freund roared with laughter and Najik left the control room, vaguely sensing that he had been ridiculed.

Harrigan gave final approval to the route for their adventure, only slightly changed from that planned earlier. "Let's head north along the wood line. Then we'll head west to see the river life five or six miles up from here. Then we'll cut across the grassy hills below the Cro-Magnon areas and follow the tree line all the way around until we get back here. We should get the best views that way and avoid the sapien areas."

"Right-O!"

"Let's do it!" Lloyd and Freund were already excited.

The group progressed, in stops and starts, a mile along the tree line. They decided to cut to the river early. As they approached it, they surprised a harem of eight huge *Sivatheriums*, which they generally referred to as "sivas." The bull siva was irate to have its seven small-horned cows diving away into the river. It was a black-maned, dark brown and shaggy, moose-like mammal nearly the size of its relative, the giraffe.

Freund pointed at the beast as it crouched slightly and stomped the dirt threateningly. "*Ach!* My friends, we had better back off. It's going to charge!"

Lloyd shot back. "No problem! He'll get quite a surprise if he does!"

Freund was concerned about the animal. "If he doesn't knock you on your can, he'll break his ossicones! They're easily infected flesh on live bony tissue. Then, we'll have to evacuate him to the clinic!"

"Mannie's right! Let's just back off slowly. . . . Let's not invite trouble . . ."

As the bear-suits slowly backpedaled, the beast charged head-down. Each of its two four-foot ossicones looked more like sharp-edged blades than antlers. It sported a smaller, second set which looked like deadly triangular horns above its eyes. These were aimed straight at Harrigan. The siva's ossicone-studded, nearly two foot-wide head formed a frightful battering ram. Harrigan backed into a tree and the painful bump he sustained within his suit gave him but a meager foretaste of what the siva's crushing impact would be like. Harrigan's muscles tensed and his mind flooded with fear; he could not interpret his fellows' yells on the radio. He clamped his eyes shut and screwed up his face in anticipation of the jolt.

Suddenly, there was a crunch and the air in front of Harrigan's view was like thick fog. It was dust. Harrigan dropped the foot-square visor and peered out into the cloud, expecting to see the siva backing off after stopping short to scare him. In seconds, the dust cleared and Harrigan's cheek received a tremendous blow from the siva's nose. It hesitated as Harrigan, stunned, failed to close the portal. The beast stuck its snout inside to chomp. The bite just missed Harrigan's nose. Then it raked his face with its foamy tongue and abruptly withdrew.

Lloyd was upon it, prodding the siva's ribs with his partially retracted claws. The siva jumped and bucked away in another cloud of dust and joined his harem in the river. Lloyd smirked at Harrigan and adjusted his video to capture Harrigan's contorted face. Harrigan was suddenly aware of a tremendous itch in his sinuses and withdrew his arms to cup his nose.

"Ff-phh-m-n! Ugh!" Harrigan's hands were suddenly filled with the light green, foul-smelling and bubbly saliva. His right eyelid was dripping a long strand of it down to his cheek and his whole face looked Christmasy: red and shining with particles of chewed up shrubbery.

"You're lucky you've got a nose to blow, old boy! Those sivas can give quite a nip—and they like to taste their opponent's blood. Wonder if they would have evolved to be carnivorous if they hadn't died out twelve thousand years ago. I think several species were moving in that direction, by the bye!"

Harrigan was not yet ready to laugh at himself. "Isn't *that* a pleasant thought! How about you guys covering me while I wash this *spit* off my face?"

The three scientists got out and fell down laughing at Harrigan's ridiculous luck. The guards posted themselves and the trio walked over to the water's edge to wash up.

They remounted and the group continued north along the river. After a mile, they saw a group of six *Coelodonta*, woolly rhinos, crashing through the forest to reach the river. The male was nearly seven feet tall and fourteen feet long. Their huge double horns and wind-blown black manes contrasted with dark brown body fur and made for fascinating video footage. The small herd included only one male, which was first to drink. The females, almost as large, followed plowing up a muddy cove as they milled at the water's edge. The men gave these majestic creatures a very wide berth and walked another mile before Harrigan halted.

"Care for a rest, gentlemen?" Harrigan was ready to declare the rest if no one took him up on his offer.

"Absolutely the correct answer!" came Freund's response. Lloyd was already opening the access panel to dismount.

Harrigan established security for the group and began to dismount next to a large, flat boulder overlooking the river. "We need to take out the tranquilizer pistols and affix them to our belts *now*. You guards can alternate rest. But I want one of you suited up and looking around at all times, and the other no farther than five feet from your suit."

Freund felt the chilly water running by. "We should have brought some brew!"

Lloyd smiled and opened the right thigh panel of his suit and pulled out a gallon beer dispenser. "Have I got to think of everything?!"

The scientists' faces lit up and they poured the sparkling golden liquid, forbidden on the plateau, to start a late and long-desired lunch. They joked and pushed each other like kids. Freund and Lloyd grabbed Harrigan and threw him off the bank into the river. By the end of their meal, Harrigan had returned the favor twice over for each of his companions. They sat drying off and scanning the brilliant foliage, browsing herbivores and rugged landscape.

They remounted and trudged through thick woods, which extended right down to the river's edge. Soon they reached a newly reforested area, filled with saplings, which formed a wide breach in the full-grown forest. They were pleasantly surprised by a tiny, black, pony-like *Hippidion*, which bolted in front of them. Three feet tall at the shoulder, it was nearly an adult. They thought that they had spooked it from the more mature brush and turned on their video cameras again, grinning at the adorable equine.

Then, out from behind a small ridge ran its awesome pursuer. It was a fourteen foot tall, ten foot high-shouldered, *Phorusrhacus*. Bright yellow body feathers and a red and blue streamlined head plume marked it as a male. The colorful terror-bird was moving at incredible speed for such a huge predator. And still it was able to keep its three foot-long, hooked beak trained directly on its intended prey. The presence of the men in their robotic vehicles did not faze the dinosaur-descendant.

It dashed after the pony and, just as it was about to lose its prey at a steep-banked creek, it leaped forward. The terror-bird clasped the mammal in a crushing bite, raised its brilliantly plumed head and threw the squealing horse to the ground. The *Hippidion* honked once like a mule as the wind left its body. It began to flop, feebly, where it landed. The bird of prey grabbed it again, this time slamming the pony on its head. The *Hippidion* was still.

Lloyd offered a philosophical analysis of the event. "I'm sure there was no intention to be merciful, but it's better that it died quickly all the same."

The bird turned from its prize, lowered its raptor head and hissed at the men. All five were immediately intimidated, despite the protection in which they walked. The terror-bird stepped off with its meal and disappeared east through the saplings and into the low grassy hills. As it went, it scattered a herd of eighteen furry *Titanotylopus* crossing the rolling plain toward the saplings. These giant, woolly one-humped camels appeared oddly complacent and aloof. The creatures had watched the carnage from the vantage of their imposing eleven feet of height—until the gargantuan bird approached and scattered them southward. The *Phorusrhacus* disappeared chasing them but did not have quite enough speed to catch any.

Relieved by the bird's departure, the men continued northward. As they approached the river's shallow headwaters several miles north, they noticed a motionless ground sloth fifty yards away above the opposite, west bank. The twenty foot tall brown and yellow *Megatherium* was sitting on its haunches browsing in a tree. It appeared to have a baby on its back.

"That can't be a baby!" Lloyd exclaimed, reaching for his telephoto lens. "Whatever is on its back is white and tan! Let's have a look here." Each man rotated his lens into place and gasped.

Kora was now five feet tall and almost fully grown. Freund could make out her face as she sat smiling and clad with pelts upon the sloth's massive shoulders. "It's . . . it's Kora! Kevin, Kora has been allowed to leave the cave! Weren't the surrogates supposed to keep them out of view of us today?"

Harrigan was livid. "They were. That's a fact, Mannie. One second. Are you monitoring this, Control?"

"We have it, *Doctorr*. Better *moof* back and I'll contact the surrogates to *rretrieve* her."

"No, the surrogates will be subject to predation out here! We'll dart her and take her back ourselves. Then I want her surrogate to answer for this! Signal the surrogate to post herself as cave guard. We'll deliver Kora to her. Harrigan out."

Harrigan raised the right arm of his suit and moved his hand within it to disable the dart trigger's safety. He sighted Kora in the video viewfinder, activated auto-tracking and adjusted the dose to low. The first shot hit its mark and the shocked girl grabbed her thigh. The sloth did not notice the shot but did lower itself to all fours as Kora began to lazily climb down. In moments, she staggered and collapsed sitting against the beast's furry hip. It gently licked her shoulder but only managed to knock her over with its thick, two foot long tongue. Then the sloth resumed feeding on its haunches.

"Follow me and stay close!" Harrigan began to ford the shallow river, hoping he would not step in a deep wash-out.

Lloyd was not so rash. "Woah, Kevin! You Americans are too impulsive. We need a cable link before fording this!"

"You're right, Bart. Everyone dismount with pistols. Link up."

The five accomplished the task in under two minutes and remounted.

"Stay close. Let's go." Harrigan led the procession into the water and eyed Kora nervously as he progressed. No one panicked yet, despite the unexpected fact that the water began to encroach over their arms and up to the heavy suits' shoulders. They were all still dry, linked and making progress.

They were sixty feet into the river, almost half way, when the ground sloth let out a deep squeal. It dropped back onto all fours and stepped carefully sideways over Kora. Slowly and noisily, it crept toward the men and the bank of the river. Harrigan was beginning to worry but saw no actual danger. Then, suddenly, the sloth bolted north along the river bank. Harrigan was unaware the animal could move so fast, almost as fast as a bear. Then he saw it, tan, muscular and almost nine feet long. His view was no longer obscured by the sloth's bulk. It was the biggest cat he had ever seen. It was bigger than the cave lions. This silent, ten-inch fanged *Smilodon* was half again the size of any Harrigan had ever seen. He estimated that it was five times the size of Kora and almost five hundred pounds. The cat was cautiously padding its way down a damp ravine almost directly toward the adolescent, who lay help-less thirty feet from its immense fangs.

"My word, Harrigan! Do you see it?!" Lloyd was screaming.

"I've . . . I've almost got it sighted. I'll shoot it!"

Freund was already feverishly trying to raise his suit's arm out of the water to target the cat. But it was too deep. Harrigan experi-enced the same.

Harrigan raced through the water but the soldiers, tied last in the line were actually backing up; retreating to the east bank. There was no time even to order them to advance. The cat was twenty feet from the girl. It began to crouch. It suspected that its meal would be taken by the bear-like figures if it did not snatch her quickly.

Harrigan grabbed his tranquilizer pistol and pounded the access panel's latch. The chest of the robotic bear immediately flooded with silty water, momentarily pinning Harrigan to the rear of the compartment. Harrigan could see the cat, now crouching low enough to pounce, as he thrust himself out of the apparatus into the cold, murky water.

Harrigan raised his weapon out of the water as he swam, now six feet from shore. The *Smilodon* rose in a sudden leap as Harrigan's shot perforated its right front paw and harmlessly squirted its con-tents in the air. Immediately, the cat tucked its paw under itself and landed just short of Kora, on its chin, with a muffled crack. Furious at the distraction, the immense killer shook the needle out of its smarting paw and drew back to pounce again.

Almost out of the water, eight feet from Kora and twelve from the cat, Harrigan held his weapon with two shaky hands. The beast snarled viciously, bearing its two neck-slashing canine sabers and its meat-cleaving carnasial molars deeper within murderous jaws. It leapt again at Kora and landed with its front claws stabbing into her thigh. Its sabers disappeared deep below her brown and white pelt smock. She did not stir but sagged belly-up as she was picked three feet up off the ground by the still-growling cat. Harrigan gasped, despairing and fearing now for his own life.

The smock tore and Kora fell with a wrenching thud to the damp ground. Harrigan could now see that the bite had only caught her clothes. The cat crouched growling over her and looking up at Har-rigan as if to dare him to take its prey. Harrigan fired, pinning the cat's tongue to the base of its thin lower jaw. Again the round had pierced the flesh and delivered its payload to the ground. The cat was frightened and tossed the painful needle out with several shakes of its head. It was still deciding whether to take the body and run or kill Harrigan, the source of a new and alarming pain. Harrigan nearly panicked as he fired two soaked duds, which plopped ineffectually to the ground. He fired again, his last round, between the animals furious eyes. The needle stuck just inside the cat's brain case, flooding its cerebral cortex with tranquilizer.

Harrigan sighed as it hung its head lower, then drooled. But it remained standing, arching its still powerful jaws above the girl's abdomen. He knew that it might take one final bite, and such a stab would be fatal.

Harrigan leaped into the air, cocking his knees back to his chest and aiming his boot heels directly at the needle still embedded in the cat's head. As he reached the cat and kicked, it raised its head and dropped its dangerous jaw with full intent to sever Harrigan's lower legs. Harrigan's boots clanged off the left saber and wedged momentarily against its right. The wrenching impact snapped the dentition at its base. The jagged saber flew to the ground and stuck upright in the dirt. The *Smilodon*'s merciless jaw clamped shut against Harrigan's high-top boots and jeans, slicing shallowly into his skin and halting his leap in mid-air. His fall to the ground beside Kora jerked the cat's massive head back down, forcing release.

In a quivering, forced effort, the big cat rose above Harrigan. Its broken tooth socket dripped blood upon the prostrate man while its intact tooth plunged toward Harrigan's defenseless stomach. Harrigan knew he would be skewered even if the great beast passed out from the drug.

Harrigan perceived a swift lateral blur above him. It was Lloyd's dripping robot hands grabbing the tooth and yanking the cat's massive head aside, just enough for the saber to strike the dirt beside Harrigan's ribs. The cat lay motionless, asleep.

Harrigan could barely speak. "It was gonna k -h -h kill her . . . me too. Gees! Get another round into it before it wakes up!"

Lloyd got out, aimed his pistol and fired one round into the shuddering thigh of the massive *Smilodon*. "Never saw one like that, here or at Megiddo. Huge!" Lloyd paused for a moment and addressed Freund. "Good thing you jerked those blokes' chains to bring them across or I'd have never gotten close enough to jump into the fray in time!"

Freund walked up in his heavy lift suit, struggling to haul Harrigan's along. The guards dismounted to remove the cables. They were chattering some excuse about not knowing Harrigan wanted to keep crossing once the *Smilodon* came into view.

Harrigan got up, stumbled toward one of the guards and swung a fist wildly at his face. Freund jumped out and held Harrigan back while the other guard reached for his pistol.

Harrigan screamed his challenge. "Oh you wanna use that gun on me?! Come on, you cowardly scum! I can handle you too!"

Freund's tight wrist-wrench disarmed the man and brought him to his knees.

Harrigan, still yelling, grabbed the first soldier by his throat and thrust him to the ground next to the other guard. "You two miserable . . . *soldiers* . . . will return to the motor pool now. I'll deal with you *later.*"

Harrigan raised his hand to slap both guards but they ducked and scurried to their suits and shut themselves in. They turned immediately, retreated across the river and disappeared into the forest. The guard's unit commander was at the Control room and radioed Harrigan to insist on sending out two more guards. Najik had apparently been called away and Harrigan was able to persuade the monitoring officer to waive this requirement—if Harrigan would not report the officer's men to Najik. To Harrigan, all the Iraqi soldiers were worthless anyway.

Harrigan caught his breath and turned to thank his friends. "You two saved my life. Bart; Mannie. Thank you both!"

Freund treated several minor wounds on Harrigan and Kora. He even packed antibiotics into the *Smilodon*'s tooth socket. Then the three of them placed the girl into Freund's suit and they trudged off to her cave, well known to Freund.

Passing back through the forest toward the gray ridge, Lloyd spotted two small groups of totally different herbivores feeding together peacefully. Six brown, horse-like *Macrauchenia* were browsing; easily reaching twelve feet up into the surrounding trees with their abbreviated-elephantine snouts. They lazily turned their tapered heads to face the newcomers but concluded that they were safe and resumed stripping leaves off branches. Beside them, one male and six female *Megaloceros*, the massive deer, were chewing wide swaths through mid-level tree branches and chest-high bushes. Neither herd moved as the trio passed within ten yards, caught the animals on video and reached the forest edge.

Two surrogates stood at the foot of the ridge and received Kora. They both mouthed several excuses for their lack of supervision and carried her into the cave. Harrigan ignored the surrogates, except for a glare, and turned his party around for the return trip.

As the men backtracked south, about half a mile from the drugged *Smilodon*, they witnessed a *G. atlas* being devoured by seven monstrous *Canis dirus*. The men knew the six foot tall reptile to be a mighty animal and they could not imagine how the wolves had been able to catch its fleshy portions to kill it. Freund longed to be permitted to retrieve the shell for his children. That was forbidden. Instead, he and Harrigan decided to return in a month to retrieve the shell and present it to the village school as a scientific and recreational asset.

It was late, already dark, and the three turned and headed toward the river at a tired trot. Harrigan radioed back the report that they would have to cross the river to camp on the east side and cover the ten miles to the exit in the morning. They were no longer in the mood for recreation. They reached the river, checked the one-fanged *Smilodon*, still sleeping, and put the river between themselves and it.

All three dismounted and were just about to set up trip-wire alarms in the increasingly misty forest when Tykvah's voice came over the radio.

"Kevin Harrigan! You have a screaming child here who's scared to death his father is going to be eaten! What kind of stunts are you three pulling out there?!"

Harrigan rolled his eyes and hung his head, receiving smirks from the other two. "Is an answer possible for that question, Tykvah? We're fine and we'll be back by noon tomorrow."

"You're in big trouble, Kevin. And I *hate* this place! It's not fun or even fascinating anymore! It frightens me *to death!* I love you . . . and I couldn't stand it if something happened!"

A brief series of distant, low-pitched howls gashed the conversation. The men stared at each other and tried to present confident smiles and postures. Each gripped his weapon more tightly.

"It's all right, Tykvah, everything's okay. Really. Calm down and I'll see you tomorrow. I love you too. Ben's not at the mike is he?"

Ben's small voice quavered. "Daddy, I love you and I'm scared. I'm really sc- Daddy, *please* come home!"

Chapter Thirteen

BEFORE I FORMED YOU IN THE WOMB, I KNEW YOU.

—JEREMIAH 1:5

It is difficult to know when an embryo or fetus becomes a person, and when life begins. Surely the embryo is not a person . . .   — Paul Kurtz, *Forbidden Fruit*

AND IN YOUR SEED ALL THE NATIONS OF THE EARTH SHALL BE BLESSED, BECAUSE YOU HAVE OBEYED MY VOICE.

—GEN 22:18

Upper Rajdakim River,
Al-Rajda Zoological Research Preserve
0548 hours, 19 October, 2014

Dawn brought a chilly but invigorating zephyr to greet Freund as he crawled out of his heavy-lift suit in the temporary camp. Fog was beginning to dissipate off the glittery surface of the river. The men had awkwardly laid their suits side-down on the ground and slept without real comfort. Freund accessed and prepared the emergency provisions, waking the other two with smells of coffee, artificial meat and toasting bread. Harrigan rose, stiff at first from bumps, bruises and cuts, but the morning seemed to wipe away the tenseness and conflict of the previous day. He dove in his underwear below the cool river's whitening surface, accidentally inhaling water as he came up. He coughed violently but recovered quickly and sat on a rock, collecting his wits and drying off. Harrigan found himself contemplative and more relaxed with his companions.

"Bart," Harrigan quietly addressed the Englishman, "do you believe in God?"

Freund perked up and stared silently and curiously at the two.

198

"Well, yes. I suppose so. Don't give it much thought, really. I guess the whole subject makes me a bit uncomfortable. Doesn't it you?"

"Yes. I didn't mean to make you uncomfortable."

"No! That's not what I mean. It's just, well, I knew a bloke once at Oxford. Bloody pain in the derriere, he was; pestering people with guilt trips 'n having to 'get born again.' That sort of thing bothers. Not your query. Why d'you ask?"

Harrigan now included Freund directly by glance. "We study the mechanisms of life. But we still can't figure out what makes personalities; what makes people able to choose while animals are more guided by instinct. Well, I'm drifting, I guess. The reason I asked is that I had an unsettling dream, night before last."

Lloyd was curious. "What sort of dream? You don't put stock in dreams, do you? I mean, a hard-headed bloke like yourself."

"Well, Mannie, I know what you would say, I think, about this. So I'll ask Bart what he thinks and then you two can tell me if I'm just stressed or what."

Harrigan paused, looking out at the shimmering river. "It started with me staring at the bathroom mirror intently. Why, I don't know. Then, as I continued to look, I began to feel a gloating, powerful feeling. It was very intense; even enjoyable. Like nothing I'd ever felt before. Then, rapidly, my face became grotesque, evil-looking and more so with each passing second. As this was going on, I began to feel really scared. And I don't scare easily. But this feeling of power was increasing right along with the fear, and I just *went along* with it. In a few seconds, I began to feel or suspect that this odd feeling of power was false; some lie. This really got to me and I wanted it all to go away. Slowly, it did.

"My image reversed, becoming normal, and the feelings dissipated. But they were replaced by anxiety that it could all return at any moment. I turned from the mirror and everything was black. I was alone. Guys, it was *so* strange: I felt then like I was infinitely alone. It was agonizing, I felt so alone. Then I saw a saddened face, like the pictures of Christ back home." Harrigan's eyes began to water involuntarily as the very same feelings returned to him while he spoke.

"Wait! I'm feeling the *exact* same thing now. This is really strange! Like I'm back in the dream but I can see you, of course. Whatever it was, it was not a picture. I felt—if you laugh I'll throw you in the river—like I was a kid, being hugged by someone after being out in the wilderness alone for a long time. Man, it was so real; so intense." A tear fell from Harrigan's cheek.

"I know this is really far-fetched. But I woke up crying; totally unsettled. Even had to check the mirror. I felt I had to make sure my family was still there; make sure the world I was used to was still there. Is that weird or what?"

Lloyd just stared at Harrigan, amazed at seeing him cry for the first time and, seemingly, over nothing.

Freund raised his eyebrows and questioned Harrigan. "Was this 'hug' thing the last thing in the dream?"

Harrigan looked down, feeling curiously drained just from relating his story. "No, actually. I pulled away. I don't know why. And I sensed that the figure was crying; somehow feeling more intense sadness than I could fully comprehend. And I felt responsible; very unsettled. Then I woke and got up as I said."

Freund persisted. "And this is bothering you even now?"

"It has shaken me, I've got to admit. And I don't like to talk about things like this. It just makes no sense. It's got to be the power of suggestion from all your Lutheran talk over the years!"

Lloyd perked up, confused. "I thought you were Catholic, Mannie?"

Freund's tone was kind. "Well, the two churches have been reconciling; merging. The world is changing in many ways. Yes. I guess Catholic is an adequate label. Kevin, about your dreams: there may be something there. Listen, be sensitive to the gentle, lowing whisper inside you. Your own feelings and, yes, even your conscience can help you. If it's just nerves it will go away with some stress management, which I have been treating you with—to no avail. If there's more to it, you'll sense the whisper subtly yet unmistakably. And, if you're open to it and sacrifice your own judgment to it, it brings inspiration and joy."

"You've been telling me that stuff for years, Mannie. I'm not totally rejecting it but . . ."

Lloyd was feeling a bit embarrassed by all of this and itching to get back on the march. "You need a vacation, old boy! That's what I think. In any event, if we're going to see much more and get out by noon, we'd better get back at it, eh?!"

Harrigan smiled at his friends, embarrassed to have related such things. He wanted to get back and calm his family. But he was eager to continue exploring, too. The men rose to clean up the area and remount. They headed south along the river bank, observing that it offered a clearer path than the hilly grasslands.

Only a quarter mile south, however, they saw a sullen and threatening *Metridiochoerus*. Long, stiff black hair from her head to her middle spine stood up to menace the visitors. The treacherous-looking guardian eyed them from amidst her half-grown, three-foot tall piglets. The piglets had none of the four dangerous snout tusks their mother sported. But they were clearly vicious, ripping a huge six-foot catfish apart and fighting over the remains. The now more safety-conscious group walked well around the boars farther down river toward the minor falls which had formed at a boulder-strewn area during summer's lowering of the water table.

There, on a rock at the edge of the falls was a real *Ursus spelaeus*. It was trying to snatch the stocked fish, most of which were not able to breach the falls' rocky lip. The men stood in awe of the grizzly-ancestor. The noise of their stomping suits had alerted the great cave bear. It turned, stood erect, clawed the air and roared but did not attack.

Harrigan spoke slowly to his comrades. "All right. Don't provoke it! Just turn left and walk way around it—and don't do anything fast. Bart, go on. You too Mannie. I'll watch him and follow you in a few seconds." Lloyd strolled off, not immediately followed by Freund.

Despite its show, the *Ursus* had been intimidated by the three of them. When there were two men, it had some interest in charging to keep them from its fishing spot. Now, there was one. The bear rose immediately and bounded toward Harrigan. Harrigan's stomach sank.

He turned toward his friends and he screamed into his microphone. "Holy sh- . . . run!"

Harrigan tried to call to his friends, despite the thudding and jarring of his less than graceful sprint. "I hope.. these suits . . . are faster . . . than the . . . real thing!"

They were. Soon outdistancing the bear and its roars, they began to feel safe, almost invincible in these slightly awkward but thoroughly enjoyable robotic suits. They stopped near the steep river bank and laughed, needing to completely and finally purge the previous day's angst and this recent scare.

Freund spoke up, still out of breath from the run. "I have never had a better time in my life, Kevin. Thanks!"

"Same here, Kevin. I think they'll make a mint when this place is converted to a park. An absolute mint! Once you find a way to take some aggression out of those big cats, anyway!"

Harrigan drew away from sucking on his water siphon. "Well, we'll never see any of that money. They'll probably fire us all when the contract is up—and not continue any genuine research. But we have it with only minor restrictions to ourselves for a few years yet."

Harrigan hesitated, remembering that Lloyd barely spent three months of the year at the Preserve while Freund kept shuttling back and forth to Megiddo. "When will you go back to see Gertrude and the kids next, Mannie? Its for the usual four weeks, right?"

"Right. Oh, I suppose in a week or so. You and I have a lot to do Monday with Gregor and there will be at least a week of analyzing the data after that. How about you, Bart. Where are you off to next? In search of more specimens to help us keep the genetic stock diverse? Of course, there's a lot we can do in the lab to deal with any defects."

"Najik has me off next week to the South Pacific. He wants fossil *Megalanias*, perfect ones rather than Komodo dragons. And another 'charmer' rumored to be still-thriving in the outback of Tasmania: *Thylacoleo*. Looks like the wombat from hell, I gather from reports!"

Harrigan perked up, angered by the news. *"Megalania*, the giant lizard? And *Thylacoleo*, the buck-toothed, marsupial lion? Woah! Wrong. Nobody goes on expeditions or starts projects without *my* say-so! What the hell does Najik think he's going to do with killers like those? *Megalanias* would eat one of these robot suits for a snack and thylacs would be as vicious as *Smilodons!* No go, Bart."

"But, Kevin, I was given to understand by Najik that he—"

"I'll deal with that . . . Najik, are you monitoring this?"

"Yes, Dr. Harrigan, this is Lieutenant Colonel Najik. Perhaps we should discuss the matter when you return?"

"Get this Najik: Keep crossing me. I'll have your job! And if you think . . ."

"When you return, Dr. Harrigan. When you return."

"And stop monitoring our conversations without announcing yourself!"

"As you wish, Doctor. Najik out." Najik tapped his pen on his hat to make a switch-off sound and continued to sit smiling at the radio console.

Freund's voice had a calming effect. "Let's not let it ruin the day, Kevin. You'll square him away later."

Lloyd spoke up. "I didn't mean to cause a problem, Kevin."

"I know, Bart. It's okay. I'll have a word with Mon. That is, if he will take time from his presidential campaign to deal with this issue. Well, you're right. Lets salvage *some* fun this morning!"

The group pressed on, passing a pair of angry-looking, ten-foot tall mastodons in the forest. These were of the species, *Mammut americanum*. Their bulging neck and shoulder muscles and fluffy red coat made it seem that they had no necks at all. They had smaller ears than mammoths and sharp, subtly curved tusks that looked more like horns. The Megiddo Preserve had paid an astronomical sum to obtain this pair's baby a few months earlier.

Lloyd edified the group. "These mastodons possess low-crowned, conical molars for tearing up leaves, unlike their grass-eating mammoth cousins. Jungle and forest dwellers, many of them were, from the Great Lakes down to Patagonia. Strictly leaf eaters but bloody *dangerous* brutes, if you ask me."

Freund interjected a subtle admonishment. "I saw one of those brawny proboscideans gore an *Elasmotherium* on my last trip out. Something panicked the mastodons and the obstinate rhino wouldn't get out of the way. Smythe was unable to save the rhino."

Harrigan looked at his console and noticed that it was approaching nine. "Sometimes I wonder how safe we are, even in these robotic suits. Okay, let's pick up the pace, guys, if you want to see the rest of the east half by noon."

"Off we go, then, wha-" Lloyd turned and jogged into an oak tree. "Ooff! Watch out for that tree, chaps!"

The other two smirked and chuckled quietly, unseen inside their bear-suits. Harrigan rolled his eyes, imagining that he never did anything absentmindedly.

They began to trot, which was not effortless but it did take full advantage of the suit's strength amplification. Leaving the river and crossing the remainder of the band of forest, they gazed directly eastward about four hundred feet into a magnificent herd of Imperial Mammoths. This part of the plateau was hilly but offered more grass than the south. Each man stopped and flipped his telephoto lens into place. It appeared to be a large herd, by Preserve standards.

Three adult males were converging on the usually exclusively matriarchal group from different directions. These loner-bulls were each about twelve feet tall at the shoulder and had thick, white curling tusks. They immediately began to joust with one another. Their roars sounded more like freight train blasts than elephant bleating. The bulls towered above eleven scurrying females whose tusks were half the size of those of the males.

There were no babies in view. One very large female, presumably the prize over which the battle was being waged, appeared to be in estrus. Two of the females were obviously immature, at six feet in height and with no tusks. The animals ignored the expedition's presence. Most cows focused on the escalating fight, only occasionally ripping up bundles of tall grass to eat. Each member of the herd was beginning to get its winter coat. Their new coats were not yet matted from skin oil and winter's weathering. Long red and black tufts, thicker at their spines, draped the huge forms.

Lloyd was cautious. "We shouldn't get any closer. Smythe tells me the bulls are very irritable this time of year and have been known to charge. They are faster than elephants; as fast as our suits."

"Fine. We'll go around no closer than this." Harrigan adjusted his video camera before moving on. He knew Ben would get a kick out of *this* animal. The combatants' blasting roars got louder, more frequent and threatening.

Suddenly, two of the males thrust at the largest male, ripping its trunk at the base. The old mammoth hauled himself up on his hind legs but could not get far, his tusks entangled with those of his rivals. He thrust sideways then pulled backwards, freeing himself only with the loud snapping of his twenty foot long left tusk. At first, the men could not see the break. But then, as it shook its great head, the left tusk sagged and dragged on the ground. It had split beneath the skin at the skull. Blood gushed along its length from the torn flesh. The youngest bull rushed at the elder and jumped upon the sagging, bloody tusk, finally snapping it from its breaking socket and slapping it hard to the ground. The elder shook his head violently and turned, racing east toward the forest and mountain ridge. It was chased relentlessly by the next oldest but escaped, vanquished.

Freund was concerned. "Should we have Control send out a tranquilizer crew to recover him to the vet clinic, Kevin?"

"Nope. He can be treated up here. Control! There's a large aging mammoth moving toward the ridge east of our location. He's lost a tusk at the base and his trunk is bleeding. Send out a vet crew and fix him up, please."

"Yes, *Doctorr*. Dr. Smythe will be sent there shortly. *Contrrol* out."

The two victorious males did not resume the battle. Instead the youngest, who had not pursued the vanquished bull, simply turned and caught the female. The other bull had wasted his time and, noticing he had lost by default, attacked and demolished a nearby tree to vent his frustration. Harrigan considered whether to continue the video and decided it was all part of life. In moments, the herd calmed down and began to trudge north out of view.

"Magnificent creatures!" Lloyd shouted. "Absolutely unparalleled!"

The trio trotted south putting the roughest of the hilly ground behind them. As they scaled one last, modest rise, a wide, four foot tall gray cone pointed directly at Lloyd from a thicket fifteen feet away.

The image did not immediately register in Lloyd's, or anyone's, mind. "What's this here? By Jove! It appears to be an . . ."

The *Elasmotherium* sprang from the bushes with a loud, growling snort. The single, volcano-like horn raised up menacingly. Then the imposing beast halted and turned its grotesque head sideways to better view Lloyd and his companions. The rhino-like creature had never been attacked by a bear and could not recognize the man-made odors. It stood its ground, snorting, stomping and confused. The scientists could feel the vibration of each thump of its hooves upon the dusty ground. They were awed by the thick, fluffy gold fur covering the upper third of the giant's eight-foot tall body and contrasting with the long burgundy wool adorning the rest of it. The creature was nearly as wide as it was tall. They backed up slowly as a precaution.

Too late. The massive head swung straight again on its hulking shoulders and its stomping feet thrust clods of earth behind it with sudden fury. Lloyd gasped, knowing the horn's impact would knock him unconscious if it did not pierce the armored suit and gore him. It was now only five feet from ramming its warhead-like, fifteen foot long bulk right into Lloyd's abdomen. The Englishman jumped right, then inadvertently slipped left. He blew hard on the leg strength controls, leaped high and twisted in an attempt to right himself. The maneuver landed Lloyd stomach-down atop the bewildered beast.

"Yeeha! Ride 'em Bart!" Harrigan was astounded and shrieked with laughter.

Freund, initially shocked, could not resist the humor of it all. "Bart, you've been watching too many American rodeo films!"

Up and over the rise, Lloyd rode the *Elasmotherium* with his friends in close pursuit. Lloyd was too petrified to do anything but clutch to the behemoth's neck and loins. After a moment, the beast realized it had nothing to charge and was experiencing a new and frightening sensation, a crushing weight—even for this beast—on its back. It stopped short, crunching Lloyd hard into its horn and giving him a mild concussion in the process. It shook its head in fright as the other two men hemmed it in between them. At once, it bucked like a horse and threw Lloyd off to its right. Lloyd landed on his back with a mighty thud and the *Elasmotherium* rushed off into the brush, still snorting and kicking.

"Gees, are you okay, Bart?" Harrigan knelt beside his fallen comrade.

"Oh, my head! But, yes, I suppose so. What a ride!"

Freund was concerned to know if Lloyd had been injured in the fall. "Bart, is your back all right?!"

"I'm fine, old boy," Lloyd retorted. "If I can survive *that beast* with a minor bump to the bean, I can take on anything here! Not to worry! Let's move on, chaps! Where's your sense of adventure?! Oh, oww!"

Freund dismounted to examine Lloyd's head anyway. Harrigan posted himself as guard while Freund administered first aid to the overconfident British cowboy. Then, the expedition pressed on.

Again trotting to make good time, the group traversed another mile before halting in awe of what nature was like forty thousand years ago. They video-captured a pride of two massive black-maned cave lions and six lionesses, which sported more modest black manes. The big cats were all chasing a *Diprotodon* at the forest edge.

Male cave lions occasionally tolerated each other in a pride. But they only participated in hunts of large prey and the eight foot long male *Diprotodon* certainly was big.

The immense brown marsupial's white stripes were not adequate camouflage. But it was surprisingly fast and agile, terminally ripping one of the lionesses open along the rib cage with its own deadly claws. The two males finally brought it down by its neck and long snout. The huge jaws of the lion clamped the marsupial's throat closed to asphyxiate it. The females immediately tore open its gut and began stripping its ribs well before it succumbed. The men were simultaneously enthralled and aghast.

The trio reached the level grasslands about noon. After a brief walk through the grass, the explorers neared the east escalator entrance and called for an all-clear check. The all-clear was not issued, however. There was an animal obscured in the thick foliage beside the grassy forest recess, where the access door was located. A recorded saber-tooth snarl and artificial scent were automatically emitted by the escalator access itself. The audio cat roar alerted two immense tan *Ancylotheriums*. They thrust their heads out from a clump of high bushes, revealing thick, brawny necks and dangerous, raised-up claws. The confused and frightened herbivores immediately faced the source of the sound and scent. Adult ancies were known to crush *Smilodons* with their wide, three-toed hoof-claws—powered by two foot wide, muscular legs. The belligerent male approached for a fight.

"Control! Open the hatch *now!* There's an ancy up here thinking we're *Smilodons* because of *your* repellent—and he wants to stomp us!"

The grass-covered hydraulic hatch opened and the three men clambered inside, just avoiding the feisty giant. They shot video of it all but were glad to get home from their fun—physically intact.

* * *

Harrigan put off tearing into Najik until after he had had some time with Tykvah and Ben. But Saturday evening came quickly and he did not want Najik to get away with so many irritations. He walked to Najik's home in the housing complex and invited him to walk down the lamp-lit street. He stopped at a corner bench and stared Najik directly in his cold eyes.

"I know you've been copying my ciphered files. I know you've been monitoring lab work and conversations. I think you've even been responsible for keeping some of my people's scientific papers out of the journals—and we've kept to the contractual secrecy on the sapien research. I've received complaints from staff members. Several believe that they have been followed during vacations and on furloughs. Several file transfers on the Internet have registered as completed but actually never reached their destination. Now, you're usurping my authority with Dr. Lloyd. I am going to discuss these issues with Minister Mon. And, if I get my way, you will lose your command."

"Dr. Harrigan, you are most *cor-rect*. I have been *afrraid* that you or your people would try to smuggle valuable commercial secrets out of my country. We will, one day, depend for our economic lives on non-*petrroleum* industries. That *ees* why there are significant *mo-ne-tar-ry* and privilege penalties for *rrules* violations. I will be held *per-sonally* responsible for loss of any potential patent. I have feared *that* more than any discipline you might trigger. Yet, I offer you and your staff my apologies. These precautions will cease if I can get you to have outgoing *com-mun-i-ca-tions* reviewed jointly with me *beforre* release."

Harrigan was taken aback by the admission and the conciliatory tone. Still, he was not satisfied. "You have said nothing about sending Dr. Lloyd out without approval from me."

"The contract states that, *ahfter* the sixth year, species selection is the *pre-ro-gative* of the Preserve. I thought you knew that."

"The Zoological Preserve is supervised by the Project Director, and that's me."

"Of course. But anything not specifically listed as a responsibility of the *Prroject* Director becomes a *pre-ro-gative* item and, hence, controlled by a *go-vern-ment* representative: me. I do regret any misunderstanding, Dr. Harrigan. *Trruly.*"

Harrigan was stumped and steaming. "Why the hell do you want a *Megalania* and a *Thylacoleo*, anyway?"

"The first specimen of the *Megalania* was found in an unidentified dynastic structure in *thees* country. Minister Mon believes that this reptile was once a symbol of pride for *ourr* people. He feels that it is important to *rrebuild* our heritage, especially since the *destrruction* which took place under Hussein. The marsupial lion is to help keep the herbivores in check. The trees and grasses have been declining in the last *yearr* and we cannot afford to ruin *ourr* pristine plateau."

Harrigan did not see Najik's idea as even practicable. "The *Megalania* is cold-blooded and doesn't hibernate. How will it get enough nourishment to maintain its thirty feet of *hungry muscle* in winter?"

"As with the turtles though on a larger scale: *arti-ficial-ly* heated burrows. They will retain enough heat to hunt in the cold for hours from *gi-gan-to-thermy* and they can live a week on one deer."

"Listen, Najik: Two *Megalania* and six *Thylacoleos*—max. And I have veto power over your safety precautions when they can affect experiments or the other taxa. That's in the contract, too! So I want your animals to have shock chips implanted and signal emitters emplaced to keep them away from the sapiens' caves, water supplies and hunting areas. And, speaking of safety, I want Kora's surrogates disciplined for lack of supervision. I also want the rest to be more safety conscious and loving to those children. They're *human*—regardless of what *you* believe to the contrary!"

Harrigan paused a moment, wondering if he would have said this only a few years ago. He felt slightly less agonized over the sapien treatment issue. He sensed his judgment had at least improved.

"Very well, Dr. Harrigan. I agree. Now we *do* understand each other better. How do you *Amerreecans* put it? Our fences are mended between good neighbors! Right. Perhaps now we can come to trust each other, yes?"

* * *

Sunday morning was a madhouse in the Genetics and BC labs. Hundreds of accelerated-growth human embryos from around the world and from the Preserve's own ancient stocks were in meiosis. They were forming the twenty-three chromosomes of would-be baby girls' eggs. Very few of the three hundred thousand forming eggs in each embryo could be harvested and observed within the time constraints set by nature. First, it was not visually obvious which cells were undergoing the fleeting process at any given moment. Second, the chromosomes formed in under an hour beginning at slightly different moments in each of the embryos' eggs. If extracted too early, the process would not take place. Too late and it would have been missed. One new tool did help Harrigan's team overcome these obstacles, however.

The lab had developed a retrovirus which, stripped of its deadly genetic codes, could invade the embryo. It followed chemical pathways to the developing egg cell and "read the molecules" on its surface which signaled that meiosis was about to occur. Once cued in this manner, the virus released a spring-loaded "molecular hook." This hook ripped open the cell membrane; snagged and retrieved the nucleus with its still-assembling chromosomes.

A scanner indicated when that molecular hook had sprung. When it had a nucleus hooked, the virus was withdrawn from the cell. The DNA strand formation could then be observed directly. The process also revealed RNA formations and their activities as regulators. The short-lived meiotic RNA assemblages, now referred to as M-type RNA, acted to either suppress or express DNA segments. All of this activity took place during the linking together of DNA strands to form the chromosomes that would have become half of the coding required for a potential human being.

Chromosomal formation observations were tricky. Only some of thousands of simultaneously occurring link-ups could be tracked at a time. This viral incision method was first developed at the lab as a way to detect and repair genetic errors, usually caused by the inevitable inbreeding of animal stocks. It could also be employed to insert DNA segments into a selected point on any chromosome. But this technique was used today to reveal how certain traits were transmitted or archived between generations of humans.

By late afternoon all of the staff, except Dr. Gregor Ruliev, were assembled to view the results of their investigations of meiosis. Dr. Ruliev insisted on continuing Freund's behavior trait DNA project non-stop. He did not want to wait until he and Dr. Freund would be joined by Dr. Harrigan the following day.

Everyone was excited by the sweeping scope of this particular part of their research now culminating in the Genetics Lab. The analysis was swift, even as meiosis was occurring. Harrigan, especially, hoped it would turn out to be a breakthrough in this, his life's work. Harrigan, Nuñez, Tykvah and Freund stood in front of the crowd. All eyes were glued to the new eight foot square color wall monitor which displayed tabular information about more than two hundred ethnic groups.

The group names were arranged in unbordered columns and rows. The names had lines connecting them, as in a family tree schematic. Below each name, the frequency of occurrence of one of several types of RNA molecules was reported; M-type RNA in red. Beside each frequency rating, a "confidence interval" of plus or minus some number of "standard deviations" was reported. This interval provided a technical measurement of the amount of error in the frequency findings. Ethnic groups with the greatest prevalence of the M-type RNA, which had intrigued Harrigan for years, were listed in the left-most columns. The far right column, which was to list groups having a complete absence of the molecule, was empty. The far left column listed only one group, labeled "Hebrew-extracted." Next came Celtic, Arab, European, Central American, African and Asian groups.

Harrigan's face was pink and his jaw was hanging open. "I'll ... be ... *dog* ... *gone!* And so small a margin of error."

Tykvah knew he would question the results and immediately reassured him. "We've run this and checked it several times before final display. The data from the meiotic process scanners don't lie."

Harrigan was not yet satisfied that the analysis was sound and, so reserved any conclusion. He needed to check on Nuñez's modeling and analysis. "Tykvah, did you run a debug on Nuñez's model *as well as* a logic structural check constrained by *both* the modern *and* ancient genetic databases?"

"I knew that would be the first thing you'd suspect if we got any dispersion patterns at all. Let alone one as clear *as this*. I ran both twice. José's model is correct and this analysis is sound."

Freund grinned, exclaiming. "You know, Kevin, I always suspected it! Especially for a few groups like the Irish. And, now there's proof. It's just amazing!"

Harrigan looked surprised. "Why would anybody suspect that the entire world's population carries *Hebrew genes* coding for production of an RNA molecule that only shows up during meiosis?!" He jabbed a pencil in the air toward Freund. "Answer me that!"

"I didn't mean the molecule, *per se*. I mean that I always suspected that the Hebrews, dispersed many times in history to every corner of the globe, substantially assimilated with numerous other ethnic groups. This may even be a clue to why they have always been referred to as the 'Chosen People.' There must be something about that coding that mankind needs."

Harrigan still did not have his answer and frowned maliciously. "Woah! You're flooding my brain too fast! Mannie! I hate it when you don't answer the question! *Why* did you have this suspicion? And I'm not concerned with any 'chosen people' interpretation!"

"Well, I'm sorry, but historians have long suspected this. It comes first from the Bible as well as archaeological and longitudinal studies of cultures. The Celts, including the Irish, were the only people of their time to use the same chariot and war tactics as the Bible describes of the Hebrews."

"Coincidence!"

"And there's the fair skin noted for the descendants of one of the biblical Hebrew forefathers, Ephraim. Such a description of complexion is consistent with that of Nordic peoples like the Celts."

"So?"

"And the prevalence of blonde and frequent occurrence of auburn hair—like yours—in both Ephraim's descendants and the Celts is noteworthy."

"A few similarities, Mannie. You can find such coincidences in *any* two populations easily. Your hypothesis would fail any rigorous tests of correlation."

"Well, there's also the use of the surname prefix 'Ben,' meaning 'son of' in Hebrew names. Just like the Celtic 'O' and 'Mac.' Few other ethnic groups used surname prefixes with that meaning. It's found in Greek and slavic names—but you'll notice that the monitor lists those lineages as also having a high prevalence of M-RNA. There is scant record of this surname prefix *before* Assyrian invasions dispersed the Northern Hebrew Tribes—around seven twenty-two B.C."

"Mannie, there's just not enough evidence!"

"And there's the fact that they shared similar, otherwise un-heard-of, taboos about food and the like. Wait! Do I see you fidgeting, Kevin?!"

Freund paused briefly to note that Harrigan was not interrupting him any longer. "Then, of course, there are the Greek history tablets which describe a people called the 'Kimmeri' who invaded the Balkans from Turkey. Historians have long established that the Kimmeri left the Balkans to move to several points north, including Ireland, around five hundred B.C."

Harrigan was red-faced and fighting a grin. "Anything else?"

"Yes. Numerous Assyrian wall hieroglyphs peg at least one of the lost tribes of Israel as *being* the Kimmeri—the same Kimmeri written about by the Greeks."

Harrigan looked at Tykvah who, along with José, was smirking at him. Working with Tykvah and Freund, Nuñez had begun to actually read the Bible and was familiar with Freund's references.

Harrigan turned, irritated but still good-natured, back to Freund. "You're trying to see if I'll get mad or show I'm bigoted or something, is that it?! This analysis only shows that the Celts have the second greatest prevalence of M-type RNA. That's evidence but we haven't got genuine proof yet! Let's just have a look at the *generational interpolation analysis!* That will show whether there's any more evidence that the Irish and the rest of the world inherited Hebrew genes! You do the honors."

Freund knew he might be embarrassed shortly, if he was wrong. But he could not remove the grin from his face. "I didn't mean to put any distinguished leprechauns present on the spot! . . . Okay, I did mean to! And I think your reaction is a riot! Let's see if I'm right. System: Display generational interpolation analysis. Put geographic mapping on screen two."

Both screens flashed. The first now displayed the "Hebrew-extracted" name at the base and only rearranged most of the others. The family tree this produced clearly showed the genetic links between all modern peoples but, this time, in estimated chronological order of M-RNA transmission.

The second screen showed a world map. With moving arrows, it portrayed an obvious geographic pattern of transmission emanating out from the Middle East. Subsequent arrows seemed to those present to be almost identical to most of the human migration paths they had seen in high school history books. Five thousand years of genetic transmissions, which generally followed well-known historical migrations, were depicted in ten minutes and then began to replay on the screen.

Everyone's jaws dropped again. Harrigan was incredulous. "Astounding!"

Each stared at the other. Then Harrigan ordered one more screen to display. "System: Display regression on screen three."

The confidence intervals had to widen to show any links, indicating lower confidence in the regression analysis. Nevertheless, these intervals indicated that the output was reliable. Several ethnic groups were now depicted as combined or not existing at increasingly earlier points on the time line. There was no listing of Hebrew-extracted before five thousand years; instead, the label "Pre-Hebrew/Nomadic" was used. The molecule was shown to have been present in fewer and fewer groups back to as far as nearly two hundred thousand years, passing over history into and then out from the Hebrew-extracted line.

Harrigan turned to his staff and began to solicit interpretations of the data and of the analysis summaries. They batted theories, excited declarations and "what ifs" around for almost an hour. Freund's theory was that the Hebrew genes, responsible for proliferation of M-type RNA, were somehow necessary for humankind. This, of course, made for lively scientific discussion. But Freund had to admit that, even though the origin and transmission were now in little doubt, he had little evidence for his belief in its purpose. Then Freund noticed that Dr. Ruliev had been ignoring the displays and debates, despite his gregarious and talkative nature. Ruliev was repeatedly standing and sitting at his desk.

Throughout the day, Ruliev had sat calmly and silently manipulating his computer in the corner of the Genetics Lab. He had earlier said that he felt he was close to finding out what a whole series of DNA sequences, long thought to be useless, were doing in peoples' cells. In recent months, he and Freund had been tracing certain genetic sequences which they suspected influenced behavioral and personality traits. Both men suspected that some of these sequences were rendered, partially or completely, active or inactive by the M-type RNA. Ruliev and Freund had felt on the brink of significant finds. To accelerate their work, they had asked Harrigan to schedule Monday as a day to contribute the Project Director's own expertise to their work.

Ruliev could, indeed, be intense at times. Suddenly, he jumped up from his workstation and turned. He shouted at the top of his lungs to the crowd of fellow scientists, forcing everyone to be silent and listen to him.

"I've have found *eet!* Dr. Freund, Dr. Harrigan, *E-ver-y-one!* These *strrands* are not 'junk DNA,' as people have thought for fifty *ye-ars!* Most of these nucleotides code *forr* personality traits and related *prropensities*, like aggression. They're *hun-drreds* of times the *compllexity* of even those we have mapped in higher primates! Each one *ees sllightly* different . . . and one new set *ees* added each generation! During meiosis, half a new set of traits is formed and the previous sets *arre* coded to be dormant by *thees* M-type RNA! That RNA does more than prevent speciation! It preserves a record of every parent and grandparent back to . . . whoever was first! *My wonderful, fellow pioneers!* We have found the basis of human *person-hood*—and we can read that of *each* of our ancestors!"

Chapter Fourteen

The questioner asked, "what is the great perfect mirror?" [The master] said, "a broken earthen pot."
— TRANSMISSION OF THE LAMP, CHUAN 26

"The problem," she went on, "is that most parents . . . have been competing with their own children for energy, and that has affected all of us."
— Karla to James, in J. Redfield's *Celestine Prophesy*

Beware of false prophets, who come to you in sheep's clothing but inwardly are ravenous wolves.
— MATT 7.15

Northern Plateau Marshlands, Al-Rajda Zoological Research Preserve
1653 hours, 12 December, 2016

Dark clouds were imposing night upon graying, evergreen dotted terrain. Even the false light of the big rising moon was being obscured. Neither human nor animal contemplated the insidious pall deeply enough to see it clearly for what it was. The loss of light and the north wind were initially so slow that man and beast alike could easily deny both the day's end and winter's encroachment—until sight was essentially denied and the sun's warmth was reluctantly withdrawn, unrecognized, unappreciated. The warning of repeated winters seemed never heeded.

Twelve sets of predatory human eyes peered through cover of tall pines, whose draped boughs hid the hunters like a mother's apron over young bullies. They focused intently on fourteen nearly elephant-sized, brown and black woolly rhinos which were grazing a hundred feet to the west. The intent of these Cro-Magnons, males now the equivalent of fifteen to twenty year olds, was malicious and greedy.

Two irate and winded surrogate fathers, Ali, a medical doctor, and Harun, an anthropologist, were too far back to see that the line of fur-clad hunters had halted and spread out. They were trying to catch up by clomping through patches of icy mud. Sweat was washing the charcoal camouflage from their faces and staining the dark tan fur of their parkas. The pair only now realized where they were. They knew that the objects of their loose supervision and scientific study had been heading toward a spear-lined pit dug months before by the Neanderthals. The hunting party was far west of its boundaries. Harun caught his breath and called out loudly in Nostratic.

"Pit! Do not leave trees! Stupid bastards! *No* fall into—"

He noticed the Cros were no longer outdistancing him but were crouched on their haunches and fur-gloved hands under the trees just ahead.

Three of the fourteen members of the *Coelodonta* herd raised their immense shaggy brown heads and squinted eastward at the dim tree line. A large, elderly male stood three feet from the edge of a half-covered ten foot wide, canister-shaped pit. Grass blew off the creature's four foot long snout horn but, still matted and caught on the base of the smaller horn behind, fluttered and tapped against the fist-sized brown eye. The wind weakly gusted southward between hunters and prey. Oblivious to the danger, the rhino threw its head up into the breeze, freeing its eyes of the irritating shafts of grass. After staring at the tree line briefly, it considered then dismissed a dawning suspicion and resumed pulling bundles of brownish-green grass into its undulating mouth with huge, downy gray lips.

Mo'ara, the group's de facto leader, glared back at his assumed father, now running noisily into view. "Shhh! *Coelodonta!*" He turned and continued to study the herd.

The surrogates fell silent, stripped of pride for having twice already today alerted potential quarry. They advanced quietly and knelt on either side of Mo'ara, who ignored them and swept his left hand slowly forward—and held it horizontal. He was waiting for the bull to step closer to the edge before he would order the herd to be scattered. The surrogates were about to forbid the dangerous attack when they saw the intimidating beast step to the very edge of the hole. Mo'ara dropped his hand. He screamed loudly, shrilly, and rose to attack the animal. Mo'ara's shriek triggered an eleven times amplification of his shouts by his comrades rushing wildly out of the woods with multicolored spears.

The herd bolted immediately away to the southwest. The bull *Coelodonta* suddenly thrust his fearsome head up and lifted his front legs off the ground to jump and turn. The dangerous, hoof-like toe nails stomped back down, crumbling the rim. He bucked and faltered onto his chest at the edge, shaking the ground, and rolled sideways. He pummeled the pit wall with his front legs enough to launch his five ton body up into the air, precariously over the center of the pit. One kick of his mighty hind legs sent the giant leaping, rocketing, ten feet out over the trap. He fell across the opposite edge with a thundering rush of breath punched from his chest. The pit crushed inward, bringing the panicked beast within a foot of poisoned spears set upright in the floor. Tan and blackened jackets rushed at the pit, hurling spears that seemed to bounce from the woolly titan's armor-like skin.

Gouging dirt frantically from the top edge and inside wall, the *Coelodonta* raised himself upon the deteriorating rim. The fear-crazed leviathan thrust itself out and onto its side on the grass. It leaped defiantly to its feet. Bucking and hurling dirt rearward, it turned to face its stunned attackers.

The Cro did not run. Mo'ara had his kin scream all the louder and throw just two spears, to retain a reserve. Both struck the animal. One hung momentarily in its jaw while the other bounced off the base of its front horn. The bull *Coelodonta* roared and raced south to rejoin its herd. Angered at the loss, the Cro did not notice the snowfall. They stared at each other until Mo'ara broke the silence.

"You all have courage of fire," Mo'ara growled as the surrogates approached, "We defeat *Coelodonta* another day." He glared, then smirked at Harun and Ali.

Ali's voice was shaky but loud. "Now you follow us back to trail! When you do not follow us, you fail! We hunt tomorrow. You follow us!"

One of the younger Cro piped up, surly and indignant. "No! We follow Mo'ara! You are weak. You warn prey."

Harun slapped the adolescent hard across the mouth. As he retracted his hand to administer another lesson, Mo'ara gripped it painfully tight and shouted defiantly, challengingly. "No! Strike me! I disobeyed. You strike me . . . *now.*"

Harun stared deeply into the Cro's eyes and felt suddenly frightened by his own alarming thoughts. *What would you do if you knew that you had been deceived for so long? . . . If you knew how we sap your blood and study everything about you? Would you kill us in our sleep or face to face? How much longer can we keep up this useless ruse? Are we surrogates still needed anyway?*

All sixteen of the Preserve's Neanderthal and Cro-Magnon surrogates had each been increasingly plagued by such worries. Frustration, too, had been mounting for them over their own primitive living conditions, brief furloughs and the defiance of their "children" and "grandchildren."

Deep, gruff howls sounded in the distance. The snowfall became clumpy. Both reminded the hunters that they had strayed too far and were overdue at the caves. Harun placed his left hand on Mo'ara's shoulder and spoke softly. "Release me . . . son. Soon you see me never. Respect me until you may lead."

The Cro smiled at his father, releasing his hand only to brazenly spit into it, and turned to his fellows. "Gather spears. We follow Harun back. Now."

The troop proceeded north, led by Harun and trailed by Ali. They sought a path which Harun vaguely remembered would lead them east toward their caves. However, the expert trackers saw six inch wide paw prints in the deepening snow: cave lions, at least five, with one barely mature male. The pride was also heading north through the briars and barren trees.

Moments later, the roars were unmistakable. The pride, which sounded irate, confused and frustrated, was attacking something. The Cro group had scared away lions before. Harun wanted an easy way to regain lost respect and led them past several hillocks to a brushy ridge, where they beheld the vicious, deafening attack in progress.

An old, brown mottled *Daedicurus* was fighting for its life. Its deadly maced tail beat thunderously, wildly, in every direction. With sharp claws on stubby legs, it slashed back at viciously snapping lion jaws. The shell-armored mammal contorted left and right violently, squealing like a deep-voiced pig and scrambling to find any cover between trees and in ruts. It alternated between hugging the ground, legs and head tucked inward, and sporadic, active combat. But the immense black-maned lions far exceeded the egg-shaped herbivore's own impressive speed and agility.

The eight foot long male lion—surprisingly larger than the Cro had imagined from the prints—leapt upon the glyptodont's shell to get at the base of its lethal tail. Like a huge scorpion, the aging *Daedicurus* jack-knifed its tail and clubbed the great cat in its thickly muscled right shoulder. The big cat's pained bellow was deafening and threw all the lions into disarray. The snarling females backed off while the male contorted on the ground. Suddenly it sank its three-inch fangs vengefully into the middle of the offending mace-tail. Momentarily unable to rise, the big cat ripped the shelled mammal's tail muscles with its teeth and claws while the *Daedicurus* returned the gouge by severing the lion's tail with its rear claw.

This confusion served as Mo'ara's signal. He grabbed two of his kin and dragged them forward with him, shouting and screaming at the animals. The rest followed immediately, forming an intimidating cascade of hunters descending directly upon the shocked, crouching cats. The experienced hunters knew well to thrust their spears like pikes, rather than to throw them. The Cro hurled rocks and wood as they charged.

Lions turned in every direction, frightened and unsure which enemy threatened them most. The wounded male found strength to jump away and face the attacking humans. The *Daedicurus* crouched to the ground and waived its bloodied tail in every direction, splintering even ten-inch thick trees. Mo'ara reached the male lion and thrust a spear at it only to wound its cheek. The females crouched low, muscles bulging and ready to spring into counterattack. The male recoiled onto its haunches, roaring and threateningly clawing the air.

The line of hunters advanced, jabbing and shouting; faces as contorted and enraged as those of the cats, which roared and feigned attack. This final, snarling attempt to intimidate the humans having failed, the male lion turned and fled. It was followed by the females which appeared as brown and black streaks. Without losing a step, Mo'ara turned left to the *Daedicurus* and pierced its neck in one thrust. This was followed by several disabling spears to its tail and legs by the other Cro hunters. Several more penetrations to its bloody, spurting neck left the animal convulsing more and more weakly.

Harun, astounded, stared from Mo'ara to Ali and back. The only food the victors took were the animal's legs and tail. The mace was removed for a trophy. The remainder, difficult to butcher, was left for the vanquished lions or other interested predators. The Cro knew the dangers of tarrying at a kill. Dismemberment took only minutes. Everyone, even Ali and Harun, smeared blood on their faces.

Mo'ara glared coldly at Harun. "Lead us home, *great father,*" he said condescendingly.

Harun could barely meet the young man's eyes. He resumed leading the northward trek through the deepening snow.

They were unable to find the trail and decided to walk along the nearly level base of the rock ridge. The hunters were grumbling and tearing tree limbs in impatience. After awhile they saw the distant glimmer of fire: the Neanderthal caves. Ali came forward to Harun to speak privately in Arabic.

"Harun, we are not permitted to have the Cro-Magnons and the Neanderthals meet. *That* is for Freund and his people, more than a year from now."

"Each clan is aware of the other. They even know that *we* will one day leave to visit other clans, or so they think. Look, Ali. Do you desire to walk through the forest *around* their caves seven more miles? Or would you rather skirt the Neanderthal caves and have to go only three—on easier terrain? We can walk just inside the tree line when we near their caves. They will not see us. They won't even smell us until we're well north of them, if at all."

"Fine. It is on *your* head!"

The group neared the Neanderthal caves and avoided being seen by heading east just inside the wood line. Suddenly they detected the distinctive, pungent odor of sloth—and heard Nostratic speech. Harun led the group to the right, deeper into the woods. After a few moments, he noticed angrily that he was alone except for Ali who was trudging sleepily behind him.

At the base of the rock ridge, directly below the two Neanderthal caves, three figures sat conversing. Kora, her surrogate father, Abdul, and her mate, Rhahs, were scraping large roots to contribute to the evening meal. They were comfortably warm with their parkas open to the snowy, thirty degree weather. Neanderthals were naturally tolerant of the cold. Robust physique, extensive body hair and thick blood enabled them to easily cope. Abdul's own hairy insulation was due to hormones. Drugs enhanced his blood's heat retention. His barrel chest, muscular physique and temporarily altered skull features allowed his "progeny" to believe that he was one of them. He grew to hate this charade more each day. He hated having to teach these usually-gentle sapiens to hunt and kill because they resisted him. He even hated Kora's pet, now nosing at him for attention.

Kora's sloth, which she had named Yom, often found roots for her. Yom lay now at her feet with its huge tongue lapping the air and occasionally shoving Abdul's arm. It had a keen sense of smell and, as a huge male with lethal claws, made Kora feel secure. She had earned its loyalty years ago by recovering it from its dying mother. She had weaned, fed and caressed it. The animal almost never ceased to poke its nose at them in hopes of loving scratches. Kora and Rhahs were distracted and irritated now, however, having to listen to Abdul give them yet more orders.

"It is near time, Rhahs. Soon, you lead clan. I go away. I teach predator hunting. You refuse. You must not fear hunting predators. They must fear you."

Rhahs remained silent, rubbing the sloth's ears. Kora spoke instead. "Predators are over all animals. Predators proud. If we hunt predators . . . we try to be over all. That is bad. Not for us. We should not make ourselves high over all. One day you will say we must be higher, higher over even the sun. No! We are not high. Not for us to be over all. We are not like the sun."

Abdul was confused. "The sun?! I do not know of this. Make me know . . ."

The sloth began to lick Abdul, who recoiled from the gentle animal and its smelly saliva. He dismissed Kora's comment to focus on his point.

"Kora! Send away Yom! Send away now! And listen to *my* words. We must be high over all animals. No animal, no fruit, no choice should be forbidden. Our will is highest!" Abdul paused, irritated that Kora ignored the command. He heaved Yom's huge head out of his lap and began again in exasperation. "Kora, Rhahs, you should have power . . . over all animals. I—"

Just then two spears struck the sloth on its shoulders, narrowly missing the three humans, as a blood-curdling whoop blared out of the darkness. The animal's flesh was not merely thick. It had a layer of tough, cartilaginous disks. Yom was only stung but he squealed loudly and fled with surprising speed, continuing to grunt and squeal.

Kora screamed for her clan as Mo'ara ran oblivious into the midst of the three to pursue Yom. Rhahs stood immediately and extended his great, muscular arm. He caught Mo'ara in the chest, knocking the wind out of the tall Cro-Magnon. The Cro leader was shocked as much by the blow as by the Neanderthal's extensive body hair and appearance. He reached for Rhahs's throat, succeeding only in yanking hair out by its roots in Rhahs's neck. The two were quickly surrounded by eleven more angry Cro.

A dozen Neanderthals were streaming down out of the cave toward the fight. The two groups faced off, screaming and threatening each other with clubs, fists and spears but instinctively allowed the leaders to battle alone. Rhahs snatched Mo'ara's spear away and thrust it viciously into the Cro's face. It penetrated a quarter of an inch into the tip of Mo'ara's nose before he managed to push it back. The two struggled and Mo'ara finally managed to pull Rhahs toward himself to throw him tumbling backward. He kicked Rhahs squarely in the stomach and the big Neanderthal landed with his head on a rock in the snow. Scrambling to his feet, Rhahs grabbed the thick hair draping from Mo'ara's forehead and cocked his arm for a devastating punch.

His blow would have broken several bones in Mo'ara's face but it was held back by both of Abdul's strong arms. Harun, breathless, rushed up and stood between the belligerents. Ali joined him and, along with all eight Neanderthal surrogates just arriving, managed to gain some control. The fight was quelled. Mo'ara, temporarily humbled, was made to admit that he was wrong. As reparations, he agreed to relinquish two *Daedicurus* legs—but actually surrendered only one. The surrogates, tired of the entire affair, acquiesced to this as sufficient.

The surrogates sent the Neanderthals back to their caves and parked the Cro-Magnons at the edge of the woods. Then, all ten moderns present walked up the face of the ridge to speak privately in Arabic.

Harun addressed his grumbling countrymen and women. "As the Americans say, this is the last straw on the camel!"

The others looked puzzled and he continued promoting his point. "I am *not* going to put up with this place and these surly, dis-obedient *freaks* for another minute. . . . At the most, for no more than another few months. I mean that they are ready to be on their own *now*. Are we scientists or baby sitters?"

Ali expressed the same sentiment. "I've had enough, too. Even though the Cro-Magnons are almost a year younger, they are ready to be on their own. The willful bastards think they are in charge and I'm sick of it! And I'm sick of Najik!"

"I'll tell you what I'm sick of . . ." Faqizade, one of the Neander-thal surrogate mothers, interjected. "I'm sick of these muscles and hair and only two weeks away each year. And I just *know;* I can sense that someone is monitoring us when we are outside the Pre-serve."

Lishazad, another Neanderthal surrogate mother looked wor-ried. "There's no proof of that, Faqizade, and at least they don't monitor us through these walking stick communicators."

Harun was getting angry that any of them would dissent. "Do you really know that they don't? Najik is a slave driver! Look! We must act together. You have a year to go and we on the Cro side have eight months beyond that. Both clans are good at hunting and have everything they need to live. To these ignoramuses, this place is Eden. To me—and I know you all feel this way—this is hell!"

Abdul contributed rationale. *"And* our work is no longer of scien-tific value, in my opinion. All they want is physiological specimens anymore. Blood samples, brain tissue extraction, egg and sperm. What do they need us here for, if all their work is in the labs? Let the Westerners take over!"

Ali became almost loud enough for the Cro to hear him. "We de-serve our bonuses *now!* Harun and the rest of us on the Cro side have already decided how! Tell them, Harun."

"I've already spoken with the other Cro surrogates. They are ready to *strike* and they are with me on this. Najik and his superiors are afraid that premature publicity about the sapien portion of this project will cause them international embarrassment; all kinds of trouble. All we have to do is threaten to inform the press if they do not shorten our time of service and accelerate our bonuses. I say that we should send the Cro back *alone* via the safe north ridge route and leave one surrogate pair with the Neanderthals. Then, the rest of us should take the raft to the escalators and give Najik our ultimatum. We'll be in brand new homes in the best neighborhoods of Baghdad by Ramadan! Who is with us?"

Abdul smirked. "I am. But what do *you*—or anyone else here— care about Ramadan, Harun?!"

"Why do you mock me? I just meant that we should negotiate no more than two more months in this place! That is all I meant, Abdul! Now, who is with us?"

Harun stared satisfied into unanimously nodding, uniformly nervous faces.

* * *

Harrigan and Tykvah sat talking in their spacious gas-powered sedan speeding south toward increasingly darkening Baghdad. Harrigan viewed Freund's decline of Mon's invitation to the state dinner as rude. Freund was already on a plane to Megiddo for a four week respite instead.

Tykvah complained about the vehicle. "All this money and we can't own a quiet, reliable electric car here."

"They've gotta sell their oil someplace! But you're right. I don't like governments mandating what I drive either."

"Are you sure the reservation is secure, since we missed checking in earlier?"

"No problem. We're set for late check-in. Hope Ben's okay."

"I'll call now and check on him. And, Kevin, thanks for listening to Mannie and me about the sapiens' safety and living conditions. I thought before that, when I started to put Ben first and work only part-time, you'd lose respect for my opinion on the Preserve."

Harrigan smiled at Tykvah. "You're great at two things and I'm only great at one. Where would Ben and I be without 'Superwoman?'"

Tykvah squeezed Harrigan's neck and called the baby sitter. All was well at home, so the pair sat quietly with their own thoughts, staring into the cloudy night.

At least, Harrigan thought, bored with the desert's dark scenery, *an affair like this is a non-confrontational way to sell Mon on better treatment of the sapiens. Bugs the heck out of me when Tykvah and Mannie double-team me on this issue. Worse when they're right!*

Harrigan broke the momentary silence. "No use going to Najik any more. The spineless worm can't make a decision and wouldn't make the right one anyway. I'll bet he's squirming right now, knowing that he wasn't invited!"

The dinner was a grand affair. Gold flatware bracketed gleaming china. The wines were the finest and the rack of lamb was the best the Harrigans had ever tasted. They were seated along with ten others at a large round table. The Harrigans sat between Penter Wonn, an elderly gentleman serving as Deputy British Consul, and U.S. Ambassador Azhi Chorazin, accompanied by her quiet husband and her daughter, a recent graduate of San Francisco University.

The comely woman of twenty-three wore a low-cut, black spun-wool dress. She listened to the polite introductions and perked up from her bored expression. "Are you *the* Dr. Harrigan? The one who started the Megiddo Zoo and that secret prehistoric animal farm here in Iraq?"

"Secret? It's not secret; just closed to the public for awhile yet. But thanks for recognizing my work, Miss . . ."

Her mother glared at her, knowing her daughter would speak in a display of rebelliousness. "I've taken a new name from my faith. Cabreem Sadeh. Like it?"

She batted her eyelashes and directed a pouting grin at Harrigan, winning her fierce glares from Tykvah.

"Uh, yes. That's very nice, Cabreem, to show dedication to your faith. What religion is it?" As soon as he had asked the question, Harrigan realized that it was considered gauche to bring up religion at such gatherings.

"It's Wicca. I felt inspired reading that new book, *Twelve Truths, One Objective.* You see, the goal in humankind's spiritual and physical evolution is to become hyperaware; to vibrate as one with the sentient universe. Any of the twelve truths will lead you there: mine is White Witchcraft. Another path is Gnostic Complexity Theory, a third is—"

Wonn, indignant and offended, rose violently. He spilled Chardonnay down the side of his tuxedo. "Stop this claptrap; counsel by words without knowledge! One must have insight to give it!

226

Such empty things are empty! There is only one truth: God so loved the world that—"

"Ah! Look, they're serving Turkish Coffee! Let's all sit and have some, *quietly!*" Harrigan interrupted forcefully, changing the subject to avoid the discomfort of this argument which his poor judgment had ignited.

After dinner Harrigan excused himself from the table, leaving Tykvah to endure the civil but still not friendly conversation. Tykvah now quietly had Wonn finish what he was going to say earlier, for she felt very curious and had a lingering sense that it was consequential. She switched to Harrigan's chair and listened.

At the head table, Harrigan managed to gain Mon's attention, and Hassan's seat. Mon led him to a private room, with Hassan in tow, after small talk.

Mon spoke in a level tone that left Harrigan uncertain whether there would be conflict or agreement. "I *underrstand* from your letter, Kevin, that you want me to order Najik to reinstall the sound walls and halt the use of *embrryonic* tissue in *ourr* research. You want the surrogates trained in *betterr* parent-hood, or something like that, too."

"Ismail, it is in *your* interest to preclude injury to the sapiens. We are learning so much about their physical strength, immune systems, genetic influences on neurology and behavior. The comparative studies between Neanderthal and Cro-Magnon continue to reveal an immense amount about our own genome's evolution, especially since the Cros are so close to ourselves. But we don't need to subject them to so much danger and such Spartan living conditions."

"Have any of the sapiens complained, *exprressed* a need for hot and cold running water, closets or food *pro-ces-sorrs?* Or the *embrryos* either, for that matter?"

Harrigan stared irate, galled at Mon for the cynicism veiled by lack of intonation. He continued trying a conciliatory approach.

"Ismail, you must agree that the sapiens need a genuine sense of family to develop societal structures we can validly study."

"You could be correct about the surrogates' commitment to their *childrren*. Najik has *apprraised* their performance as somewhat *unsatis-factorry*. But experts agree that most parents are psychologically violent; controlling of their children. This is an insight I have personally experienced. Yet I have developed . . . well *enough.*"

Harrigan felt oddly distracted. His eyes floated past Mon's to a small photo on the wall. It showed a bearded, stern-faced man in his fifties with mesmerizing eyes. Its brass placard read simply, 'Belial A. Mon.' Harrigan felt inexplicably uneasy but dismissed the involuntary diversion. He snapped his attention back to his host. "You had a tough childhood, Ismail?"

Mon's stare was almost hypnotic and Harrigan was feeling a bit sleepy from the food and wine. "Kevin, there has *neverr* been a substitute for *strress* in developing *strrength.* You have already found that *envi-rronment* can affect genetic coding within egg and sperm. Would the sapien studies be valid, especially as to physiological and genetic results, if we *rremoved strresses* which actually existed during the time of these sub-species?"

"No, I . . . I guess not. Well, it's . . . hard to say, actually."

Harrigan was debating within himself; questioning which was more important: his research, his life-long passion to explore and create—or the lives of the sapiens. He felt tired and a splitting headache was growing in his brain. Harrigan was mustering strength to contradict himself when Hassan's pocket phone rang softly. Hassan left the room and returned within moments to address Mon.

"Sir, it is Najik. He *rreports* that the surrogates have left scant supervision with each clan and have confronted him to demand early bonuses and dismissal."

Mon raised his eyebrow and then frowned as Hassan continued his summary of Najik's call.

"Sir, Najik states that they have *thrreatened* to expose the sapien research to the press if their demands are not met. He also reports that an *unsuperr-vised* Cro hunting party is now five hours overdue at their cave. I feel we must send a platoon to recover them."

Mon glared at Hassan and excused himself, bringing Hassan to another room. He returned, grinning broadly. Hassan emerged sweating profusely and looking extremely worried. He scribbled notes on how he would redeem himself by disciplining Najik for permitting such a mutiny to develop.

Mon addressed Harrigan. "I have complete *con-fi-dence*, Kevin, in your ability to judge the situation. Colonel Hassan feels that Lieutenant Colonel Najik needs . . . to be counseled on how to better manage civilian employees. Najik will be gone for a week or so when you return to Al-Rajda. What do *you* recommend, Kevin, should be done in the *interrim?"*

Harrigan perked up, concerned for the sapiens. He turned to Hassan, who was scowling jealously at him due to Mon's snub, and sought key information. "Colonel Hassan, did Colonel Najik indicate that the surrogates would be willing to go back, locate and recover the hunting party?"

"He says they *arre* most penitent, now that they know the Cro-Magnons may have become lost."

Harrigan turned his eyes to Mon. "Troops, alone or in large number with surrogates, would destroy the Cro's natural behavior patterns. The project would be nearly ruined. So I must disagree with Colonel Hassan. I recommend promising to let the surrogates go, with bonus, in a month or two if they cooperate now. I would call immediately to send Lloyd in with *a few* troops in heavy lift suits to escort the surrogates. Lloyd speaks Nostratic but knows to avoid contact. I will join him myself if I can get a plane back."

Harrigan felt proud, having shone brightly while Hassan and Najik were impotent. He believed that he would be rewarded one day.

"Again, Kevin, you have *prroven* your good judgment and leadership. You have my authority and power to *prroceed."*

* * *

The Harrigans were dropped off ten miles south of Al-Rajda by Mon's plane. Harrigan refused to disclose to Tykvah any of his conversation with Mon, except to inform her of the crisis. Harrigan kissed Tykvah and was taken by jeep to the motor pool. She was returned by van to their home. She was intensely worried for her husband, in many ways. It was 4:14 a.m.

Bleary-eyed but energized, Harrigan fired questions at the motor pool sergeant. "Where are the Cro now? And where is Lloyd's recovery party? Why aren't the two guards I wanted suited up?"

"Sir, please! *Observerrs* atop the west ridge summit are *mo-ni-toring* everything! Twelve Cro males *arre* near the northernmost yeti cave, almost the north-south midpoint of the west ridge."

"Yetis?! The Cro will be torn apart! They're just boys, for God's sake! Where is Dr. Lloyd?"

"Doctorr Lloyd left an hour ago with eight surrogates and three soldiers. Your escorts *arre* already waiting atop the west *escalatorr.*"

Harrigan donned the mechanical suit and rushed up the escalator panting; envisioning the worst. He was alone in the dim, cavernous tunnel which housed the huge conveyor. He felt very ill at ease and simultaneously thought of his odd, unsettling dreams and of the conversation he had had with Mon just a few hours ago. He dismissed the turmoil from his mind by focusing on the task at hand. But as he stepped out onto the plateau, he sensed the blue-white snow descending everywhere as if it were a blanket of guilt covering him.

Harrigan and the guards tried to move quickly on the plain beside the southern forest buffer. They hoped to catch up with Lloyd's slower group members, most of whom were on foot. The wind's howl was surprisingly loud, even inside the insulated robotic suit. Snow continued, whipped up and driven, along with that already on the ground, by the fierce winds of the plain. One of the surrogates with Lloyd was squinting and screaming into the microphone of his walking stick. Both Harrigan and Lloyd could hear the attempt but could not understand the wind-garbled words. Lloyd's group was three miles west of Harrigan and was slowly approaching the ridge south of the yeti caves.

Harrigan, shouting into his mike, called Lloyd on the radio. "Bart! Don't wait for us. We're approaching you as fast as possible but you've got to get to the Cro before they freeze—or get too close to the yeti colony!"

Lloyd was deathly afraid of the yetis. They always seemed agitated and more aggressive around him. Still, he overcame this time and again to participate in this project which so fascinated him. He hesitated and replied to Harrigan's transmission.

"I understand. Roger and all that! Just about had a mutiny on my hands getting these surrogates to keep going after we left the escalator. Seems the blighters weren't too keen on this weather. I can certainly see why, what with this blizzard! Since visibility has gotten so bad and we've not a moment to lose, I'm going to have them ride along on the outside of these suits. That will prevent losing any of them, too. Can't even understand them yelling at their communicators."

"Good. Go ahead. And keep me posted!"

Lloyd halted his group, climbed out of the heavy-lift suit, donned his *Megaloceros* skin parka and pulled the surrogates over to his and the guards' suits. He yelled his instructions, that his party was to move carefully due to the danger of branches to their riders, and returned to his controls.

"Dr. Lloyd, Dr. *Har-reegan*. This is Control. We *arre* unable to track the Cro youths any longer in this *storrm*. The last infra-red sighting was one-half mile *norrth* of the yeti cave, heading south along the tree line. Dr. Lloyd, your party *ees* but a mile south of them now."

"I copy, Control!" Lloyd seemed excited by his mission.

Twenty minutes later, Lloyd could make out a dull glimmer through the blue-gray wisps about him. It was up the ridge to his left. The storm was abating fast and a hint of the full moon glowed in the gray predawn sky.

"Kevin. I think I've got them! Looks like a fire in the cave above. I'll dismount and head in with the surrogates."

"Excellent! I knew you could do it! You're a regular *Army Ranger*, Bart! Keep me posted. I think we've been moving faster than you. We're near the yeti caves, I think and—"

Harrigan felt the pain of the five foot fall in every square inch of his face and front. Then came a second thud. His guard likewise tumbled over the safety lip of the plateau cliff, landing on his side on top of Harrigan. The second guard halted inches from the edge.

"Of all the freekin' luck!" Harrigan yelled as he squirmed to right himself and the fallen guard. "Where the heck are we?"

Lloyd began to shiver as he closed up his parka and shouted into the microphone in the butt of his dart gun. "I can barely hear you, Kevin. We're on foot with the surrogates. We're almost up to the cave so I've got to keep quiet now."

Moments passed as the only sound was the wind and Harrigan and his guard grunting to climb back up onto the plateau. Then Lloyd's voice came screaming through the speakers.

"My God! I've got to . . ."

Lloyd, the surrogates and the guards peered into the cave unnoticed. Five huge yetis lay bloodied and still, jumbled in a heap near the front of the cave. Twelve grunting, mumbling Cro youths sat cross-legged around a fire in the back, eating thoroughly singed meat and jostling with one another. Lloyd pulled his companions back outside the cave.

"Control, this is Lloyd. Release anesthetic in the north yeti cave *straight away!"*

"Yes, sir . . . activated."

Twenty silent minutes passed as the gas dissipated and Ali examined the Cro.

Lloyd resumed transmitting. "Kevin! Where are you? Are you lost, old man? Better get up here right away. Half our yetis are dead. The Cro have . . . Well, Kevin you've got to come and see this! I've gassed the lot of them. Ali says there is no frost bite or major injury. I'm about to double check their condition myself. If I find that Ali is correct, recovery to the clinic won't be *necess'ry*. I'll have the surrogates revive them and return to their own cave soon after sunrise."

"Concur. I'll meet you at your location momentarily. Don't revive them until I get there."

Lloyd had posted guards to prevent the other yetis from approaching the cave and had generally placed the situation well under control. Harrigan joined Lloyd just after dawn and confirmed for the still-agitated surrogates that Najik's midnight promise of early release for them would be honored. After the two men were sure that the Cro-Magnons' injuries were minor and properly treated, they told the surrogates to return north via the safer and easier ridge route. Harun, Ali and the Neanderthal's surrogates were ordered to avoid Cro contact with the Neanderthals on the return march. The three pairs of Neanderthal surrogates with them were to leave the group upon nearing their own caves. Around eight in the morning, as the sun began to shine through the few remaining clouds, Harrigan and Lloyd departed with the guards for the research complex. The two men were soon sitting, exhausted and drinking coffee, in the research center lunch room.

"Bart, you saved me. I dropped the ball but you picked it up. I owe you."

"Thanks, old boy. There is one favor I'd ask, if I could."

"Ask it!"

"Simone and I want to get married. And I'd like to spend most of my time here at the Preserve."

"You and Kairaba?! That's great!" Harrigan thought for a minute.

"Yes. I can arrange that. It'd be nice to have you here more often. You can keep me from falling off the blasted plateau!"

Lloyd laughed with Harrigan. "Thanks, Kevin. Thanks for the chance to prove myself, too. I mean I've always been so awkward, even clumsy some might say. No one ever saw fit to trust me with a life-and-death responsibility as you did this morning. To lead people, to fight the good fight, as it were! And that's what it was to get the surrogates to help with the recovery. Quite a handful, that lot! Had to fight them tooth and nail. They hate the Cros and Neanderthals."

Harrigan began to feel shamed, confused and unsure of himself.

"The good fight? The key is knowing who and what to oppose, I think."

"What d'you mean? Sounds like you've gotten some of Mannie's philosophy. And, yet the man seems to have an insight I wish I had."

"I think . . . I believe the surrogates hate the Cro because they are so much like ourselves. Bart, there are patterns of human behavior, like fighting or rationalizing, that either control us or are chosen by us. I can't tell which. Those Cro saw the yeti and reacted without thinking. I've done that, maybe more than most people. I have always seen myself as a tough *in-charge* ranger-type. I'm just like those Cro-Magnons. They're too ready to fight and never exercise good judgment. That's my problem, Bart. It hit me like falling off a log—or a safety cliff. Man, getting lost out there was really embarrassing!"

"Don't be so hard on yourself, old boy. You're overtired, that's all. You aren't the wrong-thinker you believe yourself to be—at all! You are a man of vision, Kevin Harrigan! You are a man who can see through the likes of Mon. The greedy bastard has no true interest in science. All he wants is money from turning this research preserve into a park. No, Kevin. I must disagree, my friend. You are a man of good judgment and keen insight."

Harrigan lowered his eyes to the floor, not consoled by his now-closer friend. He was unable to quite sort out his feelings or pinpoint the sources of his deep, frightening ache. "Bart, those sapiens are human just like you and me. And yet I created them as if I were a god. The sense of that power and the potential to improve the *entire* human genome is intoxicating . . . and it's *shameful* to me. Yet, I'd ruin *everything* if I took any steps to improve the sapiens' lives, if I let them realize *what* they are and *who* created them. I can't do anything for them . . . and it rips at me . . . inside. I . . . I can't see clearly to determine what I should prize . . . what I should fight for. I'm a coward on some *deep level.*"

Harrigan paused, recalling Freund's counsel and searching for any insight that he could now draw upon. He wondered aloud if there was any truth in Freund's nagging. "Mannie says I rationalize, choose to ignore uncomfortable issues that challenge my beliefs. He says I don't have a merciful attitude, that I refuse to sacrifice my own paradigm, and can't see the truth—whatever that means. Bart, I can't tell if the enemy I have to fight is my own work . . . or Mon . . . or myself. I imitate God in this place. But I sense I've got to make a choice . . . soon." Harrigan's eyes were glassy with tears but he would not let one fall.

"Or maybe you need to rest! Look here, old man! The whole staff, myself included, admires you. Just consider the evils you've overcome, the suffering your work will one day avert, the insights you've attained! Great things by anyone's standards! As to frailties, well my friend, you're no different from anyone else."

Chapter Fifteen

... IN THAT PLACE THERE WAS A GREAT DRAGON, WHICH THE
BABYLONIANS REVERED.   —DANIEL 14.23

The first essential for success is a perpetually constant and
regular employment of violence.   —A. Hitler, *Mein Kampf*

IF ONE OF EVIL LIFE TURN . . . TO ME, COUNT HIM AMIDST THE
GOOD . . .   — BAGAVAD-GITA, ch. 9

The Abscome Residence, Alexandria, Virginia
0721 hours, 13 February, 2017

Michael Abscome's promotion to the Congressional Liaison Staff
of the CIA was, for him, a relief after years of hard field work. He
had removed his personal office items to his home Friday and
packed the car for a celebration trip to the mountains. But he had
not moved into his new Washington, D.C. office. An unexpected call
to an early budget meeting was making him rush. He and his wife,
Ann, were darting between the study and his garage loading boxes
and files into the trunk.

Ann was helping him load various items into the old 2012 Chrys-
ler LHS, whose early model electric engine was less than reliable
and which he planned to trade-in. "Goodbye, Michael. See you tonight!" She got only a symbolic kiss from her rushing husband.

"Bye! Got to run. I knew I should have moved all this stuff into my
new office over the weekend! I'll have to leave it in the car and go
straight into the meeting, now. *And* the traffic will be . . . Oh no! I
forgot to print off my E-mail from the 'work' account and I
need some of that stuff for the briefing at eight! I'll catch it in
the car. Ann! Get me the laptop and a handful of memory pens,
please."

Abscome set a box of files in the trunk while Ann rushed through the halls after the devices.

"Thanks! Love you! See you tonight!" Abscome drove down the manicured driveway and made for the George Washington Parkway. He plugged the laptop into the dashboard with his right hand and drove along the tan pavement through bleak, wet forest. Touching the Internet icon and then the 'unclassified work' folder, he voice-verified his access code and listened for the files sent to him during the previous night. The first two files were necessary for the meeting. After scanning them briefly on the head-up display, which was integrated into his windshield, he copied them to six of the pen-shaped memory devices. Abscome did not expect a third file. He accessed it and noticed that it had been a character-by-character text transmission that was not encoded.

"NUÑEZ TO ABSCOME: IRAQIS DUPED HARRIGAN. MASS VECTOR DEVELOPED. ACCELERATED AGING FOUND. LONGEVITY FOUND. MUST TAKE ACTION IMMEDI"

Abscome frowned at the words glowing dimly above his dashboard and grumbled to himself. "What is Nuñez trying to pull? Cutoff messages! Wants to play 'secret agent' after all these years!"

He knew he could not ignore it. Yet, huge volumes of new information for closed cases had inundated the agency daily for decades. He reflected with satisfaction that there was now an automated system, based on artificial intelligence, to evaluate doubtful tidbits of intelligence like this. The system was called TEDE, or Trailing and Extraneous Data Evaluation. It was perfect for the torrents of predominately useless leftover leads which had previously bogged down agents, especially reassigned ones. Abscome spoke exasperated commands to the computer. "Move file three to TEDE. Priority: low."

* * *

It was just after midnight as Nuñez sat, still dressed in khaki slacks and a red shirt, at his computer in his chilly bedroom. The walls were crowded with giant pictures of scenes from all over North America, especially Mexico. His window was open to the cold but he was sweating profusely as he stood up from the desk in his bedroom. He regretted having sent the message via phone mo-

236

dem. Yet he had been petrified by what he saw on his screen. He had hacked into secret files that he traced to a computer at the Ministry of the Interior in Baghdad. He tried to reassure himself, repeatedly, that his snooping was not traceable, owing to modifications he had made to his communications program.

But, in fact, Nuñez had been detected and his message had been cut off while he was typing three full pages of text. The text included a list of forty-one political and military leaders from seven Arab nations who were all but puppets; controlled by President Ismail Mon of Iraq. The Iraqis, already entering the back door of his two story gray brick house undetected, believed that the transmission had not been sent at all.

Nuñez heard something. A thump. A second thump. His mind raced and he told himself again that no one could have detected his transmission. Weapons were not permitted in the housing area. He felt defenseless. He stepped quickly to his bedroom doorway and peered around the corner. The soldiers were staring directly at him from half way up the stairs. Nuñez jerked back inside the doorway, just missed by a tranquilizer dart which whizzed by his head and stuck in the woodwork. He slammed the door and locked it. Nuñez dashed toward the window. The door burst open and a needle shot through his collar into his neck. Consciousness faded.

Nuñez awoke confused and slightly nauseated. His right arm stung. Someone was withdrawing a syringe from it. Nuñez tried to interpret his new surroundings. It appeared that there were trees blocking the sun against a black sky. *No*, he deduced, *that's the moon; bright against the clear night sky*. Another soldier was standing by him holding what appeared to Nuñez to be a fat pistol. Still another soldier in a neat, tan uniform was standing with his back to him. Nuñez was on his back, freezing, damp and bound spread-eagle to four trees at the edge of a clearing. There were hissing and grinding noises, which sounded to him like heavy hydraulics, somewhere near. One of the old but now refurbished sloth-tractors was parked twenty feet to Nuñez's left and its engine was humming softly.

"Ah! Dr. Nuñez." Nuñez turned his head to the right and saw that the soldier who had had his back to him was Lieutenant Colonel Najik, still speaking. "That was a quick recovery! Thank you for *co-oper-ating* so well."

Nuñez's speech was slightly slurred. "What are you . . . Why have you . . ."

"Just a few more moments, *Doctorr*, and you will be . . . yes, that is the term . . . 'wide awake.' More awake than you may desire, I am afraid."

Nuñez was recovering his senses rapidly and began to pull at the hemp which bound his limbs to four trees at the edge of the clearing.

Najik took a pocket knife from his belt and selected a very thin blade. He reached down and jabbed it about an eighth of an inch into Nuñez' right arm.

"Aaah! What are you doing?!"

"Thank you, *Doctorr*, I simply wanted to know if your were able to feel that minor cut acutely."

Najik motioned to one of the soldiers and a carpenter's vice clamp was placed and tightened onto the sides of Nuñez's head. Two soldiers held each side of the clamp, immobilizing Nuñez's head.

"Now, *Doctorr*, you are about to see—quite unavoidably at each moment, by the way—how I have decided to deal with spies here *weethin* my command."

Nuñez realized he might have a chance for clemency now. "Najik, I'm not a spy! I quit years ago. You have old information."

"Oh, now, *Doctorr!* Do you believe that I am a fool? Permit me to help you see things better."

Najik took a bulb-shaped object from his pocket, flipped a switch on its shiny white side and waited a moment. He motioned for the two soldiers holding the vice to move between Nuñez's arms and chest and he knelt at Nuñez's head, staring at the computer scientist with an evil grin. He reached for Nuñez's right eyelid, causing an involuntary wince. Najik pulled the lid outward with his left hand. In an instant, Nuñez realized what was about to happen and shuddered, sucking in air in a loud gasp. The electric scissors seared and smoked as they slowly, tediously sliced through the upper lid yet never touched the downward-turning, trembling eyeball.

"Haa-ooh! Aaah! Unngh!" Nuñez's screams actually hurt Najik's ears.

"There! Almost no blood but I am sorry for the scratchiness of the *cau-ter-iza-tion.*"

Nuñez began to scream a prayer in Spanish. Najik immediately quelched the words by cutting his lip and starting on the other eye. Najik did not speak but fully enjoyed Nuñez's pitiful screams—even his own resulting ear pain. He noticed that Nuñez was able to rotate his retina almost below his remaining eyelids. He began, with unexpected glee, to cut the lower lids as well. In a few moments, Nuñez could make himself stop screaming, even when his eyes moved in their excruciating sockets.

"What are you going to do now, sadist? Leave me here, unable to move while some saber-tooth cuts me to *pieces?!*"

"No! Of course not, Dr. Nuñez. I have no intention of keeping you tied up, unable to move!"

Najik turned off the hot scissors and handed them to a soldier. Nuñez breathed a nervous sigh of relief, for the clear implication was that he might be untied and at least able to try to escape.

Najik took the fat pistol-like object from another soldier and held it over Nuñez's left knee. Najik held the drill whirring for a moment to allow Nuñez to anticipate the pain. Then Nuñez felt it pushing and tearing at him as it failed to make a guide hole and danced around on the slippery patella, his protective knee cap. Finally, Najik held it firm enough for the hole to be bored, and at a slight angle from the artery so as to avoid causing Nuñez to bleed to death. Najik employed methodical, push-in, pull-out iterations until the base of the drill bit struck the knee cap. Nuñez began to pass out from the pain but one of the soldiers gave him a second injection of stimulant. The agony of the second knee being drilled through did not lessen his awareness of the first's.

Nuñez's screams became hoarse and weak. His body contorted less and he was nearly limp as Najik moved toward his shoulders. Boring into the shoulders, unlike the knees, did not entail the drill skipping and deflecting on bone just below the skin. The drill went in smoothly between the end of the clavicle at the shoulder and the arm at the ball of the humerus. This caused the drill to only graze and rut the joint, as the bit was guided between tough ligaments and bone into the sensitive arm pit.

Nuñez could only moan, cough and tear. Najik stood and stared with vicious contempt at Nuñez's hideously disfigured and contorting face. "Well, Dr. Nuñez, I must be *trrue* to my *worrd* . . . Untie him and remove the vice!"

The mechanical sloth's top closed and it moved off, oddly not diminishing the hydraulic sound he heard earlier. Nuñez moaned, managed a few screams and quivered uncontrollably. He tried unsuccessfully to turn on his stomach. Agony. He attempted to wiggle, to crawl toward the softly gurgling sounds of the river, which was five hundred feet away at this point. Searing, repetitive pain.

Nuñez still tried to think of a way to survive. But he had to ask himself, *What would I do if I made it to the river, anyway?* His pain was only slightly quelled by the cold and he began to hope that he would just lose consciousness and bleed to death peacefully. His ears were ringing less as his blood pressure began to slowly drop.

The hydraulic-sounding hiss was clearer now that Nuñez was alone. He nervously considered what it might be. *I've heard that sound somewhere. Can't place it. Almost hydraulic . . . No. I heard that sound in the veterinary clinic once. It was an animal . . . being anesthetized. Yes, its wound was being stitched and its breathing sounded just like that . . .*

"Oh my God!" Nuñez's desperate, hoarse shout lacked volume.

Heavy thuds began to vibrate the ground in a quick, uneven pattern. Something was glistening off to his right. A swish. Several. Pounding. He remembered. But it was a baby then in the vet clinic; seven feet long. He turned his head to face the noise. The sight emerging from the black background of the horizon was well beyond his horrified expectation. There were two. The two immense *Megalanias* were over thirty feet long. Their wide, fast-approaching heads were three feet wide and four long. They raced straight at him with long, shark-like serrated teeth reflecting the moonlight. Nuñez glimpsed the massive ten-inch claws and thunderous bulk rocking from side to side as the horrors approached.

Nuñez was unaware that he was screaming again. Every muscle in his body was involuntarily flexed-tight, regardless of pain, to its limit. His breaths were shallow, frantic gasps. Nuñez sat up and turned his head away to the left. He forced himself to recall Freund's earlier, persuasive, and now comforting insight. *Within the 'moment' of a human life*, Freund had assured him, *suffering and death only seem like tragic abandonments. But if offered up, they transform into eternal joys. 'Eloi, Eloi, lama sabachthani?' was a lesson in divine irony!*

The first of the giants to take its share cocked its head sideways and severed Nuñez across his forehead and abdomen with one slam of its jaws. The *Megalania's* shining triangular teeth and purple forked tongue were Nuñez's final visual images. Nuñez had found his life.

* * *

Several researchers were driving into the motor pool early to begin their most extensive observations of the Neanderthal and Cro-Magnon clans yet. It would not be light for an hour but Dr. Ina Singh's expedition was already assembling near the vehicle bays as Najik's sloth-tractor emerged from the west escalator to park.

"What brings you here so early, Colonel?" Singh was curious but could not take long to talk.

"Good *morrning*, Dr. Singh! Control alerted me last night of the *Megalanias* were *under-nourrished*. So I took out a team to kill a *Megaloceros* for them."

"You, personally? And in the middle of the night in a tractor?!"

"Yes. I too am personally *fas-ci-nated* by these animals and almost never *exper-rience* the plateau. They are least dangerous at night, of course, and I did not want to have to put on that bulky heavy-lift suit to keep any *strraying* sapiens from *observrving* us."

Singh perked up, worried. "*Were* any sapiens so far from the ridges and *did* any observe you?!"

"Not to worry, Dr. Singh! I even had the men use night sights to check, to be certain that we were not *observrved*. Your work today will be in the north, yes? Quite dangerous there unless you will be only on the ridges. Are you *observrving* both clans?"

"Yes, both. As you can see, we have tranquilizer rifles and in-ear communicators but these are all well disguised." Singh turned her head sideways. She pointed at the barely noticeable plug in her ear and at a branch-like object in her right hand. She continued her impromptu briefing. "A tractor will take us to an unobserved point and will be used as our base. We're hoping to make a *most* amicable contact by presenting ourselves as a tribe. We will stay half a day with each of the two clans for our first contact. They need to get used to us by means of a number of short visits and modest gifting. We hope to eventually stay with them several weeks at a stretch so as to observe their societies in detail. It's *quite* important to observe how they have been developing, organizing; that *sort* of thing—now that the surrogates are gone."

Najik's eyes lit and he grinned. "Yes. That's right! The surrogates are *all gone* now. Well, they waited nearly five years for their hard-earned reward. It was a pleasure to *prrovide* it to them! The best of luck to *you Doctorr.*"

Najik turned and walked through the doors to his office. At his desk, Najik created a computer-assisted forgery of a hand-written emergency leave request by Nuñez, citing the deaths of both parents. Bogus travel documents were also created. A week later, Najik would similarly forge employee termination papers, based upon Nuñez's supposed desire to remain in Mexico to carry on family business. The communications section of the Interior Ministry's Special Activities Division would respond to staff calls and correspondence as if Nuñez were still alive.

Singh turned back to her group and began to check costumes. There was no make-up, as this would be detected at close range. They anticipated that their appearance as a different-looking tribe would not significantly influence sapien behavior as long as their technology and culture remained hidden. This was based on the fact that both clans had already seen each other's differing appearance and no behavior changes seemed to have arisen. Her group of modern humans would be dressed in *Megaloceros* skins and carry what looked like ordinary walking sticks.

Singh had selected Dr. James Fong, the geneticist, Dr. Stefan Woj, Preserve Zoologist, Dr. Carl Smythe, the biologist/veterinarian and Dr. Claude Olivier, Paleo Lab Director. She had wanted Dr. Freund along but he had to return to Megiddo to visit Hans, who was in the hospital with appendicitis.

They all climbed into the tractor with their Iraqi driver and the guard, received clearance and proceeded up the east escalator. Moving through the east half of the plateau was the only route Harrigan would approve, given their lightly-armed status, because it avoided the feared *Megalania* burrow. They emerged onto the foggy, evergreen-spotted and wind-blown plateau. Blatant crows and blustering gusts were the only sounds in this damp, snowless winter environment. The expedition passed the point on the river where, nearly a quarter mile to the west, the *Megalania* burrow was situated, well concealed.

Fearing that the monster could cross the river to them, Singh tested the signal emitter as they rode northward. Everyone cringed at the hissing roar her action produced. This verified that the *Megalania* was on the opposite side of the frigid river. Singh placed the device inside her fur parka. They passed quite a number of fascinating animals and a few vicious kills to reach their destination. Their tractor came into view: a tree-lined and scruffy clump of foothills at the base of the crux between the two major ridge lines.

Singh and her companions tied the gift pelts to their parkas and dismounted, leaving the guards secure inside, and headed west toward the Neanderthal caves. They had wanted to observe both groups simultaneously but Harrigan had directed that they stay together. Singh walked first in line, after arguing with Olivier who did not think a woman should walk point.

Singh and Olivier had been developing a sometimes-romantic, sometimes-stormy relationship. Olivier had even once brought her to his boyhood home in beautiful Lyon, France. He had also taken her to Paris to view the marvelous artifacts of the renowned eighteenth century anatomist, Georges Cuvier. Singh had learned enough about leadership from her mentors, Freund and Lloyd, to deal effectively with her chauvinistic boyfriend.

They trudged two miles through brambles and wet bushes to get within sight of the caves. Along the way, visibility was at least sixty feet in this environment of leafless saplings and trees. The researchers were moving into the thicker evergreen areas. The caves were up the bare ridge face a hundred feet beyond the limit of the pines. Singh's group had almost reached the flat, open rock near the caves when they heard a low, bubbling sound like a small gas motor at idle. At first the sound emanated from rustling trees between them and the ridge, then it seemed to be behind them as well. Out of both the north and south now they heard branches snap followed by light thuds upon the ground. The bubbling grew louder and seemed to surround them. Singh drew everyone into a circle.

The expedition was not the only group to hear the odd snarls. Reddish-blonde and brown heads began to pop out of the two cave openings. The researchers heard the growls getting closer. Suddenly the bushes rustled and parted violently. A rabbit dashed past them in the undergrowth followed by an immense black and gray blur.

The marsupial had bounded like a giant, elongated squirrel past the circled—and encircled—group, to within thirty feet of the horrified researchers. It momentarily ignored the humans its pride had tracked. It sported black stripes on thick, gray fur in the pattern of a tiger. And it was big. Easily a hundred and fifty pounds and almost five feet long, excluding a short-haired, yard-long tail. It had dark, front-facing eyes atop a vicious snout. The eyes blended into black diagonal stripes on its rodent-like head, which was armed with two adz-like buck teeth curling downward from the center of its angry snout. Its face, thin and streamlined, seemed only to exist as a socket for massive incisors and crushing molars.

Fong caught a glimpse of the distracted animal's murderous head. "It's . . . It's a thylac! One of those—Oh my God! It's coming back!"

A pang of fear shot through Singh as she grabbed for her emitter and found the holster empty.

The rabbit had only delayed the attack, which came coordinated between four of the six horrific marsupials. The three attacking males and one attacking female rushed out of the brush seventy feet away on two sides to cross the sparse forest toward Singh's expedition. They moved at amazing speed.

There were two half-crouching on tree limbs seventy feet off. Each was a mother sheltering one kitten in her pouch. Though this maternity was not previously evident to anyone, it was today entirely unanticipated. Harrigan had not quite understood this species' reproductive processes. He incorrectly believed that these animals were sterilized; that their babies would be grown *only* in the lab and therefore all offspring would receive the safety chips.

Singh swallowed hard and struggled to control the panicking scientists. "Backs to one another. Now! Like this!" Singh threw Smythe from his forward, aggressive stance backward into his comrades to tighten the circle.

Her voice was high-pitched but nevertheless conveyed the commands effectively. "Fire!"

The branch-shaped weapons were difficult to aim accurately. Each fired a shot. They were fairly quiet weapons but together made a resounding "Bbbbang." Three thylacs racing through bushes fell in their tracks into damp leaves. But one male, leaping tree to tree, reached the group.

It launched itself through the air at Woj. He mustered the nerve to fire again as the marsupial lion sailed toward him, now five feet away. Its long ripper-claws on the inside of its stubby front paws were fully extended six inches. The monster's regular claws, each three inches long and half an inch thick, extended forward. They were aimed straight at Woj's chest. Yet it was the hideous, alien face and murderous, gouging front teeth that made Woj blanch and lose consciousness. As the nightmare struck Woj's chest, its muscles collapsed and it went as limp as its intended prey. Both fell to the ground, unconscious.

Woj woke immediately, sore throughout his torso, to concerned faces.

"I *yam* dead?"

"No! *Yor* not dead, *mate!* Can *ya* move?" Smythe was feeling Woj's ribs and nervously looking around for the other two *Thylacoleos*.

Woj was not concerned with his pain. He got up and grabbed his rifle.

Everyone was shaking and could see the two mothers retreating deeper into the woods. Singh ran to the downed animals, kicked each and yanked out the syringes from them and from two trees. She gave them back to each man and had everyone place them at the back of their magazines. As she did so, she informed the control room and their base that there were no casualties.

"We must get to the ridge now!" The trembling in Singh's voice was barely under control as she swiftly led them the rest of the way up onto the rock flats.

There, racing toward them on slightly-bowed stubby legs was a mob of club- and spear-waving Neanderthals. The scientists blanched and halted.

Singh whispered commands to her fellows. "Kneel! Hold your heads down!"

The Neanderthals started screaming and quickly surrounded them, slamming their weapons on the ground and glaring both out into the forest and down at the frightened moderns.

Suddenly the mother thylacs appeared behind the group at the edge of the forest. The animals snarled and seemed tormented, then left of their own accord, feeling threatened by the Neanderthals.

The Neanderthals turned their attention to their guests. The researchers stared up at the sweaty, hairy crew for several minutes before Olivier broke the silence with a Nostratic greeting. "We—our clan—come to trade. We want peace!"

Olivier studied the Neanderthal faces and found no anger. Once he realized that the Neanderthals were not going to club anyone, he was excited to attempt to assume the role of spokesman. "Friends! We chase animals. We give you pelts!"

Singh glared at him, recovering her authority. But she now felt forced to give up her spare pelt as did the rest of her party. Her group was picked up bodily and taken to the clan's main cave. They were set down in the broadest portion of the first cave. It was smelly, cluttered and connected to a second, also shabby, cave. The walls and some parts of the ceiling had a few black, red, yellow and green animals painted on them. Most of the painting was rudimentary. The hand outlines looked accurate, however, for these had been made by placing hands on the cave walls and spitting or jabbing paint all around.

The community was now composed of thirty-eight adults or young adults and thirty-one children. This was two more than Singh was aware of from the hasty transition briefing which had been provided based upon the surrogates' notes. Singh and her group tried to smile—and even received several grins in return—but the surroundings and the unceasing jostling from inquisitive Neanderthals made things difficult. She stared at a large male among her hosts and recognized him to be Rhahs, their leader. She gave him a nervous smile and addressed him in a respectful tone. "We visit. We are friends. You like pelts?"

The Neanderthal's voice was husky and a few vowels sounded shallow, vaguely like nasal humphing. "Pelts? You are black-hair; long-leg woman. They will come for you! You are like Khayni. They will attack for you!"

Singh had not seen anything in the records about Kora repeating anything from her subconscious to her fellows, let alone that odd "Khayni" word. The surrogates reported that no clan name had ever been adopted by either the Neanderthal or by the Cro-Magnon. The two groups' only contact ever reported by the surrogates was the Rhahs and Mo'ara fight incident, which they characterized as minor and amicably resolved. Hence, this comment by Rhahs confused the researchers.

Singh glimpsed Kora smiling radiantly at her from a ledge. Singh kept her own thoughts unspoken. *None of the other Neanderthals evidenced the vocabulary, memory or trances that Kora did when she was younger. The reports of trances ceased a year ago, retracted as misinterpreted by her surrogate. So odd! Why? I wonder if the reports were truthful! And where did this 'Khayni' word originate?*

Singh turned to reassure Rhahs. "No attack. No one comes for me, or us. We are not Khayni. We will visit Khayni soon. We like to visit you now!"

The furry man smiled but looked confused as he touched his guests' differing complexions. "We are friends to you. We are Abli. You have many colors? You name your clan. Now."

Singh was taken aback and did not know what to call her people. She stared nervously at him as his grin slowly became a grimace. Then Woj spoke up, employing a derivation of the English word 'friendly,' which was completely unlike its Nostratic counterpart. "We are *Friendli*, our people's name is! *Friendli* have many color skins. Many colors; one clan."

The researchers gave Woj a look of complete disbelief and exasperation. But the label and explanation helped. The Neanderthal smiled again, sang something unintelligible to his people around him and split up Singh's group to be physically dragged around the cave and introduced to every member of the clan. Kora did not recognize Singh at all. Singh anticipated this. Kora seemed to be treated like some informal queen. The 'Friendli' were informed, though they already knew, that the male whom Singh and Woj had been addressing, was named Rhahs.

Once the pleasantries were exchanged, Singh and her comrades were hauled back to the center and given cooked meat. They had to accept. Singh grimaced as her male companions tore into the shreds with gusto and were handed bowls of water. Then she relaxed a bit and, now concerned, noticed the Neanderthals' hands. Several of them had the first, and sometimes the second, segment of one or two fingers missing.

She inquired of the leader, who himself was missing the tip of his small right finger. "Rhahs, finger short. Why?"

Rhahs jerked Singh to her feet and dragged her back out to the entrance. He pointed to the sun and then to a filthy, blood stained and painted boulder outside. "Fire speak inside us. Fire save us from animals. Fire warm us; clean meat. We must give back. We give *ourselves* back."

He stuck his abbreviated finger in her face and stared at her firmly. She was shaken and unsure how to react. Singh felt intensely nervous and wanted to leave.

Rhahs took her back inside. Singh told her colleagues what she had seen and had them all depart with her. The scientists made as congenial an exit as they could and noticed more smiles than frowns on the way out. They reached the sloth-tractor with sighs of nervous relief and fatigue all around. Singh found and carefully secured her signal emitter. They rested awhile, discussing what the finger observation could mean.

Fong was not shaken by the revelation. He spoke his mind in his typical quick, choppy manner. "Obviously, it's a natural fascination. A precursor to religion sparked by the most constant and unreachable thing these people can conceive of: the sun. It might even be some subconscious effect of their last set of physical exams a year ago, or of periodically gassing them in their sleep."

Woj disagreed. "No. Ina said Rhahs indicated *daht* the fire spoke to them. As you say: 'plural.' More than one of them had the same experience. Rhahs seems to associate fire with the sun. There's at least some insight in such an association. Maybe they have—or think *daht* they have had—genuine religious experiences. And they're only able to liken it—or symbolize it in terms of something they know exists yet cannot physically touch. The sun may be only a symbol of their god. The sacrifice of a finger at least proves sincerity."

Smythe was incredulous at Woj's insight. "It's no great leap of thought to associate fire and the sun, *chum*. This is just a recurrence of the most common primitive *wership* known—something we *moyt* ought to expect anyway. You can't conclude that these people are in touch with some deity!"

Woj was irritated at the criticism. "I didn't exactly say *daht!* I just said they are sincere in their beliefs. And the sacrifice is no—what is in English?—shirk."

Singh stopped all conversation. "Look: We *shall* discuss this later and accumulate more observations in the months to come. At the moment, we have to get up to the Cro-Magnon caves or we will find ourselves unable to get back by dark!"

The group tied more gift pelts to their own and trudged uneventfully three miles east to the Cro-Magnon caves. A pair of sentries observed them as they approached and one scurried into the northernmost cave. In moments Singh's group was surrounded by a dozen fairly modern looking, threatening males.

"Friends! We give you pelts! No hurt you. No hurt us!" Singh elicited a peaceful, if unfriendly, response from them.

The pelts were confiscated and placed in the rear of the cave, where fires illuminated far superior, more detailed and colorful, drawings to those which the five had seen two hours before. But there was one thing more in the paintings which disturbed Singh and her companions. There was a painting of a spear being thrown by long, thin figures into a crowd of clearly short-legged figures.

The scientists had seen many Cro-Magnon young, now adults, in the lab. They had also viewed the caves briefly during the occasional gassings. They knew that these people had a slight but definite Mongol appearance and had been curious as to why. This had originally perplexed Harrigan. He had once predicted that the Cro-Magnons would look almost exactly like modern Caucasians. Geneticists had long suspected that modern humans arose from Cro-Magnon stock.

Recently, Harrigan and his team had confirmed the suspicion: They conclusively traced *every* modern race and lineage directly to the Cro-Magnons. They had also found that all modern races—especially the Europeans, Semitic and Indian peoples—had inherited at least some Neanderthal genes. The data had caused them to theorize that the ancient root line, *Homo erectus*, of both Cro-Magnon and Neanderthal may have continued to evolve contemporaneously with the other two sub-species. They suspected that it might have therefore contributed greatly to modern man's genetic makeup. This was, for the researchers at Al-Rajda, a solved mystery. This Cro-Magnon clan which Singh was investigating offered insight on the instincts and behaviors of early modern man. The immediate mystery, however, was the intentions of the clan now confronting Singh and her uncomfortable friends.

Singh tried to spot the leader, Mo'ara, among what she knew were thirty-nine adults and twenty-seven children, but she was unable. The Cro did not have much more body hair visible between their warm pelts than modern humans. They were uniformly black-haired and sporting prominent cheek bones. The males had sparse beards and the females had little more body hair than modern women. Their complexion was tan and they had long, detached ear lobes. They pulled curiously at Woj's blonde hair, pinched and scratched at Singh's very dark skin and poked at Fong's tighter-looking eyelids than their own.

Singh, disturbed by her experience with Rhahs, could not help but ask some of the Cro about any rituals they might have. She stared at the comparatively rich art, including stencils of hands which were not mutilated, on the cave walls. The best animal and sapien pictures were the highest up: The children must have practiced on the base of the walls. She knew the Cros were more advanced, at least in art and dexterity, than the Neanderthal. Singh wondered what she might learn by asking the Cros about the Neanderthals. She spotted Mo'ara, recognizing the Cro leader and his surliness from the surrogates' reports.

"You are Mo'ara? Leader? You know short-legs, yellow hairs?"

Mo'ara flashed his brown eyes at her and spoke. "Short-legs, Abli, bad. Take our animals."

Singh inquired further. "Are you Khayni?"

Mo'ara eyed Singh suspiciously for a moment and answered. "We are *strong* Khayni! You have many faces! You are what?"

Singh grimaced at Woj for a moment and answered, using the English-derived label as a necessary lie. "We are *Friendli. Friendli* have many faces but do not fight. *Friendli* trade; grow food."

Mo'ara frowned and dragged Singh to the nearest fire. "No! *Fire* make food grow. Ash *from fire* grows green. *We* make fire happy!"

Everyone hushed and watched as the Cro leader took some drying meat from outside the cave and a rotting piece from a nearby pit. He held the fresh meat, skewered on a spear, to the fire and threw the spoiled morsel onto the coals. After a moment he withdrew the skewered meat, blew on it and stuffed it in his mouth as he spoke. "Fire make all animals; give *all* to Khayni. Fire make Khayni. We give back to fire."

Woj was intrigued by the similarities and contrasts between the two clan's odd rituals but kept silent. Singh could make no sense of any of this but she and her group played along. They were allowed to visit for only a few minutes more and then were put outside the cave.

"Keep a friendly attitude nevertheless!" Singh reminded her fellows in whispered English.

As they left, Olivier thought he saw a spoiled spot on one of the drying strips of meat and bent over to examine it. Immediately, a spear from their lone escort sliced into the back of his head. He momentarily pressed his hand to his cut and then rose, his face contorted in anger. The escort rushed him. Olivier caught him by the tight-necked hide tunic and threw him tripping head-first into the rock ledge. Singh turned to try to calm everyone but saw almost the entire clan picking up weapons and rushing out at them from fifty feet back in the cave.

Singh yanked a smoke bomb from the base of her weapon and screamed at her companions. "Run! Base: Drive out here with a sound gun. Now!"

Smythe and Fong deflected spear thrusts to knock the approaching outside guards to the ground. All five ran down the ridge as a loud pop blocked the cavern aperture with thick black smoke. They made it into the forest hoping that any lurking danger ahead was not worse than that behind. They estimated that they had only a quarter mile lead on their pursuers and three quarters of a mile to go, if the tractor was making good time. They were gasping for air as they ran, all realizing that they could not possibly be faster than the angry Cro-Magnons. Tree branches ripped at their faces but their worst fear was of running into animals.

They made it over a small ridge and, with the deciduous trees now bare, could see the tractor racing toward them. They were all tempted to rest. Woj turned and glimpsed four Cro only fifty feet behind and closing fast, spears in hands.

"Day arre on us!" were all the words Woj's heaving chest could emit.

Down the spur they jumped and tumbled. Knowing better than to try to narrow the distance from the Cro by running back up the other side, Singh yelled to her group. "Go left. Down left!"

They maintained their lead and rounded to the less-steep end of the next spur. There, thirty feet ahead was the disguised tractor.

Singh yelled into the air as she began to cup her ears. "Sound blast! Do it!" The others knew what was coming and held their ears, minimizing but not at all eliminating the pain.

The high-pitched blast tripped the four pursuers and they went flying on their faces into the wet leaves and briars. The main body of pursuing Cro stopped short and held their ears, screaming. Singh was exhausted as she leaned against the open thigh hatch of the tractor. Olivier pushed her while Fong pulled her in and the door was secured. Immediately the tractor pivoted and appeared to run off into the forest, leaving the frustrated and smarting Cro-Magnons behind. Heading south toward the east exit, the five dressed Olivier's cut head, caught their breath and flooded themselves with water.

Olivier was livid. "I hope those barbarians die and rot out here!"

Singh shot him a weary but irritated look. "We have to win them over, Claude. Those barbarians can teach us more about ourselves than we may want to know."

Chapter Sixteen

All philosophy ultimately dovetails with religion—which is . . .
reducible to history. All history is . . . reducible to biology.
Biology is . . . reducible to chemistry. Chemistry is . . .
reducible to physics. Physics is . . . reducible to mathematics.
And mathematics is . . . reducible to philosophy.
—Ed Bishop & C. Pellegrino's First Law

what is born of the flesh is flesh . . . what is born of the
spirit is spirit. —john 3.6

Freund Residence, Megiddo, Israel
1809 hours, 15 April, 2018

Harrigan and Freund sat quietly sipping iced tea on Freund's ve-
randa. The evening chirp of grasshoppers was relaxing. The sitting
position made Freund's mild paunch noticeable but Harrigan, still
muscular at forty-two, felt no air of superiority. Both men had
given up plucking their few gray hairs and neither would use hair
coloring. It was a restful Sunday evening; a reward, for the trip from
Al-Rajda which they, Tykvah and Ben had begun earlier in the day
had been long, irritating and tiresome.

Tomorrow's burial of Tykvah's father would not be pleasant. She
had been trying to get Harrigan to quit and settle with her relatives
in Israel. More importantly, she wanted him to get Mon to allow a
safer, more humane Preserve for the sapiens. Harrigan hoped that

a month's vacation would calm Tykvah's agitated state. The two families would spend most of this break together.

Evening breezes were just warm enough to be pleasant and they carried the scent of a wide variety of roses and other flowers. These were the product of Gertrude's favorite hobby. Inside, Gertrude was helping Tykvah take her mind off her father's death. They were preparing a fancy beef diner, watching the children, unpacking bags and wondering why they could not recruit the help of their too-soon relaxed husbands.

Harrigan stared at the orange and pink, post-sunset clouds above the houses. "Thanks for taking me along to Mass, Mannie."

"Did you get anything out of it?"

"No." Harrigan smiled and laughed, flashing his bright, hazel eyes and revealing slighter crow's feet than Freund's own.

Freund joined him. "Would you admit it if you did?"

Harrigan smiled wryly. "No, guess not."

"Those dreams still bothering you?" Freund held his glass to his mouth and returned the grin.

Harrigan suddenly grimaced at Freund as if his most private thoughts had just been read. "Yes. Let's not discuss that, okay?"

"Just asking, *touchy!*"

"Sorry. I didn't mean to be a jerk! Hey, Mannie, do you hear from Nuñez anymore?" Harrigan took another sip.

"Nope. Last letter was months ago. You know how it is. People lose touch; get wrapped up in their routine. His family has that big cattle ranch north of Mexico City and he gets to be head cowboy. I'm sure he's doing okay!"

"Now José is one interesting guy! Scientist, spy, lived in lots of countries and now running a ranch . . . You know, Mannie, sometimes I think I wouldn't mind retiring myself. Mon owes us his life but you wouldn't know it from trying to get him to return a call or respond to a letter. The contract's up soon and Mon finally responded to my note about it. He promised that we can continue our work after the park conversion, but the jerk didn't address any of my concerns."

"I don't trust him, Kevin. At all."

"Well, for what it's worth, Nuñez told me a year ago that he was *beginning* to think the CIA might have been right after all: The Iraqis would steal whatever they could from our work, but they're no threat to anyone. That's my judgment as well. It's just that I'm getting really tired of their sneaky monitoring and arguing with me over safety and sapien issues."

"I appreciate you fighting those battles, Kevin. But are you saying that you're gonna hang it up? Tell Mon and his bureaucrats to take a leap?"

"Are you kidding? We've only scratched the surface! Do *you* want to quit?"

"No. Got the fever. It seems every time we discover something new, it raises more questions."

The two sat silent, contemplating the fantastic mysteries they and their team had tapped.

"Mannie?"

"What?"

"You know those parallel processing neurons you isolated in brain tissue?"

"Ah! Yes. Here we go again! You're going to get mad at me for my interpretation of the results."

"No, no, no! Why don't they work that way in primates other than man?"

"They do. But to nowhere near the extent as in humans. First, parallel processing is the basis of choice in that it permits the brain to think and solve problems in several ways simultaneously. It lets us anticipate the future. Humans are persons *because* their brains evolved capable of contemplating the results of their actions on individuals and on society. When a species is capable of choosing because it can anticipate ramifications of decisions – and this is made possible by parallel processing—its members *become* persons. They are aware of others as persons.

"Second, personhood exists independent of time because it's not physical. So, babies don't await a soul until the point when they can think by parallel processing. Rather, they get it when their genetic coding *as a personality* is completed: The *potentiality* for a person is created at fertilization. That physical potentiality *attracts* the endowment of a soul, forming a human being, analogously to how ions attract to form molecules in *our* observable world."

"Mannie, I was going to say that *the first part* of your theory *might*—only *might*—be correct. If you'd let me have a chance!"

"Oh. Sorry. But what do you mean 'might?'"

"There are just too many strange pieces of evidence falling into place, like Kora's memories and everyone getting M-type RNA through the Hebrew dispersions. And, yet, there's no proof."

"If there were proof of God's nature and yours, you'd never ask for faith. And you need faith to open the eyes of your heart; to endure to the end. If he were overt, you could not freely choose to trust and love him; defer your will, your judgment to his. You would view sacrifice and repentance as a requirement, not an act of reciprocal love. And then, well Kevin, you'd *really* miss the boat!"

"Mannie, I really did try this faith thing. There have been times when I thought I felt that 'whisper' you talked about. But it just doesn't stick. I cannot accept a few coincidences as evidence of this spiritual world you say exists. Have you ever seen it? Have you ever experienced it? Have you ever touched it?"

"No. *It* touches me. *It* even gives me the ability to accept it. And only faith will save you. You simply ask for faith and you will receive it. But for such a request to be genuine, it must be a sacrifice one's own imperfect will to God's. You cannot gain your life if you will not let go of it."

"Too deep! New subject! I wanted to tell you: I finally learned to use that genetic progression model Nuñez left behind."

"What does it predict? I thought he abandoned that line of research."

"Looks like he kept at it on his own time. His model extrapolates the human genome into the future, based on the past data we've assembled. The darn thing predicts that the personality microsatellites cannot continue to be added to each generation endlessly. It predicts a definite number of generations before no more archived strands can be stably added to the lengthening chromosomes. Past a certain point, the M-RNA stops adding new personality codes. The cumulative effect of so many chemical bonds causes segments to break down."

"Break down? As in random, freak-like mutation?"

"No. It triggers a cascaded expression of the already-archived personality sequences, starting with the most archaic."

Freund dropped his tea and did not pick up the glass. "Kevin, do you mean to say that successive future generations could start to produce identical copies of ancestors in the order of original occurrence?"

"That's his theory. His notes even predict that ended lineages would regenerate because the process progresses from the most ancient sequences forward."

"But, Kevin, what about repeats?"

"He's also got something in his notes about an algorithm that steps in. It appears to preclude the problems of multiple regeneration of a particular ancestor. He was working on this part of his model just before he left. He never discussed any of this with me. It makes no sense to me but he likens it to the same algorithm that keeps people now from producing babies which are copies of the parents or of anyone else. A process we still don't fully understand."

Freund's eyes flashed. "That's it! There must be a mechanism that keeps people from being copies of anyone else. But it can't be a physical one because its functioning would indicate a sensing or awareness of the genetic makeup of every human being, even those distant in space and time. Even though every egg and sperm around the world starts off with most of their genes being identical, no one—not even what we call identical twins—has ever been found to be genetically *identical*. This is fascinating! I'd like to see his notes and the model."

"Mannie, I think Nuñez was *way* off the mark with this algorithm thing. It's just a computer projection."

Freund smiled hopefully and reached to recover his glass when Harrigan resumed. "But there is *one thing* that checks out perfectly with lab trials I've done."

Freund froze, concerned that such a fantastic computer projection could be empirically observed in real life. "And what's that?"

"The regeneration cascade can actually be triggered."

Freund stared at Harrigan in horror, lapsing distracted into both English and German. "Triggered? *Mein Gott!* What do you mean, 'triggered?'"

"Certain changes to the aging and longevity genes can cause them to produce a mutated M-type RNA. In animals, where the levels of M-RNA are minute, the mutated M-RNA speeds maturation and also produces ancestor species. But in humans, that mutation works slightly differently because human M-RNA preserves only personality sequences. In the first generation affected, it kills males by accelerated aging. In females, it codes their future progeny for fast maturation.

"The mutated M-RNA then reverses the *archiving effects* of normal M-type RNA, one set per fertilization. So, it would theoretically regenerate exclusively ancient ancestors from the point when human M-RNA first started to preserve personality sequences. How far it could go and how far back the first such sequence might have been is conjecture."

"Do the Iraqis know about this?"

"No. Just you, me and Nuñez. Mannie, stop staring at me like that! The odds of *exactly* the right genes being inadvertently modified in *that* way are so small . . . Well, Mannie, it just couldn't happen."

* * *

Later in the evening, in the Neanderthal caves, Kora and Rhahs tucked droopy-eyed children into their grass-stuffed pelt beds. Sleeping areas were organized in family groups along the cave walls. When Rhahs was asleep and she was about to doze, she noticed the familiar scent of roses outside.

Kora got up and exited the cavern. She made her way almost up to the cliffs and squatted on her shins, facing the forest in a small hollow of rock seventy feet above. Her auburn-blonde hair fluttered in a light breeze upon her protruding brow and hung well-combed over her ears and furry shoulders. Starlight glinted off Kora's eyes as she began to tear, smiling and holding her palms outward toward the sparkling mist forming above the trees. The woods became silent.

The mist rapidly became radiant and Kora's eyes rolled up and back into their sockets. Her breathing became shallow and her face began to reflect the shine. She listened inwardly to words which graced her and responded verbally in Nostratic. Kora's voice began a tremulous whimper and her smile disintegrated.

"I fear! This is not known to me. These ones I do not know. Pain. Killing. Who are these? How could—"

Kora fell silent and her smile began to return. Her shaky voice recovered and built into a sanguine proclamation.

"You do as sun wills. I do as you ask: *One last call* to Friendli. Prepare the way. It *must* be. I will be not afraid."

* * *

Harrigan lay asleep beside Tykvah in Freund's guest room. His eyes shook wildly beneath their lids and his arms twitched as if he was about to reach out. Silvery droplets of sweat beaded on his forehead and intermittently rolled off into his slightly thinning hair. The image in his mind was simultaneously fearful and comforting. Harrigan's lips began to move and his shaky, gruff tone woke and startled Tykvah. She listened, becoming more unsettled with each word.

"Must not let this be! No. I can stop—I *will* fight this! How could you let so many die?! I don't underst—"

Harrigan was silent and his muscles relaxed. His eyes remained closed as suddenly his hands cupped his face and he almost woke himself. His voice softened to a defeated, worried tone.

"Another chance? I must choose . . . so soon mankind will . . . ? But I am—"

His hands drew away from his face and he stared at Tykvah through the blur of his tears. He sat up into the half-darkness to her almost-reassuring embrace. Tykvah hid her own fearful reaction to what she had just observed and tried to soothe her husband.

"Kevin, you're drenched, you're shaking! Bad dreams. It's okay now. I love you. Be calm, now. Everything's going to be fine. What was it about, anyway?"

"I . . . I can't remember. It's faded. Gone. But everything is *not* fine, Tykvah. Not at all."

* * *

The following morning in Baghdad, Hassan's enterprising young Computer Science Chief had come in early to intercept him and gain his attention. The CS Chief had tried unsuccessfully to get Hassan to read and discuss his report on Friday. Hassan sat at his desk, read the report and gazed up smiling. Hassan stood up and walked over to shake the visitor's hand.

"Thank you," Hassan said softly. "You have worked long and hard and this will not go unnoticed. You may go."

Hassan was on the vid-phone before the young man had even left.

"The Presi- I mean the Premier, please."

A dark, stern face appeared on the monitor. "Yes, Hassan, what is it?"

"Congratulations on your restructuring of the government, Premier Mon. The Congress was worse than useless!"

"What have you called me for, Hassan? I am quite busy!"

"Sir, I wished to tell you this immediately. We have found and eliminated the deception which Harrigan has been using. FGR is now available for our researchers to employ in genetic trait identification, removal and insertion techniques. It is quite helpful in constructing and mass-producing virus vectors. These can carry programmed gene sequences for insertion into any host.

"It has helped us better identify and produce aging sequences, so it can now be used as a mass-target weapon! We have already used it to isolate strength and intelligence genes. Our modifications to FGR have also enabled us to construct sequences which code for all of the traits you require."

"Excellent, Hassan. Are delivery systems practical?"

"Yes, sir. But it will take a bit more refinement. We have debugged the duplicate FGR program and equipment here in Baghdad. They work and there are no more errors. We are presently on the verge of mass producing the virus vector. It kills males by fast aging if they are producing testosterone at adult levels. It also responds to several female hormones to seek and effectively fertilize any newly ovulated egg. Such fetuses mature very fast with any of several traits we desire to encode them with. It can produce workers for your new order."

Mon was elated but maintained his emotionless facade. He thought silently for a moment and then wondered whether Harrigan and his team should be killed or kept on, just in case more useful discoveries could be obtained or, otherwise, to avoid Western suspicion.

"Hassan, you have accomplished the assigned goals well, though later than I required. Still, I must credit you. I will remember you when the time comes. In your judgment, do you feel there is a reason to keep Harrigan and his staff?"

Hassan was about to compliment what he misinterpreted to be Mon's order to kill Harrigan and his staff. But before he could do so, he noticed an aide approach Mon and whisper something into his ear. Just then Mon nodded at the aide and tried to conclude his conversation with Hassan.

Mon was distracted and becoming impatient. "Hassan, I must go. Well done!" He turned away, forgetting to turn off the phone.

Hassan called after him. "Oh, sir, shouldn't we move in anti-aircraft units since Al-Rajda's cover as commercial research may be lost without the foreigners?"

Mon did not hear and had to leave. "Uh. What? Yes, a fine job. Goodbye."

The screen went blank. Hassan grinned widely, chuckling softly to himself. Not having listened, he thought he heard what he wanted.

Hassan's voice took on a smooth, self-satisfied quality as he made another call. "Al-Rajda Facilities Commander, please."

Najik greeted him. "Good morning, Interior Minister. How may I serve you?"

"The Premier wishes that Harrigan and his staff be disposed of. Permanently. They are no longer necessary."

Najik's tired expression brightened and he leaned forward to the lens, causing the image of his grinning face to fill Hassan's monitor. "Excellent, sir! It would be most practical to deal with the staff tomorrow, unless you wish otherwise. Harrigan, his wife and Freund, however, are being monitored in Megiddo but they will return in four weeks. I trust the Communications Section will intercept and handle any calls they might make to their staff . . . until I have the Harrigans and Freund back here?"

"Fine. I will alert the Communications Section. You may conduct the operation as you wish and report success to me."

"Yes, sir. Will there be any change in operation of the facility?"

"Maintain it as usual. Your technical contingent will grow and the sapiens and animals will be useful to them. By the way, I'm sending an anti-aircraft battalion. Remember that *you* do not command it!"

* * *

The following morning, ten Al-Rajda staff members, eight children and four spouses awoke to a deafening explosion north and west of them. It was a recording played from a trailer on a hill just northwest of the housing area. Their communications screens all flashed and Najik gave the foreign personnel an alert via the inter-coms. The Iraqi staff was ordered to stay inside.

"Attention staff and *fam-ilies!* A Kurd terrorist attack has been *in-ter-cepted*. Their aircraft has been destroyed *prrior* to reaching us. However, the explosion of their *or-di-nance* has completely col-lapsed the northeast *rridge*. Animal escape is possible. All person-nel and dependents report *immediately* to the motor pool shelter. Do not bring any belongings. I *rrepeat . . .*"

The four families and six single staff members were almost fran-tic. Calls flooded in to the Control Center with questions about ter-rorists, escaping animals and the like. All inquiries simply received a repeat of the order. With car bumpers banging, children scream-ing and shirt-tails hanging out of jeans, every staff member and their dependents assembled in the cavernous, exhaust-filled ga-rage. Twenty soldiers had them assemble alphabetically in family groups.

Once it was verified that all were present, the soldiers ceased the charade and got rough. Najik did not trust some of his men to participate in the carnage that was about to be ordered. So he had his executive officer, Major Saddam Bhaszdi, assign thirteen as hall and exit guards. Most of the rest of his command was ignorant of the operation. The remaining seven trained their weapons on the incredulous, furious and increasingly frightened group. Children squirmed and cried. Angry adults alternately attempted to curse and reason with their captors.

Najik motioned to Bhaszdi and the officer began to have his men split the group into two lines of eleven each. They kicked and prod-ded the two groups into the cargo holds of two tractors. The tightly packed and now deeply frightened people quieted slightly. Two guards in each tractor kept the civilians under control while Bhaszdi and Najik had their drivers head up the west escalator.

They headed for the grassy plain and drove north two miles along the edge of the greening forest. Continuing toward the *Megalania* burrow, the vehicles halted just within sight of it. The soldiers kicked the civilians out of the vehicles and dismounted, except for the drivers. These were ordered to face south and act as predator spotters. Both groups now became one angry, huddling rabble. Most adults knew exactly where they had been taken. Lloyd and several of the researchers kept eyeing the guards' weapons and exchanging nods. He squeezed Kairaba's hand to comfort her. Some of the researchers and all of the children completely broke down, screaming and pleading almost unintelligibly for release.

Najik tested his signal emitter and received a hissing roar from the burrow's opening, as expected. Those who had been unsure where they were now neared panic with the realization. Najik had his men line up facing north toward the sobbing, frenzied group. The crowd began to slowly back away from the soldiers until they realized that this would only bring them closer to two pairs of monstrous jaws. The volume of the crying and vengeful cursing increased with this apprehension. Someone in the back of the group suddenly fell; dropped down into the earth as if swallowed by it.

Then came the roar, muffled at first. The earth underneath the screaming civilians burst up in a splash of dirt, grass and flailing people. They were tossed back toward the burrow and outward from the eruption of soil. The soldiers were stunned.

Thrusting aside clumps of clay and sod, the *Megalania's* massive head rammed up and out at the soldiers from a previously unknown extension of its burrow. A civilian had fallen onto its scaly neck and was tossed into the grass with a painful thud. He scrambled to his feet and dashed to rejoin the others. The vicious reptile received several ballistic shots but advanced out of the hole with lightening speed, thrust forward by its scaly tree-trunk legs and ripping claws. The researchers scrambled toward the forest to escape the creature, free themselves from the heaped-up dirt and remain together.

The drivers turned and fired at the *Megalania* but stopped, realizing that they had no effect, and put their tractors into reverse gear. Najik hammered on the signal emitter but this only seemed to make the monster lash out even more. It swung its massive bulk, freeing its tail from the ground. It bit the legs off a tripped soldier and impaled one soldier through the chest with a front claw. It hissed and roared in agony as Najik held the button down continuously. The soldiers were already retreating into the tractors.

Suddenly the men in one of the tractors found themselves launched into the air, sailing straight for the tormented *Megalania*. Their vehicle was tossed on its side with one mighty jerk of the second *Megalania's* head. The first beast snapped at the broken and prostrate soldiers. Najik and Bhaszdi dashed up the side ramp of the remaining vehicle, already with its top secured by two soldiers, and slammed the close button. The vehicle sped south in reverse gear, trampling the second lizard's tail and causing it to scurry away from the pain source.

Parents and singles alike yanked children and ran for the concealment of the trees, not daring to look back. The four remaining soldiers' anguished screams each halted abruptly in turn. These were followed by a calming of the *Megalanias'* grisly shrieks. But the escaping staff and family could still hear the monsters' hissing, glottal chomps and gulps all the way to the river.

Najik was quivering violently. The two men with him were screaming and arguing over how to maximize the vehicle's throttle without breaking tracks or gears. As they approached and entered the escalator, another frightful thought gripped Najik: He would not only have to answer for the loss of men but, worse, for the escape of the civilians. His mind raced, plotted and silently planned out false reports he would have to make. Finally he decided to report that the mission had been accomplished. Since he could track down his victims eventually, he further resolved to send out patrols each day until he knew that every civilian had been eaten or executed. Even if his facilities were inspected, he reasoned, there was no practicable way for his ruse to be discovered.

He was already planning sweep patterns and lamenting that he could not obtain heavy weapons or helicopters for his facility without revealing his activities. *Probably*, he thought, *the job will be done for me by the animals. After all, how long could they survive defenseless on the plateau? As for the Harrigans and Freund, they will come right to me in a month. I can take my time with all of these 'mice.'* Najik smiled to himself again and began to calm.

Lloyd did not like the responsibility that fell to him to lead the group but he accepted it. He did not have to attend children, he was the group's senior member and he had proven his mettle as a survivor and outdoorsman. Lloyd now commanded respect. He wisely kept Singh with him and quickly verified that they were all accounted for and fit to travel. He considered heading east or southeast to scale the ridges or rappel down the cliff to escape in the spare cars at their homes. He was quickly reminded that even he would not be able to scale the steep, machine-hewn ridge or de-

scend the treacherous southern cliff. He adopted Singh's suggestion that they take refuge with the Neanderthals and disable the
cave's gassing and observation devices.

They stayed close to the river on the fearful trek north. Lloyd
maintained that they could intimidate any predator along the way
with threatening noise, superior numbers and club-wielding aggression as a group. "Plan B" was to rush into the river and hope
that no predators followed—or lurked beneath its surface. They
did not need "Plan B" but discovered, four times on their eight mile
journey, that "Plan A" worked well, except against the wolves.
These predators were encountered near the caves.

The *Canis dirus* were more attracted by the children than intimidated by this group. The researchers and their families narrowly
escaped the vicious pursuers by darting and diving into the Neanderthal caves. Their primitive hosts were only temporarily frightened to see modern clothes. The wolves did not follow the group in
but other, more vicious animals in uniforms would pursue these
foreigners there in a matter of days.

Chapter Seventeen

THEN THEY WILL HAND YOU OVER TO BE TORTURED AND WILL PUT YOU TO DEATH, AND YOU WILL BE HATED BY ALL NATIONS BECAUSE OF MY NAME. —MATT 24.9

. . . the Bible and the Testament are impositions and forgeries . . . —Thomas Paine, *The Age of Reason*

YOU KNOW HOW TO INTERPRET THE APPEARANCE OF EARTH AND SKY, BUT WHY DO YOU NOT KNOW HOW TO INTERPRET THE PRESENT TIME? —LUKE 12.56

The White House, Washington, D.C.
1442 hours, 21 April 2018

No one at the long conference table in the crisis meeting room deep beneath the White House was conscious of how grim and tightened their expressions had become over the last two hours. Secretary of State Wayne Crystal was sweating and occasionally shifting in his chair as he received the President's merciless glares. He felt as if his wrinkly face might actually melt down over the bony Adam's apple of his pencil-like neck. His concentration had often been interrupted by the fact that the President was, at forty-four, a stunning, long-haired brunette. Now, however, Crystal was being pointedly reminded that the President's beauty in no way impeded her ability to cut through his rhetoric. Neither did it mitigate the force of her wrath.

President Sheryl Cox glared at Crystal. She needed to verify her understanding of the Secretary's just-completed and exceedingly semantic report. "Are you *actually* telling *me*, Wayne, that the Israelis are so intimidated that they will not assist us . . . and that the Turks and Saudis are telling us to take a leap—*even* after you

266

kissed their feet all last year?! You told me they were on board with my regional stability program."

Crystal swallowed hard, now paying the price for his earlier boasts of accomplishment. "Madame President, the Israelis feel that they should not antagonize Mon, especially since the Mediterranean could easily be closed off from Morocco. He has a subtly dominating influence in every Arab nation and several other strategic countries in the world. Iraq's total control of nuclear weapons in Iran, Pakistan and Kazakhstan place it in a considerable position of strength vis-a-vis the Israelis and even us. We have no true allies in the area from which to threaten or stage military operations and the nuclear option is not realistic. Under the circumstances, I'd say that Mon's got all of us by the ba . . . ah . . . b-by way in which he has manipulated even our allies."

Crystal's *faux pas* did not escape Cox. She ignored it and grimaced fiercely at the shrugging advisor. "I decide whether the nuclear option is realistic, Mr. Crystal."

The Secretary thought he could regain credibility with an idea he had been considering in recent days. "Uh. Well, Madame President, we could offer to buy oil while having the U.N. threaten Mon with sanctions if he fails to hand over the facilities, software and hostages. Use *both* the carrot *and* the stick. He has shown a willingness to negotiate disagreements we've had with him in the past."

Cox shot an incredulous glare at the frail statesman. "Crystal, do you not realize that this man could destroy the genetic stability of the entire world? Mon could kill millions—perhaps billions—while leaving his own and his puppet regimes to sweep the rest of us off the planet. Do you think someone who would develop the potential to subjugate the world would negotiate away such a capability?"

"Uh. S-so, are you advocating a military threat?"

Cox was so angry she could no longer look upon Crystal, whom she now intended to replace. But she did answer him. "This nation has long had no credibility in its threats. Let cowards issue threats."

She focused on her CIA Director and National Security Chief and double-checked their previous joint report. "James, you're certain that Al-Rajda is the only location at which these genetic weapons can be manufactured—and that no stockpiles have yet been generated?"

James Fording, CIA Director, stood. He reactivated the wall

monitor he had used earlier in the meeting and pointed to blurry photos. "Yes, Ma'am. We're certain. Our satellites and our electronic surveillance in Baghdad both agree on this. The Iraqis have *only just* developed the vectors. They have not had time to reconfigure Harrigan's program and equipment for mass production of virus weapons. We're still watching Harrigan to see if he leads us to any new information about their genetic warfare program. We don't think he's knowingly on board with them . . . and letting him return to Iraq risks his life. But we have no choice since monitoring where he goes could reveal whether an additional facility exists. We're as certain as it gets, in this business, that the only Iraqi genetic weapons potential is at Al-Rajda."

National Security Agency Chief Dixon Merriweather rose to interject. "We can't figure out why, Madame President, but satellite reconnaissance shows that the researchers—and we're not sure they're hostages yet—are hole-up in one of the caves above the plateau. Two small patrols have gone out after them so far. The first patrol went out in five robotic suits but was completely knocked out with boulders and, apparently, snares. A twenty-one man patrol on foot approached the caves, but was routed by these ape-men the researchers have there. That patrol never made it back either. Nevertheless, we think it's just a matter of time before the garrison or reinforcements finally capture or kill the researchers. They've got children with them too. As for the Iraqi scientists, they are continuing to work at the research complex."

Cox addressed the group. "Gentlemen, does anyone have reason to believe that we have overestimated the Iraqi threat?"

The room was silent.

Cox turned to General Frederick Mepps, Chairman of the Joint Chiefs of Staff. "Fred, I want *every* hostage, *every* child, *every* Iraqi scientist; *every* piece of hardware and software removed from Al-Rajda and brought back here. Who do you have and how soon can it happen?"

The officer's stern, monolith expression never changed. "A composite of men from the Seventy-fifth Rangers and a squad from Delta Force, Madame President. They can be rehearsed and ready in days, but I understand that the vehicle will take three weeks. They'll need some civilian specialists along as well, but that has already been coordinated."

"Fred, there is no margin for error and I believe we'll get—*mankind* will get—exactly one shot at this, short of a nuclear exchange. Gentlemen, if Fred's people want *any* item of support, I want it provided before you draw breath to say 'Yes.' This meeting is closed. Begin now."

* * *

Najik's third patrol, led by Major Bhaszdi, was no better motivated than the disastrous prior two. Najik was not sure how he would eventually explain the destruction of five out of seven robotic suits. For now, though, that was less of a problem than the stubborn researchers and their apish friends. His worry was that Hassan might learn that the researchers were still alive and he would be caught in his lie. Hassan had not yet bothered or visited Najik and, apparently, was busy trying to secretly import equipment for improvements to the Baghdad facility and conversion of Al-Rajda to a production site.

So Najik took his time, gave his men rewards and promises of rewards. Now his third patrol was assembled and on its way. It was much bigger than the others. Fifty-eight men armed with rifles and more ammunition than any of them wanted to carry. They nervously emerged on foot, following two tractors out of the east escalator to avoid the *Megalania* on the plateau's west side. The lined-up formation moved north through tall grass and parallel to the margin of green along the Rajdakim River.

Driving and trampling through thick weeded grass and bushes, the parade flushed hundreds of noisy quail. Constant and foreboding "caws" from crows and ravens also taunted the nervous troops. Increasingly tense, the men shot at every fleeing animal they saw. Five miles into their march, however, the line of tense troops fell into disarray. They were surprised by a wary and retreating pack of growling wolves. The canines saw that they were vastly outnumbered and immediately bolted out of sight.

Bhaszdi decided to take no chances even though he could no longer see the pack from his open tractor. "Slaughter the pack! Fire into the woods," he shouted, "Over there, somewhere."

The dismounted soldiers' forty-five automatic rifles managed to wound just one wolf. The din stopped when Bhaszdi himself threw one of the precious few hand grenades, which only he carried. This particular grenade was the only 'concussion' explosive among those left over from the unit's days as a combat outfit. The deafening explosion tore through the air. It retained almost all its force and volume as it reflected off the ravines, hillocks and, ultimately, the east ridge and back at the grasslands. The echoes seemed to come from every direction, except the true source of the blast.

From the far edge of the plain the soldiers heard a faint rumble. Most assumed they had triggered an avalanche at the ridge but saw nothing to the east except low, rolling hills. They moved on. The rumble increased. Brown dots began to be visible, bobbing up and down, to the far right of the patrol. What had moments before been only a rumble, now rapidly grew thunderous. The dots became clearer. At least a hundred massive black and brown blurs, with gray lines out to the sides, were vibrating the ground: buffalo stampeding at amazing speed.

These were the fearsome *Bison latifrons*, some of which were seven feet tall at the shoulder. The panicked men could not be kept in formation. Soldiers sprinted north to get out of the path of the mass of animals, now fifty yards away and clearly identifiable. The bison careened toward them at almost forty miles per hour. The animals were spread over a hundred yard front to accommodate the over six-foot long horns extending from each side of their locomotive-like heads.

The immense horned beasts now changed direction, rushing along the low ground southwest toward the forest and the river, just south of the last running man. For a moment it looked as though the entire military formation would just escape trampling. Suddenly the herd veered again, northwest, directly into the escaping soldiers. Screams and shots rang out as bison and soldiers alike tumbled, wounded, crushed or dying in the grass. The soldiers turned left into the woods and away from their accompanying tractors. Barely slowed by tree limbs, bison crashed into the woods. With horns snapping on tree trunks and acting as splintered clubs, the animals thrust toward the river decapitating, goring and trampling men along the way. Pained and frightened bleating from the herd mixed horrifically with soldiers' frantic screams and wails.

In seconds, the bison were through to the river and away. The woods and grass were strewn with dead and expiring men and beasts. There were moaning soldiers reaching out bloody arms, begging for help. Snorting *latifrons* thrashed legs and horns to raise themselves but gained only further injury. The tractors halted and turned back to pick up nine surviving soldiers, who had been in the lucky front of the formation. There were nineteen survivors able to walk, of which ten had been in the tractors. First aid and pain killers were quickly administered and the still-dangerous wounded animals were destroyed.

Bhaszdi, shaken and nauseated, radioed Najik. "Colonel Najik, sir! I . . . I request to have the patrol withdrawn! You must have monitored the stampede. Colonel! Most of my men are dead! The wounded are suffering so that I cannot . . ." The patrol leader could no longer contain himself and vomited over the side of the tractor. "Hmm, ahh. Sir, please!"

Najik was unmoved. "You will put yourself and your patrol back together, Major! I can, um, I must now send you men whose loyalty you will have to enforce through iron discipline. I will send two more tractors of men as reinforcements. You will send back one tractor at the scene now . . . with the dead, wounded and their weapons. Do you understand, Bhaszdi?"

"Yes, sir. I am loading the casualties and weapons into the tractors now. B-but it would be unwise to send them back before . . . the replacements have arrived, sir."

"Very well, Major. Najik out."

After a few hours, the reorganized patrol drove northward. Three tractors now carried the entire contingent of thirty-seven very demoralized troops. They reached the hilly forested area at the marshy headwaters of the river and halted for a map check. Heading west across tiny gurgling creeks and small wooded ridges, they passed a foreboding point. The area was that to which Najik's previous, unsuccessful recovery crews had dragged the last patrol's damaged heavy-lift suits and bodies, now skeletons. Shivers gripped the gasping drivers and everyone scrambled to peer, profoundly intimidated, at the sight. The soldiers, unaware that they had been observed as they passed this point, continued their trek.

Approaching the Neanderthal caves, Bhaszdi saw a small, telltale billow of smoke issuing from the top of both entrances. From inside the tractors, they lobbed in several small tranquilizer gas canisters, donned gas masks and dismounted. Next, Bhaszdi threw his last few hand grenades into both interconnected caves. The troops heard nothing after the explosions. But Bhaszdi knew the cavern was extensive, so he made the decision to enter.

"You ten privates and you three drivers post here, outside the caves. Lieutenants Harif and Karut, take your men into those caves. The rest of you follow me inside."

The officers and men stared silently at Bhaszdi, as if about to refuse the order. Then, one by one, they all turned on personal search lights and crept inside. With no resistance at the entrances, the two groups merged back into one in the main cave. The rear of the cavern had at least three main extensions. Impatient, the patrol leader assigned eight men to each and moved in. They followed fresh tracks and blood stains, for over half an hour, so deep inside that radio communication became impossible.

Bhaszdi thought he heard something crack several times but was unsure. What was beginning to irritate him, though, was that by now he and his men had been inside for forty-five minutes and had seen no researchers. It was worrying him that he had neglected to set any rendezvous time for his three groups already in the cave. In addition, it was beginning to dawn on him that all of this might be a trap. Bhaszdi's stomach knotted.

He turned abruptly and barked one command on the run. "Come out of the cave-extension!"

As they emerged into the main cavern, he heard a hiss behind him. Bhaszdi turned and noticed fire in the three passages. Then three explosions in quick succession almost knocked his group to the ground. Dust and debris were everywhere. Small boulders rolled out of the passages.

He and the squad with him frantically checked the two passages that still held soldiers.

"Harif?! Karut?! I order you to come out now!" Bhaszdi collapsed on his knees on the cave floor, sobbing. "I said, I order you! Come here!"

Two of his men grabbed Bhaszdi and raised him to his feet. Fear and shame both slapped him back into reality and he knew that sixteen men had been sealed-in permanently. Bhaszdi sensed panic now like never before and ran out of the cave, followed by his surviving seven men.

What the shaking leader now observed outside the cave turned his stomach with oppressive revulsion and wrenched his bowels with stark fear. Every man in his outside contingent was dead and the tractors were engulfed in flames. Each corpse had been speared through the chest or shot, presumably with captured rifles. Heads had been bludgeoned unrecognizable into sappy lumps of bone chips and brain matter. There were no weapons or ammunition containers anywhere in sight.

Lloyd and four other jeans-clad researchers, accompanied by six Neanderthals in fur loin cloths, were running away into the woods below—but this was no consolation. Bhaszdi and his small squad were alone and outnumbered.

Bhaszdi could not keep his voice stable. "East! Run east! F- Follow me into the woods."

As the Iraqis darted off the sloping gray rock, Lloyd emerged from the forest below and to the Iraqi soldiers' right. The troops veered left, fleeing north toward the tree line there. As Bhaszdi and his men scurried, Lloyd assembled a line of several researchers back out on the rock. They were taking careful aim. Bhaszdi flung himself at the ground, yelling for his men to do the same. One soldier caught a bullet and fell silent. The remaining seven men crawled desperately twenty more feet to the forest. Inside its concealment and partial cover, they ran headlong eastward.

Pursuit was swift. Lloyd and his rifle-equipped comrades, Olivier, Smythe, Woj and Ruliev—plus the spear-toting Neanderthals—sprinted along the rock to where Bhaszdi and his men had entered the woods. In moments, the researchers were outpacing the Neanderthals and gaining on the Iraqis.

Bhaszdi now began to hear what seemed to be loud cheering in the forest to the south. The whoops and shrieks intensified. Bhaszdi realized he had no choice but to turn and fight. "Get behind that log," he yelled, winded, "there: at the top of the ridge ahead! Train your weapons at the bushes . . . to the right. The researchers will attack from the bushes south of us!"

Bhaszdi glimpsed Lloyd's men burst running from the brush behind, west of him. Lloyd and his men saw Bhaszdi's trap and immediately flung themselves into a ravine. Three of the trailing Neanderthals tumbled sideways, inexplicably stuck through with arrows in their sides. The screams and chants out of the south were now becoming deafening. A mass of twenty or more Cro, dressed only in tanned leather lap covers, rushed over the remaining Neanderthals, spearing and clubbing the three wounded ones to death.

The Iraqis watched as Lloyd's men killed two of the surprise attackers and scattered the rest back through the woods. Bhaszdi and his men ducked low as Lloyd and Olivier directed slow, constant fire on the Iraqi position to allow Smythe, Ruliev and Woj to evacuate two surviving Neanderthals back toward the caves. Bhaszdi had his men save their ammunition and simply observe. Lloyd and Olivier alternated firing and retreating as they followed the rest of their group back toward the caves. Soon, the woods were quiet.

Bhaszdi had no intention of counter-attacking the researchers and Neanderthals that day. He now realized that he might be able to win a potentially critical ally: the Cro-Magnons. He had been only vaguely curious about these sapiens before and now recalled that the surrogates had taught them language. The only language the researchers had in common was English; so he reasoned that the Cro-Magnons spoke English. Bhaszdi could speak that language fairly well.

He radioed Najik. "Colonel! Colonel, we cannot fight in the manner of these people and the Neanderthals. But the Cro-Magnons apparently hate and attack them. I can show the Cro-Magnons that our troops also wish to destroy the Neanderthals and scientists. Then, we can launch one—finally effective—attack with fresh troops in a few days. The Cro-Magnons will be happy to be fodder for us, I feel certain."

"Yes. Do *that*. Do it now, Bhaszdi. Offer them one of your weapons and win them over. Promise them food and supplies if they will help. I will send a tractor now with food and to pick you up at their caves. You may withdraw *if* you have their support."

Bhaszdi led his men due east. The Cro-Magnon caves were three miles away and Bhaszdi encountered only one animal attack, from several *Thylacoleos*. He had almost panicked when his signal emitter failed to repel two. At the last moment, his men wounded and scattered the snarling beasts.

The Iraqis reached the ridge just as night was beginning to fall. But they were not warmly greeted. Several Cro-Magnon warriors jumped and disarmed them. The primitive warriors spoke no English or Arabic. Bhaszdi and his men spoke not a word of Nostratic. The soldiers were bound hand and foot and dragged into the ornately painted cave. There, a young Cro-Magnon boy was painted with wide yellow and orange stripes and was also bound; nearly immobilized. The boy lay sobbing and squirming on a pelt-covered ledge, surrounded by brightly feathered adults holding stone axes. Quite a few Cros were crying while the remainder of the clan was chanting excitedly.

Then one Cro-Magnon voice rose above the rest. It was Mo'ara. He wore the feathered skull of an immature *Phorusrhacus* as a mask and he had red straps draped across his chest. Mo'ara commanded everyone's attention, silencing his clan while releasing the boy from the ledge.

Bhaszdi tried unsuccessfully to glean meaning from the Cro-Magnons' speech. The officer felt optimistic that he and his men would be released, since the boy was being untied and tension in all the Cro-Magnon faces was clearly dissipating.

Mo'ara, the clan's leader and shaman, rendered his judgment of recent events. "We warred again today. But two Khayni died! Our sacrifice . . . *angered* fire. Boy make fire happy. Now, no kill boy. Now, make fire more, *more* happy. Sacrifice *seven* Friendli!"

Chapter Eighteen

YOU HAVE SHED MUCH BLOOD, AND HAVE WAGED GREAT WARS;
YOU SHALL NOT BUILD A HOUSE TO MY NAME, BECAUSE YOU
HAVE SHED SO MUCH BLOOD ON THE EARTH BEFORE ME.

—1 CHRON 22.8

. . . right consists in the superior ruling over the inferior and having the upper hand.

— Callicles to Socrates in Plato's *Gorgias*

IT IS NOT SPEECH WHICH WE SHOULD WANT TO KNOW; WE
SHOULD KNOW THE SPEAKER.

— KAUSHITAKI UPANISHAD, 3.8

Cape Canaveral, Florida
0318 hours, 14 May 2018

President Cox had directed that the commando raid into Al-Rajda be made at the earliest possible moment. It was dubbed Operation Mars Scope to enhance secrecy. Two storm systems off the Florida coast would delay the operation several days if it was not launched well before dawn on 14 May.

The researchers, including Freund, Harrigan and his family if possible, were to be evacuated by Mars Scope. This was planned to be within an hour of Harrigan's anticipated return to Al-Rajda. The contingency that Harrigan or any traveling companions might delay or deviate from the route between the Baghdad airport and Al-Rajda had been considered. In that event, a special CIA unit was to report the suspect location which such a deviation might betray. The unit was also to intercept Harrigan's party and forcibly spirit the group out of the country. Cox was satisfied with the arrangements and gave the order to initiate count-down.

NASA's family of cone-shaped Delta Clipper rockets and the X-30 transport had been considered for this mission. But the Delta Clipper could not be armored at the most vulnerable spot, the bottom, because its engines were there. The X-30 was deemed unreliable. There was only one other possible vehicle for this mission.

An old standby, the space shuttle, was now entering four decades of use. The newest generation was about twenty percent larger, eighteen feet longer, more maneuverable and had a more powerful propulsion system than its turn-of-the-century predecessor. With improved fuel and engines, solid rocket boosters were no longer used. The intention to develop one which could take off horizontally from natural terrain—after a launch and reentry—had been held secret for just such a need as this mission. The *Quest* was the only model with this capability, and still it had required several structural changes. Its ceramic heat shields had, for this mission, been augmented with a layer of honeycombed armor. After three weeks of feverish reconfiguration, the *Quest* was now poised vertically upon the launch pad.

Its profile was almost triangular, rather than tapered, and its fuselage had been widened over the wing frame for this mission. The additional area created by the fuselage and wing enhancements accommodated an enlarged passenger cabin and a pressurized cargo hold. A red drop-off fuel tank with its own motor would help power initial launch. The *Quest* carried a reserve of fuel and liquid oxygen internally—just enough for a second launch from earth under good conditions.

Countdown was inside fifty seconds as Mars Scope Commander, Army Lieutenant Colonel Bryce Fulton, took a quick look around. He surveyed the seventy-four highly trained soldiers and technicians under his command.

Fulton was forty-four and older than his three fellow Battalion Commanders in the Seventy-fifth Rangers. This was because he had taken time off to complete studies as a Rhodes scholar. Fulton was a no-nonsense African American of six feet, five inches in height. He was composed of three hundred ten pounds of cool but dangerous muscle and brain. As a West Point student, Fulton had been Harrigan's Cadet Battalion Commander. Now he felt very uncomfortable that a fellow graduate had, knowingly or otherwise, put the world in danger. As the countdown reached thirty seconds, extreme fear at being launched into space agonized Fulton—though it was not discernible on his square-jawed, self-disciplined expression.

Fulton's Executive Officer was no slouch, for his part. Major Ronald Jasper was every bit as tough and ready. However, his function on this mission was to remain at the *Quest*. Jasper was in command of the reserve team, designated Team Foxtrot, and its various communications and other equipment.

Fulton pushed a button on the microphone extending from under his camouflaged helmet and gave his trusted NCO In-Charge, Command Sergeant Major Joe Di Nucci, a private call. "So, 'Airborne Joe,' are you ready to get space-borne?"

Di Nucci's tan face showed his nervousness and he appreciated the diversion from his tense thoughts. "All the Way, Colonel! And then some!"

Di Nucci's physical build and educational background bore similarities to those of his commander. Di Nucci enlisted in 1996 to move beyond poor Italian-American roots and was quickly recognized as a bright leader. He turned down Officer Candidate School but rose through the NCO ranks, eventually completing both Bachelor and Master of Science in Engineering degrees under Army educational programs. He transferred from his combat engineer specialty to the Rangers for the challenge and became Fulton's Company First Sergeant in 2012. Di Nucci and Fulton were badly wounded together two years later in the bloody Cuban Re-liberation Action.

The main difference between the two men was personal. Di Nucci was a vicious fighter because his sense of duty led him to eschew safer assignments. However, Fulton was a consummate soldier because he thrilled in crushing an enemy.

The passenger bay had no windows. But for this mission, Fulton had requested and received a luxury for himself and his men: a large television monitor at the front of the passenger hold had been installed for morale purposes. Its audio output channels, controlled by Fulton, were tuned to each man's helmet-mounted communicators. The monitor displayed most of what the pilot, Colonel Ed Richmond, could see. For now, the audio was limited to the countdown sequence. The screen showed a tiny sliver of moon in east of a partly cloudy sky, and lights on the vehicle tower's retracting gondola.

Pre-ignition at "T minus" twenty seconds brought the thrusters up to deafening power, rocking the vehicle and making everyone on board, except the Navy and Air Force crew, jump in their seats.

Four. Three. The noise and vibration increased, further shuddering passengers. Two. One. The *Quest* lifted thunderously off its pad.

Nothing could be heard above the din of the engines. The whole cabin vibrated violently and most of the men, pinned forcefully back in their seats, were so shaken that they lost track of the words in their thoughts. These men were tough but they had never dreamed that any soldiers, let alone themselves, would be launched into space. The anti-nausea pills worked perfectly but some soldiers felt, nonetheless, as if they were on a roller coaster as the soaring shuttle began its normal slow roll to topside-down.

After about five minutes, the vibration and roar began to abate.

Di Nucci looked at his men from his vantage point at the rear. "Anybody who's sick or got a problem, sing out—and don't be shy!"

The tense troopers began to stir but there were no voice responses.

As gravity lessened, the feeling of being upside-down diminished. Pulses began to decrease to almost normal and tense muscles relaxed significantly. They were moving at eighteen thousand miles per hour. The screen showed the dark black of the Atlantic Ocean and the sparkling hint of a light source behind the earth's curvature ahead. The image was upside down because the camera was also upside down so that the men began to get the impression that earth was above them. Five minutes more and the only sound was their own breathing. In twenty minutes, they began to recognize the dim, glinting lights of cities in Europe and Africa. The thin corona of earth's atmosphere became visible and the horizon increasingly brightened.

Soon they could see that they were directly over the eastern Mediterranean coast, where it was already dawn. The shuttle rolled slowly over, replacing their view of the planet with star-studded black. The roller-coaster feeling returned.

Fulton encouraged his troops. "Men, we're now approaching Iraq. Reentry is imminent. No enemy aircraft have been scrambled. We're gonna hit 'em too fast for the slow fighters they've got in this northern sector to catch us! We're gonna hit 'em hard and get out double-quick."

Dan Gallagher

Sequined black space on the monitor gave way to wispy blue caused by reentry; of necessity a steep descent. Fulton looked at the local time readout on his watch: 6:52 a.m., verifying that it would be light enough, and not too foggy, for the *Quest* to maneuver and land safely. He realized that, in pieces or intact, they would all be on the ground in about eight minutes.

He touched a control button on his wrist band and menacing, ominous-sounding classical music began to build inside every helmet. One by one, the men began to grin, clench fists and make threatening grunts.

The civilian computer team leader next to Fulton leaned over at the officer, puzzled. "What the heck is *that*, some kind of 'attack' music?"

Fulton smiled. "It's by Holst. The piece is called 'Mars, the God of War'. Very effective. Watch the troops as we begin to land!"

Indeed, the technician noticed a look of confidence, even ferocity on every face he could see. He had expected fear, despite the generally smooth glide down, but observed the most intimidating expressions he had ever seen. "Wait, I remember that piece now," he said, "Colonel, that's 'Mars, the *Bringer* of War'."

Fulton frowned at being corrected and snapped tersely. "To each his own, *Civilian!*"

The shuttle's approach was inclined nose-down as it banked right to approach from the less-guarded north. The music's volume increased to thunderous levels. The mountains of northern Iraq jutted up onto the screen. Music combined with the video image of their steep approach to the plateau to give the men a powerful impression that they were swooping like eagles down upon unsuspecting prey.

Indeed, they were on no radar screens and had no vapor trail. But the prey was not unsuspecting for long. The *Quest* had been tracked by infrared optics and heat-seeking SA-23 missiles were now being trained directly on it. Twelve missiles lifted off simultaneously from their box-like mounting a half mile south of the research complex. One giant exhaust billow could be seen on the troops' screen.

A red light and alarm signaled in the cockpit and the passenger bay. Richmond shouted over the music. "Missile in route! Brace for evasive flight!"

The *Quest*'s nose lurched upward, pinning everyone weightily in their seats. The plateau on the screen dropped suddenly from view, replaced by clear, blue sky. The technician grabbed Fulton's arm, screaming. "We have no countermeasures! We were supposed to have total surprise! We can't take a hit!"

Fulton was far from unruffled but he extracted his arm and tried to calm the civilian. "Stop! Relax! The best they've got here are SA-23s. One of those isn't powerful enough to penetrate the belly armor! They'd have to hit us with at least *ten* simultaneously and the Iraqis aren't that smart!"

* * *

Harrigan and Freund found that they had to return alone to Baghdad. Tykvah had refused to reside in Iraq unless Harrigan radically enhanced safety in the preserve and vastly improved conditions for the sapiens. Harrigan had begun to realize the propriety of her demand and, the night before departure, made an appointment for himself and Freund. Early the next morning, the men dressed in conservative suits and left with Tykvah and Ben for the airport to pitch this difficult sale to Mon. But the Harrigans still argued over previously broken promises on safety and research ethics issues as they boarded the airliner in Tel-Aviv. Suddenly, Tykvah rose from her seat and left the plane with Ben just prior to departure.

Before leaving Baghdad airport for Mon's office, Harrigan used a public phone to let Tykvah know his flight had arrived safely. "Hi, Babe. Sorry I've been so noncommittal. But I'm going to do it! Don't have time to talk. We're here, safe and sound. I'll let you know the minute we're successful and, then, you and Ben get out here! Love you! Bye!" Harrigan and Freund grabbed their small bags and ran outside to the ground transportation queues.

The two were completely unaware that they had been followed from the Baghdad airport by two groups of observers. One was sent by Hassan and one by the CIA. Both tails were completely surprised to see the two men take a cab uptown and disappear into the Office of the Premier of Iraq. The best the CIA operatives could do was circle the stark five-story black marble building. The Iraqis reported directly to Hassan as Harrigan and Freund entered the building and took the elevator down to the executive offices.

Harrigan pressed the elevator control button and spoke to Freund. "It's amazing Mon agreed to see me when I called him yesterday. This shouldn't take long, do you think, Mannie? Hope he doesn't get mad that we're a bit late. It's just after seven now!"

"He'll have to get over it! And, no, it shouldn't take long unless he has us wait *on him*. But he won't like us stonewalling him on the sapien research. We'll just tell him we have more data than we can possibly digest in years and that a moratorium on human research and removal of the predators is the only way we'll accept a continuation of the contract. You still agree on this?"

"Yes, Mannie, I told you I agreed!"

The pair reached Mon's offices and were ushered through to his private suite. The fifty foot square room was generally utilitarian. An immense rug covered most of the floor. The hundreds of flowers woven into it looked vaguely like faces and were a drab red and brown, like blood stains almost dried. The furniture was plain and squarish. Its sand colored walls, however, were adorned with a multitude of paintings. These consisted of past Babylonian and Iraqi leaders, battle scenes and artists' impressions of now-crumbling vestiges of the once-grand architecture of this land.

Mon's secretary stood at the door awaiting her cue to provide refreshments. The aroma of strong coffee permeated the room where Mon sat scribbling on papers even as they crossed to the center of the room. He put down his pen and got up from behind his massive black marble desk.

"Good *morrning*, gentlemen. Please join me at the coffee table. I trust you had a pleasant flight?" He shook their hands firmly and all sat to be served.

"Yes, thank you, Premier. Dr. Freund and I would like to propose a solution to the problem of the sapiens' . . . difficult living conditions."

"Ah! The sapiens. You know, Kevin, I have been wondering how committed you *rremain* to this part of the research. I suppose we must discuss this, as the contract must either be renewed—or not. Let us find an arrangement which meets both *ourr* needs, eh? What do you *prropose?*"

Freund mustered a smile and spoke. "Premier, we have more

data and observations than we can digest in several years. The embryo research should be discontinued and is unnecessary due to the data backlog anyway. Further, we feel that the sapiens are becoming stressed, aggressive. Perhaps because of the constant threat of predators . . ." He trailed off, looking to Harrigan to sell the demanded terms.

"Ismail . . . *your* research is paramount. That is why we don't want to risk the sapiens any longer—and we want to focus on analysis of the data we've already collected. For the benefit of the project, we think you will agree that there is only one course of action: Permanently remove the predators, establish a moratorium on zygotic and sapien research and bring the clans slowly into the modern world."

Mon silently studied the men's eyes. "You realize that this would *severrely* reduce the marketability of Al-Rajda as we convert it to a research *parrk*—and its scientific reliability as a laboratory, if we keep it as a closed research facility. The sapiens would eventually learn of us and our world anyway, ending valid behavioral study. However, we must continue physiological and genetic testing. Therefore, gentlemen, I am unable to *fully* agree. But *if* the predators can be segregated and the sapien physiological and genetic studies continued, then I can agree. Perhaps delaying conversion to a *parrk* would help."

Harrigan looked at Freund, who was grinning with optimism, stopped himself and asked for clarification. "Premier Mon, do you mean to say that we can expose them to the modern world yet deny them the freedom to live in it? And continue to experiment on them?"

Mon showed much less irritation in his tone than he felt. "Their desire to live in the modern world does not exist unless we show that world to them. I mean that they continue to live on the plateau, they become aware of things like construction of one-way viewing tubes but they *arre* to be kept in that world. And above all, gentlemen, the physiological and genetic research must continue."

Driven by an awakening sense of guilt, Harrigan rose to force his point. "Premier Mon, we must have a moratorium on sapien research and give them their freedom . . . or my entire team quits and the rest of the world learns why."

"Now, now, Kevin. Let us not threaten and fight. The *contrract* ends in a few months. We have time. It is better now to consider our positions privately, where each of us might accommodate the other, and return to the subject with the benefit of such *con-tem-plation*. There is a solution somewhere. Please, let us end this discussion agreeing to negotiate in good faith another day soon, eh?"

Freund stood to join Harrigan and stuck out his hand, unhappy to leave the issue unsettled but anxious to leave Mon's presence.

Mon rose for the pleasantry and offered an appeasement. "Until a better time, then, gentlemen. As a token of my continued esteem, please, I will have my helicopter return you to Al-Rajda."

Harrigan grumbled a weak refusal. "We have a plane chartered. Thank you, no."

"Dr. Harrigan, I would consider it a constructive gesture if you would accept. It is as fast as any commercial plane and far more comfortable."

Harrigan acted appeased. "Fine, Ismail. Thank you."

The two men left down the long hallway to take the elevator up to the rooftop helipad. Harrigan was very dissatisfied with the meeting and was considering simply persuading his entire team to quit. Two floors up, Harrigan punched the stop button and stared at Freund.

"Mannie, there's only one way to settle this with Mon. We have to go back and just tell him that our position is an *ultimatum!*"

"I was hoping you'd say that, Kevin. I don't see how he can refuse since he knows we could bring world opinion to bear on him with one press interview."

Harrigan nodded, frowned with new determination and sent the elevator back downward. The elevator door opened and Harrigan and Freund were greeted by Hassan's smiling face.

"Ah! *Therre* you *arre*, gentlemen! What a surprise. And what may I do *forr* you?"

They both gave Hassan suspicious looks and tried to brush by him. Harrigan gave an impatient response. "Yes, good morning. Excuse us, Colonel Hassan, we have an appointment with the Premier."

"You must think me quite a fool, *Doctorr*. You are here to pester the Premier but none of your concerns matter *any longer!* By the way, all *com-mun-ica-tions* go through me. It is I who *shortly* have the only morning appointment on his schedule. Therefore, *I know* that you *arre* without an *appoint-ment*. But at least you can be useful to us!"

Hassan stepped back as two soldiers rushed into the elevator and sprayed gas almost directly in the scientists' incredulous faces. The guards carried the quickly sagging bodies down the hall to a room adjoining Hassan's office. The soldiers set them down on a couch. A guard used an eye dropper to place one drop of clear liquid into each of Harrigan's eyes. He carefully replaced and tightened the dropper into its cylindrical bottle. The other guard dabbed a swab into a beaker containing a pink syrup. He touched the saturated probe to the inside of Freund's nasal cavities.

The soldier fumbled with the cap of the beaker and dropped it. Hassan looked impatient and cursed in Arabic. "You, idiot! Get the sterilization foam and clean that up!"

The guard bolted out and returned with a red, thermos-sized canister which emitted white foam over the spilled substance. Hassan left with the other soldier to prepare for his seven thirty meeting with Mon. Within seconds, Harrigan and Freund's eyes began to flutter open as the remaining guard cleaned the floor.

The guard cleaning the floor at Freund's feet never knew what hit him. A bloody brass lamp dropped from Harrigan's hand to the floor as Freund reached for the man's pistol.

"Mannie, we've got to warn the staff."

"Why didn't Mon just arrest us, if Hassan was going to do this?"

"I don't know. Maybe Hassan's starting a coup and Mon's next! The staff could be in *grave* danger! Whatever's going on, we've got to get to Al-Rajda *now!*"

Shaking their woozy heads, the two bolted for the elevator and headed for the roof landing. The pair tried to appear unflustered as they approached the pilot standing at the aircraft stairs. He greeted them warmly and ushered the two bewildered scientists aboard. The aircraft took off and headed north out of the city as Harrigan and Freund, wondering if they would have to use their weapon, gazed suspiciously at the pilot and copilot.

After a dozen minutes, Hassan and the soldier exited his office and stepped briskly down the hall toward his appointment. Hassan could barely contain his glee as he finished his routine morning report to Mon.

"And, finally, Premier, it is an immense pleasure to report that Harrigan and Freund have become subjects in our virus trials!"

Mon glared incredulously at Hassan. "What did you say, Hassan?"

"Those foreign pigs were attempting to come to your office and—"

Mon's stare told Hassan that something was wrong or misunderstood.

Hassan almost pleaded for confirmation that he had done the right thing. "Sir, I thought that, since these *useless irritants* had come to waste your time—or perhaps worse, their deaths should at least be useful in testing the new vectors."

"You thought *what*, Hassan?! Harrigan and Freund were here to discuss terms of possibly continuing their research. They seemed fine in my office. They may have been returning to accede to my conditions. Who knows what we might have gained? What have you done?!"

"But . . . Uh. Premier, did you not ask me to dispose of all of the researchers, now that we have everything we need from them?"

"I most certainly did not! Some of the researchers might have continued to assist us in several areas before realizing how they were helping us. You imbecile! How many have you killed?! Do Harrigan and Freund know that you have tried to kill the others, or them?!"

Hassan's voice was low, weak and throaty. "All of them are dead, sir. But Harrigan and Freund are unaware of their comrades' deaths and that they have just been infected. There is a serum. At Al-Rajda. There is a good chance all traces of the agent just administered can be eliminated."

Mon opened his mouth to issue orders to deal with this dilemma when his aide ran in, holding a black box which had a small monitor but no keyboard. The aide whispered into Mon's ear and spoke a command to activate the screen. Mon's expression appeared at first to be alarm but quickly turned to an evil grin.

He snatched the black box from the aide and spoke to an adjutant whose face appeared on the screen. "Prepare my jet transport and a company of guards. Tell Joint Forces Commander Akkad that I want him to scramble two squadrons of fighter-bombers, armed to bomb troops, to Al-Rajda. Send in Sahgrim's parachute brigade *as a minimum*. Then, have Akkad join me in my plane immediately!"

Mon turned to Hassan's guards. "Begin administering this serum to Harrigan and Freund! Escort Colonel Hassan, who is now under arrest, to my plane and handcuff him to his seat. Put Freund and Harrigan with the prisoner. But allow them to wake and make them feel comfortable! I will be along shortly."

The bloodied guard stumbled into the anteroom to Mon's office. "They have escaped! They have escaped, sir!"

Mon slammed the intercom button on his desk. It transmitted directly into the pilot's earphones. "Premier Two, this is Mon. Where are you and are Harrigan and Freund aboard?"

Mon's desk speaker crackled with the muffled vibration of helicopter rotors. "Sir, we are about fifty miles north of Baghdad, en route to Al-Rajda. Harrigan and Freund are onboard."

"Place them under arrest and tell them that this action is by Colonel Hassan's orders. You will land where you are and follow my plane when it reaches your location. Do you understand this?"

Harrigan and Freund listened closely to the pilot's voice. "Yes, sir. *By order of Colonel Hassan*, arrest them . . . wha-!" The background noise on the desk speaker silenced abruptly.

Mon's aide was unaware that all of Iraq's gunnery and missile controls received a radioed identification code which rendered them unable to fire upon Mon's personal aircraft. "Shall we have Premier Two shot down, Premier?"

"No. Have them intercepted when they land at Al-Rajda. I will have to personally speak with them there. Now, let's get to the plane."

* * *

A dozen SA-23s screeched up through the air toward their quarry at the same speed the *Quest* approached the plateau: nearly a thousand miles per hour. The shuttle was thirteen miles from its hoped-for landing point on the alluvial plain below the plateau. The SA-23s were now within two miles of the unarmed spacecraft. There were twenty-eight seconds until impact.

One missile began to trail, waiver and head east toward the sun. Eleven were on course and fifteen seconds away. Air Force Colonel

Richmond reached for the oxygen and fuel purge control levers. He flipped up their bright red safety covers. The copilot stared at this action in horror. There was a single liquid oxygen tank and a single fuel bladder together containing barely enough oxidant and JP-13 to reach orbit in adverse weather. Purging even a small amount of fuel would likely strand them all. He started to yank back Richmond's hand and halted, shutting his eyes. The Colonel jerked the levers down once then quickly back up.

Heat streaming off the underside of the shuttle ignited the evaporating oxygen and fuel which formed a long trail out from the engines. Every missile immediately flashed directional correction retros and seven of the them veered horizontally, under and past the Quest's dormant engines. Four missiles struck the glider's belly at an oblique angle, all in a row near the aft. The shuttle tipped violently forward, almost vertically careening toward craggy mountains just north of the plateau's rock perimeter. The troops gasped in terror at the sight of the merciless terrain thrusting up into their screen. A split second later, seven almost simultaneous explosions were heard thundering behind the diving aircraft.

Colonel Richmond strained to control rudders and retro thrusters to right his craft. It was leveling out but heading straight for the jagged northern edge of the plateau ridge. He fired all three engines, further depleting fuel. Scraping over the top, the Quest sent shock-pulverized stone bursting off the ridge. The men were screaming and cringing but as the green plateau and its river landmark came into view, they began to regain control of themselves. Everyone surged forward in their seats at the tug of parachutes slowing the shuttle's approach into the plateau.

The copilot activated the intercom. "It's okay! But we can't get near the buildings. We're going to land on the plateau, the contingency landing site."

Troops sighed, regaining confidence from the good news and the motivating music. But Richmond was fidgeting with the landing gear controls. Only the front wheel was responding. He retracted it immediately and quickly glimpsed the fast approaching ground below. Trees were rising swiftly up out of a dissipating fog which blanketed the grass and shrubs of the northern semi-swamp. Already alerted by the blast, cranes were soaring up off the marshes, eagles were fleeing the trees and other animals were visible running south. There was no time to do anything except skid to a stop on the plateau.

Richmond tensed and yelled into the intercom. "Brace for *collision* touch down! Hold on!"

The shuttle struck hard on its belly in the hilly, lightly forested and very marshy north. Morning fog formed a swirling, hazy path churning up and away from the craft's shaking frame. Dirt and tree limbs flew through the air beside and behind the shuttle. The troops saw the plain in front of them punch up and down violently on their screen. In a moment, they emerged from the wisps of fog and skidded two miles to a halt on grassy, level ground.

The mission had called for landing on the semi-arid plain, approaching too fast and then too low for the SA-23s. Now, however, they were on top of the plateau—a situation planned for but not seriously expected. At least they had landed, now oriented southward along the west side of the plateau, a half mile from the river. The music, near the end of its last movement, was distracting enough to help the troops calm. They were thankful just to have landed intact and immediately reached for their seat releases to get up and go to work as they had rehearsed. The commandos had little time now to entertain the obvious worry that, depending on the *Quest*'s condition, they might not be able to evacuate.

Everyone's attention was suddenly caught by the video monitor as the external camera and microphones were inadvertently activated. Panicked animals' snarls, yelps, screeches, roars and grunts blared in a deafening cacophony into each helmet. From left to right, the screen was filled with animals stampeding, bounding south and west away from the shuttle. Some fell as they ran, flailing to get up or avoid trampling by mammoths and *Coelodonta*. The troops were shocked and awed despite the advance briefings about this place. Awe quickly gave way to a more dominating concern over their mission.

Fulton addressed the force. "Men, you were briefed on this contingency. If this aircraft cannot get out, we blow the research facilities and attempt to exfiltrate with the hostages. I will evaluate whether we get out together by air or dispersed in teams on foot. For now, put your faith in the crew of the *Quest* and assume the aircraft *will* transport us out! Let's move!"

He started to issue various teams their orders when Colonel Richmond addressed him on a private circuit. "We should be able to launch off this plateau, Colonel Fulton. I'm just not sure how far we can get. If there is to be any chance, though, you'd better send a team out to kill that SAM site!"

Had they landed at the intended location, they would be near the river below the plateau and sending Alpha Team and two helicopters north to pick up the assumed hostages. Now the situation demanded one of the on-ground contingency plans. Given the previous encounter with SA-23s, Fulton decided it was well worth a try.

Soldiers were already unlatching personal equipment drawers under the seats. Fulton punched a button on his wrist band and the roof over them opened up to the sky. Di Nucci was already directing movements and crews which, in turn, were opening the large stowage lockers, handing out huge black, canister-like rifles and other equipment. The large crane running the length of the shuttle's right side shot up and was hauling up one of two folded-in helicopters up off collapsed, boat-like pallets in the rear cargo compartment.

Everyone silenced momentarily as Fulton barked out the contingency plan they had already rehearsed. "Copter assembly teams: assemble your aircraft and carrier pallets. Air Team One: Drop off Bravo team and the technicians on the roof of the complex, post me and Charlie Team; then knock out the SAMs. Air Team Two: Drop off Delta and Echo, then stand by on station to assist Air Team One. Foxtrot, maintain security and communications here. Alpha, you and Command Sergeant Major Di Nucci get to 'hoof it'— on foot. Let's do it!"

Fulton moved with Team Charlie to personally control the intricate operation at the research facility. He temporarily detached a pair of soldiers to blast a gap in the southern tree line through which the *Quest* would take off, in case it could not get airborne before reaching that point.

It took five minutes for the two helicopters to be unfolded and completely assembled. Each Air Team had a gunner and a pilot as crew. The Air Teams flew off, each towing a boat-shaped armored pallet full of men. The twenty-four troops and technicians in each pallet stared and held out their weapons, amazed at the hundreds of frightened animals over which they soared.

Air Team Two dropped off six soldiers at each escalator entrance on the plateau as Air Team One continued south. After using exploding rounds on a *Smilodon* which ran threateningly too near the trap doors, the men of Team Delta focused attention on both escalator entrances. This team was from Delta Force, whose members were trained to operate a wide variety of foreign electronics, equipment and, if necessary, vehicles. They immediately unlatched and propped open the sealed hydraulic doors and shot their way into the motor pool with standard ballistic rounds.

Once Delta was out of danger from the cat and successfully inside the escalator, Air Team Two left them and followed Air Team One out over the cliff.

The almost sheer, four hundred foot drop-off at the southern end of plateau cliff passed thrillingly under Air Team One and its troops' view. The Americans had no time for sight-seeing, however, as they were already taking sporadic fire from Najik's panicked troops. The din of the helicopter's rotors was now interspersed with rapid and single fire shots and a few explosions. The Iraqis outside the research building were handily dealt with by wide-arc fleshette rounds judiciously expended by the commandos with deadly accuracy.

Air Team One dropped off its five civilians and the seven Team Bravo soldiers on top of the research building. These men set focused-blast cutting charges along the edges of the roof of what they knew from intelligence briefings was the Genetics Lab. They would enter on Fulton's command, once the front offices were secure. Air Team One's helicopter moved off to pound the building's front with rapid fire from its chin turret. Windows and doors were shattered, preventing Iraqis inside from threatening Charlie Team.

The twelve men of Team Charlie and Fulton jumped out of the low-hovering helicopter's pallet and stormed the building with amazing ferocity. Once they were inside, the aircraft spun around southward and fired three metal-seeking missiles at the SA-23 sites spotted on the way over the cliff. It popped up periodically to acquire and destroy more SA-23 launchers.

Air Team Two now flew over the cliff and east, past the river. It set Echo Team down behind the deserted houses and sent missiles crashing into the nearby troop barracks. Its chin turret mowed down those who were already running out. The helicopter returned to land behind the homes, concealed. Its pilot listened to the situation on the radio.

Several Iraqi troops on foot and in jeeps began streaming out of the tunnel to escape through the main gate several miles away. These were killed to preclude their return to threaten Echo Team. The house nearest the north-south road and entrance to the access tunnel was then secured. The tunnel was the only covered and concealed entrance to the research complex. So, Echo began wiring the tunnel for remote demolition. Echo members also set up several listening devices in the area and acted as guard against land assault.

Di Nucci and his Alpha Team had moved out swiftly north toward the Neanderthal caves. The *Quest* was only four miles from the caves, so the soldiers were running hard every step of the way. The shuttle's violent landing had cleared nearly all animals from the north third of the plateau, especially on the west side. Di Nucci's team progressed without interruption. They would reach the forest edge in just over twenty minutes.

The noise of the explosions and sonic boom, and then sight of the shuttle's landing, alerted everyone in the sapien caves. The researchers quickly realized that the craft they saw was for their rescue. They gave quick and tearful good-byes to their confused and frightened friends and ran out of the cave. As they did, an arrow pierced into Lloyd's arm from the tree line at the base of the ridge. Kairaba screamed and tried to pull Lloyd down out of sight. He pushed her and threw several of his fellows back into the cave. He immediately caught another arrow in his thigh. Turning to fire on the attackers, he stopped himself and held his fire. Lloyd could only see shaking trees.

Suddenly, pebbles and rocks began to pelt him from directly overhead. He realized that the Cro-Magnons were both above and below them. The Cro must have gotten past the sentry when everyone came inside after the shuttle was identified. Singh refused to pull the arrows out of Lloyd, asserting that this could exacerbate his bleeding. He pulled them out nevertheless, unable to keep from screaming, and she dressed the wound.

After awhile, Lloyd could glimpse through gaps in the foliage that the American soldiers were running toward them. The Cro-

Magnon could see that these soldiers carried the coveted fire weapons and departed. Hoping that these new 'Friendli' would leave via the route by which they had come, the Cro moved silently southeast to conceal themselves near the boot-trampled grass. The Cro-Magnon, well concealed with pelts and green paint manufactured from their copper-oxide finds, lined up twenty-seven warriors on a small, bushy hillock at the edge of the forest. Seven of them had rifles.

Lloyd and the other researchers rushed out to greet the men they hoped would take them out of this place. They could only trot back to the shuttle, because of the children and Lloyd having to be helped along.

Sadly realizing that they were being left behind, Rhahs turned to lead his clan back to the safety of the cave.

"No!" Kora pulled him back forcefully. "Rhahs! We must go! We must teach Friendli to choose love. One final call to prepare the way. We must follow Friendli now!"

Rhahs stared curious at her for a moment. Then he squeezed her hand. "Rhahs trust Kora. Rhahs trust flower-voice you hear."

Kora and Rhahs now led their pathetic and confused band of Neanderthals to follow their departing friends. Lloyd and Di Nucci had no reason to force them away. However, the knowledge that these primitive people were supposed to be left behind—to Iraqi experiments or wrath—was wrenching to all the moderns now running hard southward. The Neanderthals' deepening confusion and sense of abandonment grew as they became outdistanced. Then, after a mile's jog, alarm seized the moderns as they peered into the distant, southern horizon.

"Jets!" yelled Di Nucci. "We've got to run faster!"

He called for a helicopter. "Mars Scope Commander, this is Alpha Leader. We see the fast-movers. We're three miles from home. Need choppers! Over."

Fulton denied the request reluctantly. "Negative, Alpha Leader, you'll have to run. Choppers needed out here."

Di Nucci had his men lash children to their backs and sprint. Two soldiers helped Lloyd hobble fast. *At least*, Di Nucci thought as they took the route through the previously boot-trampled grass beside the wood line, *we might be able to take cover in between some of those little hills up ahead.*

Harrigan took the pistol from the unconscious copilot while Freund jammed his weapon into the pilot's smarting ear. Freund pulled the headset down tight around the pilot's neck. Harrigan finished binding the copilot with his and Freund's neck ties. Both men took off their suit jackets to gain better freedom of movement. Harrigan returned to sit in the vacated copilot's seat and growled at the pilot.

"You speak English?"

"Yes." The headset tightened around his neck made him hoarse.

"Get us to Al-Rajda yesterday!"

The man looked puzzled at first, then pushed the throttle controls all the way forward. The engines whined louder and all three men were thrust back by the acceleration. Harrigan and Freund quickly regained their positions and control of the pilot.

"No tricks," Freund warned angrily, "or *you* die and *we* fly this thing!"

The aircraft took only thirty more minutes to come within view of the concrete landing site, ten miles south of Al-Rajda. The hut adjacent to it looked deserted and the pilot started to descend. Harrigan grabbed his arm.

"No you don't! Take us to the research building. We're gonna pick up some passengers!"

Just then a red light flashed and a buzzer sounded in cycles. The pilot spoke unperturbed. "Missiles deactivate near *dis* aircraft. Electronic *rrecog-nition.*"

In seconds, the missile was visible, hurtling at them in a smoky arc from the left front. Another red light flashed and the buzzer became constant. The pilot became immediately frantic.

"*For-reign* missile! It will hit!"

"Foreign?!" Harrigan and Freund blurted simultaneously.

The pilot jerked back the controls and spun the craft into a dizzying vertical loop. The engines shut down as the helicopter finished its maneuver, plummeting from rotors-down to wheels-down. Then it struck center of the river. The cockpit was underwater in seconds, just as the missile skimmed over the slowing rotors and plowed into the east bank, blasting a massive hole and throwing mud everywhere.

Harrigan fought the pain in his strained back and grabbed Freund, unconscious, from the rushing water. The pilot was dead, his chest pierced by a control lever. Harrigan surprised himself, actually considering saving the copilot but he knew he had only moments to get himself and Freund out. He slammed the cabin door shut, allowing water to flood the cabin through the destroyed windows. He swam out, pulling Freund behind him.

On the bank, Harrigan began to perform mouth to mouth resuscitation when Freund rolled over and violently coughed out volumes of water.

"Hih-ummm! Ck-cuhh! I don't k-h-hiss on the first date!"

"Fine with me! Come on! We've got to get to the vehicles or radios or something. Get our folks out and head north into the mountains."

The two rose to their feet and saw the smoldering remains of a shredded Iraqi truck-mounted antiaircraft launcher. Fifty feet away, there were dead soldiers and a drab green jeep. They ran toward the vehicle and jumped inside. Harrigan started it while Freund gathered up two rifles, ammunition and a set of binoculars. They sped east for cover in the low, rocky river bank. Now less vulnerable to fire from their left and right, they headed north toward the research complex. Freund stood to look ahead.

"Kevin!" Freund shouted as the windshield repeatedly bounced his bruising chest and arms, "There are two small helicopters at the building! Never seen ones like that before. There are soldiers on the roof and—"

Suddenly the roof of the research building exploded. The sound of the blast followed in a second, revealing a distance of about eight hundred yards, and the smoke cleared quickly.

"I can't tell if they're Iraqis or what. Now they're disappearing. I guess they're going down through the roof. Anyway, I can't see them anymore."

Harrigan continued to drive, steering hard to avoid jogging the vehicle into the river yet staying as low on its banks as he could. They had driven to within a mile of the damaged building when rifle fire began to ping off the jeep's grill and, then, shatter the windshield. He spun the jeep almost sideways and stopped. Harrigan and Freund scrambled out and peered north from under the bumper.

Harrigan grabbed Freund's arm. "Where's that shooting from, the building?"

"No. Look in that water drain up ahead!"

They both saw soldiers and recognized them as Najik's men. The shots were coming from seventy feet ahead; from five helmet-less Iraqi troops kneeling visibly in a rut leading into the river.

Harrigan grabbed Freund again and whispered. "Do you remember the first Florida patrol?"

"Yeah! There's nothing else we can do."

Freund continuously fired at the five, trying to keep them ducking. Harrigan crept back from the vehicle and then up the bank into thick grass. He continued to crawl low to the ground until he was behind the Iraqis. From the edge of the grass, he gained a perfect line of sight on each man, all of whom still fired at the jeep sporadically.

Harrigan considered his options. *Do I really need to kill these guys? We worked side by side with these guys for years. And we're not even sure what's going on here! Mannie would advocate mercy over sacrifice. Could be right.*

Harrigan fired at the men's feet and yelled one of the few Arabic words he knew, "Stop!"

The men froze. They realized they were in an untenable position and turned slowly, weapons down, to face Harrigan. Freund moved in on them. They looked nervous. The pair disarmed them and stashed their weapons in the jeep. They could get no answers from the men as to who was fighting whom, so they pushed the hapless soldiers into the cold river and motioned for them to swim away. Harrigan and Freund now sped off toward the research center, where small arms fire and explosions continued unabated.

Chapter Nineteen

be who says that a dragon is singing in the dry woods
is he who truly sees tao . . . purity is in the impure.
                                                    —ts'ao-shan

Hail, Caesar! Those who are about to die salute thee!
                              —Gladiators' Salutation, *Suetonius*

. . . shall not god bring justice for his elect . . . will he
delay long over them? i tell you he will bring about
justice for them speedily. however, when the son of
man comes, will he find faith on the earth?
                                                    —luke 18.7-8

Al-Rajda Zoological Research Preserve; Two Miles North of the *Quest*

0907 hours, 14 May 2018

Di Nucci and his men were moving slower now that some of the civilians were carried on soldiers' backs. But they were still making progress. The Neanderthal clan, also carrying their children, were running at top speed and keeping pace forty yards behind Di Nucci. The jets and puffs of smoke were becoming more than dots in the southern sky. Di Nucci was now getting nervous; wondering silently. *What if the satellite reconnaissance was wrong and there are Iraqi soldiers in the woods? Where did those Cro-Magnons go? What if some predators weren't flushed from this area? We're running right along the edge of the woods and can't even see inside!*

Then the shower of spears, arrows and rifle shots erupted from his left. One of his men fell but the rest threw their passengers to the comparative safety of the rutted ground. The Neanderthals dove into the grass. A bullet struck Di Nucci in the side of his thin flack jacket, stinging as if it had entered his chest. He was unsure of any casualties but had no time for that consideration.

"Near ambush! Fire! Attack through it!" Di Nucci's command was slightly later than his men's well-trained reflexes, which set them already to the counterattack. Alpha Team charged immediately—as if by instinct—turning left, firing and charging into the woods at the small ridge.

The Cro had kept low behind the hill and trees. But automatic fire and explosive rounds from Di Nucci's men was shockingly effective and overwhelming. The twelve soldiers were on the hill before half of the Cro-Magnon warriors could escape. Three of the seven rifles fell to the ground beneath the corpses which had, seconds ago, fired them in life. The Cros' other rifles were dropped during escape. Di Nucci led his men crashing through the woods beyond the firing line to briefly pursue their attackers. He saw three additional dead Cro in the woods ahead.

"Halt! No time to chase 'em! Check casualties!" Di Nucci was already running back, leaping past six more dead Cro-Magnon to get to the cringing civilians.

Lloyd and other adults checked wounds and comforted screaming children. He called to Di Nucci. "I'm not sure about your people, but none of mine are bad."

Di Nucci turned to his men for the hoped for signal that none of them were seriously hurt. A sergeant yelled to Di Nucci while swiftly dressing a wound at the back of a fellow soldier's neck. "Alpha is 'all up,' Command Sergeant Major. Penquist has a nasty cut but he'll be all right. Most of us have some pretty mean bruises under the body armor but no major casualties."

Di Nucci was quick. "Good. Load 'em up and let's go."

The Neanderthals had almost closed the gap with Di Nucci's group but were ignored as he continued the trek, sharply focused on his mission. Nevertheless, he hoped that the Neanderthals would, somehow, fare well after they were left behind. The modern children were still crying and screaming for the adults to wait for their less fortunate, primitive friends.

Di Nucci scowled expectantly at the southern sky, where he no longer saw any jets, and blurted out as he ran. "There'll be more fast-movers for sure. I hope the XO can deal with them!"

Harrigan rolled the jeep to a stop just south of the waterfall and slumped forward against the steering wheel. Freund could just see the top of a helicopter half a mile westward.

Freund looked over at Harrigan and pulled him upright. "Why are you stopping?"

Harrigan was slow to respond. "Just . . . I'm just kinda tired and my vision is getting a little cloudy, that's all."

"We're getting too old for this stuff, you and I. Let me have a look at your eyes." Freund held Harrigan's eyelids open and peered as closely as he could. He found his own attention span slipping as he inspected Harrigan's right eye and momentarily forgot whether he had already examined the left one.

"Nothing I can see without a scope. Look, are you okay to make it to Najik's office? Maybe we can use his monitor to find out where everyone is."

"Right. I'm fine. That's the best place. If there are soldiers any-where, they'll be in the control room, not Najik's office. You know, Mannie, this shoot 'em up stuff was fun twenty years ago. But now. . ."

Freund finished the sentiment. "Now people are really dying. Let's go."

Harrigan and Freund got out, crouch-running and crawling through the grass to reach the side of the building and Najik's win-dow. It was closed and still intact. They peered inside. The room was empty and unlit. Freund tried to slide the window up. It was locked. They cracked the panes with the butts of their rifles as qui-etly as they could.

"Hawlt! Stop or I'll *farr!*" A southern U.S. accent confused the pair but froze them in place. They turned their heads to see two burly soldiers advancing at them from around the front side of the build-ing.

"Well, well! You two look just like your pictures. Drop your weap-ons and put your hands behind your heads!" The sergeant mo-tioned for his companion to quickly frisk the pair and rush them around to the front of the building.

"You're Americans?" Freund needed some verification.

"Both of you keep your mouths shut and get moving!"

Harrigan was angry but uncertain at the soldier's inexplicable unfriendliness. "What the hell is going on? Where is my staff and their families?"

"You can speak with Colonel Fulton in a minute. *Move!*"

The pair were pulled and shoved inside the smoldering, dusty building. No lights were on at all. They moved through the gloomy halls to the Genetics Lab, joined by several other soldiers along the way. They could still hear explosions and small arms fire from the direction of the motor pool. The lab was lit by rays of sunlight streaking through smoke which billowed out through a huge, jagged opening in the roof. Broken ceiling tiles and shards of building materials were strewn everywhere. Several men were unbolting the FGR modules from the floor while others were using acetylene torches to cut components free. The sergeant ushered them over to a huge black man speaking into a microphone which hung from his camouflaged helmet. Fulton stopped speaking abruptly and grimaced as he noticed the pair.

"Never thought I'd see the day! Harrigan and Freund!"

Harrigan squinted, confused. "Do I know you? What's happening here?!"

"You ought to know me, you self-important son of a bitch! Always second-guessing the cadre. Always had the right answer. You were the tough Ranger-type. Gonna reform the world in your image. Well, *I'll* fight *for* you while you keep silent!"

The proclamation struck Freund as blasphemous paraphrasing of Exodus 14:14 but he dismissed it as coincidence. He started to protest and defend Harrigan. "You're wrong! He's changed—"

Harrigan took a swing at Fulton, who immediately countered by wrenching Harrigan's arm and punching him squarely on the cheek. Harrigan collapsed, unconscious. A guard threw a bandage over Freund's head and pulled it tight into his mouth, tying the ends behind his head.

"Get these two out of the technicians' way and *of my sight!* Put them . . . What's the most secure room outside this one, Sergeant?"

"The southeast corner office, I'd say, sir."

"Put them in there. Post one guard with them and one in the hall. Then clear these Iraqi *boy scouts* from the rest of the building!"

* * *

Up on a tall platform in the *Quest*'s cargo hold, Major Jasper stared coolly at the jets rushing off the southern horizon. He looked down at his radar scope. Eleven soldiers stood out on the Quest's wings with long, green tubes on their shoulders and crates containing more at their feet. Eight bright dots shone on this screen. They were almost at the screen's white ring, which was a computer-calculated projection of the best engagement range.

He screamed two words into his microphone. "All launch!"

The high-pitched roar of eleven shoulder-mounted anti-aircraft missiles was essentially simultaneous and almost deafening. They were thousands of feet up into the sky before any of the soldiers could throw the spent canisters down and reach for more. The men did not have to spot their target: Jasper was quickly moving a light pen on the surface of the scope to connect his new dots to the enemy ones. The computer took over control of the missiles from there. Wispy missile exhaust trails immediately began to diverge.

Jasper saw ten more targets approaching another computer-generated guide ring. He did not have to look at his trusted men to know that they were at the ready again. "All Launch!"

Another volley screamed into the sky toward the south and east, chasing now panicking Iraqi jet crews.

Nine more jets appeared on the screen, moving toward the gauging rings. As he prepared for the next volley, the first ring disappeared from the screen: There were no longer any aircraft for that first, very effective, lock-on to track.

"All launch!"

Missiles screeched yet again from the commandos' launchers. Jasper's men were mounting their next volley, noting nervously that they each now had remaining only one missile poised on their shoulders and four boxed. The launching and destruction continued. In moments, the empty crates were thrown off the shuttle into the smoky, rutted clay. The men stared tensely at their team commander.

Jasper hesitated, jerking his light pen over the radar screen to allocate every last missile to a target. He glanced nervously at the reserve crate below him on the deck and had his men relax for a moment.

"All clear!"

Jasper smiled as his men cheered and whooped. He was nervous despite the clear radar screen. Only a single crate of eight missiles remained.

Air Teams One and Two were approaching the shuttle with their gondola-like pallets full of wire-strewn computers and a few soldiers. Jasper's men guided these into the cargo bays, opened the pallets' armored sides and tipped out the contents. The choppers left and returned filled with soldiers and twelve handcuffed Iraqi researchers, most of whom had bandages on their heads and bodies. Jasper looked at his watch and climbed higher, up onto the *Quest*'s still-hot engine covers. He looked through his binoculars: Di Nucci and the civilians were less than a mile away.

As he turned, his stomach filled with acid. The southern sky was again filling with aircraft; obviously many more than eight.

Off-loaded troopers from Charlie and Bravo Teams continued to secure the hardware in the cargo bays and clamp the gagged Iraqi scientists into seats. The helicopters were gone, returning southward to pick up Echo and Delta Teams and Lieutenant Colonel Fulton, who had monitored the situation with a direct radio link to Di Nucci and Jasper.

Jasper ordered distribution of his remaining eight anti-aircraft missiles while studying his radar screen. He saw five supersonic aircraft and fifteen large, subsonic jets. He called to his men.

"Yentik, Ross and Taft: Hold! The rest of you standby to launch . . . *Launch!*"

Five missiles thrust off, screaming at the jets. Jasper again worked his light pen and watched his screen. The five targets disappeared. He waited. The larger aircraft were still approaching, not scared off. As seven of these approached the deadly ring on the scope, the helicopters popped up over the far-off cliff edge and sped toward the shuttle.

"Remaining missiles: Launch!"

The three streamers closed on the fifteen transports. Jasper knew that this was a clear indication to the Iraqis that the Americans had spent their defenses. Yet there was nothing more he could do.

Additional Iraqi fighter-bombers were already scrambled from other air bases. These would not be on station for another ten or twelve minutes. The transports would be over the Preserve in five.

Jasper checked with Richmond and received a tentative "go" as to their ability to take off again. The astronauts were dubious of the prospects of reaching orbit, however.

Jasper kept his men informed of his assessment of the air situation as he radioed Fulton, "There are bombers or troop carriers within five minutes of us!"

* * *

Mon was not interested in the objections of his Joint Forces Commander as the two men sat at a situation monitor in the cabin of the Premier's jet. Mon's plane had flown in behind the transports that carried Colonel Sahgrim's reinforced parachute brigade of three thousand men.

"General Akkad, if you fail to get Sahgrim's troops on the ground at Al-Rajda immediately, the Americans will escape and we will have little bargaining power with their government. We will also be uncertain of how much they know about our work here. Losses from missiles or parachuting mishaps are secondary considerations. Is this clear?"

General Akkad knew better than to even disagree, let alone show anger, with his Commander-in-Chief. "It is most clear now, Premier Colonel Mon. Thank you for clarifying my instructions."

Akkad reluctantly turned to his microphone and ordered hundreds of his men to what he knew was certain death. "Sahgrim, transports are to continue at maximum speed. There is no time to wait for more fighter/bombers. Acknowledge."

The speaker on the console was silent for a moment. Then came the response. "I . . . Yes, sir. I understand and will comply. Sahgrim out."

Mon turned from the console and walked forward through the plane toward Hassan, who was gagged, bound and struggling weakly. He had the guards move Hassan to an aft cabin, excused himself and followed Hassan into the cabin. He shut the door behind him for greater privacy.

"You have one chance to live, Hassan. Do you understand me?"

Hassan stopped wiggling and nodded.

"You may be able to redeem yourself with me. I would like that

303

better than killing you for ruining my plans with your ineptitude, wouldn't you?"

Hassan nodded rapidly.

"We must diffuse this crisis, *old friend*, or fight a war for which we are not yet ready. The Americans will surely not stop at one raid. And, there may also be world opinion to consider if other governments feel we are a threat. We must calm their fears. Therefore, you must do *exactly* as I tell you . . . if you wish to live. Here is what you will do after we land . . ."

* * *

Fulton acknowledged Jasper's 'five minute' warning and turned to the civilian technical team leader. "Everything secure on those pallets?"

The man provided Fulton a response by telling the helicopter pilot to lift out the pallet. "Ready to go. Take it away!"

Fulton issued commands to his other team leaders. "All teams, pull in now. Guard detail, bring Harrigan and Freund to the Genetics Lab."

The guard detail did not respond. Fulton's expression changed to alarm.

"Guard detail! Come in!"

There was still no response.

"Damn! Captain Marsh, you and four men come with me!"

Fulton and the others raced to Najik's office. The area smelled of sulfur and eggs. The hall guard was unconscious and the room guard was trying to get up from the floor.

"Where are they?!" Fulton was frantic, waiving his pistol and darting his eyes into every corner of the room.

The room guard could barely speak but tried valiantly as he pointed toward the floor. "Gas . . . canis-ter. Iraqis. Trap door!"

Beside the entrance, a rug was partly rolled back. The steel trap door would not open. Fulton had his men blast the floor, first with rifles, then grenades, finally with some remaining explosives. It served only to chip into the thick concrete and mangle the steel.

Jasper called Fulton again. "We have *zero* time left, sir. Recommend you leave now. We'll be swimming in paratroopers, bombs and air-to-ground missiles any minute!"

304

Fulton swore, but this neither gave him access to his stolen prisoners nor bought him time.

"Get out! Everyone get on the pallet *now!*"

* * *

Di Nucci was now twenty yards from the *Quest*. The Air Teams landed just east of the shuttle and off-loaded Delta and Echo Teams. The off-loaded men rushed out to help Di Nucci's near-exhausted Alpha team haul in and load the civilians. Lloyd, limping badly, shoved Kairaba into a seat and buckled her restraint. He gave her a quick kiss and rushed to help seat others.

Fulton addressed Richmond on a private channel as he approached the *Quest* on the last helicopter load. "Richmond! Can we make it out in this thing?!"

"The simulations show we can get airborne if we can attain four hundred ten or more miles per hour by the time we reach the edge."

"Is that a 'yes,' Colonel?"

"Yes."

The shuttle bay doors were closing and the fuel pumps on the engines were beginning to whine. Nearly everyone was strapped in. Singh, Olivier and Lloyd were at the side emergency door, looking worried and resisting a soldier assigned to seat them.

The Iraqi transports were already landing troops around the river and housing areas below the plateau. More transports were pouring out hundreds and hundreds of troops, now two thousand feet directly over the lower plateau. Parachutes and planes were so numerous and packed in together that they rapidly darkened the sky. Several canopies collided, dooming their tangled jumpers to plummet to their deaths. In moments, troops were on the ground all over the plateau on both sides of the river. Paratroops who landed in the open managed to avoid the pandemonium of crowding, fighting animals in the southern wooded areas. But *Smilodons* and other predators crouched hidden in the grass.

Lloyd screamed at Fulton and ran out of the emergency hatch to pull in the Neanderthals who had managed to run up to the wing. "You can't take off! *Bloody hell*, you've got *people* in the engines' blast area!" He pulled a young sapien male into the shuttle as Olivier led several of the researchers back out to retrieve the straggling and breathless clan.

Fulton responded swiftly. "We have *no* time, Doctor. Get back in your—"

Fulton could not believe his eyes as more civilians now exited the shuttle. Olivier, Singh and five of their cohorts darted past the Rangers and exited the *Quest*. They were running back to pull more clan members ahead. A shower of Iraqi bullets cut their route back inside. Fulton rushed out with a handful of men and two Improved Squad Automatic Weapons. The crew-served weapons were fired from the operators' sides as several soldiers dashed for more ammunition and shot off grenades from their huge rifles. Di Nucci ran out onto the shuttle wing with five more soldiers and, along with those already outside the door, decisively silenced most of the nearby Iraqi fire.

Fulton did not intend to let his mission fail. He grabbed one of the big machine guns and tried to force Lloyd and the researchers to abandon the Neanderthals. He fired over their heads. "Get back in *now* or you're dead." Di Nucci believed that the threat was only a bluff and so did the researchers. He shoved a Neanderthal in through the door and ordered the researchers to hurry.

Fulton fired again. Two Neanderthal adolescents being pulled toward the wing by Singh and Kora fell, their chests and necks burst by Fulton's rapid fire. The women shrieked and Lloyd jumped Fulton from behind, knocking him to the ground. The enemy fire was growing again as the last of the clan, being almost carried by Olivier and Woj, reached the wing. Everyone was firing at the Iraqis or dashing back in the door. Di Nucci grabbed Lloyd off Fulton and threw him at his men who, in turn, shoved him inside.

Fulton got up, receiving a bullet through the cheek; then two more through the eye and nose. Di Nucci grabbed him and screamed for his men to get inside. Di Nucci tried to pull his commander back into the shuttle but took a bullet in the arm pit, just where his body armor had a sweat gap. He lost his grip on Fulton's lifeless body as his men dragged Di Nucci inside and locked the access.

The whine of the engines starting was deafening. The rapid clang of small arms fire and the thundering din of grenades on the hull was mounting to alarming fury. Troops thrust nineteen of the Neanderthals into seats but there were twelve screaming adults still standing who had no place to sit. Di Nucci had his men push them into the cargo hold and secured the latch. He knew that they might be injured but at least they were inside. Di Nucci collapsed into his seat with sweat and tears covering his face and blood trickling down his side.

The *Quest* was receiving powerful mortar fire now and many more direct grenade hits as its three giant engines roared to full power, thrusting it rapidly southward. One mortar round on an engine would slow them, causing the craft to halt or careen off the cliff and crash. A shot on key seams might blow the vehicle open. But the pilot's console indicated that the *Quest's* physical integrity had not been breached.

Outside in the grass, an Iraqi paratrooper held the sighting device of his small bazooka-like missile launcher trained on the *Quest's* engines. He fired. The arm-sized missile pierced the hull at the base of the top engine, blasting its primary fuel pump. Fuel flow to that engine was automatically shut down.

Suddenly the words "Number 1 Fuel Pump Inoperable" pulsated in red on Richmond's status monitor. Richmond blanched and the copilot gasped.

"We can't reach take-off speed without *all three* engines!" The copilot was near panic.

Richmond's finger immediately flipped the auxiliary pump switch. It operated briefly, then shut down. "Damn! Why would it shut down?!"

The craft had only two more miles to reach a minimum speed of four hundred ten miles per hour and his computer projected complete failure to attain this goal. They were moving at less than half the necessary velocity. Colonel Richmond forgot to shut off the troops' monitor; he could concentrate on nothing but his instruments and throttle levers. He thought about halting the craft before they crashed below the cliffs but could not cope with the thought of failure and capture. Richmond teased more speed from his two remaining engines. It was still not fast enough. The craft and its passengers were continuously jarred by the uneven runway.

The cliff edge was now only a mile away and the *Quest* was at two hundred eighty miles per hour. A half mile away: three hundred forty miles per hour. Richmond gasped as his vehicle went off the edge and they were moving at just three hundred eighty-eight miles per hour—too slow! Some of the commandos screamed to witness the ground drop off below them as Iraqi soldiers and rocket launchers below the plateau burst onto their screen.

Richmond fought to maintain his composure, anticipating the imminent crash of his craft.

His mind raced feverishly for saving ideas as they plummeted toward the rocky ground. *The electrical breakers! They caused the auxiliary to shut down!*

Richmond grabbed for the breaker box access and could not quite reach. He screamed at the copilot. "The breaker! Hit Auxiliary One!"

The copilot fumbled to open the panel. But the shuttle was losing altitude. It was now a hundred feet from impact, plummeting fast with its nose slightly skyward. Thirty feet. Ten feet.

"Open it!"

The copilot's finger reached the breaker and reset it immediately before the impact. The impact ripped open the soft earth beneath the ailerons and the engine housings. It spewed old, blackened bones and charcoal-dirt up into the air in a grisly burst. The softness of the ground at this point avoided critical structural damage. The pump warning on the monitor disappeared, just as the tail struck and deeply rutted the ash-filled ground. In that same instant, the number one engine ignited as furiously as the other two. Thrust was still increasing rapidly and the bounce did not appreciably change the shuttle's momentum or orientation to the ground. The vehicle skipped once and remained aloft. It reached a hundred feet up, then four hundred. The *Quest* was soaring away, but Richmond could not yet breathe normally. He looked at the copilot for the fuel sufficiency recalculation report.

"With the clear weather and the weight changes, Colonel Richmond, I think we can—we might—attain a *shallow* orbit."

Richmond nervously smiled back. Then the radar alarm cut his confidence to shreds. There were several incoming missiles. He increased the angle of the ascent, partially presenting the remnants of the belly armor to the threat that was below and ahead of the shuttle. The *Quest* was now over two miles high but moving at only fifteen hundred miles per hour. The missiles could reach three thousand miles per hour if the fighter/bombers which fired them had been moving at two thousand.

"Incoming at fifty miles and closing, sir." The copilot was dripping sweat. "Our airspeed now at twenty-seven hundred. There's nothing we can do! They're going to hit! We're at full thrust now!"

"Steady. We might just be able to . . ."

The radar screen was of no use tracking anything within a few miles but the digital readout extrapolated time to impact. "Computer says impact in eight seconds, Colonel!"

"Airspeed?"

"We're at . . . We're at thirty four hundred! We're gonna make i-!"

The explosion behind and below the shuttle cracked the exhaust vents. For a moment, everyone thought they would tumble from the sky. But the vents held and the *Quest* continued to gain speed. All fuel soon expired and the engines were silent just as they attained sufficient momentum to escape gravity. The monitor showed light blue sky fading fast to foggy black. The only vibration remaining was from retro rockets adjusting the craft's direction. The Indian Ocean became just visible through the cockpit windows.

Richmond relaxed his white-knuckled grip on his controls and murmured to his puzzled crew. "And the waters were like a wall to them on their right hand and on their left."

Cheers reverberated through the craft. By everyone's opinion, the sight signaled that they were finally saved. They were in an unsustainable orbit—and that only barely—but would make their way to an emergency landing site in Australia.

Chapter Twenty

AND A GREAT AND STRONG WIND WAS RENDING THE
MOUNTAINS AND BREAKING IN PIECES THE ROCKS BEFORE THE
LORD; BUT THE LORD WAS NOT IN THE WIND. AND AFTER THE
WIND AN EARTHQUAKE, BUT THE LORD WAS NOT IN THE
EARTHQUAKE. AND AFTER THE EARTHQUAKE A FIRE, BUT THE
LORD WAS NOT IN THE FIRE; AND AFTER THE FIRE A SOUND OF
A GENTLE BLOWING.   —1 KINGS 19.11-12

Imagine there's no heaven. It's easy if you try. No hell below
us; above us only sky.   — John Lennon, "Imagine"

. . . YOU WILL WEEP AND MOURN . . . YOU WILL HAVE PAIN, BUT
YOUR PAIN WILL TURN INTO JOY.   — JOHN 16.20

The Central Plateau,
Al-Rajda Zoological Research Preserve
1003 hours, 14 May 2018

Iraqi soldiers in the field felt grossly humiliated by the Americans.
They were furious at the insult which the raid represented and at
having sustained so many casualties. Four among them were killed
by the shuttle's back blast and two were crushed beneath its hull.
The charred body of Lieutenant Colonel Bryce Fulton, however,
was collected for removal without further mutilation. Yet, collecting the dead and wounded from this plateau was about to prove far
more harrowing than the brief battle.

The shuttle's departure had frightened animals from the southern plain and forested areas. Most fled west and north. But the
Megalanias stayed crouched and agitated in their burrows. There
had been no time to brief the Iraqi paratroopers on the hazards of
the plateau. Now, a platoon of forty paratroopers was assembling

from the men's scattered landing points. They were very near one of two burrow exits. The platoon leader, a lieutenant, decided that the mound of dirt around the hole would make a convenient rallying point for his men. Standing on top of the mound, he began to call them.

Hissing and grinding sounds in the pit made the officer quite nervous and he summoned his platoon sergeant to investigate. The NCO affixed a floodlight to his rifle and crawled inside without hesitation. In seconds, he was back out again, feet first. Feet were all that remained, for the monster had snapped up the dutiful sergeant. The gargantuan lizard climbed out of the hole, arched to point its head skyward and opened its jaws to let gravity pull in the rest of the dead soldier. The lieutenant fell backward, aghast, and scrambled for the forest. His men followed and hundreds around the area bolted for the woods as well. The *Megalania* did not pursue the men but crawled back in its burrow as fast as it had emerged.

They could not forget the sight nor lose the terror it had infused in them. Hundreds of men dashed farther into the woods, unaware of the many horrors which crouched hiding in the trees and thickets. The herbivores' instincts had led most of them to stampede across the plain and northward. Their reactions to fear were almost uniformly to flee. But most of the predators had merely shifted positions within the concealment of the forest. Now, predators from all over the western plateau were concentrated in the woods close to the river and along the ridges. The panicked soldiers were running straight for one of these concentrations.

The lieutenant, a fast runner, was leading the way to the river. Branches slapped his face with every step. Passing a thicket, he noticed something large and yellow in his peripheral vision. Then, he thought he heard something pounding heavily on the ground behind him. His men suddenly screamed out unintelligible warnings. He turned and beheld his pursuer.

The massive *Phorusrhacus* beak filled his entire field of vision. It had a long red, serpentine tongue and it started to screech. He dove to escape the bite—successfully. But the bird's talon struck through his back and exited above his stomach. Both bird and prey tumbled over several times and the talon ripped back out.

For an instant, the lieutenant thought he might escape the prostrate, thrashing bird. But his ripped diaphragm would not allow him to breathe. The terror-bird rose to its feet and stepped beside him. The young officer raised his head, unable to resist a look at the nightmare. Its beak was over his shoulders and crunching through his ribcage as the shots came. The bullets ripped the bird apart in a bloody five second explosion. Four men pulled the convulsing lieutenant from the raptor's jaws. The lieutenant became almost limp and his eyes had bulged outward. It took another couple of minutes for the officer to die of suffocation. The platoon leader's men trained their weapons outward and stayed where they were, afraid to move in any direction.

Other troops were beginning to notice several fearful predators lurking in the grass. Acting on their training to use cover and concealment, torrents of soldiers rushed into the deadly woods. Roars of terrifying *Ursus*, vicious *Smilodons*, dire wolves, cave lions and other predators heightened to a maddening cacophony as more and more men invaded the hiding places of the frightened animals.

Agonized human screams echoed through the woods along both sides of the river and through numerous gaps in the foliage. Men could be seen being tossed bloody into the air or viciously torn open. Panic spread along the woods on both sides of the river now, around the edges of the plain and even onto the grasslands.

Twenty-eight hundred men all over the southern half of the plateau were now firing at anything that moved; even inadvertently killing their fellow soldiers. There was no longer anything like unit coherence. Men cringed in pits and ruts; others ran headlong off the cliff to the safety of the barrier ledge or into the river. Immense predators pursued them everywhere. *Meiolania* simply waited for their meals to swim out to them.

The submerged, rock-like prongs at the falls were originally designed to halt animals before they went over the edge and became caught in concealed steel nets within the falls. This barrier-sieve was now clogging with half-drowned men and segments of bodies. As soldiers cleared from the plain and as the smell of blood permeated the atmosphere, the *Megalanias* ventured back out of their burrows.

The pair had not been sterilized in the lab. Instead, they had been periodically gassed and their eggs were removed. But the extent of their burrows and nesting in recent months had, in fact, not been known to Dr. Smythe or the veterinary crews. The babies were every bit as vicious as the parents which had abandoned them to a far end of their tunnels. Now eight, deep green, twelve foot long juvenile *Megalanias* emerged from small burrows and headed for the river's edge.

These vicious animals amplified the panic of both men and beasts. The lizards lifted their hideous bodies and rocked left and right in a fearsome, surly gait as they ran—searching out prey. With each step, they thrust their stabbing, pronged claws outward sideways from huge feet. They raced for the water's edge and followed the river south toward the greatest concentration of soldiers. Troops managed to kill one young *Megalania* and tried, ineffectually, to flee before the others.

Soldiers at the cliff edge lost all nerve as the adult lizards approached. The jump was only five feet and about a hundred soldiers were already cringing, huddled against the minor cliff base. Furiously counterattacking the source of so many stinging bullets, the two giant monitors lost their recognition of the boundary and fell over the short cliff edge. The lizards were unhurt by the five foot tumble. Everywhere the pair beheld injured animals which had ignored the barrier this morning. These were carrion to be scavenged on any other occasion. Now, however, they vengefully eyed hundreds of terrified humans.

The *Megalania* scooped up and tossed soldier after soldier without even swallowing. The lizards took a huge number of rifle shots and began to succumb. As the reptiles began to retreat, now limping and floundering from small arms fire, they became frantic. They were losing blood and had too little strength to scale even the five foot cliff to escape north to their burrow. Suddenly, the pair turned east, trampling several paratroopers. Flailing their dangerous limbs and whipping their massive tails, the *Megalania* ran straight off the cliff to land thunderously beside the river below.

Some of the soldiers had run north, avoiding almost all the predatory animals. They were ambushed by the undaunted Cro-Magnon. Now the Cro again had weapons but retreated confused to their caves. This would only become their demise in the hours to come. Remnants of the airborne brigade eventually called for airstrikes on the caves, permanently sealing them.

Control of the enlarged brigade as a unit was completely impossible for the entire morning. Within two hours, most of the predators had been either chased north or killed. Of just over three thousand paratroopers, more than two hundred perished during the assault, twenty-six died from American action on the ground and four hundred eight died from animal attack. Scores were desperately wounded and dying. Hundreds of the shattered brigade's members were in shock.

* * *

"Najik to any Iraqi units. Come in!"

Several radio operators responded simultaneously, rendering that channel too crowded for communication. Suddenly Mon's voice silenced everyone who was speaking on that frequency.

"Mon here. Najik, where are you? Where are Harrigan and Freund?"

"I am beneath my office, Premier. And I have captured both of the *Western pigs!* They are unconscious. But we are unable to exit the shelter. It has been damaged."

Mon's plane was landing. He had Hassan taken under guard to Najik's residence and ordered Akkad to get the trap door open. A hydraulic winch had it open within twenty minutes. Mon ordered the scientists placed in the clinic and treated well.

When Harrigan and Freund regained consciousness, they could barely walk. They were made to sit in wheelchairs to be moved to the clinic, where electric lighting had just been restored. The clinic was still intact but the pair was aghast at the destruction they glimpsed as they passed through the halls to the opposite side of the building. Several hallways, especially those to the labs, were strewn with rubble. Soldiers were already busy cleaning up. Mon arrived at their room just as Harrigan and Freund, weak yet able to speak, were being helped into their beds. Mon quickly asked Harrigan and Freund the favor he needed.

"Gentlemen. This affair is truly grave and tragic. Colonel Hassan, an officer whom you know I trusted for years, has attempted to abuse your work by directing our scientists to develop genetic warfare research behind *all* our backs. He has been unsuccessful in this. However, I am grieved to convey news to you that this *trraitor* has killed your fellow researchers ..." Mon paused as Harrigan's and Freund's jaws dropped. The two men's eyes began immediately to water.

Mon resumed pressing his point, ". . . and he has triggered an American commando attack. I have come *per-sonally* to diffuse the *sit-ua-tion*. Equally as heinous, gentlemen, Hassan has injected you with '*horrmones*' which cause rapid aging. If there is anything left of the laboratory, you two must be *trreated* here, and quickly, my friends! We have no time to lose to avoid war—and to save *yourr* lives! For you two can help avert a worldwide disaster. You must—I *implorre* you—state before a video camera that there have never been genetic weapons developed at Al-Rajda."

Despite the fact that—to the best of their knowledge—this was true, the pair politely and repeatedly declined.

Mon kept a warm and patient facade. "Perhaps showing you a video tape—which I am told Hassan himself has made—will convince you of *my honor;* convince you to reconsider. I will have it shown to you when I receive it. But I must go now. Your help is absolutely *crritical."*

Mon left abruptly for Najik's residence.

Harrigan turned to his old friend and counselor. "My God, Mannie what have I done? *So* many lives lost! I've been a colossal fool to believe Hassan all these years, thinking I was in control and able to fight all my own battles. I should have been listening to you all along!"

Freund looked Harrigan in the eyes. "I wouldn't trust Mon either, if I were you, Kevin. Evil blinds us to its nature and intentions all our lives. It tries to make the right choice seem wrong."

* * *

Mon met his personal aide, numerous guards and Hassan at Najik's residence. General Akkad had set up a command post outside and was trying to gain control of his troops on the plateau. Speaking privately to his aide and three guards, Mon issued instructions on how Hassan was to be rehearsed and dealt with. He instructed the aide to use Najik's study to tape a video which Hassan was to make. Mon reassured Hassan about how he, still the Special Activities Chief, would be restored to favor. Then Mon handed him a pistol and left.

The Iraqi Premier left the house and walked briskly into the command post. He had Akkad's men leave the area and spoke with Akkad privately. "The Americans must be convinced that they have attacked us based upon *incorrect intelligence.* Have the Foreign Minister go to the U.N. with all the evidence we can make to demand an apology, the return of our researchers and reparations. The world *must* remain convinced that we are no threat. I even want you to have Harrigan and Freund returned *to the very doorsteps of their families* as soon as the virus is totally untraceable in them and they are fit to travel. We cannot afford to attack too soon or lose the genetic warfare option before it is fully operational.

"We must, Akkad, nevertheless be prepared in case the West threatens or mounts any form of attack. Have each nation around Israel go *secretly* to a level one alert. Have the Syrians find an excuse to put mechanized units into Lebanon along the north-south highway we built. Have the Turks *visibly* revive the West's guilt over Balkan Muslims. They can then strike Greece if we have to go all the way. We can hold Israel and the Balkans hostage. In this manner, we can stop or ward off any attack."

Akkad responded, worried. "I will return to Baghdad and execute your instructions immediately, sir. Some of these preparations are already underway. Uh, by the way, Premier Mon, I trust you know that the doctors estimate that the serum has only a sixty percent chance of working."

"Yes, I am aware of that. At least they are unaware of their counterparts' activities in Baghdad. Regardless, you must assure that all genetic evidence of their infections is *purged.* Give them aging hormones after purging so that the Americans will believe their condition was caused by more *conventional means* than genetic manipulation. *Only then* can they be returned. By the way, are you sure our own kidnapped researchers will not talk?"

"The researchers have been conditioned to experience genuine memory loss of their classified work upon kidnap and similar events. There are therapies which—in a variable number of months, depending on the person—can overcome this. It is out of our hands now, Premier."

"Indeed, General Akkad. Hassan's people inform me that they only need a year or so to complete a sufficient inventory of virus weapons. Let us hope that we can buy enough time to develop our destiny unmolested."

Akkad saluted, briefed his officers and left for Baghdad. Mon remained at the command post awaiting the production of his video tape and continuing to communicate with his officers.

Inside the house, Mon's aide handed Hassan a paper and had him practice his lines. He even had Hassan fire one blank to reassure the nervous colonel that he was not being double crossed.

"Look, Colonel, if the Premier had wanted to kill you . . . you would already be dead! Point it at my chest and fire, if you do not believe me!"

Hassan hesitated, pointed the weapon at a lamp and fired. The lamp was splattered with red ink, but intact.

The aide smiled. "Now, can we get this done? There is no time to lose if we are to avoid an escalation of this crisis with the Americans."

Hassan practiced his lines fairly convincingly. The aide, however, had him try several times more. Hassan tried his lines yet again, suspiciously pointed the weapon at the aide and fired. The sting of the red ink capsule pelting Mon's aide between the eyes was half of the sting Hassan received when the privileged junior officer slapped and rebuffed him.

"Did you think that would be funny? Perhaps I should inform the Premier of your chicanery!"

The aide wiped his face with a towel obtained by one of the camera men as Hassan groveled in apology, finally believing that the video set up was genuine.

He tried his lines again, once he and the aide had regained composure. The script called for him to look repentant and to speak in his native language. "I am Colonel Fezhil Hassan. I have betrayed the trust of my country by unilaterally—*without the knowledge of my government*—attempting to conduct genetic warfare research. The research was only recently begun and has been completely unsuccessful. Inspections of the site raided by the American force will be permitted. I wish to show the world the depth of my sorrow and shame at bringing undeserved suspicion upon my honorable and peaceful government. Of my own volition, I will now end my life."

Hassan raised the revolver to within a few inches of his temple.

He flinched a bit, knowing it would hurt. He pulled at the trigger, telling himself to convincingly fall over when he felt the ink pellet burst.

Hassan was momentarily able to perceive the bullet. In the split-second which remained of his life, Hassan also began to sense an insight which he had long sought. He had a sense of falling into clearer and clearer understanding of an unspeakable immensity; a seething and insidious malice, reaching up to claw and pull him further into itself. He felt this, oddly, accelerating.

* * *

Around 11:00 a.m., Mon returned with the video to the clinic for another attempt to convince Harrigan and Freund to help him. An accompanying soldier wheeled in a television and played a video tape which Mon said would shortly be released to the press. The tape was played and Harrigan and Freund watched with stunned but clouding minds. Both men cringed slightly to witness Hassan's suicide. They fell silent, considering the situation and their plight.

Freund was extremely suspicious of Mon and mentally debated the facts during the speech which Mon's aide recorded as a conclusion to the tape. *Mon certainly appears to be genuine in his assertions—and the tape was immensely convincing. We haven't actually seen any Iraqi scientists develop harmful pathogens. Perhaps the American government made a mistake. We aren't in chains or being shown off as hostages. The communications system in the building is plausibly inoperable. And the Iraqis certainly have good reason to deny Kevin and me use of the military radios, given the priorities of today's crisis. But it sure looks as if Mon doesn't trust what we might say on a real-time communications link to the outside world.*

Mon interrupted Freund's contemplation. "Gentlemen. Please do *rre-consider* my humble *rrequest.* I implore you to tell the world that this is but a scientific and commercial venture. You know that this is a *trrue* statement and that your *tes-timony* would help avoid an escalation of today's tragedy—a tragedy solely caused by Hassan. *You* will save lives!"

Freund was as civil as he could be and mustered his slowly-ebbing concentration. "Premier, you must consider that we cannot cooperate—even with a friend—when the U.S. has chosen to act as it has. There must be a good reason and we cannot cooperate, even though we believe your motives to be honorable."

Harrigan echoed the response.

Mon appeared not to be perturbed; his words even sounded re-assuring. "Well, gentlemen. I must *rrespect* your wishes. *Please do rre-consider* my plea for your important help . . . later. In any event, I *prromise* that you will be home in a few days. I am told by the doctors, however, that the only cure for your—so viciously induced—*horrmonal* imbalance *must* be manufactured and administered fresh here at Al-Rajda. But now, gentlemen, I must leave you to return to Baghdad."

The two scientists continued to wait alone in the room, its window being their only link with the outside world. They fought the sedatives which they had been given along with the serum. Around 3:00 p.m., they saw numerous medical evacuation helicopters arriving and departing. Road traffic was fairly thick. Harrigan and Freund could just barely see the dead *Megalanias* in the distance.

At supper time, a soldier delivered a warm meal of shredded chicken and gravy. A military doctor and nurse followed and increased the doses of intravenous medicine which they called "counter-hormone factor." Freund had never heard of such a serum. The doctor's answers to Freund's pointed questions indicated that the serum had been obtained from lockers in a part of the clinic which Freund had never used. The doctor claimed that the lockers also contained the only apparatus which could make more. Harrigan and Freund were told that what was left of this facility was the only place that could produce their medicine.

When and how, Freund wondered as he weakly chewed scoops of mushy chicken, *had the Iraqis developed such a medicine without being observed by me?*

Freund was tiring fast and did not articulate or pursue the questions. Harrigan was already asleep, his meal left uneaten. The two slept through most of the next day, still given excuses about not being able to call home. They had been degenerating; gravely affected with an unfamiliar condition, only apparently caused by Hassan poisoning them with hormones. Yet neither man gave up hope.

Chapter Twenty-one

War Situation Room, Baghdad
0551 hours, 16 May 2018

Ismail Mon stood waiting for the communications channel to the White House to open. He was furious that NATO forces, including nuclear weapons, had been placed on a second level alert for two days now since the raid. He was fatigued and even more tired of hearing from Sheryl Cox. He presented his disciplined poker face to the camera and eyed the large wall monitor which was about to show the President of the United States.

Cox's sneering face suddenly flashed on the screen without the traditional protocol image of the Presidential Seal. "Good morning, Premier Mon. I hope it will be that. Please listen carefully. You will order the following three actions without delay. One: stand down all Islamic League forces. Two: release your hostages. And, three: permit inspections of Al-Rajda and *any* other site the inspectors want to see. Do it now. You have no choice."

Mon sounded apologetic. "Madame *Prresident*, you have been most *catastrr-ophically* misinformed about our activities. In addi-

320

tion, I cannot control all of the forces currently on alert. The Turks inform me that they will no longer tolerate abuse of Balkan Muslims. The Syrians have long had trouble in the Bekaa Valley of Lebanon and with Israel. Morocco is worried that it will be attacked by your forces near Gibraltar—which are postured most aggressively, I *must* say. I will, however, offer my government's 'good offices' in attempting to quell the situation. Our *doctorrs rreport* that Harrigan and Freund are still suffering from having been poisoned with *horrmones* by that *traitor, Hassan*. I will return them to Megiddo this very day *if* you will return *ourr* people! Iraq, as you can easily verify, is at *no* level of alert. What more can you expect of me—especially after your recent attack into the very heart of *ourr* nation?"

"I am not a diplomat, Premier. So I do not negotiate. Listen closely and watch your screen."

Cox turned from the camera and had it pan toward a large computer screen. It depicted the Middle East from the Indian Ocean to Mediterranean Sea. Then she turned back to the camera, allowing herself and the screen to be viewed by Mon.

Cox glared at Mon but spoke to her military leaders via simultaneous communications link. "Initiate preemptive strike operation 'Mars Disinfect.'"

Mon stared, silently intimidated. Then the President's screen began to show lights moving away from fleet symbols. His own private monitors began to light up with notices of cruise missile launches.

Cox resumed. "You will be unable to intercept *all* of these *very* powerful *conventional* warheads, Premier. You have means to verify that they are not nuclear, including watching them destroy hundreds of your installations during the next thirty minutes. I will be able to recall them to their carriers—*for later use, if necessary*—only within the next three minutes. *You*, therefore, have less than three minutes to issue *valid* compliance orders to each demand."

Mon knew he was not quite ready for this. He hoped that, once he complied, the Americans would either fail to inspect his own office building or eventually acquiesce to respecting the sovereignty of it. He had no choice, given his confederation's current state of military readiness. Yet he still had Israel, the West's only foothold within his realm, completely surrounded. The superhighway near

Megiddo represented fast, easy access southward into Israel's interior for the time when Mon would be forced into brinkmanship again. His immediate objective was to gain time until his genetic weapons were ready to be employed en masse.

"I agree. Each demand will be immediately *ac-com-modated.*" He waited as Cox recalled the missiles, then continued to address her. "You will have a difficult time proving to the world that your attack upon our country; abduction and continuing detainment of our *civilian commercial* researchers, was justified. In the end, President Cox, the international community will force you to pay *dearly* in reparations. This *trransmission* is ended."

* * *

The guard returned from Harrigan and Freund's room to sit staring at his two monitors. One critically important screen showed any detected levels of retrovirus and DNA changes in Harrigan and Freund, while the other displayed video of the two scientists in their room. The two sick men he had just visited looked as if they would be dead very soon. However, the unique lab equipment showed that the two had been purged of the deadly DNA strands and virus since the night before. At that time, the guard had replaced their serum with something else which the doctor had provided.

The soldier listened with no interest to the pair conversing. He sipped his coffee, called for his relief and waited for it to arrive. He smiled with some satisfaction as he heard boots approaching through adjacent hallways. The guard perked up, knowing that he might have to be able to render some evidence of his eavesdropping, if a superior demanded one.

The guard now paid attention to both the data monitor and the video screen. He listened closely and heard Freund address Harrigan.

"Kevin," Freund said in an insistent tone, "lets talk about something besides this hell-hole, for cryin' out loud! I think about how the heck we got here and even farther back—and everything's getting confused. I *know* I should remember more details of what you're so agonized about, Kevin, but it's not falling into place. Are we prisoners of war? No, wait: We've never been in a war! But, I feel like . . . did all this start with the Army Medical Corps, somehow?

No. No. Can't have. And what about these species preserve projects? That's where we are but . . . Kevin, I just can't get it straight!"

The soldier laughed and spoke to himself under his breath. "These patients are *senile!* Completely *gone!"*

He rose to greet his relief, which he could hear about to round the corner into his hallway.

Just then, his platoon leader arrived instead—along with Colonel Najik. The guard, visibly fearful of Najik, held his best salute and was dismissed without any report being required of him. Najik and the lieutenant briefly stared at the data monitor.

Najik restated the data on the screen. "There: Not a trace! Are they fit to travel?"

The lieutenant looked perplexed. "I don't know, sir. Uh. I assume so."

"Fine. Get them ready to depart. Don't waste time with their personal effects now. Have all of Harrigan's former staff's belongings, everything, packed up and shipped to Israel by tomorrow. The Premier is sending his personal plane for these two and it should be here any minute. I'll be presenting them to their families and the authorities when we land at Megiddo. Now, let's have a last look at these two."

The officers briefly visited the scientists, informing them that they would be returned to their families and the authorities in Megiddo. Najik smiled broadly and told them that they would be much better soon. The colonel disappeared and the lieutenant called for soldiers to carefully move Harrigan and Freund outside. There, the faint aroma of charcoal dust stirred up by the wind replaced the clinic room's smell of alcohol, pulverized concrete and sweat.

As the young officer escorted Harrigan and Freund out of the bullet-scarred building, he received a printed message from his company commander. He read it and smiled. When the plane arrived and rolled near to the building, Harrigan and Freund were loaded on board. The Lieutenant looked around for Najik, who came running out carrying nothing.

The junior officer blocked Najik's way to the aircraft's loading ramp. "Excuse me, Colonel Najik. These orders regarding you came directly from the Premier's office. The captain will escort Harrigan and Freund. You are to remain here. By the way, you are under arrest."

Najik's stomach wrenched tight and his breathing quickened. He was handcuffed, hauled inside to his office and set before his computer monitor. Several officers and men had crowded into the room. One of them reported to Mon's aide on the screen and, in a moment, the face of the Premier appeared to Najik and everyone standing behind him.

"Ah. There you are, Colonel Najik. Despite the idiocy of Colonel Hassan's order for you to kill the researchers, you sacrificed courageous soldiers in the course of covering up your lies to him."

"But, sir, I captured Harrigan and Freund for you!"

"Again, you lie. One of your men whom you had guarding you in your unauthorized bunker accomplished that. You should have died fighting along side your men."

"But—"

"Silence. Had I issued an apology for the Western researchers' deaths, I would have lost credibility with world leaders—and this almost occurred. In addition, you demonstrated complete ineptitude as a tactician. Your own subordinate commanders have suggested a solution and I concur. Mon out."

Najik looked up at the soldiers' vengeful faces and blanched. Immediately they rushed him and dragged him from his desk. The officers and NCOs nearly killed Najik with their fists before their new commander ordered them to stop and take him to the place on the plateau where he was to be officially disciplined.

Najik was not familiar with the location and did not know, at first, what to expect. He was hauled out on a pulley, suspended by his wrists from a tree limb and left. His soaked feet dangled only a few moments, just reaching a submerged ledge below the surface of the dirty, amber pond.

* * *

Harrigan and Freund sat unguarded, slumping but tightly belted into the aircraft's plush chairs, and stared out the window. The morning fog was gone. They were glad for the news that they were headed home. The frail and wrinkled pair felt utterly without energy. Harrigan had to take several labored, gurgling breaths every few words.

324

Harrigan smiled ruefully at his life-long friend and spoke in a low, scratchy tone. "Mannie, what a tough R- c- hm- Ranger I thought I was once. Now . . . I'm helpless. Others had to fight a ba- hh- battle . . . that I caused."

Harrigan paused, very short of breath and aching. "I don't . . . feel I'm gonna make it . . . Mannie. You?" Harrigan was suddenly wracked with coughing and spit up some blood.

It took Freund, deep in clouded but deliberate thought, a moment to realize that he was being asked a question. His voice was slightly more stable than Harrigan's. "No. I don't think we have much time left. I believe we're dying . . . old friend. The serum may have been bogus . . . or just not effective. And, Kevin . . . stop berating yourself!"

Freund paused and related his earlier thoughts to Harrigan. "I think *all* our work was stolen, Kevin, and *perverted*. They've turned it to a weapon they *think* will destroy whole races and peoples. But, my God, Kevin. It could be . . . even worse than that . . . or it might just be how God will implement his plan. Mankind's own evil, giving most people a second chance—or maybe just the purgatorial: everyone *except* the most innocent and the most evil—we cannot know. All I know is that death makes God seem cruel . . . until seen as birth, a passage home."

"I'm not sure I underst- Oh my God! Mannie!" Harrigan was taken by a shocking thought and more coughing. "Do you think . . . Mon could trigger . . . the reincarnation of just about every human back to . . . Adam and Eve? As in Nuñez's model?"

"Kevin, we can't really know. The thoughts of God, no one knows. But, yes: That could be the mechanism, the way M-RNA ultimately operates. Mon *could* start a genetic cascade. His evil unwittingly serving to implement God's resurrection of mankind."

"It still makes . . . no sense in my judgment." Harrigan held his breath to avoid more racking of his lungs. "Why would the same actual soul come back from . . . what, from some *purgatory?*"

"Mercy. A second chance. No one should ever know for certain, in life. Otherwise they'd squander their lives—*intending* to reform and get redeemed *the second time* they were born."

The two men were silent, contemplative. Freund noticed the phone in the back of each seat. "Kevin, maybe we can call home!"

Harrigan's drooping face lit up, momentarily energized. "Ben;

Tykvah! But we have to warn . . . maybe we can get word out fast through them."

Freund reached for the phone and got a dial tone. Then this was interrupted by what he assumed was the Iraqi copilot's voice.

"You may not call out, *Doctorr*. I'm sorry. We will be in Megiddo in about an hour, however."

Freund reported the results to Harrigan. "One of the crew says 'no out of country calls.' Kevin, do you believe . . . what all these years I've tried to . . ."

Harrigan was already thinking along those lines. His eyes flooded with tears to sense that Freund was still concerned about Harrigan's immortal soul.

Freund began again in a subdued tone. "Kevin, it seems we've come so far, yet not quite far enough. We can never truly merit redemption. Yet, that's what makes grace so amazing: It isn't that we love God, but that he loves us. We have to offer genuine appreciation in the precious time we're given."

"Yes. Mannie, it amazes me. I've let myself be so . . . h-h-umh . . . horribly duped . . . more by my own priorities . . . rationalizations and perspective of self-importance . . . than by Mon's lies. I was so wrong. I deserve to rot . . . to burn in hell . . . forever."

Harrigan let loose a series of coughs and tried to regain his voice. "Maybe I can warn Mon . . . about the fire he's playing with. Stay his hand. I can't let the human race . . ."

Harrigan grabbed the phone and waited to speak with the copilot, who responded immediately.

"Doctor, I said no calls!"

"Bu-h-h-t: I must speak . . . to the Premier."

There was silence on the line as the copilot considered the request, technically not forbidden. He completed the connection to the Premier's staff office and a recorded message provided instructions, first in Arabic, then in English.

Freund rested his head upon the wide seat-back and shut his eyes. He felt a sudden sharp and, to him, almost audible 'pop' inside his head. He sensed it as hot and brief.

Harrigan listened closely to the phone hand-set, trying to understand the instructions. "You have reached the administrative offices of the Premier of the Republic of Iraq. Please dial the extension of the party you wish to reach. If you don't know the extension, press the keys which correspond to the first three letters of the party's last name."

Harrigan's tears, combined with rubbing, had cleared his eyes just enough so that he could make out the letters and numbers on the key pad. He pressed the key for M: 6. He had to scan the keys again for O and realized that it was the same button. He started to complete the dial but hesitated. His expression tightened in fear, then relaxed. Harrigan thought, momentarily, about Freund's statement that God's plan might be implemented even through Mon's unspeakable potential. Harrigan considered his own will as compared to such a plan. He set the phone hand-set back into its cradle. *Forces larger than myself*, he thought, *seen and unseen.*

"You know, Mannie . . ." Harrigan's feeble voice was cracking. Glistening tears were streaming down his face. His cough was impeding his ability to breathe; more so with each unsuccessfully expunged clump of phlegm. "You're right . . . no proof of God. Still, listening to the whisper . . . sacrificing *my* judgment . . . what would be *my* choice . . . risking what *I* have loved . . . to accept faith . . . is enough to gain hope . . . and return a love I don't deserve."

There was no response from Freund. Harrigan tried to turn his head toward Freund but burst out in more coughs; this time unable to pull air back in. He shuddered with the pain. Harrigan could endure the pain but the fact no longer made him feel superior. As he managed to turn his head, he saw that a truly appreciated and loyal friend was gone. Again Harrigan struggled to clear his lungs; to draw in air, but was unable. He closed his eyes and thought of his family, Freund's family; humankind's rebirth. The pain in his lungs increased but was not more than he could bear.

The plane was almost an hour away from landing. Yet Manfred Freund and Kevin Gamaliel Harrigan were home.

end